CRÉ-WITCH CHRONICLES

JOINED IN SPIRIT

SARAH HEGGER

Cover: Deranged Doctor Design
First Electronic Edition: July 2023

ISBN: 978-1-990731-15-0
ISBN: 978-1-990731-14-3

❀ Created with Vellum

ACKNOWLEDGMENTS

Thank you to Susan Lynne for her medical know how and corrections. She did her best, the rest was—regrettably—up to me and any mistakes are mine.

A huge thanks for my super proofers for this series: Anna Sharpe, Iola Marieke Morgan, Debbie Fuller, and Gigi Hall Rivera. You've been an instrumental part of this journey.

Also to the members of the Sarah Hegger Collective, and the @Home Collective. You guys keep me writing away. So, really, you only have yourselves to blame for this one. The chronicles have been a journey and I'm so grateful you joined me for the ride.

And to Brent, Olivia, and Caitlin. You know why, and if you don't, it's because I don't tell you enough how much your love and support means to me. I am blessed.

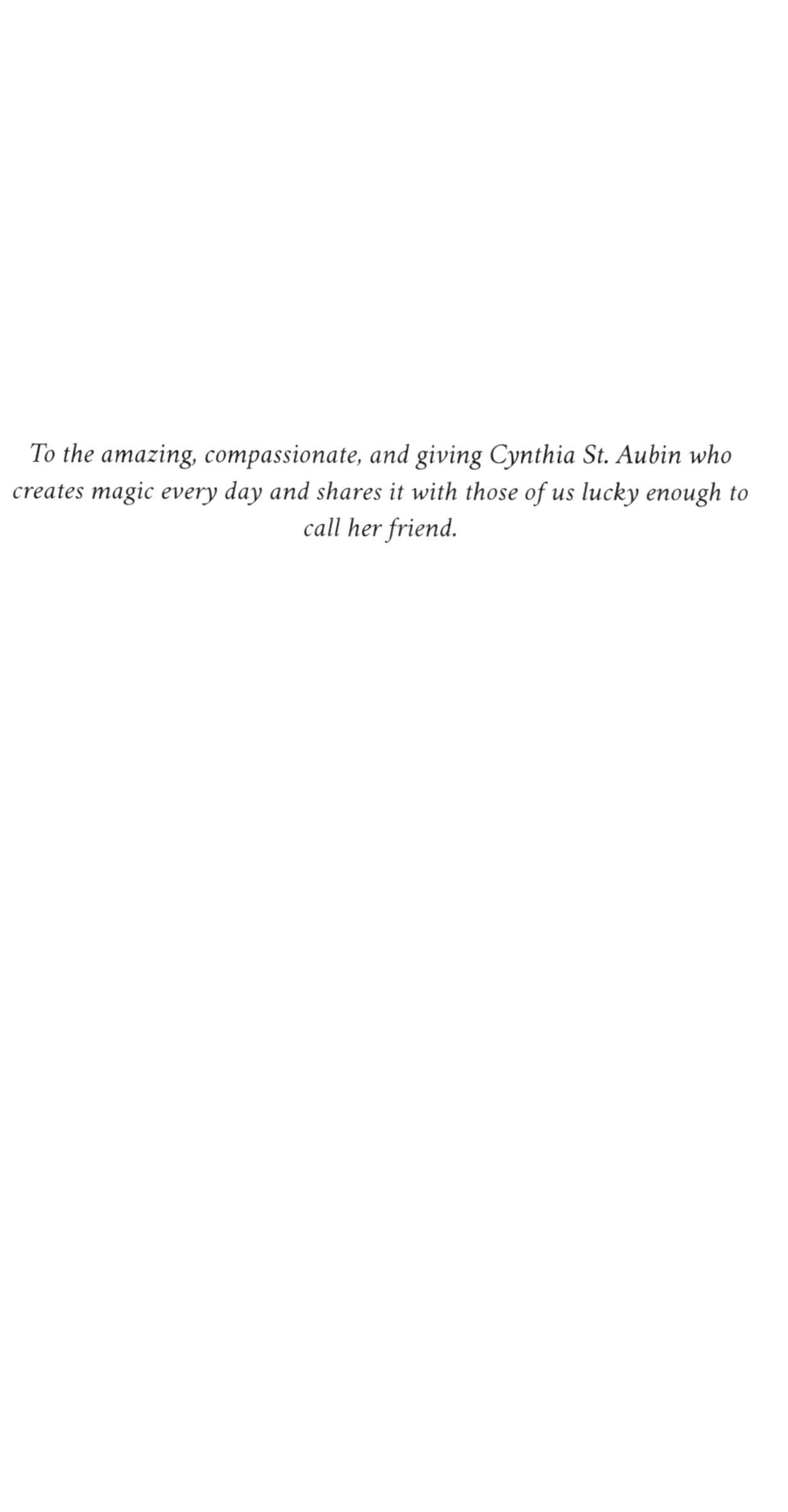

To the amazing, compassionate, and giving Cynthia St. Aubin who creates magic every day and shares it with those of us lucky enough to call her friend.

CHAPTER ONE

Fiona's belly tightened as the car wound up the familiar road out of Greater Littleton to Baile. Not a road she'd ever thought to travel again, not like this anyway. Jack drove, and Mags sat in the passenger seat beside him, their entwined hands resting on his knee. Beside Fiona, Emma, Mag's coimhdeacht, stared at the mighty castle, lost in her thoughts. Not happy thoughts if her grim expression was any indication. If Fiona had to guess, and such an exercise seemed masochistic, she would say Emma's thoughts centered around wringing her neck. No, that wasn't Emma's style. A quick bullet to the head was much more likely.

For a moment, Fiona was transported back in time to that journey hundreds of years ago when her parents had first brought her to Baile as a girl. Her mother had worn a determinedly cheerful expression, glancing back at Fiona from the front of the wagon with a tremulous smile, her plain face showing her battle between loss and resolve.

Fiona had been delighted by the turn her life had taken.

Her parents had been confused and a little intimidated by a daughter who did inexplicable things—make fire leap in the grate, light a candle with a click of her fingers. Frightened by the possibility of her "unholy" abilities being discovered, her mother had hidden them from the rest of the villagers who lived near their small, prosperous, farm.

"Don't ever let anyone see you doing that terrible thing, Fiona."

"Hide what you do, girl, or things will go worse for you."

About the time their village priest had begun to eye her from the pulpit on Sundays, her father had heard about Baile through a traveling minstrel. Fiona had lain in bed that night pretending to be asleep while they discussed her future beside the kitchen hearth.

"We can't keep her here," her father had said. "You know what will happen."

Her mother had sobbed softly. "But she's twelve, barely grown." And then a soft wail, muted so as not to disturb her. "She's my child."

And the only one her parents could have. A hard childbirth had robbed her mother of the opportunity to bring more children into the world. All rather typically, her father would have preferred a boy.

Even then, Fiona had known she wasn't destined to scrabble her existence from the soil or serve on her back beneath some sweating brute whose children she would raise and whose house she would clean.

Fiona had looked at the great, beautiful castle standing sentinel against a chilly November sky and wished sturdy Mabel, fastened to the traces of their farm wagon, could go faster.

Fiona was special. She'd known it since her first memories. She had a gift, a blessing, and her fate lay in the luring dance of flame and heat. Her purpose was enmeshed with the burgeoning power that crackled beneath her skin. And here, in this place—Baile Castle—lay the key to unlocking her future.

Then, like now, Baile's wards prickled across her skin.

Fiona gritted her teeth against the rake of cré-magic rejecting the blood magic she had been using since she'd betrayed the coven for Rhiannon. Frankly, she was surprised the wards allowed her through at all. She'd been holding her breath, half expecting to go up in flames the moment the wards touched her.

Pain speared through her, and she dug her nails into her thighs to stop from crying out. She'd get no sympathy from the occupants of this vehicle. They'd be more likely to revel in her pain. And they had good reason. She'd been front and center in their battle against Rhiannon and fighting for the opposite side.

Sensing something, Emma turned and looked at her, gray eyes locked on her with glacial intent. "I'm not taking my eyes off you."

Fiona sneered back. She knew well Emma would kill her with the barest provocation. Fiona had lived with death stalking her for too many years to feel any real fear at the prospect. Since Edana's death, the idea of death had transformed into something perilously close to wishful thinking.

"Baile." Mags breathed and leaned forward. "I'm home."

Fiona remembered feeling like that about Baile. She recalled the lift of her heart, the gentle thrum of Goddess through her body, the warm embrace of a magic grounded in life and harmony. Now it felt like the scrape of metal on metal inside her and set her teeth on edge.

The pain centered in her chest and pulsed like a suppurating wound. Fiona breathed through the pain. She'd wielded blood magic often enough to know that pain well. Blood magic was forbidden to followers of Goddess, as it drew its source from the life force of its victims. It was the antipathy of cré-magic, and cré-magic fought its corrupting influence. But Rhiannon had taught them all how to master the pain and bend magic to the power of death.

The shadow cast by the gatehouse dimmed the interior of the car.

"Give me an excuse," Emma murmured. "Any excuse, and I will end you. Gladly."

Emma would have to stand in line, however. Fiona smiled grimly to herself. Roderick and Alexander waited within Baile with even more reason to see her dead. Then there was Warren, who wasn't exactly chairing her fan club.

Fiona wasn't sure why she was coming here. Yes, Rhiannon knew by now of her betrayal and would be even more merciless than the coimhdeacht of Baile, but Fiona didn't fear her or her retribution. The manner of Rhiannon's retribution would be commensurately grisly with the extent of Fiona's betrayal, but death came eventually and ended the suffering.

No, that wasn't it. She was here because she had to be. Like she'd known as a girl that her purpose rested with Baile, she knew that now. Her future was still inextricably tied to the ancient castle and, once again, she was at a crossroads.

"Look." Tears streamed down Mags's face as she pointed to the people spilling into the bailey from the kitchen. "There's Niamh and Warren, and Sinead and Alannah. And Taylor looks taller." She turned to Jack, her face alight with joy. "Don't you think she looks taller?"

"She looks happy to see you." Jack gave her a fond smile and kissed her knuckles. "They're all going to be well made up to see you."

Mags leaned forward, the seatbelt straining against her slim shoulder. "And doesn't Andy look like he's fitting right in? And there are some new faces."

Gravel crunched under the tires as Jack nosed forward and parked.

Emma stuck by Fiona's side as people surrounded Mags. Crying, laughing, hugging, and exclaiming all blurred into a barrage of noise, the joy palpable.

Then the greetings turned to Jack. Thumps on the back, great manly hugs, and questions raised without waiting for answers.

Tiny, blond, and fae pretty, Maeve stood on tiptoes and cupped Mags's face, studying Mags with the intensity of a mother checking her child over and counting body parts. Then Roderick shifted Maeve gently aside and lifted Mags into his powerful arms.

Mags squealed and giggled as she returned the embrace.

Were those tears in Roderick's eyes?

Fiona wouldn't have believed it unless she'd been standing there and seeing it. The first coimhdeacht, the toughest of the world's tough guys, shedding tears like a big baby as he cradled Mags.

Amongst the knot of swirling, laughing people, Fiona picked out Bronwyn. A slight swell to her belly announced her pregnancy. She looked tired but well. Rhiannon had wasted countless lives on getting her hands on those twins Bronwyn was incubating—the culmination of a prophecy so old even Rhiannon didn't remember where it had come from.

The son of death shall bear the torch that lights the path. And the daughter of life shall bring forth water nascent and call it onto the path of light. Then they will bear fruit. And this fruit will be the magick. The greatest of magick and the final magick.

Fiona's chest tightened as her gaze fastened on Bronwyn's pregnant belly. An odd, unraveling sensation like yarn loosening from a ball of wool gripped her lungs. She breathed deep to alleviate the growing pressure in her chest.

Alexander noticed her first and hurried to Bronwyn's side.

The unwinding sped up in Fiona's chest as she met his hostile stare. Hatred hardened the handsome aquiline perfection of Alexander's face, and made his eyes the same cold, dark onyx of Rhiannon's. "Fiona."

"What?" Roderick stilled and turned toward her.

A wolf slunk up beside Niamh and growled, its fangs gleaming white and deadly.

"She saved me." Mags stepped between Fiona and the growing menace.

Warren reached behind him and palmed a handgun. "How the fuck did Baile let her in?"

"Look." Mags held her hands out placatingly. "She's been taking care of me for all this time. It would have been a lot worse without her…"

A low buzzing in Fiona's ears drowned out the rest of what Mags was saying. She shook her head. Mags was pleading for her life, and she needed to pay attention.

Her attention snagged on Alexander, still scowling at her, his fury hot and naked.

The pressure in Fiona's chest built, painful enough to force a gasp out of her.

Emma spun and shifted closer. "Don't fucking move."

Fiona had stepped closer to the Baile folk.

Emma dogged her.

Fiona blinked and the scene in the bailey came back into focus.

They were all still glaring at her murderously but listening to Mags as well.

"Let's go inside," Alannah said. "There's a lot that needs discussing."

"That bitch isn't setting foot in Baile," Roderick growled.

Maeve laid a restraining hand on his arm. "Trust in Goddess."

And then Fiona saw her. Goddess. Incarnate now in a teen girl with chestnut hair. Goddess glowed from within the girl, pearlescent white light surrounding her.

"*Yes, my toy,*" Rhiannon whispered in her mind. "*Fulfill your purpose.*"

Power surged through her muscles, and Fiona lunged, the knife from Roderick's belt somehow in her hand.

A woman screamed.

A huge body was suddenly between her and her target, and Fiona plunged the knife into his chest. Blood magic surged like flaming tar within her, shot down her hand and infused the knife. Its handle pulsed red and then black. Thick, oily darkness oozed into the flesh split by the blade.

Alexander's dark eyes widened as they met hers. Frowning, confused, he glanced down at the knife sticking out of his chest. And crumpled.

A bellow of rage shook the bailey. Birds escaped into the air. "My son."

Roderick's sword cleared his scabbard and arced through the air in one fluid motion.

Everything slowed down and Fiona catalogued the events one by one.

Roderick's sword.

Warren's gun.

Alexander lying at her feet, his blood seeping over the sandy floor of the bailey.

A weeping, desperate Bronwyn, with her hands pressed to Alexander's chest, trying to stem his blood.

Faces frozen in shock.

The descending arc of Roderick's sword.

"Well done, my toy." Rhiannon laughed. *"Now you die."*

And Roderick's sword bit into her neck.

CHAPTER TWO

Fiona's head sailed four feet from her body and splatted on the bailey. Roderick dropped his sword and fell to his knees beside Alexander, his son. His chest felt like he'd cleaved it in half with his sword. This couldn't be happening. He'd only discovered his son, was only now learning to love the man he had become. They hadn't had enough time.

Dimly, the screams and cries of the other Baile residents registered, but he didn't spare them a glance.

Sobbing, and muttering incoherently, Bronwyn was trying to stem the blood flow with her hands. "Help me." She looked at him with tortured eyes. "I need to save him."

Blue light pulsed from Bronwyn's hands as she drew water. The sea lashed against the rocks far below, and honey and sage filled the air—sickeningly sweet.

"No," Goddess screamed and yanked Bronwyn's hands away from Alexander. "You cannot touch him."

Bronwyn fought past her. "I need to—"

"No." Goddess's voice echoed around the bailey. White light streamed from her, and she seemed to swell and vibrate with power. "He is infected, and you must not touch him."

Staring at her in confusion, Bronwyn lurched for Alexander again.

Emma caught her slight form and held her. "Stop, Bronwyn. You need to stop."

"Bronwyn." Hannah was suddenly kneeling beside Alexander. She had a shirt in her hand and was pressing it against the blood.

Alexander's blood. His blood.

Roderick fought the rising panic, trying to reason, trying to act. He turned to Goddess. "Do something."

"I cannot." Tears streamed down her face. "I cannot touch that knife. It is from me, and it will end me."

Hannah's gaze fastened on Bronwyn. "You need to calm down," she said, her voice ice and calm in the tumult. "You're no good to him if you lose it."

Rage rose in Roderick, and he nearly reached for his sword again. How dare the woman demand calm from them.

"Brother." Warren's strong grip manacled his shoulder. "Breathe, brother. You fucking need to breathe. We need you." Warren's grip grew painful. "We need you. Alexander needs you to get it together."

Maeve dropped to her knees beside him. "Roderick." Her sweetness surged down the bond and wrapped around his heart. "Roderick," she whispered.

Tears streamed down her wan face. Her tortured blue eyes fastened on his and held him. The tender force of her will anchored him.

Bronwyn was nodding at something Hannah said. She swallowed and stretched trembling hands toward Alexander. "I'm a healer. I'll heal him."

"No." Goddess's voice rang across the bailey. "Don't touch that wound." She swayed and Kate caught her arm to steady her. She stared stricken at Alexander. "If you touch the knife, you'll sever his soul from existence forever."

Bronwyn blinked at her, blue water magic sparking and glowing between her fingers. "I have to heal him, or he'll…" She choked back a sob.

"You can't." As if gentling a wild creature, Goddess approached and crouched beside Alexander. "That knife is blood magic. If you remove it and attempt to heal him, he will die." She gently shifted Bronwyn's hands away from Alexander. "And the blood magic will transmute through you and take your children with it."

Bronwyn shook her head as if trying to dislodge Goddess's words.

With preternatural calm, Hannah stared at Goddess. "What are you saying?"

"Fiona drew blood magic into the knife and wound." She grimaced. "And that knife staying where it is, is all that is keeping him alive."

"But he is alive?" Hannah put her fingers against the pulse in Alexander's neck.

Goddess pressed a hand to her mouth. "He lives. For now. But every beat of his heart takes the blood magic deeper into his system."

HANDS TUGGED Bronwyn away from Alexander. She tried to fight them off, but they returned with gentle, but insistent, pressure.

"Bronwyn, lovely." Warren's voice rumbled in her ear. "You need to let us move him."

She shook her head, not daring to speak. If she opened her mouth and let the words come, they wouldn't stop. All her will was required to keep Alexander here, keep him with her.

Inside her belly, Regan and Rian radiated waves of alarm.

Their miniature heartbeats accelerated, their terror for Alexander washed over her in waves.

"Bronwyn," Warren said again, his hands manacling her arms and pulling her away from Alexander. "Please, lovely."

Niamh's face wove into focus on the other side of Alexander's limp form. Tears tracked down her cheeks, her green eyes awash as she wept silently. "We've got him, Bronwyn. We're here."

"No." The word blasted out of her on a sob. Some tiny part of her whispered how she was not being rational, how she needed to get a grip—for her babies, for Alexander—but all she could manage was another head shake.

"Bronwyn." Hannah's precise, efficient tones penetrated the numbness. "You need to step aside so we can get him to the healer's hall."

Didn't Hannah understand? Bronwyn couldn't leave him. If she moved from Alexander's side, she would lose him. She was all that stood between him and death. All that stood between him and the slow seeping evil, right this minute, making its way through his blood.

"She's in shock," Hannah said to someone over her shoulder. She gave a grim nod to someone behind Bronwyn.

Bronwyn was bodily lifted away from Alexander.

If they took her away, Alexander would die. Bronwyn screamed and fought the hold, kicking and striking at whatever she could.

"Stop it." Hannah's voice cracked. "You need to calm down. For those babies, and you're upsetting him."

Was she? The dispassion in Hannah's tone felt like a slap in the face. Bronwyn looked at Alexander.

His face was twisted in a rictus of agony. His glazed gaze searched the area around him for something. Her. He was looking for her, worried about her. She had to calm down.

She found Hannah's calm blue eyes in the storm. Hannah

nodded. "Take a deep breath for me," she murmured. "I don't want to sedate you, but I will if I have to."

Sedate her? Render her incapable and unconscious. Every fiber in Bronwyn roared in protest and she went limp in Warren's hold. "I'm okay." Mirroring Hannah, she took another deep breath. "I'm calm."

"In the healer's hall," Hannah snapped to Andy. "There's a gurney. We need it. I want to move him as seamlessly as we can."

Andy ran toward the healer's hall.

Warren's hold on her arms loosened, but he hovered nearby, ready to act if necessary.

"Roderick?" Bronwyn searched the faces around her. "Where's Roderick?"

"Maeve has him," Warren said. "He's worried about you."

"Tell him..." Bronwyn swallowed and tried to finish her sentence. She wasn't fine. She wasn't okay. She wouldn't be okay until Alexander had that awful thing out of him. He had to be fine. She would accept nothing else. "Tell him we need him."

From where he stood with an arm around Mags, Jack nodded. Roderick was a doer, a person of action, he would need a quest to keep him from losing his mind.

Andy returned with the gurney.

"Right." Hannah stood. "We don't want to dislodge that knife." She pointed. "Warren, Jack, Mandla, you're the strongest. Andy, lower the gurney."

People flew to obey Hannah's instructions.

Bronwyn stood to the side, helpless and trying to stem the rising panic.

Tenderly, slowly, and with loving care, Alexander was lifted onto the gurney, and the gurney raised.

"Hold his hand," Hannah said to Bronwyn. "Hold his hand and let him know that you're with him."

Bronwyn slid her hand into Alexander's. The touch almost broke her fragile composure. How many times had they shared a touch like this? How many times had Alexander laughed down at her, love in his dark eyes, and wrapped her hand in his. He'd made her feel safe, cherished, adored, and now his brittle hold on life threatened to take that all away. "I'm here." She pressed a kiss to his forehead. "I'm here."

His hand tightened briefly on hers. His voice rasped as he whispered, "Little witch."

Under Hannah's instruction, they rolled Alexander into the healer's hall.

Mellow, honeyed light streaming through the windows and the astringent bite of the drying herbs centered her. She was a healer. This place stood testament to her blessing. She pressed a hand to her belly and sent loving, reassuring thoughts to her babies. Their babies—hers and Alexander's—and he would live to raise them with her.

"Blessed." Goddess touched her arm. The infinite compassion in those fathomless silver eyes speared past her defenses and into her heart.

Bronwyn's voice caught on a sob. "Why?"

"Trust." Goddess touched her cheek. "Trust and love."

She didn't have any words, so Bronwyn nodded and followed the gurney to a bed.

Hannah supervised the transfer of Alexander from the gurney to the bed, and then glanced at the coven members clustered into the room. "I need everyone to give us a moment," she said. "I'll give you an update as soon as I've examined him." Her eyes gleamed with determination behind her frameless glasses as they met Bronwyn's. "Are you okay enough to help me? Emergency medicine is not my specialty, but I know enough."

"I'm fine." Bronwyn looked at the beloved faces around them. "We're going to need some room to work."

Hannah had a pair of scissors in her hand already and was cutting Alexander's shirt away.

For a moment, Bronwyn wanted to protest. He was so

vulnerable, and she wanted to protect him, and then she moved to fetch supplies to clean away the blood. Pulling on protective gloves, she was nearly overwhelmed by the idea of cleaning up Alexander's blood. No, she needed to stay calm. She needed to think of it as *the* blood, not Alexander's blood.

For all the times he'd stood between her and danger. And for all the times this powerful man had taken on her burdens to spare her, Maeve held Roderick to her breast and rocked him like a baby.

His hands clung to her hips, bruising in their hold.

After he'd slain Fiona, she'd brought him here to their bedchamber and sat him on the bed. She'd stepped between his thighs and wrapped her arms around him and let him express the maelstrom that threatened to break him. He wanted to go to the healer's hall, but Hannah and Bronwyn needed room to work. There would be time enough for Roderick to see Alexander.

His pain buffeted her through their bond, and she absorbed it. He had no words to express his grief, and he didn't need them, because she felt every moment of it.

Regret tinged the heavy, metallic aura of Roderick's grief. He hadn't known Alexander was his son until a few weeks ago. They had only now begun to explore the new relationship between them.

He was grieving, and regretful, but also raging. It built inside him like an unstable, molten core. He wanted to kill Fiona all over again.

Maeve had seen violence many times, but the image of Fiona's head cleaved from her body lurked behind her eyes. The sickening *thwomp* of it hitting the ground still rang in her ears.

As she rocked him, Maeve stroked his dark hair. His tears

wet the fabric of her shirt. He would hate for anyone but her to see him like this.

In his long life, Roderick had so rarely been the one afforded the luxury of succumbing to their emotions. Always, he stood stalwart between the witches and danger. Always, he provided the leadership and the rudder that the coven needed.

"My Maeve." His broken whisper almost undid her. His need for her was palpable and consuming.

Maeve kissed his head. "I'm here."

"I don't know what to do," he rasped. "I was too late to save him."

"He lives, Roderick." She soothed the taut muscles of his back. "He lives, and there is still hope."

"I can't…" He pressed his face into her middle. "Has she won?"

"No." She pushed her resolve through their bond and cupped his face. Turning his face to hers, she met his ravaged stare. "She will never win, because we will not allow it."

"My son." He pressed his eyelids together. "She took my son."

"No." She pressed her forehead against his. "Listen to me, Roderick. He lives, and for as long as he does, there is hope. How many times have you told me never to give up hope?"

He flinched. "But—"

"No." She tightened her hold on his beloved face. "We never give up. We fight on, and we need you in that fight."

With a shuddering breath, he rested his cheek against her belly. "Okay." He gave a small nod. "We fight."

Through their bond, she felt him calm and grow grimly determined. There was a hard edge to his resolve that frightened her, a single-mindedness that would not be swayed. She tucked her concern away before he could sense it and wiped his face with her palms. "Bronwyn and those babies need you," she said, hating that she needed to press him but knowing that duty would lead Roderick back to the light. "You promised him you would take care of them."

He stiffened and then nodded. "And I will." His hands tightened around her hips briefly, and then he released her. "Enough."

Maeve stepped back as he stood. He was so much taller than her, she had to crane her neck to maintain eye contact. The contrast between his intimidating physicality and the terror for his son that roiled within him struck her. She slid her arms around his waist and rested her cheek to his chest. "We will get through this, Roderick. Together."

"Always." He rested his cheek on top of her head. "You are the best witch a coimhdeacht could serve."

A GRIM BAILE sat down to dinner that night. Nobody thought, or perhaps even noticed, that Alannah had cooked the meal. Bronwyn had been persuaded to rest for a couple of hours, and Roderick sat with Alexander.

Alannah had sent Maeve to Bronwyn with her dinner on a tray. She needed to eat, for the sake of those babies. For the first time, she was glad Thomas was not here to experience this with them.

"I saw it," Mags said as she stirred her spoon listlessly through her leek and potato soup. "I saw the vision, but I didn't know what it meant."

Jack nudged her spoon as Emma said, "Eat. You're too thin as it is."

Obediently, Mags put a spoonful of soup in her mouth. Her breath hitched and she swallowed. "Why did I bring her here?"

"Because you're compassionate." Jack put his arm around her shoulders. "Because you're a better person than she deserves." He grimaced. "Deserved."

"And I was standing right next to her," Emma said, her gray eyes fierce. "She moved so fast I didn't even know what she was going to do until it was too late."

"There's no point to this." Kate dropped her spoon in her bowl with a clink. "Could have, would have, should have. It's always so easy after the fact to decide what we could have done better."

So true. Alannah added freshly baked bread to the table. She had avoided cooking since Thomas had left. Memories of the hours he'd spent in the kitchen with her were too painful for her to broach.

Sinead touched her wrist. "You okay?"

"As well as can be expected." She turned and fetched the butter. The attack on Alexander brought her own loss to the surface. The look of unadulterated pain on Bronwyn's face as she'd knelt beside Alexander would haunt her when she tried to sleep tonight. Had she looked like that the night Thomas had disappeared?

With a gentle smile, Sinead squeezed her wrist.

The door opened, and a tired Hannah walked in.

"Charlie went to bed an hour ago," Taylor said. "He had dinner first, and then I read him a story."

"Thank you." Hannah slid her fingers beneath her glasses and rubbed her eyes. She took a seat at the table. "I don't have a lot more information, but he's stable for now."

Alannah slid a bowl of soup in front of her. "You're doing your best."

"But emergency medicine is not my specialty." Hannah grimaced. "I told Roderick as much, but I'm not sure how much he's absorbing."

"He's in shock." Alannah had never seen Roderick anything less than rock solid, impenetrable as Baile itself.

Picking up her spoon, Hannah gave her a weary smile of thanks. "I've added a few more items to my supply list," she said to Andy. "I'll add more items as I need them." She sighed. "It's been a long time since I worked in accident and emergency. I feel like a green intern."

Andy nodded. "Whatever you need."

"A trauma doctor would be nice." Hannah shrugged and tore a chunk of bread from the loaf. She ate mechanically, as if she was fueling the machine rather than enjoying her food.

Alannah couldn't remember when her cooking efforts had received less appreciation. Nobody had any appetite tonight.

Beside Kate, Dhara huddled in a guilty heap. She definitely knew more than she was saying. None of them, including Dhara, knew how blurred the line was between her and Goddess.

Baile wanted answers, and they looked to Goddess for them. While Goddess occupied a frightened, shocked fifteen-year-old girl.

CHAPTER THREE

"Ah, bollocks." Andy lowered his coffee cup as the police vehicle eased into the bailey two mornings after Alexander had been struck down. He'd gotten up early to get the jump on Hannah's newest list of supplies. The last thing Baile needed right now was the police here again.

He wasn't surprised when the burly form of DCI Lennox heaved himself out of the passenger seat. His sidekick, Constable Acharya, turned off the ignition before joining Lennox.

Jack was back, and so were the coppers. Coincidence? Andy had a sinking feeling it was not. On a deep, steadying breath he opened the kitchen door and managed a neutral smile. "DCI Lennox." He nodded in the man's direction. "Constable Acharya. What brings you here this morning?"

"Mr. Braithwaite." Lennox hitched his trousers over his middle-age spread. "We've been expecting a call from you."

Andy hid his trepidation behind his smile. "And why is that?"

Acharya dug a notebook out of his pocket. "We have it on good authority that Mr. Jack Langham and Miss Madeleine

Cray were seen driving through Greater Littleton two nights past at seventeen thirty."

"He means half past five." Lennox threw Acharya a hard glance. Then he tried an oily sort of grin in Andy's direction. "These young blokes, always so eager."

"I'm afraid we had a little excitement recently." Andy hoped never to live through another afternoon like it. A low constant ache in his chest kept Alexander and Bronwyn in his mind. And those twins Bronwyn carried. Andy felt powerless in the face of their need. "We didn't have a chance to give you a ring."

Lennox raised one craggy brow. "Excitement?"

"Indeed." Andy had no intention of answering the DCI's question. He wouldn't know where to begin. At least not in any manner that wouldn't result in all of them coming closely acquainted with the local police station. "But as you're here now, you have saved me the effort." He stood in the kitchen doorway, effectively barring the coppers' way. Unless they had the documentation, the buggers could stand outside like the vultures they were. "Jack has, indeed, just returned."

"Then we'd like to speak to him." Lennox glanced pointedly toward the inside of the kitchen. "If that would be convenient."

It was so the bloody opposite of convenient. "It is my under-standing that Mr. Conrad Lester has returned to his home."

"Is it?" Lennox cocked his head. "And how did you come by that information?"

"Like you, Detective." Andy allowed himself a small moment of smugness. "I have my sources."

Lennox pursed his lips. "You're an interesting man, Mr. Braithwaite." Somehow, Andy sensed that was not a compli-ment. "You worked for the VOA previously, and were assigned to investigate this castle, in fact. You handed in your notice suddenly and without warning and took up residence here." He shoved his hands into the pockets of his pants. "I don't suppose you'd have an explanation for any of that."

The explanation would not be one Lennox would comprehend, so Andy leaned his shoulder against the doorjamb and gave the appearance of thinking through Lennox's request. He blamed the upset of yesterday for the brusqueness of his tone as he replied, "No, I don't think I will explain. And as far as I'm aware, none of my actions require, or are worthy of, police interest."

"Hmm." Lennox's sharp gaze traveled over the castle. "Yet, every time I come here, I find myself with more questions."

Andy didn't bother to reply to that obvious attempt at intimidation. "Also, unless you have probable cause relating to Mr. Langham, it is entirely at his discretion whether he answers your questions."

"We have the bullet casing." Acharya had a go at playing bad cop. With his open, fresh face, it failed to raise so much as a quiver of apprehension. "We also have traces of human blood near the location of said bullet casing, and an unexplained car accident."

"How unfortunate for you," Andy drawled. "Are these your grounds for questioning Mr. Langham?"

"It's all right, Andy." Jack spoke from behind him. "I have nothing to hide."

Acharya tensed as Jack's big form edged past Andy into the bailey.

Lennox stayed cucumber cool. "Hello, Jack. Fancy seeing you here."

"Not really." Jack strolled into the bailey. "As I'm sure you know, I live here now."

"And I find myself interested in knowing why." Lennox studied Jack through narrowed eyes. "We'd like you to come with us and answer some questions."

"Okay." Jack strolled toward the vehicle. "Let's get this over with."

"Jack?" Emma appeared tense as a hunting leopard behind Andy. "You don't have to go with them."

"I know that." Jack shrugged. "But I have nothing to tell them, and the sooner I get on with telling them that, the sooner they'll stop showing up on our doorstep."

Andy wanted to argue, wanted to toss Lennox and Acharya out of Baile on their ears, but maybe Jack was right. With all that was going on, they didn't need the continued police scrutiny.

Emma and Jack exchanged a long look. Finally, Emma nodded and stopped beside Andy. "I'll see you later."

"Count on it," Jack said, as he opened the back door to the police vehicle and climbed inside.

Lennox looked at Emma then Andy. His keen eyes searched for answers before he turned and went back to his vehicle.

"Jack will be fine," Mags said from beside Emma.

Andy didn't know whether Mags knew that because she had her strange way of knowing things, or whether it was wishful thinking. Given what had happened to Alexander, he didn't want to ask. He would rather go on believing Mags *knew* Jack would be all right.

Emma and Mags remained beside him as the police vehicle drove out of Baile.

Determination hardened in Andy's gut. "I need to get on with sourcing Hannah's supplies," he said. "And then I'm going to nail down where these police orders are coming from."

Emma nodded. "Let Sasha know if he can help."

"Will do." Andy poured himself another cup of coffee before he went to his study. In the office Baile had given him, the old castle felt weary and sad, as if it too held its breath while Alexander fought for his life.

MAGS DIDN'T LIKE WATCHING Jack be led away by the police. Letting him out of her sight felt wrong on so many levels. They'd only just found each other again.

"Hey." Emma put an arm around her shoulders. "Jack's an old hand at dealing with the police; he'll be fine."

Mags managed a nod. "Yes, he will."

"Hi." Dhara wandered into the kitchen looking sheepish. "So, she"—she jabbed a thumb at her own chest—"says you guys need to, like, bond or something."

Mags couldn't help but stare at Dhara. The girl had the most beautiful, pure white aura, but blending inside that blinding white light were the more usual, muddier shades of a human girl. Also, she couldn't get a read on Dhara. With most people, she got something, some hint of what the future held in store for them. Dhara, however, was a complete blank, and she got an idea of what non-seers saw when they looked at other people.

Emma glanced at Dhara and grimaced. "We know, but now might not be the right time."

"She"—Dhara tapped her breastbone—"disagrees."

Neither Mags nor Taylor had received even the slightest vision or seeing to suggest that Goddess would reincarnate in a human teen. It felt like failure to Mags. With all the precognition, she'd not been able to prepare Baile or Kate and Dhara for what waited in their future. Guilt gave a nasty twist through her belly. She had seen Alexander's trouble but had been unable to interpret it in time to be of any use.

The energy in the kitchen shifted, and Dhara's eyes glowed silver. Goddess had taken over their shared body. "Blessed," she said to Mags, "you must bond with your coimhdeacht."

"Oh, boy." Emma stared at Goddess like she was conflicted between bowing and laughing. "That is some freaky shit."

Goddess took Mags's hand and then Emma's. "There is no need for ritual anymore. Tell me, do you accept this bond?"

"So, Emma doesn't need to get naked in front of the rest of

the coven?" Mags remembered Warren's vehement objections to doing that.

"No." Goddess smiled. "Do you accept your bond?"

"I do," Emma said.

Mags nodded. "I do."

Light spilled from Goddess like the tide washing up the shore. It engulfed the three of them and then scattered as tiny droplets that settled into Emma and Mags.

The coimhdeacht markings on Emma's arm flared and grew darker.

And then Mags felt her. The strong, fiercely independent, loyal, and determined woman who was her coimhdeacht.

Emma's eyes gleamed as she touched her solar plexus. "It's you." Then she chuckled. "Bugger it, Mags, but your thoughts are a jumble, and that has nothing to do with your blessing."

CHAPTER FOUR

Warren eyed the hectic glitter in Roderick's eyes with trepidation. He glanced at Mandla through the Landy's rearview mirror to see the big South African giving Roderick a similar look. There was an air of menace surrounding Roderick that made Warren not want to be taking a drive with a large, edgy bastard who had super strength and a huge sword.

"Where are we going?" When Roderick asked him to drive and roped Mandla and Emma into their mission, he hadn't asked any questions, but now he wanted to know.

Roderick's jaw firmed. "The hospital."

"Hospital?" Emma sat forward and rested her forearm on the back of Roderick's seat. "Why do we need a hospital?"

With a growl, Roderick said, "Because that is where there will be a doctor of the sort Hannah needs. I asked Andy to google it, but he said he already knew where we could find a trauma doctor." He worked the unfamiliar term carefully out of his mouth.

"Find a trauma doctor?" That innocuous phrase seemed to carry the weight of hidden intentions, and now Warren definitely wanted those out in the open. "And by find a trauma doctor, you mean what exactly?"

"Drive." Roderick rapped the dashboard. "I will tell you when we reach the hospital."

Yeah, no, Warren wasn't feeling reassured.

"How is Alexander?" Emma asked softly.

Roderick grunted. "He ails."

Two days since that fucking rotten night, and Baile held its breath. Roderick and Bronwyn spent most of those days in the healer's hall with Alexander.

Putting the Landy in gear, Warren drove them out of the bailey and onto the road to the village. What the hell! It beat waiting at the castle for Jack to get back from the police station. Warren only partly understood why Jack had gone along with the coppers so readily. Jack had said it was the fastest way to get them off his back. As a past offender, Jack would always be first in the police's crosshairs when something suspicious had taken place. With Alexander's condition, he argued, it was best for everyone if they comply and not garner any more attention.

Andy didn't think Jack's compliance would do it. The police were on the hunt, and someone higher up was pulling the strings to make sure the hunt stayed hot.

Emma cleared her throat. "Not to be rude or anything, but you do know what a trauma doctor is?"

"No." Roderick folded his arms and sunk his chin to his chest. "But I know what I need to know, which is that my son needs one."

They all shuddered as they crossed the wards. Mandla rubbed his coimhdeacht markings, and Warren experienced the same tingle as the other man.

The crazy in the bathrobe had gathered a couple of friends. They all turned as the Landy cleared the wards, leaped to their feet like aliens had landed and ran toward the Landy.

Warren pressed hard on the accelerator, and they scattered.

Mandla turned in his seat to stare at their diminishing shapes through the back window. "Will they be a problem?"

"Not if they stay this side of the wards," Emma replied in a tone that promised she would make sure of that.

The village green was awash in people. Warren thought he might have spotted Gresby and Cressida amongst the throng. The musty scent of sage permeated the Landy, and Mandla sneezed. It looked like a bank holiday with the number of people milling about. And beneath the sage, Warren picked up the unmistakable stench of blood magic.

With Alexander so ill, Warren didn't want to go past his former manor house, so he stuck to the main road out of town.

"Turn left at the next junction," Emma said as she tracked them through her mobile. "The hospital is about twenty clicks and on the right."

Warren had the nasty feeling he wasn't going to like where this mission was heading.

———

SIMON CHECKED the clock over the nurse's station. Fifteen minutes to the end of his night shift. After tonight, he had a whole two weeks off to look forward to. The night had been long and full of the usual crazy brought on by Friday night. He should have been excited about his holiday. Instead, he was filled with the familiar dread of how to fill all those empty hours. His ex had been one hundred percent right about him, galling as it was to admit. He didn't have a life outside of this hospital and this A&E unit.

His parents had left for their annual pilgrimage to Greece, and he could go and see his two brothers. The thought flattened his mood even more. His brothers had wives and families and made him feel like a sodding loser. And they talked about bloody animals all the time. Simon had no issue with animals, he'd love to have a dog, but he drew the line at verbally dissecting creatures great and small over the dinner table.

"Doctor Lewisham?" A bright-eyed, perky intern cornered him as he turned from the nurse's desk.

Behind the desk, Maureen groaned. "Makes me tired just looking at her."

Maureen was a veteran of A&E and had seen more interns come and go than the average medical program. Come to think of it, she might have been here when he'd been an intern.

"Doctor Lewisham." The intern tucked a tendril of hair behind her ear, her light brown eyes glowing up at him with the fervor of a new physician. "Can I please consult with you on the spinal in eight?"

Had he ever been that young and arrogant? His ex argued he was still arrogant. Simon suppressed the urge to snap at the intern. "Did you mean Mrs. Carlisle?"

"Be gentle, Doc." Maureen chuckled and peered at him over the half-moon lenses of her readers. "You were once a snotty upstart."

Yup, Maureen had definitely been one of the nurses to break him to heel as an intern.

"Um." The intern pulled the chart out from beneath her arm and scanned it. "Yes, that's right. Mrs. Brenda Carlisle."

"She has a name," Simon's tone barely avoided being a snarl. "She is neither a medical condition nor is she a bay number."

The intern blinked at him. "I just meant—"

"I know what you meant." He took the file out of her limp hands and strode away. "But we treat people here. Remember that."

"Yes, doctor." Her feet pattered behind him. "I only wanted to know if I could be in when you examine eight—I mean, Mrs. Carlisle."

"No." He stopped before the curtain and lowered his voice.

"And she has a possible spinal injury. Also remember that she is still awaiting her diagnosis, and she is frightened and in pain."

Irritation flashed through the intern's eyes. "No? You mean I can't attend with you?"

"That's exactly what I mean. I don't believe no is a word that allows for much interpretation."

"But—"

"Stitches." Maureen slapped a file against the intern's chest. "Rudy Grey, eight years old, playing with a pocketknife."

The intern opened her mouth to argue. A spinal injury was so much more interesting than stitches, but she thought better of it, took the file, and scuttled away. There was hope for her yet.

Maureen looked at him before she tugged the curtain back. "Ready?"

Schooling his features into a professional mask, Simon nodded.

Pale and sedated, the middle-aged woman lying in the bed looked up. Her dull eyes fastened on him as if he could offer her salvation.

If only. "Good morning, Mrs. Carlisle. I'm Doctor Lewisham, and I understand you tangled with a garden fence."

EMMA'S PHONE pinged an incoming message from Andy. They were parked outside A&E, the faint glow of the illuminated Emergency sign creating pockets of shadow inside the Landy. Jesus, this was a fucking horrible idea.

Her gaze met Warren's and he grimaced. No, Warren didn't agree with what was about to happen. But yes, Warren would go along with it. She tapped Roderick on the shoulder. "That's him."

A tall, fit man walked across the parking lot, stuffing his

arms into his coat as he walked. He was dressed in hospital scrubs, and he walked like a man with the weight of the world on his shoulders.

"Simon Lewisham," she read off the screen. "Thirty-four. Divorced. No children. Nobody will come looking for him for two weeks."

When Roderick had announced his plan to get Hannah a trauma doctor, none of them had known exactly what he meant. Now they did. Unable to dissuade Roderick from his quest, they'd at least managed to get him to agree to finding the best candidate for a spot of dawn abduction. Andy and his magical internet fingers had unearthed who they needed. It was scary how quickly Andy ferreted out information from cyberspace. Emma had been praying he didn't find a likely candidate—but, nope!

Warren sighed and turned to Roderick. "Look," he said in the tone of the last reasonable man on the planet. "Are you sure you—"

"Aye." Roderick yanked on his door handle.

"Okay." Warren leaned across him and slammed the door shut again. "Then at least let's do this the smart way."

Emma snorted at that one. Smart abduction was an oxymoron.

Glancing at her, Warren nodded. "Do it."

Here went nothing.

Emma eased out of the Landy, Mandla right on her heels. Mandla vanished into the shadows and let her stride toward the unfortunate Doctor Lewisham alone. On his way to the doctor's parking lot, the good doctor was about to experience a very bad morning. If she didn't think Roderick would go full rogue on this, she would never have agreed to carry out the mission.

The rumble of the Landy's engine assured her Warren was easing into place for swift retrieval.

"Simon Lewisham?"

He stopped and turned at the sound of her call. Dark hair and lighter eyes in a classically handsome face that had grown craggy around the edges. A slight frown crinkled his brow as she approached. "Yes."

"I'm Emma," she said with a smile. "We met a couple of weeks ago."

His frown deepened as he tried to place her, doubt mingling with civility on his strong, clean features. "I'm sorry, I can't quite remember…"

"Right." Emma stopped in front of him. "You probably meet so many people, it's hard to remember. Emma." She held out her hand. "Doctor Emma Fletcher."

"Dr. Fletcher?" Some of his uncertainty fled. His glance flit to a dark blue sedan parked nearby. "What can I do for you?"

So many things. But Emma kept that to herself as she shook his hand. "I took a chance you worked the night shift last night."

Mandla loomed behind Simon.

Some instinct warned Simon, and he half turned, but Mandla covered his mouth and dragged him against his chest.

Simon's eyes flared in alarm, as he struggled against Mandla's hold.

Emma stepped forward and jabbed him in the neck with the sedative Roderick had lifted from the healer's hall.

Simon slumped.

The Landy's back door flew open, and they bundled him inside.

Neat, quick, and tidy, and over before anyone was any the wiser.

"Drive." She clapped Warren on the shoulder. "One trauma doctor acquired."

CHAPTER FIVE

Bronwyn looked from Roderick to Warren, then Emma and Mandla, before finally looking down at the inert form restrained on the bed beside Alexander. "You did what?"

Warren cleared his throat. "Hannah said she needed a trauma doctor."

"And you…" Bronwyn pressed her thumb and forefinger into her eyes. None of them would look her in the eye. "You kidnapped this poor man?"

"We…waylaid him." Emma winced and stepped back. "If it helps, nobody will miss him for a while."

Nope. That didn't help at all. Bronwyn's exhausted brain refused to process the information. She glared at Roderick. "Why?"

He folded his arms and scowled. "Hannah said—"

"I got that part." Fury swelled inside her. She couldn't fucking deal with this shit right now. They'd kidnapped a doctor. Kidnapped. A. Doctor. "What the hell do you expect me to do with him?"

"Maybe heal him first." Mandla finished fastening the restraints around Simon Lewisham. "We had to give him something to knock him out. Not too sure we got the dosage right."

Oh, this kept getting better and better. "You drugged him?"

On top of the drugging—and the kidnapping, lest she forget —they had restrained him. After abducting the poor man, they were now tying him up. She barely managed to keep her voice below a bellow as she said, "Let him go."

"Not a good idea." Mandla shook his head. "He's going to be upset when he comes 'round."

"He has every right to be," Bronwyn lost the battle and yelled. "You kidnapped him."

Roderick's jaw set in a stubborn line that made her want to punch him. "You need him. Alexander needs him."

And Bronwyn lost what few wits she had left. "You had no right to do this. Don't we have enough to deal with right now? Don't I have enough to deal with?"

"What's going on?" Hannah stumbled into the healer's hall, pulling her hair into a tie as she walked. She stopped dead and pointed to the doctor. "Who's that?"

"Ask them." Bronwyn was about to go hysterical if she stood there any longer.

Hannah looked at Warren for an explanation.

He took a deep breath and averted his gaze. "We got you a trauma doctor."

Glancing at the doctor, Hannah gaped at Warren. "Why is he tied to the bed?"

"Oh, this is the good part." Bronwyn dug her nails into her palms, so she didn't take her temper out on Hannah. Warren deserved no such consideration as she snarled at him, "Tell her!"

"We...er...brought him here." Warren shifted. "Not entirely voluntarily."

Insane laughter bubbled in Bronwyn's throat. She didn't have the capacity for this. Alexander could be—no, she wouldn't think that.

"We drugged him and tossed him in the Landy." Mandla looked like he was reciting the day's weather. "You might want to check on him, because we didn't exactly have time to measure the dosage."

"Jesus." Hannah breathed. "Oh, fuck."

"Well put," Bronwyn snapped. "Take him back."

Doctor Simon Lewisham chose that moment to groan. His eyelids fluttered open and then closed again. His breath wheezed through his teeth.

The healer in Bronwyn took over and she approached him. "Doctor Lewisham? Simon?"

Hannah joined her on the other side of the bed. She lifted his eyelids and checked his pupils. Then she took his pulse. She made a face at Bronwyn. "Whatever we do or do not do with him, you need to heal him."

"I will kill you for this." Bronwyn scowled at the idiots standing around the healer's hall. "And then I'll reanimate you and kill you again."

"You're upsetting Alexander." Roderick glanced down at his son.

The stark terror in his face gave Bronwyn the hold on sanity she needed. Roderick was suffering along with her. That didn't mean she could or would excuse what those morons had done, but it did give her a glimmer of understanding.

Water surged through her in the familiar scents of honey and sage as she drew on her blessing. She swayed as the effects of the sedative passed from Simon to her.

Warren grabbed her elbow and steadied her.

And then the drug was transmuted into the earth.

And Doctor Lewisham woke up.

SIMON'S first thought was that he must have been in a car accident or something, because he was lying on his back on what resembled a hospital bed with a bunch of strangers staring down at him.

But he didn't remember even getting into his car, and he didn't hurt. He just felt confused, and his mouth tasted vile.

A pretty redhead leaned over him. "Doctor Lewisham? Simon?"

"Who are you?" He had to work to get moisture into his arid mouth. "Where am I?"

The redhead glared, but not at him. He turned his head in the direction of her scowl. Three men stood shoulder to shoulder, big buggers too, and all of them eyeing the redhead nervously. A blond woman stood beside them, and she looked vaguely familiar.

"You're in a heal—hospital." The redhead touched his arm. "You're in a hospital."

"Of sorts." The blonde grimaced. "But you are safe."

Simon tried to move, but his wrist snagged on something. He tugged harder but he was caught. His brain took a while to catch up with the evidence his eyes provided. His wrist was restrained. He gave an experimental tug on the opposite wrist, and then his ankles.

Ball clenching fear rushed through him. He was tied down with a bunch of strangers staring at him. He battered the fear back and forced himself to think. Information. He needed information.

"What hospital?" He turned his gaze back to the redhead.

She sighed. Something about her eyes bothered him. They were the eyes of a woman in pain. "It's not really a hospital. It's a healer's hall, and you're inside Baile Castle."

That name rang a distant bell. He struggled through the cotton wool in his brain to place it. "Who are you?"

"I'm Bronwyn." She pressed a hand to her chest. "And I'm a healer."

One of the men, the big man of color, cleared his throat. "Might want to avoid names."

Bronwyn's strange vocabulary caught him off guard. "You're a doctor? Have I been injured?"

"Not physically." Bronwyn scowled at the men again. "But you have been…er…you've suffered from our actions."

"Doctor Lewisham?" Another woman peered down at him. This one wore glasses and scrubs. He drew comfort from the stethoscope around her neck. "I'm Doctor Hannah Maxwell."

"Hannah Maxwell?" That name also sounded familiar, but his brain was still treacle. "So I am in hospital?"

"No." From the cluster of men, the one with the cropped blond hair stepped forward. "Look," he said. "There really is no easy way to tell you this, but we kidnapped you."

That couldn't be right. Then again, he was being restrained. "Kidnapped me?"

"Yes." The man nodded and looked contrite. "We're sorry about that part."

Deep down, outrage stirred in Simon, but he was still in too much shock to register it. "Why?"

"We need your help," the man said. "And we didn't have time to explain."

Fury washed over Simon in a blinding wave. "Like fucking hell!"

"Quite right," Bronwyn snapped at the blond man. "And now what, genius?" Her American accent morphed into a terrible version of a British accent. "A touch of torture? A spot of coercion?"

"Now, we explain." A huge bastard with frigid eyes and dark hair stepped forward. "Now we explain that we need him to save my son's life."

Hannah blew a long breath. "Oh boy."

Some twisted part of Simon demanded clarity. "Let me understand this," he said, still flat on his back because they'd fucking restrained him. "You kidnap me, tie me up, and then believe that I will help you?" That same twisty bit in his brain actually stepped outside himself and laughed its ass off.

"My son is dying," the big bastard said.

Oh, well then, as long as there's a good reason for kidnapping me. Before he could air his inner sarcasm, Bronwyn went pale, her right hand cupping the slight rounding of her abdomen.

Simon had seen plenty of pregnant women use that gesture. An unwelcome tendril of empathy squirmed inside him. Then he noticed the man lying on the bed beside his.

The first thing he noticed was the fucking knife sticking out of the man's chest. He glanced at Hannah. "Um…you are aware…" He tried to wave his hand in that direction, got stopped, and jerked his head.

"Yes, I'm aware." Hannah pulled a face. "But it's complicated."

It was a fucking knife in the man's chest, and if it hadn't nicked either the aorta, pulmonary artery, or coronary artery he'd be amazed. Judging by the lack of blood, that knife was keeping the man from bleeding out. "He needs surgery. Is that why I'm here?"

"Um…sort of." Hannah wrinkled her nose and looked at Bronwyn.

Bronwyn drooped, all the anger draining out of her to be replaced by what looked to be grief or worry. Could she be attached to the injured man?

"You need to do something." Simon yanked against his restraints. "Or that man is going to die."

"Like I said." Hannah stepped back. "It's more complicated than that, but he's not in any immediate danger."

"Why is that man tied to the bed?" A woman's voice sounded from over to his right. It was sweet and husky and everyone turned to face the sound.

So often, a person's voice didn't match their appearance. In this case, the woman was everything her voice promised her to be. Long, auburn hair framed the most perfect bone structure he'd ever seen. Above the full curve of her mouth, a straight nose rested beneath eyes the color of spring irises. His breath caught and he stared. She held a tray in her hands and her long, slim legs were encased in jeans.

Those eyes were on him, and a slight frown creased her creamy brow. "Bronwyn?"

Bronwyn sighed and looked at the big man. "Ask Roderick."

The newcomer looked to Roderick, whom Simon presumed was the big bastard beside his bed. "Roderick?"

The blond man answered. "Hey, Alannah. What are you doing here?"

"I brought Bronwyn something to eat." She raised the tray. "She didn't make it to breakfast this morning, and she can't skip meals."

Alannah. Her name was Alannah. An inexplicable warmth spread through Simon's chest. He experienced the disorienting jolt of *deja vu*. He knew her from somewhere, but he was also painfully aware that he'd never met her before. Simon would have remembered Alannah. And he had the distinct impression that now that he had met her, he would never be able to forget her. All this in less than five minutes. It must be whatever sedative they'd given him.

She moved like sunlight through water to between his bed and the man with the knife wound and put the tray down on a small table. The distinct waft of roses and something more—woodsy and sweet at the same time. She smelled like Christmas morning.

Christ! What the hell had they given him? It was buggering with his head and making him fanciful.

"You need to untie him," she said, and those indigo eyes

found his. She stilled and blinked at him, and then gave her head a tiny shake. "Untie him, Warren."

Simon forced his mind to put the pieces together. Big bastard went by Roderick, blond man by Warren, which left the barnlike man of color and the attractive blonde woman as yet unnamed. The blonde woman he had seen before but his sluggish brain refused to cough up an answer. A hazy memory of her approaching him in the hospital parking lot surfaced and then disappeared before he could get clarity. He concentrated on what he did know. Hannah and Bronwyn he had clear, and Alannah.

"Nay." Roderick crossed his arms. Impressive biceps flexed along with some well-developed flexors along his forearms. "We cannot risk releasing him."

"This is inhuman." Alannah gestured toward Simon. "You can't do this."

"I've already done it." Roderick thrust his chin out.

Alannah huffed. "Then undo it."

"Nay."

"Um…Alannah." The attractive blonde stepped forward. "We acquired Doctor Lewisham in a rather unorthodox manner."

"Doctor?" Indigo eyes rested on his face again, and he swore he almost felt sunlight on his skin.

Hannah sighed. "I made an offhand remark about needing an emergency medicine specialist to help Alexander."

Knife wound was Alexander. Simon stored it all away for when he got out of here and turned in this fucked up bunch to the police. He'd make it clear he told the coppers Alannah had wanted him set free.

Alannah pressed a hand to her mouth.

Mesmerized, he watched as her lips split into a grin she tried to suppress. "Oh, Roderick, you didn't?"

Now Simon was not feeling quite as charitable toward her.

"He bloody well did," Warren grumbled. "And made us all accessories to the crime."

"And you too, Emma?" Alannah finally put a name to the attractive blonde. "You went along with this?"

Emma Fletcher. Simon got it now. She'd introduced herself in the parking lot as a doctor and he'd lowered his guard—more fool him.

Emma winced. "He didn't give any of us much of a choice."

"Roderick." Alannah sighed and turned back to Simon. "I'm so sorry about this, Doctor…Lewisham."

"Simon," he croaked. "My name is Simon."

She smiled, and if he hadn't been flat on his back, he would have lost control of his knees. "I'm so sorry, Simon. Are you hungry?"

Was he? He couldn't quite think past another hunger that woke inside him. More than sexual, although there was a fair amount of that, this hunger was soul deep.

Alannah's fingers were cool against his wrist as she worked on the restraints. "Why don't we all sit down to a nice lunch and talk about this?" She freed one of his hands.

"Do not release him." Roderick lurched for her.

Fierce protectiveness welled in Simon, which was beyond ridiculous given that he was the one who'd been abducted and forcibly held.

"Roderick." Alannah threw the man a pitying look. "You can't keep Simon chained to a bed if you want his help. Why don't we all have lunch together and talk about this?"

Roderick got to the other side of the bed faster than Simon could blink and stopped Alannah's hand on his other restraint. "If we release him, he will escape."

"Also report us," Warren said.

Emma nodded, as did the nameless barnlike bugger by the window.

"No, he won't." Alannah smiled down on him. "At least not

until we've had a chance to explain." Her eyes beseeched him. "Will you, Simon?"

When she looked at him like that, he'd give her his physician's hands if she asked. Simon found himself nodding. "No. I'll hear you out."

CHAPTER SIX

Sinead stood near the hairline crack in Baile's kitchen garden walls. Baile didn't crack, and she didn't get dusty. Except, apparently, she did now.

"I pointed it out to Roderick whilst you were away." Andy stood and dusted his hands against each other.

An unenthusiastic autumn sun gave breaking through the clouds a passing attempt. Around them, herbs and vegetables lay dormant for the coming winter, bare branches sticking out like pins on an earth cushion. She and Alannah needed to do some pruning but working up enthusiasm for anything seemed like a gargantuan task.

Sinead traced the crack with her forefinger. "It should have disappeared when we healed the wards."

"That's what I thought." Andy frowned. "But we are still finding the odd spot of dust here and there."

Just to confirm for herself, she asked, "And this was here before you had the big shake up when Goddess incarnated?"

"It was." Andy nodded. "Have you any idea what it means?"

"Not a clue." Belly knotting, Sinead stood beside Andy and looked up at the soaring gray walls of the keep. Baile had stood since the twelfth century and never shown signs of her age. She was a visible sentinel for cré-magic and her showing wear and tear couldn't mean anything good. More shitty news. Sinead kept her sigh on the inside. "Have you noticed anything else like it?"

"Not as yet," he said. "But this is a large castle, and small damages such as that crack are hard to pick up." He straightened the cuffs on his pale blue button down. "Debra and I are conducting a more thorough assessment of the castle."

"That's a good idea." Sinead didn't like the direction her thoughts were taking. If Baile was getting small cracks, allowing dust to appear, it had to mean something was wrong with the magic infusing every stone of the castle. Initially, they'd assumed the problems arose from the anomaly in the wards. That if the wards were compromised, it compromised the time bubble encasing the castle and preventing it from decaying or aging. If the problem was in the core magic, however, it could be far more concerning. "Alannah and I will check the wards again and do a hunt through the castle itself with our blessing, see if we find any more nasty surprises from that bitch."

"Right." Andy nodded. "Also…" He cleared his throat. "I don't wish to speak out of turn, but Emma requested a very unusual search early this morning. It was so early, in fact, that I was still asleep."

"Search?" Sinead put the mint on top of her pruning list. It was doing its best to take over the entire herb garden again.

"Internet search," Andy said. "She asked me to find a trauma specialist and to delve a bit into their history and personal particulars."

"What does Emma want that for?" And she didn't get why Andy was telling her about this. Surely, Mags would be a better person to approach if Andy had a concern about Emma. Emma was Mags's coimhdeacht. Then again, Mags could be away with the fairies on a good day.

Andy followed her through the kitchen gardens. "It wasn't for Emma, but for Roderick."

"What does Rod—" And she knew the big guy far too well to miss the relevance. "What kind of personal details?"

Andy looked uncomfortable and shoved his hands in his pockets. "Um…whether they had family, dependents. Living situation. Those sorts of details."

"Ah, hell no!" Sinead tore her eyes away from the rosemary. "In other words, he was looking for an emergency doctor who nobody would miss if they disappeared."

Andy kept his gaze assiduously on the treetops of the orchard. "That was my conclusion as well."

"Buggering buggery." Sinead had to take a deep breath. Roderick going psycho was the last thing they all bloody well needed. Sinead would never forget the sickening sight of Roderick separating Fiona's head from her neck. Thank Goddess Baile had dealt with that nasty surprise and disappeared both the body and the head. It did raise the icky issue of where Fiona's head had gone, but some questions were better not asked.

"And." Andy coughed into his fist and went back to his tree line reverie. "Roderick, Warren, Emma, and Mandla returned this morning and entered the healer's hall carrying something." He grimaced. "A large something that required both Warren and Mandla to carry it. Carefully."

And Sinead wanted to drop to the damp earth and cry. It was all too much. Alexander lying like the barely living dead. Bronwyn's inconsolable grief. Their babies who might be born without a father. Roderick's rage because, of course, the big shit couldn't face his feelings. Thomas being gone. And Noah. Or rather, no Noah.

"Sinead?" Andy blinked down at her.

She didn't realize she had actually plopped to the ground, her fingers digging into the soft soil beside her and pulling the comfort of the earth element. "Those stupid, idiotic, brainless, stupid"—she'd already said stupid—"half-baked, crack-headed, dick-brained turds." She sunk her hands deeper, and soft green light sparked between her fingers. "They had to go and make everything worse. We already have Jack being interrogated by the police. Oh, the coppers are going to love it when they hear this one."

"Indeed." Andy looked around the garden as if searching for help. "Nobody has emerged from the healer's hall since they arrived." Andy opened his mouth and shut it again.

"What?" Sinead glared at him. More bad news, what fun! "Just spit it out."

"There is still…er…the property tax matter, and I have reason to believe that is becoming more pressing."

"Great." She dropped her heavy head to her chest. Her shoulders felt like Baile was taking a load off on them. "So, let me sum it up. We have Alexander fighting for his life, and all that means for everyone here." She waved a vague hand rather than break it down person by person. "Cracks and dust, crazies on the doorstep, Rhiannon filling Greater Littleton with her army of doom, Jack being harassed by the police, the taxman breathing down our necks, and Roderick decided now would be a smashing time to add snatch and seize to the tally."

Andy's expression grew pained. "Those are the major points."

"Oh please. Hit me with the minor points while you're at it." She couldn't stand it and held up her hand before he could. "No, don't." She shoved herself to her feet. "You know what worries me the most about all this, Andy?"

He eyed her as if uncertain he wanted to know. "What?"

"I'm the one providing the voice of reason."

SINEAD STORMED BACK inside the castle, taking the back entrance to the kitchens like she normally did. She immediately tripped over one of Niamh's animals and narrowly avoided going crashing into the wall.

The badger gave her a look of deepest reproof before trotting away.

"You were in my way," Sinead called after it.

And now she was talking to a badger. She sighed and eased her muddy boots off and hung her coat on a peg.

Alannah had been working on her fuel of the future, and it hit her nose in a tummy-churning combination of goat fart and old gym shoes. Bloody hell, but Alannah needed to do something about that smell.

There was nobody in the kitchen, but the smell of fresh baked bread and roast beef filled the air with home comfort. Alannah had slipped back into her role as coven feeder like she did most things, quietly and without fuss.

The wolf pups tussled near the hearth and yipped a greeting when they saw her. They were cute enough to draw a smile. She was glad they were still hanging around the kitchen. Alannah needed all the comfort she could get.

Sinead knew her twin's heart was still breaking over the loss of Thomas, but it wasn't Alannah's way to draw attention to herself. As the only person Alannah would let near enough to see her pain, Sinead felt the responsibility for loving her sister through heartbreak. That and the unmistakable truth that she'd been the one to separate Alannah and Thomas weeks before fate had stepped in and made the gap permanent. The result would still have been the same, but Sinead bore the guilt of the extra time she'd stolen from Alannah and Thomas.

Avoiding the situation in the healer's hall, she climbed the stairs to the great hall and then took the staircase to the upper level. Andy's news of cracks fresh in her mind, she tried to view Baile critically. Tried to see any other signs of wear and tear.

Were the runners in the hallway looking more threadbare? Had the wooden banisters lost their healthy shine?

Gah! She would drive herself bonkers at this rate.

Paintings lined the hallway, an eclectic mix of work from witches who had lived at Baile over the generations, and artwork gifted to the coven by grateful people—which may or may not have been from famous artists.

And then Sinead stopped dead and stared at the small gilt framed oil painting flanked by an amateur rendition of a horse with a weirdly tiny head on one side, and a dodgy self-portrait on the other. Situated near the center of her chest, there was no way the position of that woman's second breast was anatomically correct. Ignoring those, Sinead stepped closer to the middle painting, an oil depiction of a bucolic British scene. Through trees bursting with new greenery, a pale-stone cathedral basked in the afternoon sun. A name was faintly visible in the lower right-hand corner of the work: John Constable.

Well, now, perhaps Baile had the means to rescue herself from the massive property tax jaws of death. And maybe they could knock one thing off the overwhelming list of *Fuckery Out of Our Control.*

Of course, the painting could be a fake, and nobody had ever had it verified, but Baile was packed with works like this one. It was as possible that they were sitting on a veritable diamond mine of valuable pieces.

It was worth a shot to get this one, at least, authenticated.

She stepped closer to the wall and reached for the frame.

The painting vanished, not even leaving a mark on the wall to prove it had hung there not thirty seconds ago.

Frustration roiled inside Sinead. This bloody castle was too clever for its own good sometimes. "Really?" She yelled into the rafters. "I wasn't even sure it was worth selling."

A laughably out of perspective watercolor of a vase of flowers blinked into the place the possible Constable had hung.

Growling, Sinead shook a fist at the castle and stalked down the corridor to the suite of rooms she and Alannah shared.

She slammed the door behind her.

A fire crackled to life in the large hearth to the back of the small sitting room.

"The painting would have been better," she said, but drew closer to the warmth anyway.

The weight of the morning's revelations pressed down on her, and Sinead sunk into one of the large, overstuffed armchairs in front of the hearth. Dropping her head on the back of the chair, she stared into the crisscrossed beams above her head. Tears prickled beneath her eyelids, and she pressed the heels of her hands into her eyes to stop them.

The last time she had cried, Noah had held her and comforted her.

She missed him more than she would have thought possible. They hadn't even had a proper relationship. One incendiary kiss, followed by his revelation that she was his mate didn't amount to much.

A rebellious tear snaked down her cheek.

Closing her eyes, she tried to recapture the smell of fresh air and forest that seemed a part of him, that annoying smirk that made her want to smack him, the press of his big, hard body that reminded her she was female.

Another tear joined its mutinous friend and wound down her other cheek.

She wished like hell he was here, to hold her, make her laugh, tell her everything would be okay. Call her sweet thing with that infuriating tilt to the corner of his mouth. But she'd left him in Canada, allowed him to push her away, when he was so badly injured she had only his alpha, Zach's, assurance that Noah would survive.

The door opened and Alannah walked in wearing a frown.

Sinead ducked her head to hide her tears. "Hey."

"Hey." Alannah moved closer and perched on the arm of her chair. "It's no use, you know?"

"What?" Even knowing her twin was onto her, Sinead tried to bluster her way through.

"Sinead." Alannah's tone gentled as she wound Sinead's ponytail through her fingers. "It's okay to miss him."

"I wish…" Sinead stopped that thought before its friends and family could join the pity party. She wished so many bloody things that it wasn't even worth getting started.

Alannah sighed. "I know."

Sinead pressed her head against Alannah as they studied the cheerful fire together. Alannah smelled of Bronwyn's magic honey and sage signature with overtones of herbal remedies. "You were in the healer's hall."

"Yep." Alannah shook her head. "You don't want to know what Roderick has done now."

"I spoke to Andy." And this time Sinead sighed. "And you're right, I didn't want to know."

"That poor man." Alannah stood. "I promised him lunch and a conversation, and he agreed."

A note in Alannah's tone permeated Sinead's glum mood and she studied her sister's face. "What?"

"What?" A mask slid over Alannah's features.

Yeah, this sensitivity to each other's moods and thoughts went both ways. "There's something you're not telling me."

"You're right." Alannah rubbed a hand over her forehead. "I need to get lunch on the table."

Sinead caught her hand before Alannah could stand. "Tell me."

"It's the man. The doctor." Alannah frowned and shook her head. "I have the strangest idea that I know him from somewhere, but at the same time, I'm absolutely certain I've never seen him before."

Tapping on the window startled them, and they both turned.

Kai stood on the window ledge, her falcon's beak tapping the glass and demanding their attention. She cocked her head and studied them, then with a harsh cry she took off again.

"That bird is freaky." Sinead felt three hundred years old as she hauled her carcass to its feet. "But let's feed this poor man and try to persuade him he doesn't want to see the lot of us behind bars."

CHAPTER SEVEN

Sandwiched between Roderick, Warren, Emma, and Mandla—Simon had picked up the last name on his list of abductors—he was frog marched out of the healer's hall and into a large courtyard.

Drizzle dampened the cobblestones and packed earth beneath their feet, and he peered past massive shoulders to see where they were keeping him. Gray stone walls flanked him on all sides. Square Norman towers cast even gloomier shadows over them than the weather warranted. Unless he missed his guess, he was in a castle. An honest-to-God castle. Bronwyn had said they were in Baile Castle, but he wasn't about to take anything this lot said at face value. Given where his hospital was situated, his family history, and the apparent age of the castle, Baile made sense. Of course, he couldn't be sure how long he'd been out, and it could be Hartlepool for all he knew.

On one side of the bailey, a stormy, gray sea was separated from the bailey by a stone wall lower than the soaring towers around him.

Curiosity stirred. If he was inside the mysterious Baile

Castle, then color him intrigued. He'd heard about Baile long before he'd interned in Greater Littleton's local hospital.

You couldn't live anywhere near Greater Littleton without hearing whispers about Baile Castle. Built in the twelfth century, it had guarded the bluff above the village before the village had even come into being.

Staff and patients alike let rumors slip about the place. Up until the past summer, tours had been allowed inside its walls on selected days. Simon had meant to join one of those tours, but his demanding mistress of work had kept him from taking one. Then, for no apparent reason, the tours had stopped, and the castle had been shut to visitors. When he'd asked a particularly garrulous patient one day why he didn't drive to the castle and ask the residents if he could look about, the man had told him that nobody got to Baile without an invitation.

Simon had been so intrigued by that statement that he'd asked Maureen about it. She'd agreed with the patient. People often set out to reach Baile, and somehow, never did. Convinced local lore was being exaggerated, or they were having a laugh at his expense, Simon had put the theory to the test.

Sure enough, he'd spent an extremely frustrating Sunday driving up and down the single road leading from the village of Greater Littleton to Baile without arriving at the castle.

As he'd driven, that castle had always seemed to be around the next bend, or a short way ahead, but he'd never managed to get any closer than that. Eventually, he'd given up.

"Is this really Baile?" He didn't want to tip them off that he might be onto his location.

Emma glanced over her shoulder at him. "Looks like it could be, doesn't it?"

"Sarcasm?" he drawled, not letting them see him sweating. "On top of everything else."

"You are in Baile," Roderick said, gaze fixed ahead of them.

A small herd of sheep bleated and hurried out of their path, disturbing a family of ducks.

There were a lot of animals in the bailey as well. He stopped so suddenly that Mandla swore and nearly bumped into him. "What kind of dog is that?" He pointed to a large gray and white canine slinking out of the main keep of the castle, tail down, ears flattened against the rain. Simon's survival instinct chattered at him. "That's not a dog, is it?"

"We're getting wet out here." Warren hunched his shoulders up to his ears. "Can we talk about this where its dry?"

Simon got moving again. "There are no wolves in England," he said. "They've been extinct for hundreds of years."

Roderick snorted.

"You're right," Emma said and stopped in front of a door and opened it. She motioned him forward. "After you."

On the other side of the door, a large, homey kitchen slumbered, complete with wood-burning range, copper pots dangling from the ceiling, and the mouthwatering yeasty aroma of freshly baked bread. Despite his situation, Simon's stomach growled.

And she was there. Alannah. Only…not Alannah. It wasn't just the different clothes that tipped him off, but something else, something he couldn't put a name to. But he knew he was looking at her twin.

The twin glanced up from where she was sitting at the large, rough wooden table in the kitchen's center. Her expression turned wary. "Hi." She gave him a tight smile. "I'm Sinead."

"Alannah's twin." His logical brain demanded he verify his gut.

"Right." Her eyes twinkled. "What was your first clue?"

A pretty, dark woman strode into the kitchen. She stopped when she caught sight of him. "Hello?" She turned searching onyx eyes to Mandla and raised her eyebrow. "Who is he?"

Mandla almost looked sheepish as he answered her, "Ask Roderick."

"I'm asking you." She jammed her hands on her hips and glared at Mandla.

"I'm Simon." He tried not to obviously search for Alannah as he nodded to the woman. "And I'm here against my will."

Her mouth dropped open, and she gaped at him. Then she turned her death ray glare back on Mandla. "Tell me Simon is joking."

Mandla's face went stoically blank.

"He's not joking," Sinead said. "These idiots kidnapped a doctor for Alexander."

"Oh shit." The dark woman grimaced at him apologetically.

Simon marked her as a possible ally to help him escape.

Footsteps clattered down the staircase opposite the exterior door, and a tall, willowy redhead strode into the kitchen, tripped over the hem of her floaty dress, and righted herself. "Is lunch ready yet? I'm starving." She waggled her fingers at him. "Hi, Simon." Cocking her head, she studied him with jade-green eyes. "You should take the room in the south tower. It has a wonderful view."

And the crazy kept coming. She'd used his name as well. "Do I know you?"

"Oh, no." She went to the window and peered out. "Is Jack back yet?"

"No, Mags." Emma touched the redhead's elbow and motioned her to sit. "But you need to eat."

Mags rolled her eyes and winked at him.

More people filtered into the kitchen, including a teen, a toddler, and a young girl. Sue him, but Simon wasn't getting a hardened band of desperate criminals vibe.

Yet another knockout redhead sauntered into the kitchen. She smiled warily at him and went straight to Warren and put her arms around him.

"Heya." She stood on tiptoe and kissed him.

Warren got a sappy look on his face as he stared down at her. "Heya." Then he jerked his head toward Simon. "And don't yell."

"Uh-oh." The second redhead turned and gave him a searching stare. "I'm Niamh." She approached him with her hand held out. "Welcome to Baile."

Simon snorted before he could stop himself.

Niamh looked startled and vaguely affronted.

"Uh…Niamh." Warren rubbed his nape. "Simon is not exactly a…er…voluntary visitor."

And they went through the same routine of telling the story, getting shocked and indignant responses, and then settling down again.

Alannah slipped into the kitchen with a large serving platter in her hands. She took it to the range and began piling a roast and veggies on it.

"Do you need anything?" Niamh stared at him earnestly. "You've had a difficult morning."

Simon almost laughed at that. "I need my freedom."

"Right." Niamh grimaced. "That might be a bit tricky at the moment."

Fucking hell. All Simon could do was gape at her.

"Roast beef, roasted tatties, parsnips and carrots," Alannah said and put the platter on the table.

"My apologies, Alannah." Roderick gave her a curt nod. "But I'm not hungry."

Silence clattered into the kitchen and all eyes swung to stare.

"That's okay." Alannah patted his beefy arm. "Go and sit with him."

By him, Simon presumed she meant Alexander.

Roderick left the kitchen.

The young girl leaned closer to Warren. "Roderick always eats."

"I know, chicken." Warren kissed the top of her head. "He's worried about Alexander."

"Right." She heaved a sigh and looked at Mags. "I can't get anything, can you?"

Mags frowned and looked worried. "No. His future is blank. Even the unraveling dream has stopped."

The girl nodded and helped herself from the platter.

Warren added carrots and parsnips to her plate before passing the platter on.

Simon's sense of the ridiculous nearly got away from him. He was sitting down to Sunday lunch with his abductors. That didn't stop him from helping himself to several slices of beef, a small mound of potatoes, and carrots and parsnips.

Alannah added a gravy boat and a basket of Yorkshire puddings to the table.

"Try the horseradish." Sinead pushed a small dish toward him. "Alannah makes it herself."

And God bloody damn him, but he did.

The door opened and Hannah appeared. Her gaze found him, and she nodded. "Oh good, you're still here."

Simon stopped with a fork halfway to his mouth. Like he had any choice in the matter.

The toddler shrieked and grinned and held his hands out to Hannah.

"Hello, darling." Hannah kissed his rosy cheek and took the seat beside him.

Her son?

"Gravy?" Niamh offered him the gravy boat, and he took it.

Alannah took the last seat at the table, wedged between Mandla and Warren and directly opposite him.

An air of sadness seemed to surround her, or maybe it was him being fanciful. Everyone here seemed worried and downcast, but Alannah carried a heavier load. Was she close to Alexander?

Hannah filled the toddler's plastic plate and then hers. "We should explain," she said.

Simon had the vague sense that a person in his position shouldn't be plowing into his lunch with quite so much gusto. But the meat was tender, the potatoes crusty on the outside and fluffy within, the gravy rich and beefy—it was a fucking delicious meal. "You could start with how that man is still alive."

"That's not an easy question to answer and will require a good deal of broadmindedness on your part." Hannah ate neatly and mechanically.

"Try me." His plate was empty, and he sat back. "My current situation is not exactly usual."

"Right." Hannah shot a scowl at Warren. "You couldn't have stopped him?"

Warren snorted. "Have you ever tried to stop Roderick?"

"I have." Emma looked smug and then apologetic. "He was not taking no for an answer."

"Speaking of answers?" Simon got them back on topic. Namely the reason they'd sodding well kidnapped him.

"As you could see, Alexander sustained a knife wound to the chest," Hannah said, feeding the toddler between taking bites for herself.

Simon's medical brain kicked in. "You haven't removed the knife."

"No." Hannah wiped gravy off the toddler's chin. "We are unable to remove the knife."

"Which is where I come in." He scoffed and folded his arms. "You can't expect me to perform surgery here. That man needs a hospital."

"That's not going to happen, Doc," Emma said. "They can't help him in a hospital."

He was flabbergasted by the sheer fucking stupidity of that statement. "Of course—"

"No, she's telling the truth," Hannah said. "We have to treat him here."

The situation was too dire for dancing around their feelings. "Then get ready to bury him. Because the lack of a sterile environment alone is insane."

Emma put her arm around a weeping Mags and scowled at him.

"If this was a normal knife wound, I would agree with you." Hannah didn't look as if his bluntness had offended her. "But we are dealing with the arcane." She shrugged and spooned potato into her toddler's mouth. "Magic, if you will."

Not sure he'd heard right, Simon shook his head. Then again, nothing about this morning was right or sane. "You're taking the piss."

"Language." A woman with chestnut hair glared at him from the far end of the table.

And Simon nearly lost his cool.

Alannah's midnight purple gaze met his, and his anger dissipated. "Please listen," she murmured.

"I'm a medical man." He jabbed his thumb at his chest. "A scientist. I can't listen to drivel about magic."

"But what if it wasn't drivel?" Alannah tilted her head. "What if we are telling the truth?"

"You can't be." He didn't want to think of her as insane, but magic didn't exist.

"The facts are these," Hannah said. "The wound is arcane in nature. If we remove the knife, he will die for certain. We have no idea what the long-term effect of that knife is. Bronwyn, whom you met earlier, is a healer. She takes injury or illness within herself and transmutes it into the earth. As you noticed, she is pregnant. The magic within that knife is pure evil, and if Bronwyn attempts to transmute it, she will infect her unborn children. And those children are the future of all magic and must be born." She sat back and took a breath, looking at him calmly as if she hadn't spat out that mouthful. "I'm an oncologist. I need you to help me keep him alive until we solve the arcane issues."

Simon was sure he should have something to say to all that. If she'd sounded even a jot uncertain, or even partially averted her gaze, he might have stumbled on the words to renounce the insanity she'd spouted. As it was, Hannah looked as calm and assured as if she was recounting the condition of a cancer patient to him.

His gaze sought Alannah's. None of this could be real. It was an elaborate hoax.

Yet, her gaze stayed on him—clear, troubled, and imploring.

CHAPTER EIGHT

Nofoto leaned into Mandla's strong, silent presence by her side. They'd finished lunch, with that poor doctor looking like he'd been hit by a hurricane. She was sure shock was a big part of why he got up from the table after lunch and followed Hannah back to the healer's hall without an objection.

"This is bad," she whispered. They couldn't keep the doctor here, and they also couldn't let him go.

Mandla's arms came around her and he pulled her back to his chest.

Maybe if she hadn't been able to feel his emotions, read his thoughts through their bond, his silence would have irked her, but instead, she drew comfort from him. She missed Johannes-burg, their home. Jacaranda trees would be in bloom, carpeting the roads in a mass of purple blossoms. After a dry winter, spring rains would be triggering the summer growth into an explosion of colors and scents. She missed the intense color, the raw immediacy of life in Africa. Had they done the right thing in coming here to England? She didn't belong here.

Mandla pressed a kiss to her temple.

Yes, they'd done the only thing they could. Her mother had insisted on them coming, and they had each other.

England's cold seeped into Nofoto's bones and nestled there until a hot bath banished it. Mandla laughed at how she felt the cold more intensely than he did. She didn't feel cold now, with his hot, hard body cradling her and anchoring her to this place.

As a weather witch, she could change the weather.

Mandla rumbled something inarticulate.

"I won't do it," she said. Changing the weather had repercussions. "But that doesn't mean I don't think about doing it."

He untangled them and took her hand.

Leading her out of the kitchen and up into the great hall, he strode toward the library. Nofoto didn't know how old Baile Castle was, but the magic was steeped into the stones, and it comforted her to be within the walls.

The big fireplace in the library was ablaze and pumping warmth into the room.

On three walls, packed bookshelves rose about three stories to a beamed ceiling. The fourth wall was nearly entirely windows, and the view of the village by the sea was spectacular.

She sighed as she dragged her eyes away from the view. They had work to do. As the first weather witch in centuries, she and Mandla had been trying to discover more about her blessing. Niamh had also given her several books on the history of the cré-witches, and how their magic worked.

"Nofoto?" Warren spoke from the doorway.

She turned to see him standing there with Taylor. The grave expressions on their faces made her heart thump uncomfortably.

Mandla pulled her closer to him.

"What is it?"

Taylor looked pale and miserable. She could put that down to Alexander's condition, but Nofoto's instinct whispered the expression augured ill for her.

"I saw something," Taylor said.

Warren put his hand on her shoulder and stared at her, as if trying to lend his daughter strength.

Nofoto wasn't sure she wanted to hear what Taylor had seen. Sweat prickled her skin, and her mouth dried. "About me?"

"Your family and friends. Your people in Johannesburg," Warren said.

"You need to warn them." Taylor clenched her hands together. "They need to hide. Now."

"What happened?" Mandla went still as a hunting lion.

"They're in danger," Taylor whispered. "If you don't warn them, they could die." She swallowed. "All of them."

Andy eased past them and held out a phone. "I've tracked your mother down. The number is all ready to hit dial."

Nofoto stood there and stared at Taylor. As the library tilted around her, she wanted to demand Taylor take those words back. Her mother, her friends, her little brother—all of them in mortal danger. It became hard to breathe past the constriction in her chest. Surely, Taylor didn't mean those words. Maybe she'd misunderstood what she'd seen. "No."

"I'm so sorry." Taylor pressed closer to her father.

Warren's gaze stayed steady and sympathetic as he looked at Nofoto.

That got through to her more than anything, and fear tightened her muscles. She couldn't move. She knew she had to act, but her brain wouldn't work, and her body was fixed to the spot.

"Thank you." Mandla walked her over to Andy.

Even in the face of Taylor's shocking news, Mandla was her rock. She took the phone from Andy and hit dial.

The call connected, and a woman with a South African accent spoke. "This number is no longer in use. Please check the number and try again."

Her vision blurred, and she reached through the bond for Mandla.

She felt his fear, his worry, and his determination. He steadied her and she redialed.

"This number is no longer in use. Please check the number and try again."

"What does that mean?" somebody shouted.

Mandla took her hand.

It was her. She was yelling, but she couldn't stop. Taylor was never wrong. If she had seen something, that thing would happen. Had happened? Black spots danced in front of her eyes. Taylor, Warren, and Andy lurched in the doorway.

No, it was her. She was swaying.

Sweeping her up, Mandla deposited her on a sofa and crowded in beside her. She tightened her grip on his hand. She couldn't let go or the worst would happen. "Why is my mother not answering her phone?"

"I'll find out," Andy said and left the room. "I'll contact Sasha. We'll get answers for you. I promise."

JACK ARRIVED BACK at Baile wanting a shower and to punch something. Eight hours with that bullheaded Lennox and his sneaky sidekick, trying to catch him in a lie, and him keeping a firm lid on his temper. They'd called him in for the second day in a row, wanting him to be their suspect. Good luck with that, fuckers.

There was nobody in the kitchen other than Niamh's menagerie cozying up next to the lit range. He shook his head at a duck cuddled into a big black mongrel. Seeing shit you never thought you would came with living at Baile.

The great hall lay still, the grave atmosphere of the coven residents being absorbed by the building they lived in. Lennox would have a fit if he'd seen Alexander's stabbing and Fiona's beheading, and Lennox would do his fucking best to pin it on Jack.

Knowing Emma was here to watch Mags had kept him from going out of his mind with worrying about his witch. Since her recent abduction, he hated letting her out of his sight for long. He followed the murmur of voices into the sitting room.

It was like walking into a wake, and he stopped on the threshold. His heart clenched in his chest. "Alexander?"

"Hanging in there." Warren grimaced. "Roderick, Maeve, and Hannah are with him. And the new…never mind."

Jack zeroed in on Magdalene—no, she hated when he called her that—Mags sitting beside Emma on a large sofa.

"Hey." Mags turned her pretty face up for a kiss. "How did it go?"

"Same as yesterday." He wedged himself in beside her, sandwiching her between him and Emma. As far as Jack was concerned, it was the perfect spot for Mags, surrounded by the two people who would give anything to keep her safe. "They've got bugger all and are still fishing."

"Is questioning you without probable cause two days in a row, even legal?" A frown puckered the skin above Emma's arctic-gray eyes.

That was a good one, and Jack laughed. "You'll find the law gets elastic around ex-cons."

Mags cuddled his arm and snuggled closer to him.

And Jack let his stressful day go. He'd do it all again to keep his Mags safe and sound. The leaden atmosphere in the sitting room permeated his brain. "What's going on?"

"We've had some unfortunate news." Andy looked up from his laptop.

Mandla grunted but kept his arm around a shivering Nofoto.

"What is it?" Like they could handle any more bad news.

"We got word that Nofoto's people were in danger," Emma said. "We haven't been able to reach anyone to find out if they're okay."

"Word?" He looked to Emma for his answers.

"Taylor saw it." Her brow furrowed. "But she can't get anything else, and even Sasha is not able to confirm what's going on."

His gut twisted. He looked at Nofoto. "I'm sorry."

She nodded and burrowed closer to Mandla. Jack had never seen such a tender expression on the carved walnut of the big man's face. He understood Mandla's expression, however, only too well. Jack was the same with his Mags.

His Mags, the most powerful seer in the coven. Jack looked down at her. "Did you get anything?"

Emma sucked in a breath and Mags looked up at him with tormented green eyes. "I didn't…my blessing…I can't."

"You know she can't," Emma hissed at him.

Mags as she had been that night on the boat after they'd first rescued her flashed through Jack's mind. Her fragility had shocked and grieved him. But his Mags was stronger than even she knew. "I know she thinks she can't."

"Jack." Mags's gaze beamed his betrayal back at him.

Jack hated that look, and even more hated being the cause of that look, but she'd been running scared of her blessing since Greece. Her blessing was such an integral part of Mags it was like hiding her sun. If anyone could give Nofoto answers, it was his Mags. And she was only half of his Mags when her fear of her blessing stopped her from using it. Christ, in days past, she'd see thing he didn't want her to see. "I know you're scared." He cupped her silky, ivory cheek. "I know you don't trust your blessing, but Emma is sitting right there, and she stabilizes you."

Mags pleated the sparkly fabric of her skirt between her fingers. "I can't, Jack. I just can't."

"It's all right." Emma took Mags's fidgeting hand in hers. "Nobody is going to make you do anything you don't want to."

They weren't? Jack shot Emma a glare over Mags's head. He knew what Mags had been through, that her kidnapping had left scars beneath her surface, but he also knew Mags. Her blessing was everything to her. It was what made her a witch, and she loved her witchiness. "Mags." With his forefinger, he turned her chin his way. "Look at me."

She complied reluctantly.

He hated the fear and doubt clouding her emerald eyes. He wanted to banish it forever. "Nofoto needs you to try."

"Fucking hell, Jack!" Emma leaped to her feet. "You know what she went through. You have no right to do this to her."

"That's right." Hours of Lennox and Acharya had fine-tuned his patience. "I was right there when we got to her, but she's running scared."

Emma bunched her fists. "She has every right to be frightened. She's my witch." Emma jabbed a thumb into her chest. "I can feel how much this terrifies her."

"Then you should know exactly why she needs to do this," he said.

All eyes were fastened on them, soaking up the drama.

Emma growled at him. "You share her bed, but you don't know what's going on inside her."

Yeah, three could be a crowd, and right now was one of those times. He, Mags, and Emma were an unorthodox kind of throuple. Not in the sexual sense, but it was too easy for him and Emma to tread on each other's toes. "If she doesn't do what she was born to do, then Rhiannon's won. She's taken Mags's blessing away from her."

Emma opened her mouth to argue, frowned, and then snapped her mouth shut.

"Jack." Warren—ever the peacemaker—stepped between him

and Emma. "You know it's more complicated than that. In this case, I agree with Emma."

Coimhdeacht stuck together, through thick and thin, and right and wrong. But Jack knew his woman, and he knew she had more balls than the lot of them put together. And her coven needed her. If she didn't help them, it would eat her alive. He couldn't let her slink away from her calling. She needed to know she could control this blessing, the same thing she told Taylor.

He turned his attention back to Mags and shut out the other occupants of the room. "You can do this, Mags." He kissed her knuckles. "And you need to do this." He glanced at Emma. "Emma is right here. I'm right here. We're not ever going to let anything happen to you again."

Mags's eyes went huge in her face, and she pressed her lips together. "I'm scared."

"I know you are." He kissed her forehead. "But you can do an incredible thing. A thing that maybe only you and Taylor can do, and it belongs to you. Not to Rhiannon, not to the coven, not to anyone else but you. Use your gift, Mags."

Emma inched onto the sofa on her other side. She still glared, but it had softened from her wanting to rip his guts out to a bit of minor manhandling. "I'm right here, Mags," she said.

Mags drew a deep breath, and then another. "Okay." She swallowed and got to her feet. She approached Nofoto. "Do you have anything of your mother's with you?"

"You can do that?" Taylor sat up straighter.

"Yes." Mags gave her a wan smile. "It's one of the things I still need to teach you."

And that was the other reason Mags needed to get right with her blessing again. Taylor was depending on her to teach her everything she knew. The only safe way for Taylor to use her blessing was under the guidance of an older seer.

"She has this." Mandla handed Mags a square of fabric. "It's her mother's favorite headscarf."

"Right." Mags stared at the offering for a long moment and then took it with a trembling hand. She motioned Taylor closer. "A person's belongings hold some of their life essence, their spiritual signature. It's like searching a library when you know the author's name."

CHAPTER NINE

Sinead couldn't stand the gloomy atmosphere anymore, and she slipped out of the sitting room.

Through the doorway, Alannah gave her an understanding smile.

The news was shit and getting worse. Mags had found no trace of Nofoto's mother, Lerato, but she had discovered that Taylor's vision had come true. People had died, so many that Mandla had taken Nofoto upstairs an hour ago. Nofoto had lost family and friends in South Africa. The only glimmer of hope was that they'd not seen Lerato or Nofoto's younger brother amongst the dead.

Mags had gone one further and scried for Emma's friends in Moscow. They were in danger, so Sasha had sent them all into hiding. The terrible result of her scrying had swamped the victory of Mags using her gift again. Scrying had devastated Mags, but Jack and Emma had her.

Walking through the great hall, Sinead wrestled with the twitchy sensation in her middle. She needed to do something—act. She wasn't built to sit around and wait for trouble to come to her.

She strode for the kitchen. Out of the corner of her eye, a shape caught her attention. Perhaps because she'd become aware of it so recently, but she knew before she even turned for a better look that it was the Constable.

Baile had moved it to the wall beside the library. Bloody castle was taunting her.

Well, Sinead would see about that. Human cunning against a pile of bricks and mortar—no contest.

She strode for the library, speaking as she went. "I'll just find something to read." And hope like hell nobody came out of the sitting room and saw her chatting to thin air. "That will help me sleep tonight."

The Constable loomed to the right of the library door.

Sinead opened the door and lunged for the Constable.

It vanished.

"Bloody hell," she roared at the castle. "You're doing this to be an asshole."

"Sinead?" Alannah appeared in the sitting room door. Other faces crowded behind her shoulder. "Who are you shouting at?"

"This—" She couldn't think of a bad enough insult for the castle, so she waved her arm around. "This—"

Mags shouted, "Sinead!"

Pushing through the cluster in the doorway, Taylor ran out of the library toward her. "OMG, Sinead, you won't believe—"

The wolves of Baile howled.

"What?" Sinead wasn't following, and she looked at Mags and then Taylor. Their cheeks were flushed, and their eyes sparkled. That didn't look like more awful news.

Frowning, Niamh rushed past everyone and ran for the entrance. "The wolves!"

"What is it?" Sinead chased after Warren as he pursued Niamh. "What's wrong with the wolves?"

"Pack is going fucking crazy," he called over his shoulder. "They're losing their collective mind."

"That doesn't tell me anything," Sinead yelled at his back.

Wolf pups streamed into the great hall from the kitchen, yapping and squealing as they chased Warren.

"What is it?" Alannah drew even with Sinead.

And then Sinead felt it, and she stopped dead. Her heart swelled and throbbed in her chest. Something soft and warm brushed her nape, like the stroke of a hand.

"Oh Goddess." Her words rushed out in a sob, and she pressed both hands to her mouth to stop them. Still the words spilled out of her. "Please, Goddess, please, please, please."

Alannah's eyes filled with tears. "Sinead?"

She shook her head. She couldn't speak the hope aloud for fear it would be snatched away from her.

Wolf howls reverberated through the still evening, so loud now it sounded as if Pack was right outside.

"Come." Mags took one of her hands and tugged her forward. "It's okay, Sinead. He's here."

Her feet wouldn't move. Couldn't move. If she went outside and it wasn't true, it would snap her in two.

Mags pulled against her resistance. "You can trust me," she whispered. "Your wolf has come for you."

And suddenly she was moving, running so fast she almost did a Mags and tripped over her own feet.

Twilight was falling over the bailey as she tumbled into it.

Wolves streamed around them, baying and howling, their bodies weaving around Niamh in a restless frenzy.

The shadows beneath the gatehouse shifted, and a massive, black wolf loped into view.

Hackles up, ears pressed against his head, Alpha growled. He stalked closer to the black wolf.

Sinead lurched for her wolf, but Niamh grabbed her arm and held her. "This needs to happen first."

"What?" She didn't know what Niamh was talking about. She only knew her wolf was here. Her Noah, her mate, had come for her. How was he even a wolf? He'd told her if he left his pack land, he would never be able to shift again.

She didn't understand, didn't care, she just wanted him.

"He's entered another alpha's territory," Niamh said. "They need to establish the dominant wolf."

"He's a shifter."

"Who is part wolf." Niamh smiled. "This won't take long, and they won't fight. But it needs to happen. Unless you want them to snarl at each other every time they meet."

Alpha stalked Noah and then stopped.

Noah raised his head, his lips peeling off canines longer than Sinead's finger.

The two wolves stared each other down, and then Alpha lowered himself to his belly and whined.

Noah trotted closer and sniffed his ears, batted his muzzle.

Springing to his feet like a puppy, Alpha play bowed.

Noah snapped his teeth at him, and Alpha yipped and danced out of the way.

As if released from a spell, Pack streamed to their new alpha wolf.

And Sinead stood there and bawled like a baby through it all. She barely felt Niamh and Alannah clutch her hands.

"I've never felt anything like him," Niamh whispered. "Animal and human. It's like walking around in his mind."

Warren grumbled how much he didn't like that, and Niamh blew him a kiss. "Not like you, handsome. Not the same at all."

Pack shrank back, and Noah took several steps forward. He stopped and a series of pops, squelches, and snaps came from his contorting shape.

Warren went slightly green and flinched.

And then Noah the man was there, standing naked as the day he was born, and smirking at her. "Hey, sweet thing." He cocked his head. "You just gonna stand there, or maybe get your ass over here?"

And get her ass over there she did. Sinead didn't stop until she crashed into warm flesh smelling of forest and maple, and powerful arms tucked her close.

Noah kissed the spot behind her ear. "Are you crying, sweet thing?"

"Uh-uh." She shook her head and pressed her tear-soaked face against his bare chest. "I don't cry."

"With me you do." He cupped her face and made her meet his eyes—amber eyes, wolf eyes. "My mate's tears are my honor to comfort."

Aaand there she went again. Full on waterworks.

"Um…mate?" Warren cleared his throat and thrust a pair of gray sweatpants at Noah. "Might want to put all that away."

Noah's laugh rumbled through his chest. "Shifter hazard."

"Got that." Warren nodded, his lips compressing in a hard line as he tried not to laugh. "But we got a twelve-year-old girl, my daughter, and Dhara hanging around."

"Dhara?" Joy lit Noah's face. "She's okay?"

"She's fine." Sinead gave his waist one more squeeze before stepping back enough to allow him to haul on the sweatpants. And bloody hell, the gray sweatpants thing was legitimate. She could barely get her gaze to travel north again.

"Noah," Dhara screeched and pelted across the bailey toward him. "Noah, it's you."

Noah caught her and swung her into his arms.

Blinking rapidly to stop more tears, Sinead refused to stand there and sob like a sodding leaky teapot.

Wiping away her own tears, Alannah was not helping the weep-a-thon.

"Noah." Kate approached more sedately than her sister, but her delight was as clear on her face. She nudged Dhara aside for her hug. When she stepped back, her expression clouded. "Zach?"

Noah looked grim. "I've got a lot to tell you, but he's…okay. Physically, he's fine."

"But?" Kate's gaze scoured his face for answers.

"We need to talk," Noah said. Then he looked past her at Niamh. "Your energy." He blew out a long breath and shook his head. "Weirdest thing, but I kind of want to bow to you."

"That's Niamh," Sinead said, and suppressed the surge of jealousy. The only witch Noah would bow to was the one he called mate, aka her. X-rated visions of Noah on his knees in front of her boiled through her blood. She had to clear her throat before she finished her explanation. "And she's a guardian, which means she links with animals."

Nodding slowly, Noah inclined his head. "Guardian."

"Wolf." Niamh nodded back.

Their eyes met.

Noah huffed a laugh. "Well, that's inconvenient." He dropped his gaze from Niamh's. "She told me to go inside, and I'm gonna make like a good boy and do it."

Niamh waved a hand and chuckled. "I was testing to see if my suggestions worked on you too."

"Suggestion?" Noah snorted. "It's more like putting a leash around my neck and telling me to heel."

Sinead had thoughts. "That works on you?"

"Only when she does it." Noah gave her a look that said he was onto her.

"But we should go inside." Alannah shooed them all toward the castle. "Even if it's only to find Noah a shirt."

"Oh, I don't know about that." Mags eyed Noah's naked chest. "He seems to be doing fine without one."

Jack growled and tugged his sweater over his head. It hit Noah in the middle of his chest. "Put that on."

With a smirk, Noah dragged Jack's sweater over his head.

"Now you need a shirt." Mags stroked Jack's cut pectorals.

Jack smoldered down at her. "Why don't we go and find me one?"

"Ugh!" Emma banged the side of her head with her palm. "Stop it, Mags. Stop those thoughts right now."

Sinead slid her hand into Noah's as they followed the others back into the castle. Some part of her was scared if she let go of him, she'd wake up and find him not there.

Looking around him with interest, Noah whistled as they crossed the great hall. "This place is quite something."

"She likes when people say that," Andy said. "She likes to be admired."

Nodding slowly, Noah took it all in, lingering on the tapestries hanging from rafters, the stained-glass window, the vaulted stone ceiling. He smiled down at her with those topaz wolf eyes. "The castle smells of your magic. It's like being surrounded by you."

Sinead had no problem with that and smiled back at him. To be honest, it would take a scalpel to get the grin off her face right now.

"Come on." Warren nudged Noah.

They followed Warren and Niamh into the sitting room and found a perch on a sofa.

Tugging Sinead onto his lap, Noah kept her there with a hand on her hip. For once, Sinead had no objection to being manhandled.

He pressed his nose into her neck and sniffed. He sat back with a peaceful smile. "Mate."

"You shifted?" Sinead got her first question out of the way.

"Yeah." Noah ruffled his hair. "I lost my connection to pack land when I left, but when I got closer to this place." He shrugged. "I could feel a new connection. It got stronger the closer I came. About when I passed those freaks on the road up here, I got the compulsion to shift, and I did."

"Noah didn't think he could shift once he left pack land."

Kate explained to the room at large. "There was something about the land our community occupied that made shifters possible. When they're away from it, they can't shift."

"It's the wolves here." Niamh motioned the pups chasing each other into the sitting room. "They hold the magic of this land in their blood."

"Huh." Noah looked intrigued. "So it works kind of like we do. They were born on the land and the magic resides in their blood?"

"Something like that." Niamh thought it over. "To be honest, that's the best explanation I have. Now that you're here, we can test it out and see what happens."

Now that he was here, Sinead had all sorts of plans for Noah.

"Tell me about Zach," Kate's quiet voice carried across the sitting room. "And my witches."

Noah lifted Sinead and placed her beside him. Lowering his head, he took a deep breath.

Sensing he needed her comfort, Sinead snuggled closer to him.

"It's bad, Kate." Noah met Kate's eye. "Rhiannon's people attacked the settlement. There were more waiting in the forest, and they picked off the witches and wolves as they were escaping."

Kate whimpered and pressed a hand to her mouth. "How many?"

"We've only found Corrie so far. Abe managed to keep Sage alive and Val's two kids. Along with Cole, Corrie is the only other adult witch we could find. The rest." He cleared his throat. "We think they were either killed or taken away for their magic."

"Cole?" Kate had gone deathly pale, and her nails dug into the armrests. "He came back?"

"Yeah." Noah's tone softened. "He came back for Rachel.

They're together now with what's left of the coven and the wolves."

Kate made a visible effort to pull herself together. "How many wolves?"

"Only Abe, me, Rachel, Sara, and Zach."

"Oh Jesus." Kate pressed a hand to her mouth.

Sinead's gaze met Alannah's and her own horror was reflected back at her. There had been over two hundred witches and thirty shifters in the Ottawa coven when they'd visited. The devastation was too awful to contemplate.

Alannah rose and went to sit on the arm of Kate's chair. She took Kate's hand and held it. "I'm so sorry, Kate."

Kate's face crumpled, and a sob shook her slim shoulders. "All of them?"

Noah swallowed and nodded. "Yeah, Kate. Zach is going to keep looking."

CHAPTER TEN

In the main part of the healer's hall, where Bronwyn kept her herbs and remedies, Roderick heard Hannah speaking quietly to Simon. Although he couldn't make out what they were saying, and it mattered not to him. After persuading Bronwyn to go and rest, Roderick was staying with Alexander until she got back. He welcomed the time alone with his son.

Roderick examined his son's face lying on the stark white pillow. His hair was several shades darker brown than his own, and his aquiline bone structure so like his mother's. If one could even call that heinous cunt a mother.

Very little of Roderick showed in Alexander's facial features. Roderick's stamp was in Alexander's height and shape. It was in his bond to Goddess that had called his son back from evil and into the service of Goddess.

And Alexander's life had been forfeit ever since. Alexander had been conceived and born because of the struggle between Rhiannon and Goddess. He'd already given all of himself to forces wielded above and through him. Surely, there would come a time when Alexander would stop paying the price for a battle much older and larger than all of them.

Roderick had lived so many hundreds of years that loss had become a part of his existence. Witches died, fellow coimhdeacht died, mundane humans lived their small span and died. Now, death was stalking his child, and Roderick wanted to rail against it, wanted to end it like he had ended Fiona.

The grim satisfaction of her death was overshadowed by the knowledge that when he'd killed her, he'd also killed any possible source of information about that cursed dagger in Alexander's chest. Goddess had said it came from her, and thus she couldn't touch it. Roderick could smell the blood magic on the fucking thing, feel it pulsing like a malevolent headache at his temples. His warrior blood urged him to rip it out and destroy it, to remove it from the flesh of his progeny.

His child.

The knowledge sunk like a pebble through water and landed with a soft *clink* on the bedrock of his awareness. Flesh of his flesh; blood of his blood, and beloved as such.

The missed years weighed heavily on him as he watched the ragged rise and fall of Alexander's chest. He had never seen him as a babe. Would never know if he had been an energetic lad, or a studious one. Had been robbed of the opportunity to impart his knowledge and his experience as Alexander became a man.

Instead, Roderick had tried to kill him at every opportunity presented. Dear Goddess, what would have happened if he had succeeded in ending a life so much tied to his own?

Roderick dropped his head as the overwhelming burden of the possibility pressed on him.

"I have failed you." His voice sounded rusty in the tomblike silence. "I have failed you in more ways than I can count." He had left Alexander to be raised by Rhiannon. His nights were tortured with thoughts of what that must have been like for the boy. What iniquities had she inflicted on a vulnerable youngster?

Roderick's reason grasped that he could not have done more

for a child that he didn't know was his. Regret, however, was a different taskmaster. It whispered of lost time and opportunities. Regret mixed with his sense of duty and reminded him that he had left Alexander with her, to be twisted and tortured into a shape she decreed.

He sensed Maeve enter the healer's hall and hurry toward him. In his grief and worry, Roderick hadn't blocked his emotion from her. As she approached, he was glad he had not. He needed the comfort that only his Maeve could offer.

Her hand was warmth and surcease on his nape. She eased his head to her heart.

Roderick rested there, her heat surrounding him, the slow, steady pounding of her heart a resting place for his torment.

"Hannah says you're his father," Simon spoke softly from the doorway.

Not able to take his head from Maeve, Roderick nodded.

Father. Such a common word. Such a common role. He barely remembered his father. He had only faint images of a large man, gruff of manner, and brusque of voice. A man who didn't spare the rod or the hard hand when he deemed it required. Roderick had been raised the old way, the hard way. Reared and wrenched into manhood by the scruff of his neck. He would not have raised his son thus.

Simon approached the bed. "You don't look old enough to be his father."

Roderick's answering laugh was like a jagged saw through hard wood. "I have never felt more ancient than I do now."

"Yes." Simon nodded as if he understood. He shoved his hands in his pockets. "There are very few things worse than watching your child suffer."

The primal twist through Roderick's gut made him clasp Maeve closer to him.

She wrapped her other hand around his shoulders, like he was the child and she the parent.

"You kidnapped me to save your son." Simon rocked on his heels and lowered his chin to his chest. "Funny thing, is that I can understand why a parent would do that."

Roderick would have done that and more for Alexander.

"Why me?" Simon cocked his head.

"The who made no difference to me." Roderick had no strength to temper his words. "It was your skill I wanted."

"Huh." Simon moved closer to the bed and studied Alexander. "I want to tell you something." He made a dry sound of disbelief in the back of his throat. "Why I ended up working in Greater Littleton."

Roderick wanted the man gone so he could be alone with Alexander, Maeve, and his pain.

"I came to Greater Littleton because my family came from here." Simon did not seem to require a response, which was good because Roderick had none for him. "Way back when, my family came from this area." Simon leaned closer and examined the dagger. "My mother mentioned it when we were growing up. I interned here, and after my divorce, accepted a position here. I've never really been able to explain why I felt so connected to this place."

"Your family hails from Greater Littleton?" Maeve's sweet voice fell tender on Roderick's ears.

"Apparently so." Simon put his fingers to Alexander's neck pulse. "I have a great, great, great, great-whatever grandmother who lived and worked here. I always meant to do some research about her." Simon shrugged. "But I work a lot, and I never got around to it."

"Do you know her name?" Maeve asked.

"No." Simon lifted the lid of one of Alexander's eyes.

Roderick allowed it only because of Simon's profession, but his protective instinct rose to simmer beneath the surface. Alexander was so vulnerable in his plight. If only Roderick had moved faster to stop Fiona. The moment played constantly in his mind, and with the razor precision of hindsight, he saw his own failure to act quickly.

"Perhaps it's all the odd things Hannah has been telling me." Simon picked up one of Alexander's hands and examined his nails. "But it got me thinking how strange it was that you took me and not one of the other doctors."

"Andy researched you," Roderick said. "We chose a person who would not be easily missed."

Simon replaced Alexander's hand. "Then it's not so strange after all." He shoved his hands back in his pockets. "But I've been thinking."

"Yes?" Hannah came up behind him, her keen gaze on his face.

Simon turned to her. "I have two weeks of leave and nothing better to do with them."

"You'll stay?" The hope in Hannah's voice permeated the fog surrounding Roderick.

"I'll stay." Simon huffed. "I can't believe I'm saying this, but I'm staying." His tone turned all business. "But I'm going to need x-ray capability, a cardiac monitor, cardiac leads, pulse oximeter…"

Roderick tuned Simon out. Simon's words were like a foreign language, but Hannah was nodding and making notes. All he understood was that Simon was staying to save his son.

MAEVE SAT with Roderick until Bronwyn returned. The diminutive water witch looked too fragile to handle Alexander's condition and her pregnancy. But Bronwyn had steel in her spine, and she managed a smile for Roderick as she took her place beside Alexander's bed.

Maeve pressed a kiss to her cheek. "Shout if you need

anything." She would send one of the other witches to join Bronwyn in her vigil. She shouldn't be alone.

Roderick held her hand as they crossed the bailey together. She'd been so intimidated when Roderick had first bonded her. She had never pictured the soul deep comfort that had blossomed between them.

As if her concern for Bronwyn being alone had summoned her, Niamh opened the kitchen door and crossed the bailey. She had four dogs with her, plus a squirrel perched on her shoulder. "I thought I'd go and sit with Bronwyn."

"I was coming to find someone." This was coven, and Maeve's heart filled. In her previous life, she had never fit into the coven. She'd been there, but an outsider, separated by the isolation of working her blessing and being the only spirit walker. Further, even witches were not comfortable with someone who dealt with the dead every day.

Niamh burrowed into Roderick and gave him a hug. "How are you doing?"

Startled, Roderick hesitated before returning the gesture. He grunted in response, a sound conveying both his reluctance to speak of what he felt, and his deep-seated worry.

"I know." Niamh looked up at him with a gentle expression. She released Roderick and patted his chest. "Now, let's see how our new doctor feels about animals in the healer's hall."

They entered the kitchen to find Sinead's wolf-man, Sinead, and Kate. The conversation cut off as they were noticed.

Maeve and Roderick had met Noah at dinner. Roderick hadn't said anything, but Maeve sensed he liked the shifter. Noah was plain speaking to the point of blunt, had an irreverent sense of humor, and adored Sinead.

"How's Alexander?" Sinead looked up from her perch on Noah's lap. They had barely gone a minute without touching since Noah's arrival. Maeve understood the need. If she and

Roderick were ever separated, it felt like part of her was missing until they reconnected again.

"Much the same," Maeve answered for Roderick. "But Simon has decided to stay."

"He has?" Alannah appeared in the pantry doorway. She frowned at the glass jars in her hands. "Well, that's…good, then. Good for Alexander."

Sinead studied Alannah as she walked to the table and set the glass jars on it. "I'll get those tomatoes in for you in the morning."

The twins often played their emotions close to their chest, and watching the other twin was often more informative than trying to discern what was happening beneath her sister's surface. Clearly, Sinead sensed something Alannah wasn't saying, but was that the reason for the tense atmosphere in the kitchen?

"Hmm…thank you." Alannah arranged the glass jars whilst surreptitiously studying Kate.

"You know what you have to do, Kate." Noah also kept his attention locked on Kate.

She scowled at him. "Don't act like it's all decided."

"But it should be." Noah jabbed the table with his forefinger. "I'm here now. I can watch over Dhara."

Maeve glanced at Roderick, and he shrugged. He had no idea what they'd walked in on either.

"She's fifteen, Noah," Kate snapped. "What do you know about fifteen-year-old girls?"

Sinead held up her hand. "Fairly sure I was fifteen once, and that means Alannah was too."

Kate made a strangled noise and tried not to smile. "I know that." She propped her elbows on the table and dropped her head into her hands. "It's just that this particular fifteen-year-old happens to be my baby sister."

"What is amiss?" Roderick glanced between Noah and Kate.

Kate averted her gaze and stared at the table. "Nothing. Everything's okay. You concentrate on your son."

Maeve felt Roderick's skepticism, and nudged Kate. "It doesn't look like nothing."

"It's…fine." With a loaded glance, Kate frowned at Noah. "Roderick has enough to deal with right now."

"Does it affect this coven?" Roderick yanked out a chair and sat opposite Kate. "The welfare of any of my witches?"

Kate picked at a groove in the table with her thumbnail. "Not directly."

"Yes," Noah said.

Kate glared at him.

Noah smirked back.

"Dhara?" Roderick guessed.

Kate's head snapped up.

"Kate needs to get back to Canada," Noah said. "With the commune scattered, she wants to find the missing witches. She also wants to get back to Zach."

"I never said me wanting to go back had anything to do with Zach." Kate stuck her chin out.

Noah shook his head. "But it does, doesn't it?"

"Maybe." Kate dug her nail into a small crack in the wooden table. "I mean, he can't find the missing shifters and witches all on his own."

"Right." Noah pinned her with a stare. "And?"

"And what?" Kate scowled.

Noah sighed and enunciated his words carefully, as if speaking to a child. "And he's your mate."

From Alannah and Sinead's lack of reaction, Maeve guessed they'd known of the mate bond between Kate and Zach.

Noah softened his tone as he added, "And he needs you."

"Dhara needs me," Kate snapped.

"Dhara has us." Noah gestured to the kitchen occupants. "And she is safest behind Baile's wards."

"If your people and your mate need you, then you must go," Roderick said. "Just because they do not live at Baile, it does not make your commune any less cré-witches."

"Funny you should say that, because Noah was telling me they've found a place to settle," Kate said. "A cave surrounded by the same wards as Baile."

Roderick frowned as he considered that. "Like Baile?"

"The magic felt and smelled like Sinead." Noah tightened his arms around Sinead. "We recognized it instantly."

"But you did not know it was there before?" Roderick cocked his head and studied Kate.

"No." Kate shrugged. "Or I would have moved my people there."

Alannah paused in removing the jar lids. "The magic does what it will. It adapts to what we need. At least, that's how Baile seems to work."

"Right." Roderick nodded slowly, before his gaze grew keen on Kate again. "And you are concerned to leave Dhara here?"

"Everywhere is dangerous for her, what with Goddess being part of her." The words tumbled out of Kate, and she looked stricken. "I'm not implying you wouldn't take care of her."

Maeve leaned across the table and patted her hand. "We know that. We also know that you've always taken care of her."

"Dhara shares a form with Goddess." Roderick's voice took on an implacable note. "I have dedicated my life to Goddess, and that doesn't end now."

Kate stared at the table and took a shaky breath. "I know that, but with…everything…I didn't want to add to your worries."

"Blessed." Roderick pulled his shoulders back. "Coimhdeacht guard the coven. I am the first coimhdeacht, and I am first a coimhdeacht. You may leave Dhara with us and do what needs to be done. My son would expect nothing less of me."

CHAPTER ELEVEN

Sinead stood by the window as Noah prowled the suite she shared with Alannah. It was like bringing home a dog from a rescue with the way he investigated corners and peered behind furniture. She even caught the telltale flare of his nostrils and she'd bet he was sniffing stuff.

She didn't know how she felt about the sniffing. It made her want to check her armpits, even knowing that it would make no difference because his sense of smell was so much better than hers.

"If you lift your leg on that couch, I'm going to put you outside."

Noah flashed a grin at her. "You really make me want to bite you when you say shit like that."

"Huh." She might not mind a bit of judicious biting, in the right places. First, though, they needed to settle matters between them. They'd parted ways in Canada without having a conversation about the mated thing. "Why don't you sit down?"

"Why?" His eyes narrowed, and then he sighed. "You want to talk."

"Yes." She settled into one of the armchairs and motioned him to take the one opposite her.

He scowled at the chair. "Wolves are not big on talking."

"Then this is a job for man-Noah."

Noah studied the armchair and then strode toward her. Lifting her like she weighed nothing, he sat and settled her on his lap. At this rate, she might never use a chair again. "I missed you," he said in answer to her incredulous look. "I need physical contact." He grinned. "It's a wolf thing."

There seemed to be a lot of wolf things that she would need to get used to. If he was going to be around.

"So, now you're here, in England." She needed to understand what that meant, but it was difficult to concentrate with his hard, powerful body pressed against her.

"Now, I'm here." He curled a lock of her hair around his forefinger. "If you go elsewhere, then that's where I go."

For a woman who'd never kept a man around long enough to qualify as a boyfriend, even in the loosest sense, she found his statement daunting. "Then you're saying that we are a unit, from now on."

"I can't change that." He tugged on the tendril to get her to meet his gaze. "You're my mate. I have to be with you."

She retrieved her hair with a gentle tug. "Hear me out." She held up a hand. "What if, say, we don't get on? What then?"

"We find a way to get on." He speared his hand through the hair at her nape and massaged her scalp. "I will never want to be anywhere that you aren't and with someone who isn't you."

That was clear enough. "And you're absolutely fine with that?"

"You're my mate," he said, and settled his fidgety hand on the small of her back. "You are the one being who is mine."

"But what if a wolf finds their mate and doesn't like them?" After all, she wasn't the easiest women in the world to live with. "What if one mate drives the other one mad?"

"Hypothetically?" His topaz wolf eyes bored into her and called her crap.

Sinead dropped her gaze first. "Maybe not."

"They couldn't." He exerted light pressure on her back until she leaned into him. "There is nothing my mate could do to make me regret that they were my mate."

"Are you sure?" She had never been able to offer anyone that kind of commitment. What if she couldn't do that now, with him? "What if your mate doesn't like you?"

"Non-shifters sometimes take longer to come around." He pressed his nose into her neck and sniffed. "Rachel's mate rejected the bond, and they stayed apart for five years."

"So, that is a thing." She pounced on the information. "People do reject the bond."

"Shifters don't." He nuzzled beneath her ear, his deep voice rumbling against her. "Non-shifters sometimes do."

Tingles broke out down her neck and sparked in her nipples. "Rachel's mate rejected her?"

"For a time." He nipped her earlobe and then sucked it into his mouth to soothe it. "But he's with her now."

"But what if he hadn't?" It was hard to keep conversation going when he was doing mouth things to her. Hot shivers of sensation spread over her skin.

"Sweet thing?" He nipped and sucked her neck to her jawbone. "Do you need to hear the words? Wolves are not good with words. We're so much better at action." Noah growled deep in his throat.

The sound did something sweet and hot to her that made her wriggle in his lap. A primal response to his growl awoke in her. "Why don't we try the words anyway?"

"Words," he snarled, and took a deep breath. "I love you, sweet thing. I love your fire and your sass."

He was doing well, and Sinead had to blink moisture away. Allergies! She had allergies.

"More?" His tender smile curled around her heart and warmed it.

"Maybe."

"I love your indomitable spirit and your warrior's heart." His eyes glowed gold. "I love your tender soul and your gorgeous face." Now his smile became definitely wolfish. "And I adore your kickass body."

Oh my. She hadn't realized how much she needed to hear the words until he said them.

He cuddled her closer into the cradle of his thighs. The very hard cradle of his thighs. "Shall I tell you something about wolves?"

"Yes." Her voice came out in a breathy whisper. She was coming around to being more of a fan of action than words.

"We're wolves," he murmured, pressing his mouth to the pulse in her neck. "We are born to hunt."

"Hunt?" Her neck lolled to the side, giving him free access to her skin. "That doesn't sound very…evolved."

"Ummm," he rumbled. "First we track our prey."

"Prey?" She suspected she'd enjoy Noah's tracking.

His big hand covered her knee and began a slow trawl up her thigh. "Then we study them."

Studying was good, very, very good. She let out a breathless gasp as his other hand cupped her nape and positioned her head where he wanted it—her lips almost touching his. "Is this you studying me?"

"Uh-uh." Gaze fixed on her mouth, he shook his head slowly. "No, I've moved on to stage three in the hunt."

Sinead very much hoped stage three had something to do with lip-on-lip action.

The hand slid to the inside of her thigh and climbed. "Stage three is where we lure our prey."

"Is this you luring me?" It was working, as well. Her entire being focused on his mouth, wanting to feel his lips, taste him, explore him.

Noah sucked her bottom lip into his mouth. "How am I doing?"

"I'll let you know." By which she meant he was doing fantastically.

"You're lying." His hand cupped the juncture of her thighs. "I can smell your need."

Oh Goddess. Him saying that cranked her desire up another notch. "Unfair advantage."

"Wolf," he whispered. "And once we've lured our prey close enough." He pressed his hand to the seam of her trousers, rubbing her sensitive flesh against her pants. "We attack."

His mouth took hers in a bruising kiss.

And Sinead must have a bit of wolf inside her, because his mouth on hers, his tongue, and teeth, unleashed her wild side. Digging her fingers into his scalp, she captured his head and kissed him back. This kiss wasn't the tentative exploration of new lovers, but a full-frontal assault on each other's senses.

Their tongues tangled and teased, explored, and invaded.

And all the time he kept moving his hand against her thigh juncture.

Her hips responded, pushing against the pressure he exerted, seeking more.

Not breaking the kiss, Noah surged to his feet.

Mewling the loss of his touch, Sinead wrapped her legs around him and pressed into his erection. His swollen length hit her right on the sweet spot, and she moaned.

Noah walked them back until her spine connected with the wall. Then he pressed deeper into her.

Needing to touch his hot skin, Sinead burrowed beneath his sweater to the smooth silk beneath. She explored the iron bunching of muscle on either side of his spine beneath his hot skin. He was beautiful and all hers. She dug her nails into his strength.

Groaning, Noah increased the pressure of his kiss, eating into her mouth as if he wanted to absorb her whole.

"Off," she panted into his mouth, tugging at his sweater.

He broke their kiss briefly to haul the sweater over his head. He gripped the hem of her shirt and ripped.

"Oh." Sinead studied the ripped sides of her Arcane Activist T-shirt. "I liked that shirt."

"I hated it." And then he was back, his chest against her breasts, their hips grinding and pressing, imitating the act they both wanted. "It kept me from touching you."

His hands worked behind her and unclasped her bra. He spread his big, rough palms over her breasts, plumping them, learning them, finding the ways she liked to be touched.

"I need these off." He tugged at her waistband and growled his frustration. Then he grabbed the waistband and ripped the center seam. His strength thrilled her, and her panties were next to go. She didn't care, she wanted the barriers between them gone as well.

Reaching down, she slid her hand into his sweats. Hard, hot male flesh pulsed in her palm, and she pumped his length.

"I need inside you," he rasped. "Put me inside you."

Sinead didn't need any more prompting. She lined them up and sank onto his shaft.

With a groan, Noah flexed his hips and impaled her.

Her flesh stretched to accommodate his girth and then welcomed him into her tight, wet clasp.

They stilled for a moment, letting the pleasure sink bone deep into them. He was perfect. They were perfect.

"Another time," he growled. "We're going to play, and I'm going to taste and touch you everywhere, but I need you too bad. Been waiting too long to be inside you."

Sinead tightened her thighs around him, urging him to finish what he'd started.

Noah drew back and thrust.

The stone was rough against her back, her head thumped against the wall, but Sinead didn't care. Her entire being was focused on the man driving into her, one powerful thrust after another.

Desperate for more of him, all of him, she fused their mouths back together.

Noah pumped faster, harder, deeper, his fingers digging into her ass as he caught her in his rhythm.

The wet slide of sweaty skin provided their soundtrack as she urged him on with moans and incoherent cries.

Her orgasm bloomed deep inside her. "Oh please," she chanted into his mouth. "Don't stop, please don't stop."

"Never," he grated, spearing into her over and over again.

Sinead climbed so high, the drop yawned dizzying and delicious in front of her. "Yes," she screamed as her completion broke over her. Her muscles bunched and surrendered, her channel squeezing him.

On a shout, Noah pushed deep and released into her.

Ripples of sensation shot through her from their joined flesh, and she clung to him with arms and legs.

Noah's weight pushed her into the wall as he buried his face in her shoulder. "Jesus," he whispered. "Motherfucker."

Something about that struck her as inordinately funny. Maybe it was the high she was on, but Sinead pushed her head against the wall and laughed.

Noah's chuckles rumbled in the big chest pressed against her. Then he kissed her softly, gently, a sweet affirmation of what they'd shared, and whispered, "Mate."

CHAPTER TWELVE

Emma stood by with Warren and Mandla while Kate said goodbye to Dhara.

Dhara cried, while Kate did her best to remain stoic. "And remember." She cupped Dhara's face. "Listen to Roderick and the others, and if you need me, Andy knows how to contact me."

"I know." Dhara's eyes flashed silver. "Be well, Blessed."

"Gah." Kate shook her head. "I will never get used to that."

Dhara gave her a wry smile. "Just imagine how I feel."

"And I will come and visit." Kate pulled Dhara into a hug. "And as soon as things are safe again, you can come and visit me."

Emma admired Kate's optimism, especially given what she was going back to. Sasha reported that things had gone very quiet on the Rhiannon front. Quiet made Emma's skin crawl. The eye of the hurricane was always quiet.

"I love you, Katy," Dhara sobbed. "And you be careful. Do what Zach tells you."

Kate snorted and gave her sister a watery smile. "Like that's gonna happen."

Dhara managed a weak chuckle. "But he will keep you safe."

"Yes, he will." Kate nodded and tucked her sister to her side. She turned a fierce gaze on Noah. "And you take care of her too. You're the person who knows her best here."

"I will, Kate." Noah kissed her forehead. "And I'd pay good money to see Zach try to get you to do what he wants you to."

Kate shoved him and laughed. "You're the worst." She looked at Noah and her face softened. "And the best." She scowled at Sinead. "You remember that."

"Way ahead of you." Sinead slid her arm around Noah's waist.

Yeah, no prizes for guessing what those smug assholes had been up to last night. All the coupling-up around Baile was making Emma twitchy, especially since she didn't see any prospect for her. *As soon as things are safe again.* Kate's words echoed in her mind.

Emma had never lived in a world where Rhiannon didn't exist. Her grandparents had brought her into the organization when she was still a child. Nobody could afford to be ignorant with Rhiannon roaming the earth.

Mags sensed her disquiet through their bond and slid her hand into Emma's and squeezed. "Everything will be fine."

"You've seen it?" Emma studied her face.

Mags winced. "No. Taylor and I are not getting any outcomes on Alexander or what Rhiannon is up to next, but it will be fine because we'll fight like hell to make it so."

"Yeah." Emma nodded. She'd carried the weight of this fight against Rhiannon for what felt like all her life. Before she'd been working with Sasha, but now she was part of a brotherhood and a coven, more part of the fight than ever. Because now she had her witch to fight for.

Kate's instructions kept coming, and Dhara nodded and wept.

"Kate?" Noah touched her arm. "We need to go. Sasha has arranged safe transport, and we need to get to them."

Kate nodded and took a deep breath. Her face collapsed and she grabbed onto Dhara and sobbed.

"Blessed," Goddess said. "I shall guard this vessel and this witch, because she is mine."

"Right." Bobbing her head and sniffing, Kate stepped away from Dhara.

The coven members said goodbye to her in turn. Even Bronwyn was there to see Kate off.

Emma beat Warren to the driver's seat.

With a look of disgust at them for their antics, Mandla climbed into the back beside Kate and Noah.

Nofoto stood on tiptoes to peer through the car window at him. "You take care now."

Mandla nodded.

"And don't do anything dangerous."

Mandla nodded.

"Behave as if I was right there with you."

Mandla raised an eyebrow. He leaned out and kissed Nofoto. "*Sala gahle.*"

"*Hamba gahle.*" Nofoto stepped back.

Jack would stay behind with the other witches. Of course, Roderick was still there, but Emma was worried about the big throwback. Goddess, she was worried for all of them—the Baile coven and all the others like them around the world.

Beyond the wards, a small encampment had sprung up. About fifteen tents and a couple of caravans sat by the side of the road.

"It's them!" A woman shrieked as soon as she spotted the Landy.

People crawled out of tents and came running.

Slamming her hand on the hooter, Emma put her foot down. As much as a good fight would ease her tension right now, they had Kate in the vehicle.

"We should keep an eye on that." Mandla turned in his seat

to watch the figures dancing behind them in the road. "There are more than when we arrived."

"There are more coming every day," Warren said. A mobile home trundled up the road toward the camp.

Noah gave them a feral smile. "Maybe a little wolf amongst them might make them rethink their living arrangements."

"Or it could result in a wolf getting shot." Emma threw over her shoulder. "And I'm not explaining that to Sinead."

Noah growled. "They won't see me if I don't want them to."

"Let's table that option," Warren said. "We can revisit when we've got Kate safe."

It was weird to think of Warren meeting Jack through anger management workshops. The Warren sitting in the passenger seat had the coolest head of all of them and was a dab hand at heading off discord. Jack had told her that Warren used to have big trouble controlling his temper. Then again, there was something about bonding a witch that tended to smooth the rough patches in a coimhdeacht.

"Jesus." Noah looked ill. "What the fuck stinks like that?"

"Alannah's fuel of the future," Warren said.

"Nah." Noah shook his head. "That stuff doesn't smell pretty, but it's all natural. No, man, I can smell blood magic and a shit fucking ton of it."

Mandla produced a knife longer than his leg and palmed it. "Where?"

"Whoa there, Nelly!" Noah threw his hands up and leaned away from Mandla and his enormous weapon. "You gonna pillage and loot a village later?"

"Blood magic users killed my people." Mandla's voice went low and deadly.

Noah's shoulders tightened. "Yeah, mine too."

The two men looked at each other and nodded. Yeah, Emma knew a pact forming when she saw one. Rhiannon and her murderous followers had some vengeance heading their way.

"Where is the blood magic coming from?" Kate asked Noah.

With a grimace of distaste, Noah opened the window and sniffed.

"Ugh!" He jerked his head back in and made retching noises.

Emma jumped on her reflex to gag as well. "Where?"

"Greater Littleton, and the surrounds." Noah opened a bottle of water and swigged. "It's all around us."

Yeah, no, that didn't make Emma happy.

Opening the glove compartment, Warren extracted a gun and checked the chamber.

"Lennox know you're carrying that?" Emma jerked her head at the handgun.

"Nah." Warren checked the safety and then lowered it to his lap. "But then I'll just have to stand behind you. By the time he finishes stripping you of your weapons, he'll be too tired to get to me."

Emma couldn't say anything. She did have a little thing about being well armed and prepared.

As they drew closer to the village, Noah seemed to be having more difficulty with the stench. His eyes watered and he looked ready to barf.

"How does this work?" Mandla gestured Noah from top to toe. "This wolf thing."

Emma wanted to know as well, and from his silence, she guessed Warren did too.

"Sometimes I'm a man, and sometimes I'm a wolf." Noah folded his arms.

"Stop it." Kate shoved him. "Noah is one of several shifters…" She cleared her throat. "One of a few shifters now, who are able to command their form. It started a number of years back when one of the children on the commune went through puberty and developed the ability. We suspect it has something to do with the earth point being moved to the land and being inside a person as opposed to a place."

"Huh." Mandla studied Noah. "Does it hurt? When you…change."

"Like a son of a bitch." Noah shrugged. "But you get used to it, and the stronger your wolf, the faster the shift."

Warren turned around in his seat. "And the smell thing? Do you have the same senses as a wild wolf?"

Noah waggled his hand. "Yes and no. Our smell is millions of times better than normal humans, but not as good as wild wolves. On the other hand, we have better vision than wild wolves. That's where our human helps us. So, little bit of column A, little bit of column B."

"What about sex?" Mandla asked the question none of them dared.

Now you could hear a pin drop in the Landy.

Emma did her best not to look too curious.

"What about sex?" Noah cocked his head and studied Mandla.

"Do you…" He made some helpful hand gestures, tapping his cupped palm on his fist. "Like a dog."

"Ah shit." Kate dropped her head into her hands. "I can't believe we're having this conversation."

"Why do you want to know, handsome?" Noah winked at Mandla. "Interested?"

Mandla stilled, like a gathering storm, and then threw back his head and guffawed. He thumped Noah's shoulder. "I like you, wolf."

"But not that much, right?" Noah chuckled.

Mandla's booming laughter was contagious.

They all sobered as Emma slowed to enter the village.

"What the hell?" Warren leaned forward and peered at the heavy traffic. The village was gridlocked like the M25 at rush hour. "Where did all these people come from?"

"They stink." Noah gagged. "Those fuckers are everywhere."

Emma edged between a family minivan and a sedan. She

eased forward a few meters and then stopped. The crowd made her uncomfortable. In groups, humanity got real stupid, real fast.

On either side of the road, people streamed down the pavement. The village green was choked with crowds. A group dressed in fatigues wove through the traffic and joined the throng on the village green.

"Oy!" A man shouted. "It's them."

Emma's gut tightened. *There you go.* She scanned the road for an exit point.

"Fuck." Warren breathed as several heads snapped in their direction.

Cars boxed them in, front and back.

Five men shifted in their direction. More voices joined the shout, and more bodies came at them. They were stuck.

Mandla had his knife out again, and this time, nobody had anything to say about it.

Car doors opened behind them, and more people threaded down the road toward them.

Noah growled, a low menacing rumble that reverberated through his chest.

"Don't." Kate put an arm on his shoulder. "You can't shift here."

Noah's eyes glowed like a cat in the dark. He produced his own knife.

"Shit." Emma glimpsed a small gap in the traffic ahead and to her right and floored the Landy, narrowly missing a truck. The driver hooted and yelled at them. "They've got us pinned down."

They were stuck again.

"The pavement," Mandla snapped. "Jump it and go."

She couldn't, not without collecting human trophies for the Landy's bonnet. "Too many people."

Mandla grunted and produced his cell phone. After a short pause he said into his phone, "Make it rain, baby. Hard."

He'd barely hung up when the wind whipped through the village. People's hair streamed, scarves and hats went floating into the air. Walkers had to lean into the force of the wind. Litter and belongings from the village green were swept up and tossed.

On the green, people yelled and started gathering themselves.

"Come on, baby," Mandla muttered. "Bring it."

Thunder crashed overhead. A woman screamed, and their pursuers stopped and stared at the sky. Thick, rolling clouds gathered like popcorn above them. The wind increased, more thunder, and the clouds turned black. The entire day dimmed, and headlights flared on the cars around them.

Lightning split the sky and slammed the village green in a static burst.

People ran for cover. The pavement emptied as pedestrians ducked into shops and vehicles or huddled in doorways. Clouds opened and rain flooded down around them, pounding like miniature fists on the Landy roof.

Emma didn't hang about. She shoved her way in front of a silver sedan and ramped the pavement. The Landy took it in her all-terrain stride.

A few sodden pavement stragglers cried out in alarm and pointed.

Gritting her teeth and hooting, Emma picked up speed.

"Oh shit, oh shit, oh shit," Kate chanted.

"Watch out." Warren pointed to a display of tourist tat.

Emma narrowly dodged it, then almost connected a parking meter.

"Whoop!" Noah fist pumped. "Pedal to the metal, woman!"

Emma jerked the steering wheel and sent the Landy careening across the village green. Tires churned grass into mud, and the engine roared. On the far side of the green, traffic had eased enough to be moving. Spaces had opened between the cars and Emma aimed the Landy that way.

Their followers dropped far behind, and she swung left across the green. The Landy jolted off the pavement and resettled as they slid into the traffic.

Noah banged his fist on her headrest. "Let's do that again."

CHAPTER THIRTEEN

Alannah stared at the ingredients on the table in front of her—smoked haddock, basmati rice, curry powder, turmeric, boiled eggs, chicken stock. The last time she'd made this dish, Thomas had teased her about wishing he could taste it. For some reason, she wanted to make it tonight. It didn't hurt quite as much to prepare something Thomas would have loved.

She put water in a pan to poach the fish and added bay leaves.

"Hi," a man said from the door.

Alannah jumped. She hadn't heard anyone approach.

The new doctor—Simon—stood in the doorway with his hands in his scrub pockets. They would need to find him something else to wear. His brown hair was disheveled as if he'd been running his hands through it. Now that his eyes weren't burning with murderous intent, she noticed they were a lovely shade somewhere between green and brown. Hazel. He had hazel eyes.

She smiled back at him. "Hi."

His gaze narrowed on the ingredients as she added more to the table. "Are you making kedgeree?"

"Yes." Her voice came out brusquer than she'd intended. She didn't know why his simple question made her feel so defensive, but her hackles had risen. She softened her tone. "Yes, kedgeree. It's a favorite around here."

He blinked at her and took a step into the kitchen. "I like it too." He cleared his throat and rocked on his heels. "Kedgeree, I mean."

"Good." She checked on the fish before she went back to chopping onions. Her eyes teared up, and she wiped them with the back of her wrist.

"That happens because the onions release a chemical irritant." Simon jabbed his forefinger at the onions.

"They do?" She had no idea whether he was making this up or not and didn't really care. He had a nice voice—deep and soothing, the sort of voice you wanted a physician to have. The right voice to say things like *this won't hurt a bit* or *you're going to be fine.*

"They do." He nodded. "It's called syn-Propanethial-S-oxide and it stimulates the eye's lachrymal glands, and you…er…cry."

He looked a bit awkward and unsure of himself, so she gave him an encouraging smile. "I didn't know that."

"No, well, most people don't." He rolled his lips inwards and then puffed them out on a breath. "We used to blame the enzyme alliinase for the instability of substances in a cut onion. In 2002, I believe, Japanese scientists discovered a previously unknown enzyme and proved that lachrymatory factor synthase is the real villain."

His science babble was kind of endearing, and she said, "That's fascinating."

"It really is." He frowned and cleared his throat. "Would you like to know the process?"

"I would." She was barely listening, but he was so earnest, she didn't want to say no.

"Well, when you cut into the onion, the Lachrymatory factor

synthase is released. The synthase enzyme converts the amino acids sulfoxides of the onion into sulfenic acid. The unstable sulfenic acid then rearranges itself into syn-Propanethial-S-oxide. The Syn-Propanethial-S-oxide becomes airborne, interacts with our eyes, our lachrymal glands get irritated and"—he snapped his fingers—"tears."

"That's really fascinating."

He gave a rueful chuckle. "It really isn't." He dropped his head and studied his trainers. "I tend to babble when I'm nervous."

"You're nervous?" People generally didn't get nervous in her company. Never mind generally, he might be the only person who had ever got twitchy around her. "I'm sorry. You don't need to be nervous." And then she winced, because the poor man had reasons aplenty to be nervous around the residents of Baile. "What I mean is, you won't come to any harm."

"I know." He leaned his hips against the counter to the right of the sink and watched her. "You do a lot of the cooking here?"

"Most of it." She put a pan on the range hob and added butter. "I enjoy feeding people." Something she'd almost forgotten since Thomas had left. There hadn't been much joy in anything she did. "We grow most of the fresh produce here at Baile."

"Is that because of the…er…magic and stuff?" He flushed.

For a mundane, and one who'd been abducted, he was dealing well with the information dump he'd been given. "Partly." She added half the onions to the pan, and they hit the butter with a delicious sizzle. "Sinead and I have an affinity with growing things, and we can help them along. Nothing to disturb nature's balance, but our earth connection keeps that from happening." She stirred the onions in the butter. Onions frying in butter had to be one of the most mouth-watering smells in the world. "But we also tend to stick to ourselves up here." She pointed her wooden spoon in the direction of

Greater Littleton. "The villagers are all wary of us, and don't love having us around." She turned to get the cumin, curry powder, and rice.

But Simon had moved closer and held them out to her.

"Thank you." She added the spices and then the rice. "I'm sure you've heard the rumors and gossip about the witches of Baile."

His shoulder bumped hers as he peered into the pan. "Sultanas?"

"Yes, please."

He returned from the table with the sultanas and a jug of stock. "Only, not so much gossip and rumors as truth, as it turns out."

She added the sultanas. "Right." The stock steamed as it hit the hot pan. Strange, but generally people in her kitchen irritated her. "But magic makes people nervous, so we don't go shouting it about."

"Hannah was giving me the lowdown earlier." He leaned on the counter closest to the range and watched her stir the pan's contents. He had a restful way about him that must work well in his profession. "She said you and Sinead are something called wardens, and that means you deal with the earth and plants?"

"That's about the truth of it." She moved to the poaching pan and removed the fish with a slotted spoon.

Simon gestured the fish. "Shall I flake that for you?"

"That would be lovely." Sinead would often help her in the kitchen, but normally she cooked alone. True, she didn't encourage participation, but Simon seemed to know what she needed before she needed it.

She kept a critical eye on Simon as he fetched the fork and flaked the fish. She needn't have worried. His precise surgeon's hands performed the task better than she could. Thomas had enjoyed watching her cook, and their relationship had been forged in her kitchen.

Simon nodded toward her rice mixture. "I add a drop of cream to mine at the end."

"So do I." She stirred the rice and stock combination. It was odd how comfortable she felt in his company. She wasn't sure what that meant, and it disturbed her. "You cook?"

"When I have time." He folded his arms. "The hospital takes up most of my time and being on call when I'm not there."

"It must do."

He moved to the table and peeled the eggs, his movements deft and skilled.

Alannah dropped butter into another pan to start the sauce. She was curious about him. "Do you like being a doctor?"

"I do." He brought more onions, the turmeric, and ginger to her. "I was one of those lucky people who always knew what they wanted to do."

Growing up in Baile, none of them had ever given what to do with their lives much thought. They were witches, and that demanded secrecy. Added to which, service to Goddess was a thing that chose you, and not the other way around. She added tomato puree to her sauce and watched it for a couple of minutes. Then she added the cream.

"Actually." Simon grabbed a knife and chopped parsley. "My family was horrified when I chose medicine?"

"Really?" She thinned her mixture with some of the poaching liquid. He seemed the sort of son any family would be proud of. "Aren't parents usually delighted when their child wants to be a doctor?"

"Usually." He chuckled. "But not when you come from several generations of animal doctors."

She liked his deep, warm laughter. "Your parents are veterinarians?"

He brought the parsley to her and dropped it in her sauce. "Back to my great, great, greats and beyond. I broke the line when I decided to doctor humans instead." He smiled at her. It lit his serious face and made him look warm and approachable. "But I have two older brothers who dutifully went into the family business, so it wasn't a mortal blow I dealt them."

He had a nice smile—warm with a hint of mischief. They hadn't given the poor man much reason to smile since he'd been forcibly brought here.

Stepping back, he left her to combine all the components of the kedgeree. "I suppose you didn't have much choice about being a…er…witch."

"Not really." She folded fish into the rice mixture. "But I don't have a problem with what I am. It's not just something I want to do, it's something I need to do." She sifted through her thoughts. "Something I am as opposed to something I do."

Tilting his head, his steady hazel regard took her in. She got the feeling he really saw her, and she suddenly wanted to hide. "Right." He pointed to the table. "Shall I set that?"

"Sinead will be in soon." If Noah had been around, Alannah might have let Simon go ahead and do the job. Which was not the entire truth. She felt vulnerable and exposed, and she wanted him out of her kitchen. "She likes setting the table."

He nodded. "Okay, then."

Their former comfort slunk away, and Alannah couldn't think of anything more to say.

Simon nodded and walked toward the stairs leading into the rest of the keep. "I'll let whoever I find know that dinner is ready."

"Thank you." As he walked out, she almost called him back. But there was no point to that. She had no space in her life for a man with a lovely laugh and gentle eyes. "And thank you for the help."

He turned and looked at her, and there were those wonderful eyes again. "Any time."

Alannah was used to men finding her attractive, but there was something more than that in Simon's gaze. She rounded up her thoughts before they could go bounding in an unwelcome direction and busied herself with cleaning the kitchen.

A piercing whistle broke into her thoughts, and she went over to the window and looked out. High above the castle, a brown speck hovered.

"Is that Kai?" Sinead joined her briefly at the window before she began setting the table. "She hasn't been around the last couple of days."

Alannah watched the kestrel surf the sea breeze above the castle, her wing and tail feathers making tiny adjustments to keep her aloft. "She must be hunting."

"How's Alexander?" Sinead clattered knives and forks together before setting out places.

"I'm not sure." She fetched wineglasses and brought them to the table. "I haven't been in the healer's hall this afternoon."

Sinead stopped and glanced to the stairs. "But wasn't Simon just in here?"

"Oh, yes." And she hadn't even asked about Alexander, hadn't even thought to. She'd been enjoying his company and their easy chat. Guilt tightened her chest and constricted her breathing. She loved Thomas, would always love Thomas. "I didn't ask."

"Thank Goddess he decided to stay." Sinead doled out dinner plates. "I don't know what we would have done if he'd decided to report us."

It wasn't until Sinead said that, that Alannah realized she'd never thought Simon would go to the police. In fact, she'd been mostly sure he would stay. Which was super presumptuous of her, given that she barely knew the man.

CHAPTER FOURTEEN

Jack bit down hard on his back teeth as the police cruiser trundled into the bailey and stopped. He'd been half expecting them since Warren had briefed him on their impromptu off-roading as they got Kate to an airstrip three days ago. Jack might even be surprised it had taken Lennox this long to get his ass up to Baile.

The windscreen wipers swiped across the front window of the police cruiser, sending a spray of green stuff flying. Lennox threw himself out of the car and stood glaring at the sprigs of greenery now littering the bailey floor.

Cradling his coffee cup, Jack took the opportunity life had tossed at him, propped his shoulder on the kitchen doorjamb and drawled, "Decorating for Halloween, Inspector?"

"Fucking whackos." Lennox kicked at the offending sprigs before turning his glare on Jack. "I don't suppose you'd know anything about this?"

Not bothering to check his grin, Jack strolled closer to the inspector. "And you'd suppose right. Acharya into herbs maybe?"

"Step aside, please." Acharya hopped from the driver's side, evidence baggies clutched in his hand. The man must use some kind of gloop in his dark hair, because the coif never moved. Not even after hours of interrogation. Acharya was a walking testimony to the efficacy of hair product.

Lennox growled and stuck his hands in his pockets. "What the fuck are you doing?"

"Bagging the evidence…Inspector." Acharya stopped and looked bewildered.

"Christ!" Lennox's jaw tightened, and a vein pulsed in his neck. "We don't need sodding evidence bags. They threw this shit on the car." With a careful breath, he made an effort to contain his temper. "While. We. Were. In. It."

Acharya opened and shut his mouth, before trotting back to the cruiser and disappearing the evidence baggies.

"I'm no expert." Jack crouched and picked up a sprig. "But this looks like parsley to me." He examined a feathery spray near Lennox's sensible thick-soled brogues. "And that could be dill." A tiny purple bud on the silvery sprig identified itself. "And that's definitely lavender."

"Thanks for the botany lesson, Langham," Lennox ground out. "Want to hazard a guess how it got all over my fucking car?"

"Again, I'm no expert." Jack sipped his coffee, loving the moment like sun on his back. "But if I were to guess, I'd say you were the victim of a drive-by herbing." He pretended to think his statement over. "If you can call it a drive-by if you're doing the driving."

"Funny." Lennox deadpanned.

Frowning, Acharya emerged from the vehicle. "I don't believe you can refer to it as a drive-by if you were the one doing the driving."

"Right." Lennox took a deep breath, and then a second. His

gaze sharpened on something—someone behind Jack's right shoulder, and Jack did some deep breathing of his own. He'd told Mags to stay in the kitchen. He should have known she wouldn't listen, but hope sprung fucking eternal.

"Hello, Inspector," Mags trilled and hooked her arm through Jack's. "I see you've met our friends on the road."

Lennox's eyes narrowed. "They don't seem to like you much for friends."

"Nor you." Mags giggled and pointed to the herbs. "Parsley, dill, lavender, and I'm guessing oregano are all used to ward off evil spirits or witches." She cocked her head, her curtain of hair tumbling over Jack's forearm in a way that made him want to tangle his fingers in it. "So which are you? Evil spirit or witch?"

"Miss Cray?" Lennox assumed the stoic expression of a man who'd been baited by the best and lived to tell the story. "We were actually hoping to speak with you."

"Oh, I know." Mags dimpled at Lennox. "And here I am. Only, there's a nasty chill this morning. Why don't you come inside?"

Jack gnashed his teeth. He didn't want these buggers close to Mags, let alone sitting down with her over tea. And make no mistake, that was where this was heading. Mags would have them sipping tea and chomping biccies before they knew what had happened. Pure evil.

Emma and Noah ran through the gatehouse, both dressed in training gear and pouring sweat. Jack wished he'd taken their offer to join them on a run this morning. But then he wouldn't have been here to watch Mags, and he and Emma took turns making sure one of them had eyes on her at all times.

"*Whoop, whoop!*" Noah sang. Then went into some rap about the sound of the police before *whooping* again.

Chuckling, Emma punched his arm.

Noah didn't even wince, and Jack knew how hard that woman could punch.

"What do you do for an encore?" Lennox turned an unimpressed expression on Noah. "'I Shot the Sheriff?'"

Acharya stiffened and glared at Noah. "And you are?"

"Pleased to meet you." Noah stuck out his hand and grinned. "Noah Rivers. Cute car."

The effort it took Acharya to take the offered hand was almost comical and played over every line of his uptight shape.

Emma strolled past him, and Acharya didn't miss the way she filled out her skintight yoga pants as she went.

Yup, Emma did amazing things to Lycra.

Noah smirked at Acharya and followed Emma.

"New additions?" Lennox had his temper under control now, and his good cop was putting in an appearance.

Jack kept it noncommittal. "Something like that."

"Don't be annoying, Jack." Mags swatted his arm. "Jack's such a clown, Jasper. That's Noah and Emma." She leaned closer. "Noah is from Canada." She turned on her heel and motioned over her shoulder. "Come along, then. Alannah has been baking, and if we don't get in there fast, all the shortbread will be gone."

Had he called it or what? Jack followed after his witch. She really didn't give a man much choice.

Lennox took the invitation at a near trot.

Taking a moment to smooth his tunic, Acharya followed.

In the kitchen, Alannah looked up from moving biscuits from a baking tray to a cooling rack. "Hello."

Acharya stopped dead. Even Lennox looked taken aback.

Alannah would do that to anything with a pulse.

"Hey, beautiful." Noah kissed her cheek and swiped a handful of cookies.

Alannah batted at his hand with her spatula, but Noah had the reflexes of a…well, a wolf.

Jack experienced a secret moment of delight imagining what Lennox would make of that clanger if they dropped it on him.

"I've put the kettle on." Alannah beamed at the coppers.

"There's a nasty chill this morning. A nice cup of tea will warm us all up."

"No tea," Lennox snapped. "Thank you."

"Really?" Alannah looked as if he'd clubbed a baby seal to death in her kitchen. "Surely, you have a few minutes. And the shortbread is fresh out the oven."

Lennox folded. "Well, perhaps a quick cuppa."

"Lovely." Alannah's smile brought the sun into the gloomy day. "Why don't you all go into the sitting room, and Noah and I will bring tea in?"

"We will?" Noah sprayed crumbs around the kitchen.

Alannah looked at him. "Please?"

"God dammit!" Noah glared at her. "You know when you make that face, I'll do anything."

"Hmm." Alannah smirked as she went back to her biscuits. "And if you're really nice, I won't share with Sinead how I do it."

With a giggle, Mags gestured the staircase. "This way, Inspector."

"Acharya!" Lennox snapped at his gaping constable.

Acharya scuttled after them.

Whistling low, Lennox stopped as they entered the great hall. Greedily taking in all the details, he turned a full circle,

A wolf pup skirted Acharya and showed him some teeth.

Jack knew the feeling and had definitely experienced the same impulse.

"Nice place you have here," Lennox said.

"She's beautiful." Mags motioned the hall. "And all original."

Acharya walked closer to the stained-glass window. He cocked his head and frowned.

The image in the window did that to people. It depicted the first three witches goddess had called. It had featured the first four before Rhiannon had changed camps, resulting in the image feeling off and unbalanced.

"Here we are." Mags opened the sitting room door and gestured the coppers inside.

Jack would have gone with the dungeon. He hadn't seen one, but he was sure Baile must have one. If not, the castle could do what she did, and conjure one up.

Lennox, looking more like he regretted caving to Alannah, stomped into the sitting room. He didn't even wait for anyone to sit down. "You are Miss Magdalene Cray?"

"I am. Only, Magdalene is such a mouthful. Please call me Mags." She settled herself on the sofa, leaving enough room for Jack.

An invitation Jack took. He always felt better when Mags was in touching distance.

"Umm…Mags, then." Lennox stood with his back to the windows. A position that conveniently gave him a perfect view of the room's other occupants and shaded his face. "I understand you took a recent trip to Moscow."

"Yes." Mags tucked her legs up beside her and nestled into Jack. "It's a fascinating place. Have you been?"

"Er…no." Lennox shoved his hands in his pockets. "May I ask your reasons for traveling to Moscow?"

Lennox was way out of line, and Jack needed to set him right. "First, you'd need to tell her why you're asking."

"It's fine, Jack." Mags pressed her head to his shoulder. "I have nothing to hide."

If only that was how coppers worked, but Jack kept his lip buttoned.

"I went to see a friend," Mags said. "Emma. You saw her in the bailey. I needed to persuade her to come home with me."

"May I ask why?" Lennox shifted.

"No." Mags grinned. "Tea!"

Alannah glided into the room with a scowling Noah carrying a tray in her wake.

Jack swore he could hear Lennox's molars grinding.

"I'll leave you to it," Alannah said, leaving her tray and motioning Noah to put his down beside hers, she swept out of the sitting room.

Mags scooted forward and poured milk in bone china cups so fine they were translucent. Baile and Alannah were bringing out the good china. She glanced at Lennox. "Milk?"

He nodded. "We were talking about why you went to Moscow."

"No, we weren't." Mags looked to Acharya. "Milk?"

Acharya nodded.

"You were asking if you could ask why I went to get Emma." Holding the teapot lid with one finger, Mags poured. "I said I was not going to answer your question."

Jack relaxed slightly. Mags with her unique blend of sweet and scatty had the boys in blue baffled.

Lennox stepped forward. "And why is that?"

"Sugar?"

"Two."

"Because it's private." Mags dropped sugar in his tea before handing Lennox the cup and saucer. "Emma had her own reasons for going to Moscow, and I am not at liberty to share those." She turned to Acharya. "Sugar?"

"Er…no…thank you."

Mags smiled and handed him his tea before picking up the biscuit plate and offering it to Lennox.

Lennox hesitated, and then took three shortbread fingers.

At which point, Jack tossed manners out the window and grabbed his fair share. And when Acharya refused, Jack took his for good measure. Shame to let Alannah's baking go to waste. Fresh out the oven, too.

Mags handed him a cup of tea. Just the way he liked it.

The intimate details of that exchange were not lost on eagle-eye Lennox either. "Personal reasons?"

"Oh yes." Mags giggled. "And I can't say any more than that." She wagged a finger at Lennox. "So, don't keep asking, or you'll get me in trouble with Emma."

"Right." His big fingers struggled with the delicate teacup handle. "And Mr. Langham accompanied you."

"Yes." Mags caressed the word as she turned a sweet smile on Jack. "Jack comes everywhere with me."

Acharya slurped his tea and then blushed. "Sorry."

"We were given to understand you and Mr. Langham had an argument and that was the reason you left." Lennox canted forward, like a bloodhound on the trail. "And that was the reason Mr. Langham followed you."

"Oh, my." Mags picked up her tea and took a sip. "Someone has been indiscreet." She fanned her face with one hand. "It's terribly embarrassing, Inspector. Jack and I had a rather dramatic tiff."

"What about?"

"Sex," Mags said and sipped her tea.

Acharya choked on a mouthful of tea.

Lennox's cup rattled in its saucer.

And Jack might be enjoying himself. He sat back and let Mags run amok.

"Jack wanted to wait until we knew each other better." Mags sipped. "I didn't. And when he was more resistant than I liked, I got angry and stormed out. He followed." She leaned over the shortbread and took her time making a selection. "I have a voracious appetite," she said and bit into the biscuit.

"Right." Lennox cleared his throat. "And what can you tell me about the people outside the castle."

"The herb bandits?" Jack drawled, spreading his arm over the back of the sofa.

"Yes," Lennox grit out.

"They don't like us," Mags said.

Lennox shifted. "Why?"

"They think we're witches."

"Are you?"

Mags threw her head back and laughed. "You tell me, Inspector. Didn't everyone tell you there is no such thing as witches?"

CHAPTER FIFTEEN

Bronwyn tuned out Hannah and Simon whispering at the far end of the healer's hall. With all the equipment Andy had brought in, the hall looked more like a mundane hospital. Her helplessness lashed inside her, breaking like a summer storm on a windowpane. For all her blessing, and growing strength, she could do nothing to help the man she loved.

She knew what Hannah and Simon were whispering about, but she didn't let on. They tried to spare her feelings by not telling her, but she had eyes. She could also smell the growing stench of blood magic on Alexander.

Hannah and Simon left the ward part of the hall and went to where she kept her herbs. All the better to discuss the problem without her hearing them.

Bronwyn eased the sheet down Alexander's chest.

And there it was. From the mouth of his knife wound, dark tendrils crept like cracks across his chest. Nearly black where the knife protruded, they faded and thinned toward the end. But they were growing, almost hourly, and spreading their venom through him.

She knew without asking that Simon was concerned about

what the monitors were telling him. Alexander's vitals were slipping, like he was clinging to life by his fingertips and the cliff was crumbling.

The twins moved in her belly, sensing her fear, and reacting to it.

She wanted to sleep, but her worries chased her dreams, and she was too scared to close her eyes and find them leering and lurking behind her eyelids.

The words she battled into submission floated to the top of her consciousness and formed into a cohesive thought. Alexander was dying.

No! She shoved the thought away. To admit it was to admit defeat. Time and time again, they'd beaten the odds. When they'd first met, Alexander had expected to die to save her, but they'd saved him. Brought him to Baile where together, they'd built a life, created two new lives.

Her twins wouldn't be born without a father.

Fuck that. She was a healer. The strongest healer. Even Roderick said he'd rarely seen her equal.

The steady beat of the heart monitor stopped, and Bronwyn froze.

Ba-Beep.

It began again, and she released the breath she'd held.

Dhara had said if she transmuted the venom from the knife, it would corrupt their babies. But could she weigh two unborn children against the existing life of the man she loved?

Her head ached with the choice. And it was a choice. Every day she left Alexander to drift further from her, she made that choice.

She'd grown up without a father. There were worse things. The twins wouldn't miss what they'd never had. But she would.

Dear Goddess, her life without him would be barren, colorless, devoid of hope and light.

Terror choked the sobs in her throat. Her eyes burned with tears she couldn't shed.

Alexander was dying.

Pain sheared like an axe through her chest, robbing her breath, and stopping her heart. She couldn't live without him, didn't want to live without him. Wouldn't live without him.

His skin was warm and clammy beneath her palm. His life essence thrummed at her fingertips. Honey and sage perfumed the air as her blessing responded to her desire.

"Bronwyn." Roderick grabbed her wrist and pulled her hand away from Alexander. "You can't do that."

Fury tore into her, shredding her reason as she tried to yank her hand away. "Get your hands off me."

"Bronwyn." He clasped her shoulders. "Listen to me."

Listen to more words that meant Alexander would die. Bronwyn writhed against his hold. She was the only being who could help her love, and Roderick wanted to stop her.

His grip tightened. "Stop it, Bronwyn. You can't heal him, and if he was here, you know he'd forbid it."

"Forbid?" she snarled. "Nobody forbids me."

"Magic does." Roderick's pale blue eyes pierced through her rage and fright. He gripped her shoulders tight enough to stop her from moving. "You cannot use your blessing for harm."

Harm? She struggled to make sense of his words. "I'm harming him by letting him suffer when I could save him."

"You can't save him." Roderick's voice was as implacable as his grip. "And if you try, you will harm the babies."

She hurled the words at him that would shatter his conviction. "He will die if I don't."

"Maybe." Roderick's jaw tightened.

"Look." Bronwyn yanked the sheet away from the noxious tendrils working through Alexander's cells with every moment that passed. "It's growing."

Roderick dropped his head. "I know. I've seen it."

"Then you know why I have to heal him." Hope beckoned. Roderick would see reason.

"I see why you're desperate to heal him." Sadness flickered in Roderick's eyes and the downcast turn of his mouth. "And I understand. But he made me promise I would take care of you and the babies. And he would not want you to do this."

It was like crashing headlong into an immovable boulder. "You don't know that. You barely know him."

"I know because if this were me, and Maeve had to make the choice you do, I would not want her to risk our children." Roderick's eyes glistened with suppressed tears.

His threatening tears shook her to her foundation. Roderick never cried. Roderick was solid, dependable, immovable like the stone walls of Baile that sheltered them.

"Don't abandon hope," he whispered. "Never abandon hope."

The horror of what she'd almost done body slammed her, and Bronwyn swayed. Roderick was right. Alexander wouldn't want her to risk the children while there was still a glimmer of hope that he could survive. She'd almost given up on him. Her belly roiled, and she wanted to throw up. Alexander would never—had never—given up on her. Her doubt might have damaged him, tempted fate. "I'm sorry."

"You're exhausted." Roderick pulled her against his chest and wrapped his arms around her. "You're exhausted and frightened, and nobody judges you for that."

"I almost put our babies in danger."

He pressed his cheek to the top of her head. "Do you think I have never had similar thoughts? Do you think there have not been times when I wanted to abandon duty and respond to the promptings of my fear?"

She did think that. Roderick never wavered. "Have you?"

"Tahra was my first witch." His voice was a comforting rumble against her ear. "And I loved her. But she was already centuries old when we bonded and so very tired of the battle she fought. She was ready to move on."

Bronwyn didn't see the connection, but Roderick's huge body kept the nagging anxiety at bay. At least, for the moment.

"I had to let her go," he said. "I came to realize that if I truly loved her, I would want what was best for her, and not what was best for me."

For a moment, she had believed Roderick could give her comfort and guidance, but he was not making any sense and she couldn't apply what he said to her situation. "I think I'll go and rest now." She untangled herself from his arms. "Will you stay with him?"

"I will." Roderick inclined his dark head. "But you miss my point."

She was too weary to dissemble. "Yes."

"It was fear that made me want to keep Tahra with me. Fear that I would not survive her passing, fear of how much it would pain me when she did."

Too exhausted to keep standing, she sank into the chair beside Alexander. "I could have killed our children. I can save my love or save my children, but I can't do both."

"And fear drove your actions." Roderick crouched at her feet. He rested his hand on the swell of her belly. "Search your heart, the love you and Alexander share, for what he would do."

Alexander would save her, at all costs. But he would also never want to be the reason their children didn't live. If she saved him and lost the twins, he would carry that burden. And so would she.

"That thing." Roderick's lip curled in disgust as he pointed at the dagger. "That thing is killing him, but he's not dead yet. Stay with love and hope. Live in them day to day and know that you don't walk alone."

If only she could draw comfort from that. As much as she

appreciated the love and support of the coven, none of them were in her position. A sacrifice was being demanded of her.

"Trust in Goddess," Roderick said.

She curled her fingers into her palms before she raked them across his cheek. Trust in Goddess? That's all she had been doing, all any of them had been doing. Ask Alannah how those words felt about now. "Do you?" She locked eyes with him. "Do you trust Goddess?"

Roderick's sigh came from the deepest part of his being. "I'm trying, Bronwyn. I'm really fucking trying."

Drip!

Mags was aware she was dreaming as she looked around the cave surrounding her. Jack's warmth where he lay sleeping next to her told her she was in her bed in her room. The tangle of their legs anchored her.

She hated this dream, but she forced herself to stay. It was the first time the dream had come since Alexander had been stabbed. Maybe it would give her the answers she needed.

Earth, wood, and musk tickled her nose. That smell again. Every time she had this dream, she smelled it. It had no matching image or experience in her mind. It was unique and she couldn't identify it.

Drip!

The cave looked the same. Unrelenting gray stone all around her. The same twenty-foot outcropping to her left. The tumble of boulders on her right. Trying to tease out more meaning, she stepped closer to the boulders. She scoured them for any sign, any slight irregularity, any hint of what they were trying to tell her.

A second form shimmered into being beside her.

Taylor. They were walking this dream together.

"No," Taylor whispered. "I hate it here."

"Me too." Mags took her hand. "But there has to be some reason we keep having it."

Taylor glanced up at her. "Are we having it together?"

"Looks that way."

Drip! Drip!

Taylor stiffened. "The blood comes next."

Drip! Drip! Plonk!

Already, Mags could smell the coppery tang. It crept across the floor toward them.

Braziers flared to life along the cave walls, and they stilled.

"That's new," Mags murmured.

Taylor nodded and stared at the braziers. "Fire."

Wind tugged at their hair and blew it into their face. "Air," Mags said.

"Earth." Taylor pointed to the ground beneath them. The unbroken gray split, and a tiny green tendril shot out.

"And water," Mags finished as a small droplet caught the light from the braziers and sparkled.

The gray enfolded them again. The blood had reached their feet and looked obscenely red against their pale, bare skin.

Taylor lifted one foot and then the other, but it was a futile effort. The blood was inescapable. "No," she moaned.

Mags tightened her grip on Taylor's hand. "Stay with me, sweetie. Breathe. It's not real. It's just a dream."

"It feels real." Taylor whimpered.

A rumble shook the darkness as the earth-wood-musk scent strengthened. A new smell lurked behind it. Almost like sulfur.

Mags sniffed, and Taylor watched her.

"Do you smell that?"

Taylor wrinkled her nose. "It smells like matches being lit."

"Yes." That was it.

Blood pooled around her ankles, staining the bottom of Taylor's pajamas.

Mags tensed and waited for what came next—the skeins of silk that formed Alexander's face and then unraveled.

But the damp, sticky wind only grew stronger, and so did that combined smell of sulfur and the other musk-earth combination. It smelled a bit like leather.

The blood rose to their knees.

Taylor slid her arms around Mags and pressed into her. "Mags, what's happening?"

"I don't know." She put her arms around the girl. "But I do know that it's only a vision dream. It's not real. It's trying to tell us something."

Blood lapped at Taylor's thighs now, and Mags picked her up.

Taylor's blood-soaked legs fastened around her waist, and her arms manacled her neck. "I don't like this, Mags."

"Just a dream," Mags murmured, shuddering as revulsion twisted inside her. The blood was at her waist now.

Taylor clung as the blood rose higher.

"Just a dream," became a refrain Mags chanted again and again. Even as every instinct fought to escape the rising blood.

Blood covered her breasts, thick and sticky. Goddess, would it drown them?

Whimpering, Taylor pressed her face into Mags's neck.

Then came the stillness and the blood stopped rising.

Mags nearly wept with relief.

The strands of silk shot out around them, weaving and spinning in a dizzying display. Color leeched into the gray and the strands became red, yellow, green, and blue as they wove together with sickening speed. Mags couldn't follow their motions, but as suddenly as they'd began, they stopped.

Taylor gasped against her neck. "Is that…"

"Yes." Mags stepped closer to what the strands had created. The rockface reformed into a distinctive shape. "It's a dragon."

CHAPTER SIXTEEN

Simon stood beside Hannah at Alexander's bedside. Time blurred at Baile. He'd headed an A&E for years now, dealing with multiple patients, but this case was defying everything he knew. And that would be because he was dealing with magic and not pure science.

Man, he never imagined a day when that thought would enter his brain.

"The infection is spreading," Hannah said.

Dark tendrils radiating from the point of penetration had spiderwebbed across Alexander's torso, worse than yesterday, and the day before. "It's spreading faster as well."

Fuck it, but he hated losing patients, and he refused to lose this one.

Hannah took her glasses off and cleaned them on the hem of her scrubs. "What about a blood transfusion? We use them for some leukemias."

Simon was all out of ideas. All the drugs they'd pumped into Alexander were doing bugger all. "Do we have a donor?"

"I tested Roderick." Hannah replaced her glasses on her face. "He's a match."

"Theory for transfusion being to replace whatever the hell that is with normal blood cells."

Hannah nodded. "Right. Look, it's risky, but what do we have to lose at this stage?"

"Right." He was so out of his depth, yet he and Hannah were keeping Alexander alive, however tenuous the man's hold on life was. "Let's do a whole blood transfusion."

She glanced at him. "Might not be the most effective."

"Might also help us see what we're dealing with." He motioned the room around them. "We also don't have the equipment to start separating the components and it would take too much time."

"Good point." Hannah moved away from the bedside. "I'll get Roderick prepped."

***

JASPER LENNOX HAD BEEN a copper for nearly twenty-five years now. He'd worked his way up the ranks to DCI with hard work, persistence, and trust in his instincts. The same instincts that were blaring a warning at him now.

The Baile case stunk like three-day old shellfish left in the sun. The castle itself gave him the twitches. It was like he could feel eyes on him every time he went there. Funny thing, but he liked Jack Langham. The guy was lying to him, but it was more like a crime of withholding information. Jack knew something about that shooting, but Jasper had the sense he hadn't done the shooting.

Now that Conrad Lester was home safe and sound, and apparently none the worse for wear, Jasper should drop his enquiries. But that bloody gut instinct kept prodding him to keep digging.

And then there was the way Magdalene Cray had used his first name. He knew for bloody sure he hadn't used his name in front of her, yet she'd trotted it out like they were best friends. She could have googled him, but she didn't seem the type.

Those nutters hanging about near the castle worried him as well. Sure, there'd always been rumors about Baile and its residents, but that lot hadn't arrived until recently. He'd sent a couple of uniforms up there to move them along. They'd be back. Jasper knew it like he knew his shoe size.

The station house faced a commercial street. Rising above the squat shops was the graceful roof of a stately old home that records told him belonged to Lord Donne. He'd taken to driving past there on his way to and from his other cases. Lennox didn't much like what he was seeing at the manor. Thousands of people had descended on Greater Littleton in the last month, and a sizeable number of them had congregated at that estate. The village was used to the summer rush of tourists, but Jasper had never seen the like.

The newcomers had this air about them, a suppressed excitement like they were waiting for something. Jasper would bet his badge they were together in some way, but they came from all different social groups. There were the normal hemp shrouded pagans, the Wiccans, but they weren't rare in Greater Littleton. But newer types had joined them. Normal folk who should be going about their jobs and raising their 2.4 kids. Yet, there they milled, clustering mostly on the village green and the estate, and then breaking into other groups like a Sunday social.

And then there were the most recent additions, and those bastards worried Jasper the most. They were straight up fucking trouble looking for a place to happen. Their excitement had a violent edge to it that made his nape tingle. He had the uniforms doing weapons checks and generally making their presence felt, but it was like farting into a thunderstorm.

Crap was heading Greater Littleton's way, and he was missing too many puzzle pieces to be effective. Why had Donn abandoned the manor and moved into Baile without putting the place on the market? Were these newcomers connected to him in some way? That didn't sit right with Lennox, and he had no idea why. Fuck! He was stumbling around in the dark here.

"Guv?" Acharya stuck his head around his office door.

Eager little fucker got right up Jasper's nose—that instinct again. "What?"

"You wanted to be informed if anything further happened with Hermione Andover."

Yes, he most certainly did, and Lennox got out of his chair faster than his middle-aged spread should have allowed. "What is it?"

"She claims another break-in." Acharya looked skeptical. "And she's refusing to go back to her house."

LIKE THEY'D BEEN WORKING TOGETHER for years Noah, Emma, Mandla, and Warren ran through the underground tunnels to the hidden entrance behind the village green.

Mags and Taylor had both seen the same thing. Hermione and Gemma had been attacked in their home. Hermione had managed to get them both out, and they were waiting on the village green, but the coimhdeacht needed to get there now.

Warren didn't pause to check but ran straight into the underground crypts and took the stairs to the green. There may be questions later as to where they'd all suddenly come from, but the danger was too pressing to wait.

Rhiannon's followers had upped their game, and anyone associated with Baile was now a target.

Bursting onto the green, Warren assessed the situation. The bloody place was crowded with people. A woman caught sight of them and pointed. "There they are."

Heads swung their way. A group of tough-looking bruisers moved toward them.

Noah scented the air and pointed. "There."

"How did you pick up their scent?" Emma asked, but she was already moving with Noah.

"They smell like Bronwyn," he said, his jaw set in a hard line.

Warren searched the crowd for a glimpse of Hermione or Gemma, but moving bodies kept obscuring his view.

"Come on then." Mandla squared up to one of the toughs dressed in leather like an escapee from *The Matrix*.

The idiot kept coming. Too puffed up on conceit to even check his forward momentum.

Out of the corner of his eye, Warren was aware of Noah and Emma shoving through the crowd. Warren ducked a punch and returned the favor to the soft gut closest to him.

Mandla had his guy in a headlock. "Tell your friends to back up or I'll rip your head off."

Warren believed him. Mandla wasn't the chattiest bloke, which made him bothering to warn a person something that person should listen to.

Matrix hadn't received the memo and mouthed off, "I'll fucking kill you."

"Not today." Mandla twisted and the fucker dropped like a stone. Fortunately, with his head still attached.

Warren was too busy to check for a pulse.

People on the green either surged toward the fight or ran from it screaming. The coppers wouldn't be far off.

Matrix's mate snuck up on Mandla's left and connected the big guy's jaw.

With a crack of flesh on bone, Mandla's head snapped back. When he faced his assailant, Warren swore his eyes glinted red with fury.

His distraction very nearly cost Warren as two more idiots flanked him fists swinging. He caught the nearest thug's arm and wrenched it behind his back. Then he shoved him at his mate. He wished Jack could have been there, but Jack had enough eyes on him right now.

Emma and Noah were running back their way. Noah had Gemma in his arms, while Emma shielded Hermione with her body. Some dickhead got too close, and Emma downed him with a swift kick to the solar plexus. Emma had moves. She took the knees out of another attacker.

Sirens wailed from down the street and Noah and Emma increased their pace.

"Go." Emma reached him and gave Hermione a push toward the crypt entrance. "Straight down the stairs and keep moving until you find a tunnel. We'll catch up."

Noah lowered Gemma. "Run for me, sweetheart. Follow your mom."

More fuckers surged, trying to get past them to Hermione and Gemma.

The wards closed around Hermione and Gemma, and they disappeared.

"What the hell?" Their pursuers lost momentum.

Warren used the distraction to take another unfriendly down.

Emma stepped into the path of a guy at least a foot taller than her. A punt to the bottom of his nose had him staggering back with blood spurting down his face.

"Mandla," he yelled. "We've got them. Let's go."

With a disappointed glance at his group of potential victims, Mandla stepped back, but not before he'd delivered another punch.

Warren disengaged. Drawing a weapon on a crowded green was not an option.

The group closed on him, but slower this time.

"Back off." Warren didn't take his eyes off the thugs.

Mandla joined him, drawling, "Or don't."

The pace of their assailants slowed.

Emma disappeared past the wards after Gemma and Hermione.

Noah joined him and Mandla. "What do we have here?"

"Bunch of tough guys," Mandla said.

"I like tough guys." Noah showed his teeth. "I like to show them how tough they really are."

Dear Goddess, these two were enjoying this clusterfuck.

One of the circle got brave and stepped closer.

Mandla growled and closed on him.

The guy backed into his mates, almost tripping two of them up.

"Mandla, Noah." Time to close it down. Warren motioned the two of them. "Back to Baile."

Mandla hesitated then dashed for safety with Noah on his heels.

Making sure they hadn't left anyone behind, Warren backed up one step at a time. Slowly did it. If they showed fear, this lot would attack for sure.

Warren crossed the wards.

The group on the green were almost comical in their blinks of confusion.

"Where'd they go?" One of them turned and glared at the group as if they could provide the answer. "They were right fucking there."

Had to love those wards. Warren chuckled as he turned and sprinted for the crypt entrance.

***

BY THE TIME they made it back through the caverns and into the castle, Alannah had tea ready for them.

"Come and sit." She clucked around Gemma, leading her to a couch near the fire. "What a horrible thing to happen to you."

"That cave." Gemma's eyes widened. "Coolest thing I've ever seen."

"I've never seen that before." Hermione looked somewhat accusatory as she faced Alannah. "When I did the tours."

Alannah smiled back. "Well, we didn't know how much we could trust you then."

"True." Hermione slumped into a chair. "Sorry, I'm feeling rattled by what happened."

"What did happen?" Warren propped his shoulder against the mantel. "Taylor and Mags said you had another home invasion."

Hermione shuddered and accepted a cup of tea from Alannah. "They came through the back door when I was making breakfast."

"Awful." Alannah handed tea to Gemma and offered her some sort of cake. Having Alannah back on the baking was great, and Warren snagged a piece before Mandla got in there. Big son of a bitch had hollow legs.

Emma took the seat beside Gemma. "What did you do?"

"Mum threw the kettle at them," Gemma said. "And it was boiling too."

Warren was impressed with Hermione's quick thinking.

"Then we locked them in the kitchen and ran out the front." Gemma didn't seem to be too traumatized by the incident.

Hermione's cup rattled in her saucer. "They said something to me."

Warren tensed as they all waited.

"They said Rhiannon would be very glad to see me."

"Oh dear." Alannah slumped in the chair closest to him. "We thought that might be the case."

"Who's Rhiannon?" Gemma looked from one to the other of them. "And why would she be glad to see us?"

All eyes swung to him.

"Right." Warren eased himself away from the mantel.

Normally, these explanations were taken by Roderick or Alexander. Goddess, but he couldn't think of Alexander not making it. He was as much a part of Baile and the coven as the caverns. And Warren missed his irreverent sense of humor, he even missed his poncey ways and pampered accent. Roderick would be glowering and hedging, but Warren rather thought the time for that had flown past. Hermione deserved to know the reason her life was at risk. "You know a lot about Baile, and the women here, but let me fill in some blanks for you."

CHAPTER SEVENTEEN

Bronwyn couldn't decide what and who to watch after Alexander's blood transfusion.

Hannah and Simon were glued to the various machines and monitors beside his bed. Roderick kept his eyes on the black lines on Alexander's chest.

If she could have willed the transfusion to work, she would have.

After what seemed like centuries, Simon's serious face relaxed into a small smile. "Vitals are stable."

All the room's occupants expelled their pent-up breath.

"The lines are getting lighter." Roderick bent over and peered at Alexander's chest.

They all leaned in to verify Roderick's conclusion.

Hope flared in Bronwyn. The lines were receding, and the steady *beep* of the heart monitor meant an improvement.

"That's good right?" She glanced at Hannah and then Simon.

Hannah gave a small nod. "It's an improvement." She held up a cautioning hand. "But it's still early, and we're still not sure what we're dealing with."

Rhiannon, she wanted to yell. They were dealing with that

awful bitch. She'd made Alexander's life miserable from the day he'd been born, culminating in that final awful act of Fiona's. Mags said Fiona had seemed changed, or she would never have brought her to Baile. Baile herself must have sensed something, because she'd allowed Fiona inside. And yet…

She couldn't dwell on that hideous day.

Bronwyn couldn't understand how Rhiannon could have done such awful things to her child. She touched the swell of her belly. How did a mother inflict willful cruelty on their child? She knew it happened, but carrying her own children made the depth of the ugliness even more clear to her. If there had ever been any part of humanity left in Rhiannon, it was now long gone. It made her even more determined that Rhiannon would never get her hands on her and Alexander's twins.

"Was Alexander her target, or was it Goddess?" Roderick studied Alexander as he asked.

Bronwyn hadn't given it much thought. "Does it matter?"

"Not really." Roderick shrugged. "But she cannot have either of them."

"No." Bronwyn took Alexander's limp hand and held it to her cheek. "She can't have any of them."

***

TAYLOR HATED the way adults always thought you could chuck a bunch of teens of the same approximate age together and they'd automatically be friends. Like the fact that you were the same age, and in this case gender, would automatically make you besties for life.

Still, it was nice to have people around her age at Baile. Hanging out with middle-aged people all the time got boring. Not that life at Baile had been exactly boring. She sometimes wondered what her school friends would make of her now, and her new abilities. She'd love to see Becca Carlson's face if she found out Taylor could, honest to God, tell the future. Mags had told her she could read tarot as well. It was up to her which way she tapped into her blessing. Roderick said they shouldn't make money off their blessings, but Becca Carlson had been such a bitch to Taylor that she'd charge her like a thousand quid for a reading. Or maybe she should do one of those live TikToks and tell people's futures for them. If Becca joined her live feed, no way Taylor was picking her for a reading.

Gemma and Dhara followed her across the bailey. Dad had appointed her to show Gemma around, and she was starting with the coolest part—the caverns.

"Are we allowed down here?" Gemma eyed the sheer descent of the stairs to the caverns and swallowed.

Taylor didn't like to think of it in terms of what was allowed and what wasn't. When she'd first found the caverns, she'd known her mother would have a fit if she saw her, and she'd gone anyway. Goddess had wanted her in the caverns, and she'd gone and discovered she was a witch. "It's where the magic is." Or maybe not. She shot Dhara an apologetic look. "At least, that's where it was."

"It still is," Dhara said.

At least Dhara was Dhara today, and her eyes hadn't gone silver and her voice singsongy.

"Magic?" Gemma breathed and looked wide-eyed at them. "Like real magic?"

Hadn't Gemma been listening when Warren had told them all about Baile and the coven? "Well, not like Harry Potter or anything." They needed to clear that up from the start. "There would be no wand waving and sorting hats. "It's elemental magic, which means the magic comes from the four elements."

Gemma flushed. "Cool."

"The elements are like the engine," Dhara said and started down the stairs. "And the blessing is like the car."

Sort of, but Taylor kept that to herself for now. Her *car* often felt more like a runaway train. Still, if she needed to bitch to someone about that, it would be Goddess and not Dhara. Although they were the same person, but not. It got confusing.

"Were you scared?" Dhara asked over her shoulder. "When those people broke into your house."

Gemma took the stairs slowly, one at time, her hand on the cliff at her side. "A little."

Taylor would have been a lot scared if someone had tried to break into her home.

"I was scared," Dhara said. "When we had to leave our commune."

That's right. Taylor sometimes forgot that had happened to Dhara and Kate.

"Why did you have to leave?" Gemma's slow pace made Taylor want to go past her, but she hadn't been so sure of these stairs the first time she'd taken them either.

"Attackers were coming," Dhara said. "And we needed to get me and her"—she jabbed her chest—"safely to Baile."

They reached the ledge in front of the caverns.

Gemma peered into the opening. "It's very dark in there."

"You'll see." Taylor darted ahead of the other two. This was her favorite part of entering the caverns. It made her happy every time she saw it.

As she crossed the threshold, crystals blinked on from the ceilings and walls, and the soft chime of welcome sounded. With all the cardinal points active now, the ceilings gleamed with red, blue, yellow, and green light. It was like stepping into your own mirror ball.

"Wow." Light played across Gemma's face as she dropped her head back and stared all around her. "It's amazing. I never got the chance to look properly when they brought us here."

"Right." It really was amazing, and Taylor took a moment to let it sink in. It gave her this feeling of being part of something much bigger than her, something important to the world. She'd never thought she would be a girl whose future mattered to the fate of the world. She'd never thought of herself as a Katniss or a Hermione. "There are a bunch of caves." She pointed to the sigils. "Those tell the story of each witch's magic. Maeve puts them on the caverns walls when a witch dies. At least she used to." Nobody really knew what the sacred grove being gone meant. "But I like to think the old witches are watching me." She felt a bit stupid having confessed that and shrugged. "Or some such crap."

Dhara squeezed her hand. "We walk amongst them."

That last bit sounded a lot like Goddess, so Taylor checked her eyes. Still Dhara in there, but with the teeniest gleam of silver around her irises. The sharing thing got weird sometimes.

"There must have been…like…a bunch of witches who lived here," Gemma said. She put her hand out to touch and then snatched it back.

Taylor laid her hand against a sigil. "You can touch. It tingles."

Eyes shining, Gemma placed her palm on the wall. She snatched it back and giggled. "It does tingle."

Taylor led the way into the next cave. This one had even more sigils than the one before.

"What happens when you run out of cave?" Gemma gestured around them. "When you have more witches and thingies than cave walls."

That wouldn't be a problem anymore, but Taylor didn't want to add to what Dad had already told Gemma. People freaked out when you gave them the full story, and she might even like Gemma a bit. Mom said she'd had cancer, and Bronwyn had healed her. "Was it true you had cancer?" The question just popped out, and Taylor wished it hadn't. Gemma probably didn't want to talk about the cancer and nearly dying and stuff.

But Gemma smiled and nodded. "I was dying, and then

Bronwyn came." She clicked her fingers. "And just like that, bye-bye cancer."

Dhara took a deep breath and stared at Gemma. "We used to have healers at the commune, but none of them could do what Bronwyn does."

Except, Bronwyn wouldn't do anything now, not with Alexander being so sick.

Taylor didn't like to think of that day too much—the stabbing and then Fiona's head being chopped off. Mom had insisted they talk about it, like that was going to help. She kept telling Taylor she needed to process what had happened to her. Mom would totally lose her mind if she knew what Taylor saw in her visions. It was kinder not to tell her, and now that Mags was back, Taylor preferred to speak to her. Mags got it. The visions were disturbing, terrifying even, but they were also like an early warning system. Now that Mags was back, she'd also taken over teaching Taylor how to use her blessing better. "I'm a seer," she said.

"Like seeing the future?" Gemma blinked at her.

"Yup." Taylor liked how being a seer made her different, but she also knew that she would never be quite comfortable hanging out with regular kids anymore. When she'd stepped into Goddess pool when she'd first come here, that had put a barrier between her and regular people. So as much as she dreamed of making Becca Carlson jealous, that would never happen.

Gemma wandered into the next cave. "Isn't that scary sometimes, seeing the future?"

"It can be." Taylor missed being able to go to sleep and not worry what her blessing was going to cough up. Not enough to regret her blessing, but her dreams were not simply dreams anymore. "But no scarier than cancer, or a home invasion."

"Twice," Dhara added.

"Hmm." Gemma trailed her fingertips over the sigils, and

then giggled as they flared beneath her touch. "You know what I hate about cancer?"

Taylor was pretty sure the dying thing would be way up there.

"It's how people treat you," Gemma said.

They entered the final cavern. Goddess pool still glowed, but you didn't get the feeling that you wanted to bow anymore. Mainly because Goddess was about three feet away and watching Gemma.

Dhara tilted her head. "How do they treat you?"

"Like you're going to break," Gemma said. "You can't believe how many different ways they ask you how you are without mentioning cancer or death."

Taylor felt better about blurting her cancer question straight out now.

"I thought my friends would be the same when I got back." Gemma shrugged. "But they treat me differently. Like they are scared of catching cancer from me."

"I can only imagine how my old friends would treat me if they found out I was a witch," Taylor said.

Dhara pointed at her chest. "Or that I had Goddess inside me."

They all laughed and went closer to Goddess pool.

Dhara stripped off her shoes and socks and sat beside the pool. She dipped her feet into the water. "It's always warm."

Goddess pool lit up like a snapped glow stick.

"Whoa." Gemma took a step back.

"It's Goddess inside her," Taylor said and took a load off next to Dhara. "The pool reacts to her."

Gemma perched beside them and stared at the pool as if deciding if she was going to put her feet in too.

The cave was quiet, with only the distant sound of the tide and the gentle lap of the water.

"So, I guess you guys don't leave here much." Gemma wrapped her shoelaces around her finger.

"No," Dhara said. "If Rhiannon or her people catch sight of me." She drew a thumb across her throat. "So as much as I would like some freedom, that tends to keep me here."

"Right." Gemma studied Dhara as if trying to see Goddess inside her. "So, what do you guys do?"

Dhara pulled a face. "Me, not much, but Taylor is always seeing things and getting visions. Mags is teaching her how to use her blessing."

"Mags?" Gemma wrinkled her nose. "She's the tall, skinny one?"

"Yeah." Taylor didn't like that description of Mags. "She's gorgeous. She looks like a supermodel."

"They're all beautiful." Gemma laughed. "Especially Alannah and Sinead, and there are two of them."

"Right." Dhara rolled her eyes. "Double trouble. You should see people's faces when they see them. They get this kind of struck dumb expression."

"You're pretty too." Gemma flushed and stared down at her feet. "And Taylor."

"You too," Taylor said, because she didn't want Gemma feeling bad about herself. Not after what she'd been through. "I've been posting TikToks for Niamh."

Gemma's face brightened. "I follow her." She laughed. "Well, you, I suppose, if you're making them."

Taylor rolled her eyes. "Niamh is clueless."

"Is she really that good with animals?" Gemma scooted closer to her. "It's like they understand her."

"They do." Dhara shrugged. "She's a guardian, which means she's the voice for animals."

Gemma nodded and thought about that. "And Mags is a seer like Taylor. Sinead and Alannah are wardens, which means they take care of the earth. Bronwyn is a healer—thank God for that." She frowned. "But what does Nofoto do, and your mother?"

"My mother is mundane," Taylor said, although describing her mother that way seemed disloyal, so she added, "Which only means she doesn't do magic. Nofoto is a weather witch, but I've never seen her do the weather or anything."

Gemma eased one shoe off and then the other. She played with the top of her sock. "There's something I didn't tell my mother." She tried to play it off, but Taylor could see it was something big. "She worries, you know. Since the cancer."

Dhara glanced at Taylor and they both waited.

"The kids at school." Gemma took a deep breath. "A couple of them were bullying me."

Dhara looked angry. "Bullying?"

"You know." Gemma shrugged and rolled one sock down. "Calling me names. Shoving me. Stealing my stuff."

Taylor needed to tell her dad about that. Nothing around here was ever bloody simple. "I'm sorry," she said. "Has that been happening a lot?"

"It was getting worse." Gemma tucked her sock in its corresponding shoe and then peeled her other sock off. "It got much worse after the first home invasion."

Okay, her dad would definitely want to hear what Gemma had told them. Only, she would tell him not to tell Gemma's mother. Hermione was nice, and dealing with a kid who had cancer would suck.

Dhara put her arm around Gemma's shoulders. "Then you're in the right place," she said.

"I was bullied too." Taylor wanted Gemma not to feel alone about the bullying. "A group of girls at my old school hated me. There was this one called Becca Carlson, and she was the worst."

Gemma sighed. "There's always that one, isn't there?"

"Right?!" Taylor didn't get how some kids could be so mean. "She used to call me weirdo."

Gemma shook her head. "What a bitch."

"Baile doesn't tolerate bitches," Dhara said. "And she'll look after you." Then she giggled. "And we can all be weirdos together."

CHAPTER EIGHTEEN

A chill wind whipped around the corner of the manor house and tugged at Rhiannon's cloak. The pastures stretching beyond the manor had been mowed short, with patches of freezing mud clinging to the ruts and dips. The wind carried a hint of winter, and Rhiannon breathed it in. Before winter came Samhain, and she had been waiting.

Some idiot had hung cheap Halloween decorations around the elegant patio doors, and they stuck out like a canker on the face of the beautiful old house. Alexander's house, and now hers.

A glass broke in the kitchen, followed by a raucous burst of laughter.

Pigs! All of them.

She had been away for weeks now. First, keeping Mags away from Baile, and then cementing alliances she had made around the world. Cashing in favors people had been more than happy to promise with no thought for when she would collect. They were about to receive a rude awakening.

"Mistress." The minion she'd found in South Africa appeared beside her. The woman moved silent as a wraith, but she was proving useful. She was obedient and never questioned, and since all four cardinal points had been activated, had revealed herself to have a not insignificant amount of power. Nothing like Edana or Fiona, but those two had been collateral damage. She also did not hesitate to meet Rhiannon's demands for blood, even hers. "The Canadian witches are on their way here."

The lawn before the pastures was littered with furniture and broken housewares. People of this time had no appreciation for beauty. They consumed like voracious parasites, quick to replace, and quicker to discard.

She took a final breath of the crisp air. So much would change when she ended Goddess. Nothing would stand against her as she remade the world to suit her. "Clean this up." She motioned to the mess on the lawn. "And then clean up the house."

The minion bowed her cowled head. "Yes, mistress. Shall I rid the manor of the rabble?"

"Yes." They had been squatting in her son's house, defiling it with their mundane presence and disgusting habits. "Keep the ones with power but make them put everything to rights first."

"Mistress." The minion bowed.

Rhiannon didn't want useless humans here. They poisoned her triumph, made it tawdry. Her moment had been hundreds of years in the making. Plans within plans, pieces moved into place like on a massive chessboard, and this Samhain, it would all come to glorious fruition.

Fiona had proved useful one last time.

Rhiannon hadn't cared whether she struck at Roderick, Alexander, or Goddess—although a swift end to Goddess would have been fortuitous. She had known better than to chance the athame finding Goddess's heart. Roderick and Alexander would never have allowed that to happen, however, and they had paid the price for their loyalty.

Her son was dying. Reflexively, she rubbed her chest, and

grew annoyed at herself. He had been a tool, and a useful one, and she had wielded him. Alexander had served his purpose. He had spawned the children she had created him to produce and was nothing more than an impediment now. Still, she couldn't prevent the flashes of him as a boy that insisted on invading her mind and causing an ache to her chest.

He had been an endearing little boy, lively and full of questions. She had mostly left him to minions to raise when he'd been very young, but she'd taken a more active hand once his power had started to manifest. His intelligence had made him the best of all those who served her. That same intelligence had, however, enabled him to hide his change of heart.

The original attack on Baile had been the turning point.

Rhiannon walked into the kitchen, and silence descended. Minions tried to make themselves one with the cabinets. A woman stood at the sink, washing an immense collection of filthy, food encrusted dishes and pots. A man wiped the stains marring the prettily painted cream and sage cabinets. Another man worked at the range, his body shaking with the intensity with which he cleaned.

"As it was," she said. "You put it back like it was, or I will choose someone to pay the price for the damage."

She loved that she didn't have to raise her voice.

The hallway outside the kitchen had fallen still as a grave. Objects had been dragged over the gleaming wooden floors, carving unsightly trenches. A beautiful oriental rug sported burn marks and ground-in stains.

Alexander had loved this house, fussed over it like a proud mother.

The salon was denuded of most of its furniture, and she let her feet carry her to the hearth. Above the mantel was an oil painting she had commissioned of her and Alexander. He'd always hated the painting, but like the dutiful son she'd thought him to be, he'd hung it there for her.

Her beautiful son. Hair as dark as a raven's wing, eyes the color of onyx, with the hint of laughter around the corners of his full mouth. She and Roderick had created a magnificent child. They were both dressed in Regency garb, and the fine tailoring hugged his broad shoulders, the breeches clinging to the lines of his muscular thighs. He had been her finest creation.

And then he had turned.

She should have seen him turning, noticed the small signs that he had grown a conscience. With the benefit of hindsight, it was all disturbingly clear. She hadn't factored Alexander's betrayal into her plans, and she should have. Roderick had always been insufferably upright and good. But Rhiannon had trained Alexander and assumed that would be the deciding factor in her favor.

She ran her fingers over the gilded frame of the portrait. Dust smeared her fingers, and her rage spilled over. "Clean it."

"Mistress?" A woman appeared in the doorway, wringing her hands.

"There is dust on my son." She was surprised to see her hand shook as she pointed. "Get it off."

The woman scurried forward. "Yes, mistress."

Roderick. The thorn in her side all these years.

She still remembered the day he'd arrived in Greater Littleton clearly. It had been close to a millennium ago, but none of the details had faded. Of course, there had been no village here then, just the cavern and the sea, and the land that kissed the shore.

Strong, proud, and arrogant, Roderick had ridden to the land ceded him by the king.

He had stopped his horse on the promontory where he would build Baile Castle and looked about him—a conqueror there to claim his due.

Rhiannon had been for ridding themselves of him. She had hated the feelings the man stirred in her, despised how it showed her female weakness. He had made her want things she had believed long dead in her, woken desires and needs that she had overcome.

Brenna had argued that he was important, that he marked a new epoch in their history, and he must stay.

Roderick had barely even glanced at her, Rhiannon, the most beautiful of the witches. No, that day he had eyes only for Tahra. In the weeks that followed, he would fall further and further under Tahra's spell, and become the first coimhdeacht.

Perhaps Rhiannon's hatred of him had been born then. But she had been clever and hidden her resentment, worked with the other three and Roderick to see Baile rise around them. She had known her jealousy made her weak, vulnerable and she had worked to eradicate it.

It was strange, but on the cusp of her eventual victory, her thoughts had turned melancholy and reflective.

In the end, she had won him from Tahra and borne him a son. She'd stolen his seed to impregnate herself and circumvented Goddess's way of controlling her witch's offspring. Smug in her victory, she had hugged that knowledge to herself, never told Roderick.

But their son had returned to Roderick. Like with Tahra, Alexander had chosen another over her. For that alone, and not just his betrayal, Alexander would pay the ultimate price.

She sighed. Outside the salon window, men were carrying furniture back into the manor. A small group of women picked up the rubbish.

She would miss Alexander. Perhaps even miss Roderick. They had traveled a long path together, the three of them. Seen witches come and go, watched ages slide by, seen humanity repeat the same mistakes over and over again, and they had been constant. Their battle had been constant. Rhiannon had known it would come to this moment. For balance, Goddess would have to incarnate. And in those first years, she would be as vulnerable as the human child she had chosen as a vessel.

Nostalgia drove Rhiannon to call for a car.

"Roderick?" Noah stood in the entrance of the healer's hall, a towel wrapped around his waist.

Roderick applauded his modesty. As much as he didn't object to nakedness, it also didn't belong in this holy place where his son waged the war for his life. "What?"

"Rhiannon is here." Noah grimaced. "I've never seen her, but that bitch stinks of blood magic. It's like it's sunk into every part of her."

Shock held him immobile. Noah had to be mistaken. "Baile would never allow her across the wards."

"She's not across the wards." Noah moved deeper into the room, prowling like the animal he shared a being with. "She's standing on the edge of the wards." He shrugged one shoulder, clasping his towel with his other hand. "I run with Pack along the wards. We're keeping an eye on those whackjobs on the road."

Could Noah be correct? "Tall, shapely, long black hair?"

"She's stunning," Noah said. "If you like your women homicidal and fucking evil." He motioned the bailey. "Pack wouldn't go near her."

Aware he was sitting there like someone had felled him, Roderick blinked at him. "What does she want?"

"To see you." Noah rolled his eyes. "She's standing at the edge of the wards yelling for you. I took that as a sign she wanted to see you."

"Tell her…" And Roderick didn't know what to tell Rhiannon. She wouldn't be here out of concern for Alexander. He'd known that bitch for a long time though, and she might be here to gloat or to threaten. And suddenly he wanted to hear what she had to say. "Can you find someone to sit with him?" He wouldn't let Alexander battle alone.

Noah's expression softened. "Sure. I'll sit with him until Bronwyn gets back."

"My thanks."

Roderick's mind whirled as he walked into the bailey and made for the gatehouse. She couldn't touch him while he stayed within the wards, but perhaps he could end this once and for all. He almost went back for a sword, but the temptation of ending her life with his bare hands had him moving forward.

Dressed in a long black gown that belonged to a previous century, Rhiannon stood on the far side of the wards. Gently tossed about by the wind, her long hair gleamed in the fitful sun. Thank Goddess he had never taken her bait, not even at his most promiscuous. He'd cut his cock and balls off before he buried them in that poisonous cunt.

"Roderick." She smiled when she caught sight of him. "I'm not here to fight."

She might not be, but he was.

"Uh-uh." She waggled a finger at him. "You did not think I would come here unprotected, did you?"

He saw it then, the glowing black nimbus enshrouding her. He'd never seen its like. "What the fuck is that?"

"A little spell I've been perfecting. You touch it, and the magic will eat you alive." She cocked her head. "I see you doubt me."

Roderick was a hairsbreadth from sprinting across the wards and testing her words.

She snapped her fingers.

One of the unwashed idiots cowered forward. "Mistress."

Rhiannon grabbed his hair.

Black oozed over his skin. As his skin melted from his flesh, he screamed, and his eyes burst and leaked down his face.

Roderick wanted to vomit as the man liquefied in a reeking puddle at Rhiannon's feet.

"As you see." She lifted her skirts out of what remained of her demonstration.

For Maeve, he couldn't risk attacking her. And for Alexander and those precious to him, whom he had entrusted into Roderick's care. Still, temptation thrummed in his blood. There were other ways to kill her that might not mean touching her. A well thrown rock, the stripped bones of her demonstration wielded like a club. Nay, Baile needed him to act from reason. "What do you want?"

"I'm feeling sentimental today." She giggled and shrugged. "I do not blame you for your skepticism, but there it is."

Roderick didn't bother to reply.

"You cannot win, Roderick." She made a regretful expression that he knew better than to believe. Triumph glittered in her black eyes. "I have made my plans too carefully. Everything is in readiness, and I need only Samhain and the power it brings."

Gloating it was then, and a bit of threatening. She was nothing if not predictable.

"I came to offer you the chance to join me," she said. "Alexander will die unless you give him to me. I can save him, you know."

She surprised a laugh out of Roderick. "You know, more than anyone else, that I would never accept that offer."

"Not even for our son?" She pursed her full, red mouth. "Baile will fall, but we built it together before, Roderick. We can rebuild." Rhiannon let her gaze travel his length. "I have never had a coimhdeacht, but perhaps in the new world I will build, it would be good to have one by my side."

Roderick folded his arms. He had already given his answer. Nothing would change, and she knew that. "Why don't we get to why you're really here?"

Anger tightened her features, making her look like a dark

angel. "You are correct, of course. Even if you did change sides, I would never have you. I would not deign to touch Tahra's leavings."

And there it was. Roderick almost smiled. "Is that what this is about?"

Hands balled into fists, she struggled to master her temper. Taking a breath, she recovered her composure and met his gaze. "Why Tahra?"

"She had worth," he said, delighted to see the hit score. "Her beauty ran through to her marrow. You were only ever this." He gestured her from head to toe. "Treacherous and weak."

"Was it a weak witch who nearly brought this castle and its coven to their knees?" She spat. "Is it weakness now that you tremble before?"

"I've never trembled before you, Rhiannon." He let his derision color his face as he shrugged. "I've never felt much of anything for you." Taking his opportunity to wound her, even if it was small and petty, he gave a smug smile. "But it wasn't the same for you, was it?"

Her black eyes blazed at him. "I hate you."

"But you didn't always." He toed the edge of the wards and lowered his voice, making it soft and intimate. "You wanted me. Maybe you're here now because you still do. All your planning and all your vengeance boils down to one silly, jealous woman."

For a moment, he thought her fury would drive her to forget the wards and attempt to strike him. Instead, she paused before raising her chin. "Soon now, you will regret those words, and everything else that lies between us."

"Maybe." He chuckled. "But I will never regret that I couldn't bring myself near you, much less to touch you."

Roderick's coimhdeacht markings prickled as Goddess cleared the gatehouse. He moved to protect her.

Rhiannon's eyes widened. "You," she spat.

"Rhiannon." A look of profound sadness darkened Goddess's

eyes. She looked at Rhiannon with such love, it made Roderick's heart ache. "My lost child."

"I was never yours." Rhiannon's entire body quivered with the venom of her response.

"Ah, but you were." Goddess smiled, her pain palpable. "You were so filled with passion and purpose. You were a warrior witch, and my delight."

Rhiannon swallowed. "I will end you."

"You will do as you must." Goddess touched his arm to keep him from speaking. She smiled at Rhiannon like a fond mother. "You will play the part that was chosen for you long before you walked this earth. And I will play mine."

Rhiannon raised her chin. "I chose my own path."

"Did you?" Goddess stared at her, tenderness softening her expression. "And even in your brokenness, I have loved you. At your most heinous, I have loved you. And even now as you stand before me, sure in your victory and certain in your defiance, I love you."

"I don't want your love." Rhiannon's voice shook.

"But you have it." Goddess tugged Roderick's arm and turned them away. "And what has been set in motion will come to pass."

CHAPTER NINETEEN

Kate stood in what remained of the place she'd grown up, lived her entire life, and her brain shut down. The beautiful log home she'd been born in, and later shared with Dhara, lay in a crumpled, ashy ruin. Only the stone chimney stood like an obscene blackened finger against the waning day.

It was all gone. Everything. Everyone.

She'd been on the move for the greater part of three days. That dash from Greater Littleton to a helipad, from the helicopter onto a flight to Toronto, then the train from Toronto to Ottawa and finally a car journey. Sasha's people had surrounded her in a protective bubble through every mile, keeping her safe, and taking the travel logistics out of her hands.

With heavy feet, she stepped over the charred remnants of the porch stairs and into what had been her kitchen. Melted, twisted metal was all that remained of her appliances. All she had left of the hundreds, if not thousands, of meals she had created in that kitchen. The table where she had counseled people, comforted them, argued, and socialized had disintegrated into the blanket of ash coating her boots.

Deep inside, her tears dripped corrosive as acid into her heart. Kate was glad Dhara wasn't here to see this.

"Kate?" A woman who had been part of the protection detail that had picked her up in Ottawa touched her arm. "We can't stay here. We are still getting reports of a hostile element in the area."

Hopelessness swelled inside her, and Kate wanted to be five again, wanted her mother to take her hand, her father to tell her it was going to be okay. Someone—anyone—to make decisions for her. She turned to the woman. Kate had a vague memory of her introducing herself as Margo. "Where do I go now?"

Margo's gaze filled with compassion. "No friends or family?"

"They're all gone." Kate heard the quaver in her voice, felt the sobs tighten her vocal cords. "Everyone I knew. They're all gone."

"I'm sorry, Kate." Margo scraped a boot through the rubble. "It doesn't change anything, but I'm sorry."

Kate went down what used to be the hallway to her bedroom. Before it was hers, her parents had used this bedroom. Dhara had been born in the big bed her father had carved from a fallen maple. "It makes it so real," she whispered to nobody in particular.

Margo had followed her and nodded. "Yeah, it does."

"I mean, I grew up on horror stories about what would happen if Rhiannon found us." She bent and tugged a colored scrap of fabric from beneath a broken and burned timber. The soiled pink scrap had somehow survived the blaze. Kate tried to place it in the room. Maybe a small section of her drapes, or one of the squares she and her mother had meticulously sewn into a quilt. "Even when we were evacuating, it didn't seem totally real."

"It never does." Margo took the scrap from her and examined it. "I've been in our organization since I was sixteen. I've been trained, even had encounters with her people, but this past year." Margo sighed and shook her head. "Everything has escalated. We only get done in one place, and we're off somewhere new." She gave a humorless chuckle. "Fighting a war the rest of the world knows nothing about, but they will if we don't fight it."

"I think that's from a quilt my mother and I made." Kate touched the fabric with her forefinger. "It was the last one we made together before she died." She couldn't bring herself to take the scrap back. It felt like doing that would acknowledge the loss of what it had been. "Our entire purpose here was to hide the earth point from her. To keep it safe until the cré-witches could activate it. My ancestor was one of the original witches who founded this coven for that sole purpose."

"And you did protect the earth point, Kate." Margo put a hand on her shoulder. Her angular, long face looked mournful. "You kept it hidden, the witches activated it, and you got Goddess to safety."

But for how long? Kate kept the thought to herself. She didn't know how much Margo knew of the escalating pressure at Baile. If Rhiannon succeeded, Baile would be reduced to nothing more than this. All those hundreds of years of history, all those memories, and lives that had sheltered beneath the solid rock of Baile would be left smoldering and wasted, ready for the wind and rain to wash them away. For the snow and ice to cover them and bury them.

Margo's radio crackled. "We have reports of wolf activity near you, Margo. Copy?"

"Copy that," Margo spoke into her shoulder unit. "Kate? We need to go."

"Wolves?" And Kate felt him. Deep within, in the place she had spent so long not acknowledging, she sensed Zach drawing closer. "No." She shook her head. "They're my wolves. I mean, they're with us."

Her wolves. Her wolf. Her mate.

And she needed him like the next beat of her heart.

Kate spun and trudged in the direction her heart tugged. She increased her pace, almost tripping over the strewn ground to get to Zach.

Shadows shifted and coalesced at the forest edge, and wolves slunk closer.

Margo crowded close to Kate. "Are you sure they're friendly?" Her finger played with the trigger of her weapon as she eyed the approaching pack.

And then Kate saw him.

Zach stepped out of the forest in his human form, wolves slinking around him. He looked primal and powerful, and blessedly familiar.

"Katy?" His raspy voice carried through the silent settlement toward her.

The sobs broke free, and Kate stopped in the middle of what had been a central path. Her legs locked, her spine seized, and the pain ripped free in a maelstrom.

"Katy." Zach ran and closed the distance between them. He snatched her against his chest, and his arms came around her like solid bands. "My Katy," he whispered against her hair.

He lifted her off the ground and Kate clung to him with arms and legs.

A plaintive howl echoed through the silence, and then another, and another, until the mourning wolves forced the rising moon to hear their lament.

And Kate wept.

Zach held her, absorbing her pain as he whispered words of comfort and reassurance against her ear.

"We need to go," Margo said from behind them.

Zach's voice vibrated through Kate as he answered, "We have a safe place. It's a drive, but we'll be safe there."

As she clung, Zach carried her, to where, Kate didn't care. She wouldn't and couldn't let him go yet.

She was dimly aware of a vehicle and Zach climbing in with her still cradled against him.

"She'll be safer in the back," Margo said.

Zach growled and tucked her head beneath his chin. "She stays with me."

Another Kate, a past Kate, and maybe a future Kate would protest his high-handedness, the way he took control and swept her along. But this Kate needed him too much to protest.

The vehicle moved, and at some point, she must have stopped crying, because she lay quietly against Zach, letting the beat of his heart soothe her. "Noah told me," she whispered, unable to say aloud the extent of the devastation Noah had shared.

"Yeah." Zach tightened his hold. "I'm still searching for others."

Other survivors, he meant. She couldn't bring herself to ask if he'd found any.

"If they're out there." Zach kissed her temple. "I promise you, I'll find them, Katy."

And he would. Zach wouldn't rest until they knew what had happened to every wolf and witch who had called the community home.

Kate nodded and pressed her face into Zach's neck. She would think about all of that when she could. Exhaustion crept into her limbs. Jet lag, shock, and her weeping caught up with her and closed her eyes.

She half woke to full dark and the vehicle stopping.

Zach left her briefly with Margo, a blanket tucked around her like a cocoon.

"He'll be right back." Margo tucked the blanket under her chin. "We just needed a quick break, and then we'll get moving again."

A wild wolf approached her slowly, its nose working the air around her and Margo.

Margo stiffened.

Blearily, Kate registered a warm, furry body against her side. And then Zach was back, picking her up again, cradling her, keeping the disparate parts of her from shattering in a hundred directions. After years of taking care of the commune, taking care of Dhara, to not be the one in charge was a blessed relief, and Kate didn't question her need to surrender.

More engine humming, more quietly spoken directions from Zach, a couple more stops.

Dawn broke over the forest in copper and rose streaks across the sky.

Her eyes felt scratchy and gritty. The sunlight made Kate's eyes water. Margo accompanied her into the forest for a bathroom break, and then they were back in the truck. Kate climbed right back into Zach's lap and went back to sleep.

It was dark again when she woke, and Zach was climbing out of the vehicle. "You need to eat something," he said.

Kate shook her head. Even the idea of food made her stomach churn.

"Yes, Kate." Zach's voice took on that authoritative tone that normally drove her crazy and made her want to defy him just for using it. "You're running on fumes, baby."

It was the baby that did it. And Kate perched by the fire and nibbled on whatever food he handed her. It all tasted like ash and dirt, and she mechanically chewed and swallowed.

Margo and her team banked the fire and tossed sand over it to kill any stray sparks, and it was back in the vehicles again.

Outside, the forest grew thick enough to block the sky. Eerie tree shapes took form in the glow of the headlights and then disappeared into the blackness again.

Kate drank from the water bottle Zach handed her. "Where are we going?"

"Deep into pack land," he said. "You'll see what we found when we get there." His topaz gaze rested tenderly on her face. "But I promise it's safe, Kate. I wouldn't take you anywhere that wasn't."

No, he wouldn't. It went against every part of the mate bond for Zach to take her into danger. More than any of the other wolves, the protective instinct was strongest with Zach as alpha. Kate leaned into his strength now. At some future time, she would find a way to disentangle herself from his hold, and face their new reality, but for now, she wanted to rest against him and let him do what he'd wanted for years—take care of her. She'd fought his protective instinct for so long, and now it was grounding her. Zach, the threat to her independence, had become her haven.

His thighs bunched beneath hers as he shifted positions and it occurred to her she'd been using his lap as a seat for the best part of two nights and a day. "Are your legs okay?"

"I'm fine, Kate," he murmured. Stubble dotted his chin, and they must both stink, especially to his sensitive wolf nose. Even that didn't persuade her to move away from Zach. He took a deep breath. "I just need to hold you for a little bit longer, Kate."

It made her relax again that he needed her comfort as much as she needed him. As alpha, he would have felt the loss of each and every wolf.

Her selfishness stirred inside her. "Are you okay?" It was a stupid question because she already knew that he couldn't be.

Zach growled, and the sound reverberated through her. "No." His honesty surprised and pleased her. "It fucking sucks. All of this."

"Noah said Cole was back."

"Yeah." Zach huffed. "He came back for Rachel. He's been incredible. The kids already look to him for leadership."

Zach's alphaness might not like that. "And you're okay with that?"

"The witch kids look to him." His voice held a note of wry amusement. "The wolves are all mine."

And so was she if Zach had his way.

There was too much to think about. For now, it was enough that he wanted to hold her, and Goddess knew, she wanted him to hold her.

CHAPTER TWENTY

"Uh-oh." Alannah caught sight of the police cruiser once more making its way into Baile as the coven was sitting down to breakfast.

"What?" Sinead joined her at the window. "Oh, shit."

"Language," Debra snapped. "There are C-H-I-L-D-R-E-N present."

"There are," Noah drawled. "And they can S-P-E-L-L as well."

Dhara snickered and went back to her breakfast.

Tossing her a wink, Noah speared another sausage. A wolf pup, all legs and paws bounded up to him hopefully. Noah raised one side of his lip and flashed an incisor. The pup slunk away.

"But they're so cute." Taylor batted her lashes at him.

"And they are learning." Noah cut into his sausage. "And they'll eat when the alpha is done."

Taylor looked at him sulkily and eyed the pup as if she was intending to slip it something yummy.

"Don't do it," Noah said.

"But they're babies." Taylor glared at him. "They need to eat."

"They're wolf pups." Noah kept right on eating. "And we honor them by treating them as such. We respect their nature because their loyalty to us demands as much."

Taylor stuck her tongue out at him, and Gemma giggled.

Shaking her head at them, Niamh suppressed a smile. Noah was right, and she knew for a fact he'd make sure those pups were well fed after breakfast.

"What's the problem?" Warren joined them at the window and slid his arm around her waist. "Ah, bugger it."

Debra dropped her knife and fork and puffed up like an outraged hen. "Language."

"Mom," Taylor whined. "Give it a rest."

"We have standards in our family, Taylor. And foul language—"

"Totally understandable." Andy touched her arm. "Perhaps we could defer this conversation to a later time though?"

Debra pursed her lips but nodded her agreement.

Leaning in closer to her, Hermione whispered, "You're absolutely right. Youngsters need boundaries."

"Yup." Noah jabbed his fork at the pups salivating near the hearth. "Boundaries."

"Jack?" Warren spoke over his shoulder. "Your fan club is here."

"My fan club?" And then Jack got it, and he scowled. "Fuck!"

"Language," Debra shouted.

"Give it a rest," Sinead yelled back. "We have more important things to worry about."

Jack pushed to his feet, and Mags stood with him, looking at him with concern. "What do they want?"

"More questions," Jack said and drained his coffee. "I'll get my coat."

Lennox and Acharya stood by their cruiser.

"Huh," Warren said. "That's different. Are they waiting for something?"

Alannah had a horrible suspicion she understood exactly what the coppers were waiting for as two more cruisers slid into the bailey. "Probably those."

Beside her, Jack tensed and narrowed his eyes. "That looks more serious than their usual visit."

"Well." Warren squared his shoulders. "Let's find out what they want."

Never one to hang around, he strode to the door and opened it.

"Mr. Masters." Acharya gloated. "I'm afraid you're going to have to come with us."

Jack looked at Warren in surprise before returning his attention to Acharya. "I don't understand."

"Relax, Jack." Lennox smirked at Jack. "We're not here for you. Not today anyway."

"Come along with us, sir." Acharya reached for his handcuffs with a hopeful gleam in his eye. "I would advise you not to resist."

"Are you arresting Mr. Masters?" Andy shouldered his way through Jack, Warren, and a now lurking Mandla. It must have taken some impressive shoulder action on Andy's part to clear those man mountains out the way. "On what charges?"

"We have CCTV footage of an incident that occurred early on the morning of the twentieth of this month, showing a vehicle registered to this residence as being involved in a serious traffic and public safety violation."

Oh dear. Alannah glanced at Sinead. They'd heard the story about the drive across the village green from Noah.

"We understand Dr. Emma Fletcher was driving the vehicle." Acharya's eyes gleamed as he surveyed the faces in the bailey. "And she will definitely have to come with us."

Police had climbed out from the other cruisers and approached the kitchen door.

With all eyes on the central group, Alannah watched Lennox.

He didn't seem as keen on this morning's arrest as she would have guessed he would be. Instead, he was focused on Baile, his gaze taking in the outer walls, the bailey, the healer's hall, as if he was searching for answers.

"We will also need the other occupants of the vehicle to come with us and give a statement." Acharya's chest swelled like he was a man seeing his life's dream come to fruition. "You are not under arrest at this time, but it would be best if you came along with us now." He put his hand out to grab Warren's arm, took a good look at Warren, and turned the motion into a gesture for Warren to lead the way to the cruiser.

"Enough!" Roderick's shout startled them all. Followed as it was by his fist pounding the kitchen table. Cutlery and crockery crashed. A pup dashed out of the kitchen.

It was Roderick as Alannah had never seen him, and even Sinead stepped out of his path as he stalked through the door. "Leave!"

Acharya and Lennox blinked at him. The other police stopped in their tracks and glanced at each other.

"You will get in your carriages and leave." Roderick looked twice his usual impressive size. His face was a mask of fury, his eyes glittered coldly.

"Um…Roderick." Warren kept his voice calm. "It's all right."

"Nay." Roderick closed on Acharya with deadly intent. "I do not recognize your authority here. Baile does not recognize your authority. You will leave now and with not one member of this coven."

Lennox cocked his head. "Coven?"

"Out!" Roderick thundered.

"Sir." Acharya's voice shook as he straightened his uniform jacket. "I will need you to calm down. We do not want to use force but are prepared to do so if it becomes necessary."

"You understand nothing of force." Roderick towered over the man. "You puny, misguided little weasel."

"Oh shit," Sinead whispered. "The big guy's lost it."

Jack and Warren glanced at each other before stepping closer to Roderick. "Roderick," Warren whispered, eyes on the approaching cops. "They're the police. We need to cooperate."

"Nay, we do not." Roderick grabbed Acharya by the arm and turned him toward his cruiser.

"Sir!" Several police converged on him.

Lennox reached for his phone and dialed.

"My lady." Roderick glanced at Baile. "Their welcome is revoked."

Lennox, Acharya, the four approaching police and the three cruisers all vanished.

"No more." Roderick glared around the bailey. "Baile is closed to all newcomers, and we now take a stand."

He whirled and strode for the healer's hall.

Along with the stupefied coven, Alannah stared at where the police and their vehicles had been.

The healer's hall door slammed shut behind Roderick.

"Tea?" Maeve stood in the door with the teapot in her hand. She smiled serenely and went back into the kitchen.

"Maeve." As he followed Maeve inside, Warren shook his head as if trying to clear it. "You need to talk to him, calm him down. I don't know how things worked in your time, but kicking the police out will not end well." He shoved his hand through his hair. "Never mind the fact that there will be questions as to how they were here one minute and gone the next."

Maeve poured herself a cup and added milk to her tea. "Indeed, there will be questions, but Roderick will be pushed no further." Taking a seat, she located the honey in the center of the table and added a spoonful to her cup. "His mind is quite made up."

Mandla barked a laugh and yanked out a chair and sat. "That's a useful trick."

"Right!" Noah looked impressed as he went back to his breakfast.

Sinead tried to punch his shoulder, but Noah caught her hand and kissed her knuckles. He grinned up at her. "Come on, sweet thing. You'll only hurt your hand if you do that."

"You have to sleep sometime." Sinead scowled at him.

"Oh. My. God." Debra's face went puce. "I can't believe he just did that." She clapped a hand to her mouth. "We are in so much trouble now. Ohmygod, ohmygod, ohmygod."

"Not ideal." Andy put his hand on her shoulder. "Not really ideal at all."

LENNOX STOOD amongst the uniforms and tuned out their gasps and nervous chatter. No one who knew him would call him a fanciful man. They were more likely to fall about laughing if anybody should suggest even the possibility. But they'd been standing inside Baile, the cruiser's engine still running, and attempting to arrest Warren Masters and Emma Fletcher.

The possibility of the arrest had kept Acharya grinning like an alley cat at a fish barbecue. Lennox had gone along with it because the same instinct that had chattered at him before was being mouthy this morning. Still, even talking about arresting Masters and Fletcher had been overkill.

Then that big bastard, Roderick, had lost his mind, and now they were standing out on the road leading to Baile. Lennox had lived his entire life in Greater Littleton. He knew the rumors about that castle, had heard them since he could understand them. He'd lay his next paycheck that if they tried to reenter that castle, they'd find themselves driving around and around it for the rest of their natural lives.

"Did you see that?" Acharya appealed to his fellow officers. "He resisted arrest."

"Technically, it was the big one who resisted." A short, sweet-faced constable replied, patting herself down to check her body was still where she'd last seen it.

"But they resisted," Acharya crowed. "They assaulted a police officer. We'll get the AFOs up here. Then we'll see about resisting."

"Armed officers." Lennox stepped into the conversation. Acharya did not seem as surprised as the rest of them by the freaky phenomena that had just happened. "For what amounts to a traffic incident."

Acharya puffed up. "Sir, with respect, they endangered lives with that little jaunt over the village green. They resisted arrest, assaulted an officer—"

"You don't look assaulted to me." Lennox let his gaze travel from Acharya's head to his toes, and he didn't mind letting his derision show. "But we're also not standing in front of that castle anymore." He watched Acharya's face carefully as he added, "You don't find that at least a tiny bit odd?"

"Sir?" Pale, the sweet-faced constable approached him. "What just happened?"

"Magic," he said, and chuckled at the look of horror on her face.

She glanced at the others before looking at him, trying not to look at her superior officer as if he had a screw loose. "Did you say magic, sir?"

"When you have eliminated all which is impossible, then whatever remains, however improbable, must be the truth." Lennox strolled for his cruiser. He hoped the thing still worked after that zap out of Baile.

She followed him. "Sir?"

"Sherlock Holmes," he said as he opened his car door and leaned against it. "Unless you have a better explanation."

"No, sir." She drifted back to her colleagues.

Coven. Lennox tucked the word away. The big man had

definitely said coven, right before they'd been poofed right out of Baile.

And Acharya was still looking entirely too comfortable with what had happened.

* * *

RODERICK SENSED Maeve before she entered the healer's hall. "You've come to tell me I shouldn't have done it."

"On the contrary." She brushed his arms away and perched on his lap. "Of course, they are all still clucking about it in the salon. They look as if they'll be at it for a while."

He sat back in his chair to give her more space. "I have my limits, my Maeve."

"Indeed, you do." She laid her head against his shoulder. "And you have reached those limits, my Roderick."

He allowed her comforting presence to soothe his rage. "She stood there, bold as brass," he said. "Fucking stood there and taunted me." He could not fathom Rhiannon's actions, but they had infuriated him.

"She is worryingly sure of her victory." Maeve threaded her fingers with his and laid their hands in her lap.

"Aye." And that was what infuriated him the most. Then those bloody police—bah!—had entered his castle and sought to take his brothers. It was too much to be borne. From the information Andy had ferreted out through his computer, Roderick was certain Rhiannon was somehow behind the constant police interest in their folk. As she was behind their tax troubles, and all their troubles.

Maeve looked at Alexander. "How is he today?"

"Not much changed," Roderick said.

"Oh, hi." Bronwyn entered the hall and managed a weary smile that was weighted by her sad eyes. "I didn't expect you here."

"I needed to be here." Alexander would have understood his reaction better than the modern residents of Baile. He and Alexander had lived in rougher, more primal times. They both understood the might is right principle.

Bronwyn took a seat on the other side of Alexander's bed. "I heard you caused an uproar."

"He had the police removed from Baile." Maeve spared him the need to answer.

Bronwyn pulled a face. "That'll do it."

Simon came into the room, stopped when he saw them, and proceeded to Alexander's side. "I heard there is nobody in or out of Baile."

"Well, nobody in," Bronwyn said. "And I wouldn't bet on leaving here and not attracting police attention."

Simon nodded and pushed Alexander's bedsheet down. He checked the infection lines on his chest.

Roderick's innate sense of fairness chose that moment to raise its head. "You can leave. If you like."

"Why would I do that?" Simon put the device he used for listening to Alexander's chest in his ears. "My patient is right here."

CHAPTER TWENTY-ONE

Alannah escaped the intense atmosphere of the castle by going to the battlements. The coven was discussing Roderick's actions, and it was quickly descending into a raging argument. She didn't see the point. For better or worse, it was done.

Andy had been trying to get the coven to listen to him about logistics and getting supplies in and out the castle, and Warren kept trying to keep the peace, but they needed to fight it out. With Alexander so ill, everyone was tense and angry.

From this high, she had a 360-degree view around Baile. Near the ward edge on the road, the group of hecklers had grown. The police had moved them out a couple of days ago, but they were back, and there were more of them than ever. That was going to make leaving the castle a challenge.

She quested for the wards. Without Sinead's half of their blessing, she couldn't be sure, but the wards felt strained, like they were under pressure from outside. They were pulsing strong and sure, but it felt like a giant finger was pushing the balloon from one side. That would need to be looked at closer, but she'd need Sinead for that, and she wanted a few more moments to herself before she checked it out.

Up here, the air was never truly still, and a sharp wind made her tug her cardigan tighter around herself. Its chill nipped at her cheeks and made her nose run, but she loved the way the wind cleared her head.

A thin, high whistle made her look up.

Kai circled the battlements, her wings spread to catch the updrafts. She drifted down in slow circles, adjusting her wings as the wind grew stiffer closer to the battlements. Back winging, she landed on a crenellation about six feet from Alannah.

She cocked her head and studied Alannah with her piercing black eyes.

The kestrel was the symbol on Thomas's family crest. Despite her words to Sinead about not wanting to find out, curiosity had eventually driven her to investigate. To anyone living outside of Baile, linking Kai to Thomas would sound ludicrous. But the kestrel had shown up the night Thomas had left them, and she often joined Alannah in her battlement solitude.

"Hi," she said.

Kai shifted her weight and ruffled her wings against her back.

"I miss you," she whispered, allowing the constant bubble of hurt in her chest to rise to the surface. "I miss you every bloody day."

Kai studied her.

"Sinead's wolf is here." She dabbed at her tears with her cardigan sleeve. "And she's so happy. I guess you saw him arrive."

Kai bobbed her head.

Hadn't Sinead told her that she'd once had a conversation with Noah while he was in wolf form? Sinead hadn't known the wolf she was talking to was Noah, but she'd chatted to it anyway.

Kai wasn't Thomas. Alannah knew that, but somehow the bird was linked to Thomas, and she drew whatever comfort she could from that knowledge.

"She tries to play it down for my sake." The wind tugged her words away as they left her mouth. "But he makes her happy, and I'm glad for them." Talking to Kai gave her a freedom she wouldn't use with another person. "But I'm jealous as well. I look at them sometimes and I can't understand why we couldn't have had our happy ending."

A foot scraped and Kai swung her head in that direction.

"Sorry." Simon backed into the stairwell he'd come from. "I didn't know anyone was up here."

With a shrill cry, Kai flew away.

Alannah wanted to yell at her to come back. "It's okay," she said but she resented having her privacy interrupted.

Simon held up his hands. "Sorry. I was just exploring. I'll leave…" He stopped and studied her. "Have you been crying?"

Feeling exposed, she swiped at her face. "It's the wind. It makes my eyes water."

"Right." Simon shoved his hands in his pockets. He hesitated, half turning to descend the stairs and then stopped. "It's not the wind," he said. "But I can go if you want to be alone." He chewed on the inside of his cheek. "It's just that, I'm a good listener." He cleared his throat. "If you need one."

Simon was a near stranger to her, but his quiet earnestness had a restful quality that had her saying, "The view from here is spectacular."

"I thought it might be." He took a few steps onto the battlements. "It's why I came up here." He smiled. "Not to spy on you, I promise."

"I know." It didn't seem the sort of thing Simon would do. "You're welcome to share it with me."

His smile grew and warmed his serious features. "Great." He strode to the edge of the battlements and looked over. Turning a slow circle, he breathed, "Wow."

"Right." Alannah followed his gaze to the village and out to sea.

"You could see something coming for miles up here."

She couldn't resist teasing him. "I think that was the general idea. You'll have to ask Roderick. He had Baile built, you know."

"I didn't know that." Simon frowned in thought. "He looks remarkably dapper for a man of his age." He chuckled. "You could make a fortune if you could bottle what he has and sell it."

Picturing Roderick's face if someone even made that suggestion made her giggle. "I would strongly advise you not to suggest that to Roderick."

"Yeah." Simon exhaled roughly. "I wouldn't suggest a cup of tea to Roderick in his current mood." He started and looked guilty. "I mean, not that I blame him. He's dealing with a lot and seeing Alexander like he is—"

"Roderick has a temper at the best of times. He comes from a different time, and it shows." Alannah let him off the hook. "We call it getting his medieval up."

That drew a bark of laughter from Simon.

For no apparent reason, she wanted to keep talking to him for a while longer. "You're doing very well with all of this." She waved her hand to encompass Baile. "It's a lot to wrap your head around."

"Meh." He pulled a face. "That's only because you've never worked A&E. There are no end of surprises as to what people will put where, and what ideas they thought would be good ones."

Someday, she'd like to hear his stories. Humor warmed the depths of his hazel eyes.

"Truthfully, I don't know how I'm doing with all this."

Bunching his hands in his pockets, he shrugged. "The logical side of my brain keeps telling me I should be freaking out, but I'm not. There's an inexplicable sense of inevitability around being here."

A warm shiver snaked down Alannah's spine. It didn't feel bad, exactly, but it did make her want to put distance between them. "Anyway." She dusted off her hands. "I've had enough cold air for one day."

"Alannah?" The gentle way he said her name stopped her. "I really am a good listener."

"I…" Her refusal jammed in her throat. There was something about Simon that made her want to talk to him, however. It must be his doctor's bedside manner. He'd probably heard countless whispers from patients. "I don't know."

He shrugged out of his coat and put it around her shoulders. "That's okay."

"You'll be cold." She only made a half-hearted effort to return the coat. It held his body heat and smelled of rich earth and rosewood.

"Nah." He shoved his hands in his pockets. "I'm manly and tough." He quirked a brow at her. "Okay, maybe not as manly and tough as Roderick or Warren." He grimaced. "And definitely not like Mandla or Jack. Not even Noah." He sighed and motioned the coat. "Maybe you should give me that back."

Alannah laughed. She liked this sillier side to him. "Why don't we think of the coat as manliness bootcamp?"

"Deal." He grinned at her.

A beam of watery sunlight hit their battlement and bathed it in a golden glow. Even the wind died down and allowed the sun to provide some warmth. Clouds still hung over the sea and the wind whipped whitecaps onto the wave tops, like cream frosting. It seemed as if a warm bubble had wrapped around the two of them. Her coven sisters had their own troubles, and there was nothing anybody could say anyway. Thomas was gone. Her heart was broken. End of story. Yet, she found herself saying, "I lost someone. Someone I loved."

"Ah." Staring out to sea, Simon nodded and propped one shoulder against a crenellation. "I guessed it was something like that."

Despite it being warmer now, she still snuggled into his coat. "You must see a lot of grieving people in your line of work."

"Yes." His jaw tightened. "It's never easy, and people have different ways of expressing their grief."

"He...the one I lost wasn't a person."

Simon's gaze cut to her but there was no judgment in his eyes, only a calm and reassuring empathy.

She didn't know how he'd take the next part. "He was a ghost, actually. The spirit of a coimhdeacht who died here a few hundred years ago." Simon didn't move from his pillar, just watched her. "I don't know if you can even call what we had a relationship."

He nodded and moved his gaze to the sea. "I bet that makes it worse in a way."

"What?" Nobody had ever said that to her, and she stopped to consider it.

"It's like people who lose an animal," Simon said. "People around them are quick to point out it was just a dog or just a cat. Or when someone is mourning the loss of a person who is still alive, but not a part of their lives. People will say that at least that person is still alive." He turned to face her. "In your case, a ghost—so not a real man after all, and not a relationship that could be physical in any way." His gentle smile held the wisdom of ages. "But like the dog owner or the one with the missing relative, the grief is real to you. The loss is real to you."

MANDLA CAME up behind Nofoto so silently he made her jump when he said, "What are you looking at?"

"Them." She pointed out her window to the two figures on the battlement. From her room, they could see Alannah and Simon speaking. A pool of gentle sunlight caught them like their personal spotlight.

Mandla joined her at the window and grunted.

"He's a good man."

Mandla nodded his agreement.

"And she's so lovely and so sad." Nofoto carried her own grief like an iron weight in her chest. So much loss shadowed the coven, so much heartbreak. Some days it felt like they'd all forgotten how to laugh. Andy tried almost daily, but there was still no news of her mother or her people.

She'd watched Alannah and Simon talking and wanted to make a tiny difference for someone.

"The sun's shining on them." Mandla jerked his head toward the battlement bathed in buttery light. "Did you do that?"

She had, and she nodded. "He makes her smile."

"And?"

Mandla read her too well, and it drew a reluctant smile out of her. "It's hard to be romantic when you're freezing." She gave a light shrug. "So I may have given the wind a little shift to the side as well."

"Huh." He gave her the side-eye. "It's cold in here."

"No, it isn't—" And she caught the burgeoning idea in Mandla's thoughts. Giggling, she held out her hands and backed up. "Oh no." She shook her head. "Don't even think about going there."

"Cold hasn't dampened all the romance." Mandla tracked her.

She backed up farther and shook her head, laughing too much to produce the actual words. Reading his intuition a split second before he lunged, she bolted for the door.

He was on her before she could turn the handle, causing her to shriek as he flung her over his shoulder.

Nofoto banged her fists against his back and struggled—but not too hard, because the cold hadn't dampened everyone's ardor.

CHAPTER TWENTY-TWO

Bronwyn appreciated the coven's constant support and love, but the times when she could sit with Alexander on her own were her favorite. Simon had taken a break, and Hannah had been by five minutes earlier to check Alexander's vitals.

His temperature was slightly elevated, and Hannah said that needed watching, but his other vitals were stable.

They were going to try him on more antibiotics in the morning.

His skin had the clammy pallor of illness, and his eyes moved constantly behind his lids.

She bathed his forehead with tepid water again. Despite her powerlessness as a healer in this situation, she could do the small things to make him comfortable like bringing his slight fever down.

The ugly striations across Alexander's chest were obscene reminders of what they were fighting. They? She almost scoffed at the word. Her love was fighting this on his own. Goddess, she wished she could help him. But she didn't want whatever was inside him anywhere near their babies.

Her blessing, however, could be very specific and focused. Like it had found the tumor in Gemma and not touched the healthy tissue around it. She could also focus on the smallest cellular problem. It stood to reason that it worked the other way. She could avoid the infection and focus on the fever and bring it down for him.

She knew the infection was causing the fever, so instead of treating the cause, she could treat the symptom. Like a lot of over-the-counter medications did.

Before she could second-guess, she sat and touched Alexander's hand.

She fed the smallest tendril of her blessing inside him. His vascular system pulsed with the infection, and she drew her blessing away from it. Everything in her wanted to fight for him, but she knew the risk if she did. Edging forward cautiously, she dodged any cell that looked suspect and stuck to the healthy ones. Hannah had been teaching her modern medicine, and she could promote his heat loss through his skin and help bring his fever down. So, maybe looking at his skin cells? Staying far away from his torso, she fed the minutest amount of her healing into his skin cells. An area no larger than a penny, to be safe. Hannah had also said medications worked by interrupting the chemical signals that told your internal thermostat to turn up the heat.

Maybe, the brain?

She eased through his skin cells instead of using his vascular system. It was slow going and a bit like wading through glue because she didn't want to increase the power on her blessing. This was a stupid idea. Knowing how something worked didn't help you mimic how it happened. She needed to talk to Hannah and Simon.

Bronwyn began the slow process of withdrawing from his cells.

The infection twisted inside Alexander like a striking cobra.

Bronwyn pulled back but it latched on to her blessing. The harder she tugged, the tougher it wound its coils around her blessing.

And then her blessing started to imitate the infection. It replicated itself into her blessing and shot out of Alexander. Lightning fast, it traveled along the connection to her and into her body. Her inner power lashed out to fight the infection but was absorbed and mutated. Panic swept through her. She had no control over what was happening to her.

Bronwyn heaved and wrenched as it rampaged through her system. Black marks spread from where her hand touched him, pulsing and streaking over her skin.

She tried to drop his hand, but hers felt fused to his skin.

Oily, black toxicity spread unchecked through her system. Her heart beat erratically, her breathing grew labored, her mind foggy. Her vision went and then her hearing.

The infection surrounded her womb and infiltrated the cells.

Regan and Rian screamed at her internally, their tiny bodies contorting to avoid the horrific blackness surrounding them and trying to take them over.

Bronwyn's womb contracted.

The twins stilled, and their power swelled as they wound around each other. Magic, pulsing and white, built in them and surrounded them. It pushed at the darkness and then pulsed. One violent pulse that shot Bronwyn out of her chair.

Her entire body lifted and contorted before dropping to the floor. The infection shrieked through her system, ringing inside her head, and her hand dropped from Alexander's arm.

Her last thought before she passed out was that the markings were gone, her body was clear of the evil.

Bronwyn's scream made the hair stand up all over Hannah. She ran for the healer's hall. At first, she didn't see Bronwyn because the chair beside Alexander was empty. And then, she looked down.

Lying like a broken doll on the floor, was Bronwyn.

Hannah yelled. "Simon!"

And then she remembered he'd gone on a break.

Crouching beside Bronwyn, her physician's training took over. She checked for a pulse. There, but erratic. Breathing was shallow. Eyes responded to light.

She needed to get Bronwyn on a bed, but she was alone in the healer's hall.

"Simon!" she bellowed. "Anyone!"

"Hannah?" Roderick's voice came from the doorway. "What is it?"

"It's Bronwyn." She motioned him over. "I need to get her up on that bed."

Blood stained the crotch of Bronwyn's jeans, and Hannah's heart dropped. Oh dear God, not that on top of everything else. She forced back the panic. It was so much easier finding that clinical detachment when you weren't invested in the patient.

Roderick was already raising Bronwyn in his arms.

He caught sight of her blood, and his jaw tightened. "What do you need?"

"Simon." Bleeding was bad, but it didn't have to mean miscarriage. Jesus, she didn't know enough about gynecology and obstetrics.

"I'll get him," Maeve said from somewhere near the door.

"We need to strip her." Hannah worked on the clasp of Bronwyn's jeans. "We need to see what's happening."

Minutes dragged like hours as Roderick helped her.

Hannah hooked up the machines to Bronwyn. Could Andy get her an ultrasound at a moment's notice? Oh God, oh God.

She calmed a little when they got Bronwyn's jeans off. The

blood was definitely bright red, but it wasn't that much. Hannah would take whatever glimmer of hope she could find.

"Tell me." Simon ran through the door.

"I heard her scream and found her on the floor." Hannah recited Bronwyn's stats for him as Simon checked her over. He was an ocean of calm competence as he went through the steps quickly and without fuss.

Roderick stepped back and watched.

Simon was fastening the blood ox monitor when Bronwyn's eyes fluttered open. "What…"

"You passed out." Hannah grabbed her hand to reassure her and stood near her head to give Simon room to work. "What happened?"

"I…" Bronwyn frowned as if trying to remember. "I was trying to bring his fever down." Her eyes widened and tears welled. "That thing in Alexander. It latched on to me and attacked." Her entire body tensed. "My babies. It attacked my babies."

"Bronwyn." Simon's voice snapped through her rising panic. "I'm going to need you to calm down."

Nodding, Bronwyn tried her best to comply. Tears ran down her temples and into her hair as her big eyes fastened on Hannah's face. "Are the babies all right?"

"We need to make sure you're stable first." Hannah wiped her tears away.

Bronwyn shook her head. "I need to know about the babies."

And Hannah remembered something Bronwyn had told her a few days ago. "We don't have an ultrasound, but you can do it." She smoothed hair back from Bronwyn's face. "Remember you told me you can sense them, what they're feeling?"

Bronwyn took a shaky breath. And then another. She closed her eyes and tried to center herself. A frown creased her brow and then relaxed.

"They're there." Bronwyn's hand drifted to her belly. "Thank Goddess, but they're there."

"The bleeding has stopped," Simon said. He touched her belly gently. "I think we're okay."

Bronwyn's tears started again. "It was my fault." Her breath hitched. "I thought I could help his fever." Her guilt-stricken gaze found Roderick. "I heard what you said. I didn't go anywhere near that awful thing." She shuddered. "But it attacked me."

"Hush." Roderick reached her side in three large strides. His big hand cupped her cheek. "It's all right now, little witch. Just breathe."

Bronwyn put both hands on her belly. "Stay there," she whispered. "Please, please, please stay there."

"That's right, little witch," Roderick crooned. "You tell them they're all right now. Tell them they need to stay right where they are until the time is right."

"Heart rate is almost normal," Simon said. "Blood pressure still high, but that's probably shock."

"You hear that?" Hannah leaned closer to her. "You're okay." She covered Bronwyn's hands on her belly with one of hers. "All of you."

Nodding, Bronwyn found Roderick's gaze. "I'm sorry."

"No," Roderick murmured. "There is no cause for apologies."

Hannah had never seen the big man look that tender or compassionate, and it made her want to weep.

"It's over now," Roderick said.

Bronwyn shook her head and tried to stop crying. "I shouldn't have done it. Why did I even think I could do that?"

"Because you wanted to help Alexander," Roderick whispered. "Because the man you love was suffering, and you're a healer. You cannot always stop the compulsion that demands you ease someone's suffering."

"Don't be nice to me." Bronwyn sobbed. "I don't deserve it."

"You need to stop doing that." Simon stood behind Roderick. "You need to focus on the fact that the babies are fine and you're fine." He patted Bronwyn's hand. "But I am going to put you on bed rest for a day or so."

"Here?" Bronwyn sniffed.

"Right here." Simon gave her a sweet smile. "Where I can keep an eye on you." He looked at Alexander. "Isn't this where you want to be anyway?"

Bronwyn nodded and swiped her hand over her face. "I shouldn't have even tried that. It was so fucking stupid."

"Probably not your best idea." Simon's tone was gently teasing. "And my best medical recommendation would be not to try it again."

Bronwyn drew a juddering breath and nodded. She looked down at her hands on her stomach. "Never again."

———

RHIANNON SCREAMED as the blood magic made contact with the children. Her babies. Her precious babies that she'd sacrificed everything for.

"Nooo!" she screamed her desperation.

Glass shattered. Minions around her shrunk into themselves and clapped hands to their ears.

She continued screaming even as she grabbed the nearest minion.

It could not all be in vain. If that fucking witch lost those babies, all her plans would be for nothing. They were the future of magic, and she needed to shape that future with them by her side.

"Give me blood," she bellowed.

Someone jumped forward, she knew not who. Her entire being was locked on the hideous spectacle playing behind her eyes. The backlash as the babies repelled the blood magic from their womb sent her flying across the room.

A table screeched as she connected with it. Plates and glasses bounced off the table and crashed to the floor.

"Here, mistress." The bowl of blood was in front of her.

Rhiannon pulled all four elements in an excruciating burst of power that almost rendered her insensate, but she had to protect those babies. Her son would die for nothing if she didn't stop her magic from killing the thing she desired most.

She heaved the blood magic out of Bronwyn and back into Alexander. It pulsed and writhed against her control. With every ounce of her amassed power, she held it there, fusing it into the dagger. Then she wound it into a connection to her. That could never happen again.

What was that stupid, stupid girl thinking to have even brought her blessing near Alexander?

No more. Rhiannon fastened the connection to her sternum. It would take a lot of power to keep that connection through the wards, but she could not lose those babies. She would not lose those babies.

And Rhiannon settled in to watch over the unborn.

CHAPTER TWENTY-THREE

After the scare with Bronwyn, Mags went to sleep knowing she would be hit by a vision dream. Big events tended to trigger her blessing, and she wrapped herself around Jack before she went to sleep and braced for it.

The dream, when it came, was new.

First, Baile wove into focus, and then her vision telescoped into a turret and one of the small octagonal rooms at the top. She knew it wasn't hers, but it could be either of the remaining three towers. The woman had long dark hair, dark as a raven's wing, neatly braided down her back. Tall and lithe, she wore dark pants and a sweater. There was nothing remarkable about her outfit other than it didn't look familiar to Mags. But it was weird. The clothes were unfamiliar because she knew she'd never seen them on any of the coven, but more alien, like she'd never seen their style before. And then she got it. She was seeing years into the future.

In the center of the room stood a large crystal. At first glance, the crystal looked gray, but as the woman drew closer and the light changed in the vision, the crystal showed subtle lights of amber and green and blue. Labradorite, but the biggest piece Mags had ever seen. That crystal was definitely not in today's Baile.

The woman bent to examine the crystal, and Mags's vision shifted so she could see her face. High cheekbones, ivory skin, and darkly lashed eyes. She looked familiar, but Mags was also sure she'd never seen her before. The woman seemed sad, but it was an old grief that clung to the lovely lines of her face and haunted the depths of her green eyes. Putting both palms on the crystal's smooth surface, she closed her eyes and whispered, "Where are you?"

Strange markings decorated the woman's right arm. Not quite coimhdeacht markings, but something like that.

Mag's vision dissolved and sent her flying through space. Light blurred past her in speeds that made her belly roil. Everything went to absolute dark. Dark so intense she couldn't experience any of her senses, but she knew she was still moving. She kept traveling through the terrifying blackness until she wanted to scream and wake up. It felt like a tomb.

She burst into light so strong she had to blink to clear her vision. Colors danced and swirled around her, twining around each other, coalescing to form another color before splitting again. Only to reform into another light strand that created a new color, colors Mags had never seen before, so achingly beautiful she wanted to cry.

And then the light show exploded, and a landscape formed.

More of that bewildering speed dragged her over trees and grass, rocks, and sand, over a sea such a deep blue it was almost purple. The landscape looked odd, alien. The colors were just not right, and the shapes were unaccustomed. She didn't get the feeling they were unnatural however, just...other.

A large, stone building loomed toward her. The architecture had rounded edges and resembled smaller buildings clustered together that sprawled over the hillside. She'd never seen its like. It had a vaguely tribal feel to it. And then she was zooming through those umber-colored walls.

People milled about a great hall, not dissimilar to Baile's, but again, other. Not in her frame of reference. A man sat at a dinner table, and she knew it was him she was here to see.

Dark hair, tanned skin, and jewel-bright green eyes. He looked exactly like Alexander, only with Bronwyn's eyes. Mags hadn't seen it in the woman, but it was clear in the more masculine features of the vision man. He froze and cocked his head, as if listening to something, his expression growing vacant. He said something in a different language, and she didn't understand.

Around him, people yelled and ate and drank. The food didn't look like anything Mags had ever seen.

"Oy." A table companion thumped him on the arm, and the man shook his head. He ran one hand through his hair. It was his left hand, and on it were similar markings to the woman she'd first seen. He spoke again in his guttural language. Mags tried to draw closer to him, but the vision dissolved.

"Mags." Jack drew her close to his body. "Dream?"

She nodded because she had no words to describe her vision.

Jack's big hand spread on her tummy. "Was it the blood dream?"

"No." The woman's sadness lingered in Mags's chest. A profound sense of loss and hopelessness that made her want to cry. The man had seemed…lost, untethered.

"Want to tell me about it?" Jack kissed the top of her head.

She did and she didn't. "I don't know how. It was strange. It was the future, that much I'm sure of, but I didn't know the people I saw."

"Hmm." Jack's bass voice rumbled through his chest. "Like when you saw me?"

"Similar." She snuggled into his warmth. "Only I knew why you were coming."

Jack chuckled. "And who I was coming for."

She pushed the dream aside. They had enough trouble at Baile without adding what might or might not be Regan and Rian into the mix. Only if it was the twins, why were they separated? She didn't want to think about it. "Speaking of coming here for me." Mags slid one of Jack's large hands over her breast.

"Mags," he groaned her name and pressed his cock against her bottom. "You're a demanding woman."

EMMA RAPPED her head on the kitchen table. If she hit it hard enough, she might be able to eradicate the images of Mags and Jack getting it on. Goddess, but they were at it like rabbits. Again.

Now, Emma had no problem with doing what came naturally, but she'd prefer not to have a front row seat to someone else doing the wild thing. It was like watching porn starring a sister.

And there was stuff about Jack that she'd much rather not know. Jesus, the guy was like her best friend.

A rumpled, shirtless Warren appeared in the kitchen doorway. He paused when he saw her. "Couldn't sleep?"

"Nah." She'd woken when Mags had after that dream. Emma could glean glimpses of it from Mags's mind. And then Mags had decided on a far more pleasant way to spend the night. Pleasant for Mags and Jack at least. Emma, not so much.

Warren moved over to the fridge and took out the milk. He rummaged in the saucepans hanging over the range until he found the one he wanted. "Taylor had a bad dream. I'm making her some hot chocolate."

"A vision?" Emma was glad for the distraction Warren

provided. "Mags had one tonight as well. It wasn't bad, so much as it was odd."

Stopping his pouring, Warren gave her a sharp look. "That's almost exactly what Taylor said. She said it was…other."

"Yeah." Emma could draw the vision from Mags's mind, but that would involve delving into Mags's mind, and right now, she wasn't going anywhere near that. If only she could turn the emotions off as successfully.

Warren put his saucepan of milk on the stove and clanked through the canisters Alannah kept beside the range until he found hot chocolate. "So, what's keeping you up?"

"Mags and Jack." She barely suppressed a shudder. "I get way too vivid pictures and emotions from Mags."

Throwing his head back, Warren laughed. "I honestly never thought about that." He shuddered. "Yeah, but that's so much more than anyone needs to see." He dug a spoon into the hot chocolate. "You know you can tune her out?"

"What?" Please Goddess, let Warren be telling the truth right now. Salvation beckoned.

"Your witch." Warren watched the milk on the stove. "You can tune her out. You still stay connected to her, so if she gets into trouble, you'll know, but you won't have to…" He waved his hand to indicate anything Mags could get up to.

Emma needed that and now. "How?"

"Grab the connection." Warren made a motion with his fingers like he was turning an invisible button. "And turn her down."

Emma blinked at him. "Turn her down? That's it?"

"That's it." Warren grinned.

Tuning into her bond with Mags, Emma reduced the volume.

Sweet relief flooded through Emma as Mags went down to a low murmur. She was still dimly aware of where Mags was, and what she was doing, but it was no longer the live sex show happening through her body. "Thank you," she breathed. "I can't believe you waited until now to tell me."

Chuckling, Warren stirred Alannah's homemade chocolate concoction into the milk. "Roderick told me on pain of death that I do not tell the witches."

"They don't know?" Emma wasn't sure she could keep a secret from Mags for long.

"We don't want them tuning us out," Warren said over his shoulder. "We can't be effective if they tune us out. Or that's what Roderick said." He shrugged and smiled. "It could be the big guy's rampaging control issues getting out of hand."

Talking about Roderick made her think of earlier today. She checked the clock above the door. Yesterday morning now. "Close call with Bronwyn."

"True." Warren frowned. "I don't know what she was thinking to even take that kind of chance."

The need to defend Bronwyn had Emma speaking with heat. "She was thinking about the man she's losing and how much she wants him to live. She's a woman in a horrible situation who is in survival mode and watching the man she loves die."

"Whoa!" Warren held up a hand, the spoon lightly gripped in his long fingers. "I'm not criticizing."

Emma smelled bullshit. "Yes, you are."

He opened his mouth, then snapped it shut and nodded. "You're right. I was being critical." He stirred the hot chocolate. "I'm a father, and risking your child's life is anathema to me."

"She didn't risk the twins on purpose." Emma was one hundred percent sure of that when it came to Bronwyn. "She wanted to help Alexander. How would you feel if Niamh was lying there and you could help her, but the risk was to Taylor?"

Warren shook his head. "I don't even want to think about that possibility."

"There you go." Emma folded her arms over her chest. Now that the porno in her head was gone, she was ready to go back to sleep, so she stood. "Bronwyn needs our support, not us being judgmental."

He sighed as he poured the hot chocolate into a mug. "You're right. I'm an asshole."

"Maybe not a complete asshole." She liked how Warren didn't get defensive. "But we're going to need each other in what's to come, and we can't afford to be fighting amongst ourselves."

Warren laughed wryly. "Now you sound like me talking to Alexander and Roderick." He dropped his head. "Jesus, I hope he's going to be okay. I would give fucking anything to be refereeing one of their inane bouts of dick waving right now."

CHAPTER TWENTY-FOUR

Alannah found Sinead and Noah in the library. They made such a sweet picture that she stopped a moment at the library door to watch them. Sinead sat on Noah's lap, curled into his chest with her head on his shoulder as she gazed into the crackling fire.

With a look of utter contentment on his face, Noah was talking to her, telling her stories of his life in the Ottawa commune.

Alannah had never seen Sinead look that peaceful or happy. Love lit a glow beneath Sinead's skin and made her eyes glimmer. Her inner radiance made Sinead even more beautiful than ever.

Of course, she was always Sinead, so the legs dangled over Noah's were encased in clunky boots that laced halfway up the calves of her fatigues. And she even had Noah wearing an Arcane Activists T-shirt. The way it stretched across Noah's impressive chest and biceps, Alannah might one day learn to like those bloody T-shirts.

Noah turned his head. "Hey."

"Hi." Sinead moved to scramble off Noah's lap.

Alannah shook her head at her twin. "You don't need to do that."

"What?" Sinead blushed and averted her gaze. "I'm sure Noah's legs are going to sleep, and my ass was going numb."

"No, it wasn't." Alannah took a seat on the leather sofa beside them. "And we need to come to an agreement."

Noah cocked his head, looking so canine as he did, that Alannah nearly laughed. If you knew what to look for in the shifters, the animal was only just beneath the skin. "Agreement?"

"You two need to stop thinking you need to apologize for being happy," she said. A half empty glass of wine sat on the table in front of the sofa, and Alannah snagged it and took a sip. Red wine, fire burning in the grate, cold morning outside—Sinead and Noah had the perfect idea.

Sinead got as huffy as a Karen at a Love is Love parade. "I'm not apologizing for—"

"Sweet thing." Noah pressed a kiss to her neck. "You totally are."

"I'm not." But her words lacked conviction.

Noah looked at her.

Sinead glared before subsiding against him. "Okay, fine. But it seems wrong to be so happy…" She stopped and shot Alannah a guilty look.

"When I'm all heartbroken and miserable?" Alannah finished Sinead's sentence. She took another sip of the red wine. Blackberries, with a hint of chocolate and a sweet tobacco finish. They must have been raiding Alexander's cellar. "The two things aren't connected."

"She loves you." Noah tugged Sinead back against his chest. "She wants to see you happy."

"I know that." Alannah squeezed Sinead's knee. "And I love her for that. But happiness is a blessing. With all this crap going on around us, we need to take what we can, when we can." She finished the wine. "Look at Bronwyn. Even Mags didn't see what happened with Alexander coming." She patted Sinead's shin. "Enjoy your happiness and enjoy this man of yours."

Noah made a contented grumble. "What she said."

"Oh, I know you agree with that." Sinead rolled her eyes at him.

Their gazes locked, and so many tiny messages passed between them that Alannah felt like an intruder. When you lost someone, it was often the small things you missed the most. Those fleeting, inconsequential moments that cemented the bond between two beings and made you feel seen. The way you could share a joke without speaking.

"We agree then?" Alannah needed to get back to the reason she'd tracked Sinead down. "You stop hiding your happiness from me, and I'll do my best not to rip your hair out with jealousy."

Noah sniffed and looked at her. "What's worrying you?"

Wow! He'd been able to smell that. It made her wonder what else he could smell. With a chuckle she said to Sinead, "That sniffing thing might get annoying."

"Yep." Sinead nudged Noah. "It gives him a definite advantage."

Noah nuzzled her neck. "Yeah, but given how totally I'm gone for you, it all balances out."

And that was so sweet Alannah melted inside.

"Right then." She got back to business. "We need to check the wards together."

Sinead sat up, all business again. "What's wrong with them?"

"They're not right." Alannah stood and held out her hand to haul Sinead up. "They feel odd, but I'll need you to get a better read on them."

"Their scent is…inconsistent." Noah got to his feet as well. "I'm new here, so I wasn't sure what they were supposed to smell like."

They took the back door out to the kitchen gardens, stopping only to bundle up before tackling the cold day. All except Noah, who muttered something about them not knowing what real cold felt like.

Noah slowed as they walked through the kitchen gardens, stopping to examine the plants every now and again. "This is incredible," he said. "I've never seen such healthy tomatoes."

Sinead waggled her fingers. "Warden witch."

"I can see that." He bent to study a rosemary bush that was lasting later into the season than it would outside of this garden.

Their favorite spot to access earth lay inside the orchard where the soil was soft, and the old trees amplified their magic.

Alannah crouched beside Sinead, and they dug their joined fingers into the earth. An earlier morning cool from frost lingered in the soil. Roses and cloves scented the air as they drew earth. A green shimmer surrounded their fingers twined in the ground.

The wards shimmered and pulsed through their earth sense. White and crystalline, the wards surrounded Baile and her land in glowing lines. They checked the repair they'd done after pushing Rhiannon out of the wards. It looked as strong as when they'd first fixed the wards.

Alannah was beginning to think she'd imagined what she'd sensed in the wards from the battlements yesterday evening.

"There," Noah murmured as the wards contracted. "The smell changed."

"Right." Alannah pulled more earth, and Sinead fed it through the wards.

The ward lines now integrated them into the looped system, and they could sense them from the inside. From inside the wards, their true nature became clearer. They weren't solid lines but functioned more like an electrical circuit with power pulsing through them.

Sinead and Alannah waited, the wards thrumming through bones and blood.

The pulse happened again, and they followed it along the loop. A second pulse took them by surprise.

"The power is weaker where it pulses," Sinead said. "You feel that?"

Alannah nodded, because Sinead's description was accurate. The pulses were like the weak points in a stretched elastic band. Slowly and carefully, they searched the entire loop and found three more weak points.

"Let's strengthen them," Alannah said.

Nodding, Sinead drew more earth, and then more until the magic pushed at the confines of their skin. She built even more strength until it felt like they would explode from it, and then Alannah fed it into the wards.

Their magic swelled the wards and strengthened them. Only, not in the five weak points. Now the strong stretches of the wards looked even more powerful than the weak points.

"Shit." Sinead released earth and looked at her. "The wards are weakening."

"That can't be good." Noah glanced from one to the other of them. "Rhiannon?"

"Logic dictates that she must be behind this somehow, but we couldn't find any trace of her in the wards," Alannah said. They'd been through every inch of the wards looking for weak spots, and no stain of blood magic could be detected.

Sinead looked uncertain as she asked, "Should we tell Roderick?"

"Tell Roderick what?" The man himself strode into the orchard wearing a thunderous frown.

Hand in his, Maeve gave them an apologetic nose crinkle.

"You didn't smell him coming?" Sinead hissed beneath her breath at Noah. "What's the use of your sniffing now?"

"He was up wind," Noah hissed back.

Sinead scoffed. "Excuses."

Noah's growl rumbled through his chest. "You're gonna pay for that smart mouth, sweet thing."

"Bite me." Sinead grinned.

Clearing his throat, Roderick planted his feet apart and scowled down at them. "What's wrong with the wards?"

"They're thinning in places." Alannah stood and dusted dirt from her hands. "We can't find any apparent cause, and when we strengthened them, we only ended up strengthening the parts that were fine."

"What does that mean?" Maeve frowned and chewed on her bottom lip.

"It means we need to guard Baile the old school way." Noah looped an arm around Sinead's shoulders. "We need to patrol."

"Patrol?" Roderick scoffed. "Do you know how far these wards stretch around Baile's demesne? There aren't enough of us to be effective."

"You're right." Noah held up one finger. "Unless you had a wolf shifter who would get a pack of wild wolves to help."

Sinead tapped her bottom lip and pretended to think it over. "Now where would we find such a thing?"

"Or." Alannah decided to play along. "We could just sit in our castle and wait."

"You all suck," Roderick snapped.

Shock at his modern language held them all frozen for a second before they laughed. Roderick was evolving into a twenty-first-century dude.

"I'll talk to Warren," Noah said. "We'll make sure two of us are always on patrol and use the wolves to fill in the gaps."

Alannah sensed an emotional storm brewing in Roderick, and her need to smooth the waters took over. "If that's okay with Roderick?"

Roderick nodded. "Aye. Do as you will."

So, not fully evolved yet then.

"WHAT IS IT?" Maeve waited for Alannah, Noah, and Sinead to be far enough away before she prodded Roderick for what had him stirred up inside. "I wouldn't have to ask, but you're doing that thing where you block me."

Roderick did a good job of looking surprised. "I don't block you."

"Yes, you do." She patted his chest to let him know she harbored no ill feelings. "All of you coimhdeacht do, but that's not today's problem. Tell me what's got you all twisted up inside."

"You know I'm concerned about my son." He assumed a cold, forbidding mien, the one that was supposed to scare people off from digging further. At this point, he really should know better than to think that would work on her.

Maeve shook her head at him. "No. It's more than that."

He tried, for all of three seconds to tough it out, and then he exhaled, and his shoulders slumped. "They were not going to tell me about the wards."

"You don't know that." Roderick had shouldered the safety of Baile for so many hundreds of years, not being informed would have tweaked him. "And I would wager they were only trying not to burden you further than you already are."

"Am I so weak?" Vintage Roderick thrust his shoulders back and stuck his jaw out like he'd take on all comers. "Am I so incapable that I fold at the first sign of trouble?"

Maeve did love this big barbarian with his overdeveloped sense of duty. "You're getting your medieval up."

He snorted and made a face.

Sliding her arms around his waist, she tucked herself beneath his chin. You had to know how to get that granite spine of his to bend. Fortunately, she was a self-proclaimed expert in just that. His muscles lost some of their tension at her touch.

"We're coven," she said. "Part of what we do is share each other's burdens."

"True." Although his arms came around her, he was still holding something back from her.

Maeve snuggled closer, surrendering to the iron strength of him against her softer parts.

"What if they doubt me, Maeve?" he whispered. "What if they doubt me, and they are right to do so?"

Her heart broke for him as his words registered. She hadn't known him for all of his many years, but she was willing to wager that she could count on one hand the number of times Roderick had been forced to confront his own fallibility. The meeting with Rhiannon had shaken him to his center. "They don't doubt you," she said. "They empathize with you and feel for your pain." The first time she'd seen Roderick, she'd been but a child, but even then, he'd made everyone around him feel safe and protected. As she'd grown to womanhood, she'd come to resent his authority over the coven. Even after they'd bonded, she had fought his assumption of command.

She knew better now. Roderick had been thrust into his fate as much as all of them had. Only with him, he'd been living the reality of that fate for so much longer that it had become second nature. He wasn't one for many words and did not often tell her how much she meant to him. In showing her his doubt, he showed her more effectively than any *I-love-yous* all that she meant to him. That he needed her as much as she needed him filled her heart to overflowing. "Listen to me, warrior, and listen well." She tilted her head back to meet his gaze. "When I was thrown into stasis to be here in this time, who did Goddess choose to come with me?"

"Maeve," he grumbled and stared stubbornly at something over her head.

She tightened her arms around him. "Who?"

"Me." He sighed long sufferingly.

"Who is it that has seen this coven through that awful massacre, and been here to show us the way forward in this new time?'

He grunted. "Maeve, I know not of what you speak."

"Yes, you do." She poked his iron-hard side. "You are the rock on which Baile stands, and you will never falter." Going up on her toes, she kissed the underside of his sculpted jaw. "But when you feel like you might falter, I will be right by your side to remind you of your strength."

His gaze locked on hers.

Maeve could hardly credit that she had once found his pale blue eyes cold. "And you will never stand alone while I am here."

CHAPTER TWENTY-FIVE

Jack Langham had to be the stubbornest man on the planet. Emma didn't know how Mags didn't end up thumping him from one day to the next. Right now, he stood with his legs akimbo, arms braced, and his chin jutting out at a fight-me angle.

And fight him she would. It was for his own bloody good, for fuck's sake.

Fortunately, the barracks were quiet at this time of day. Noah was out running the perimeter with his furry friends. Roderick was in the healer's hall, and Warren was holed up with Niamh in their room. If he hadn't been otherwise engaged, she would have brought Warren in to referee her argument with Jack. And Mandla was wherever the hell he wanted to be, because nobody questioned the big South African about his whereabouts. Not that he'd answer even if they did. Mandla was almost as nonverbal as a monk under a vow of silence—if said monk was prone to violence.

"Jack." She tried to keep her tone reasonable and not littered with obscenities. "You can't patrol the wards."

He scowled down at her. "Why not?"

They'd been working together for long enough for him to have clued in on the fact that she wasn't about to be intimidated by a big man with a gruff voice. Big men hit the ground harder than their smaller counterparts. "Because you're not coimhdeacht. You don't have the bond, and we have no way of knowing if you're all right or not." They'd been over this at least six times by her count. She also tried not to mention that, size aside, Jack was as vulnerable as the next man without the extra abilities granted coimhdeacht by Goddess.

Jack lifted one shoulder. "I don't see how that makes a difference."

"Of course it makes a difference." Did she really have to go through buddy protocol with him? "Think about it for a second here."

Down the passage leading to the barracks bedrooms, Andy's door opened, and Debra came out. She patted her hair back into place and tucked her shirt into her skintight leopard-print skirt. Catching sight of them, she stopped and blushed. "Oh, hi."

"Hi." Emma returned her greeting with a smile. "We didn't know anyone was still down here."

Debra cleared her throat and smoothed her skirt over her hips. "No, well…here I am." She tittered and scurried past them.

Jack watched her go and then lifted his brow at Emma in question.

His effort at changing the subject was tempting, but she had to settle this with him before they went much further. "Say you're several clicks from the castle, and you come across something suspicious." She waved her hand to indicate the area outside the castle. According to Sinead and Alannah, the wards had created a huge domain around the castle. "And something happens." She held up her hand before he could interrupt her. "And don't even think of asking me what could happen. You've fought that bitch and her groupies enough times to know the answer."

Jack snapped his jaw shut.

"Right." Emma took the point win. "Because you and I both know that shit happens when Rhiannon is involved."

He opened his mouth again.

"We both know there is every chance she is involved." Jack was grabbing at straws if he thought she would buy his argument about them not knowing for certain if Rhiannon was involved in the weakening wards. "There are those nutters out on the road. The village is filling up like a brothel on payday, and it's not impossible that one of those yahoos from the village fancies his chances of getting through the wards."

"I can use a cell phone." Muscle bunched over his biceps as he flexed.

"You might not get the chance to." She understood how he felt. She would also hate to be excluded. "If you were bonded with Mags there would be no question you could go. We'd love to have you out there, but—"

"This is some exclusive bloody coimhdeacht bullshit you're pulling right now," he said.

"No, it isn't." Emma had to haul back on her rising voice. "It's being practical. There aren't enough of us that we can put you at risk."

"Right." Jack jabbed a finger at her. "There aren't enough of us. We need every able-bodied man out there we can field."

"Man?" She lifted her eyebrow. "Is this some kind of sexist thing you got going here? You're bitter because I get to go, and you don't?"

Jack scoffed at her. "You know better than that."

"Okay." She did know better than that. "I know that you know that what I'm saying makes sense. Why are you being so stubborn about this?"

"Because, Emma," he labored the syllables of her name, "I can't sit back while everyone else does their part. I can't be dead weight."

He was so off base she had to take a moment to formulate an argument. "You are so not dead weight."

"What's my contribution then?" He stepped closer to her and lowered his voice. "Being Mags's lover? Is that my sole purpose in being here?"

"Don't even go there." She slashed her hand through the air, irritated that he would even think he had no other reason to be here. "I would never have found Mags without you."

"Yes, you would have."

"Not as fast as I did." She touched his forearm, wanting to both comfort and shake him. "You kept me going when I wanted to give up. You ground Mags and make her happy. You're part of us."

"You ground Mags." He gave her a heavy look. "And I love that I make her happy, but I have to be more than that."

Emma sighed. She got what bothered him, she really did. Jack was a man of action, a doer, but putting him knowingly at risk was not an option. Out of better ideas, she hauled out the big guns. "What would happen to Mags if you got hurt? Or worse."

"I won't get hurt," he insisted. "We have no reason to believe that anyone has or can cross the wards. Patrolling the wards is only a preventative measure."

"We have every reason to believe they'll try." She had to make him understand. "Those wards are showing weak points for a reason, and we all know Rhiannon is behind that reason. To assume otherwise would be pig shit fucking stupid."

"Which is why we need all eyes on the job."

Emma screamed in her head and took a deep breath. They were going around and around the fucking mulberry bush.

Andy's door opened again, and Hermione tripped out, fastening the buttons on her blouse. "Hello, Jack, Emma." She giggled and walked past them.

"Did they…" Emma pointed her finger down the passage to Andy's room.

Jack watched Hermione walk away. "It looked that way to me."

"Together?"

Jack looked intrigued.

And Andy stepped out of his bedroom looking as prim and buttoned up as ever. He nodded a greeting in passing at them before hurrying off to take care of whatever Baile and her coven needed him to.

"Well, that's new," Jack murmured.

"And none of our business." Emma got him back to the discussion at hand. "Now, back to you going on patrol."

Jack was still staring after Andy. "Do you think anyone else knows?"

"Back here." Emma snapped her fingers at him. "It takes all types, and we don't get to judge."

"I wasn't judging." Jack glared at her. "But even you gotta admit that's interesting."

She nodded, because it totally was. Andy, Hermione, and Debra's possible relationship would have to wait for another day, however. "Look, Jack, I—"

"I've got an idea." Jack turned back to her.

Emma braced herself to shoot him down. "What?"

"I go out with you," he said. "We go as a team, and you keep eyes on me at all times. That way, if you get into trouble, I'm right there for you."

"That's…" Actually, not a bad idea. Teams were always better than individuals, and if she went with Jack, it meant Warren and Mandla could team up, and that left Noah with his fur army. "A good idea."

Jack pressed his advantage. "So, you agree. You and I patrol together?"

"I agree." She held out her hand to shake on it. "And you

know there isn't another soul in this castle I'd rather have on my team."

THE LAST TIME Rhiannon had stood in the former school hall, Alexander had been by her side. That night, when he had been so resistant to the blood sacrifice ceremony, she had assumed he was getting ambitious ideas about usurping her. She should have paid better attention, because the real answer had been there to see. Alexander had been repulsed by the blood magic. That must have come from Roderick.

She pushed the memory of that night aside and prepared for her gathering of the faithful. More and more minions poured in every day, and tonight, she was going to give them a show.

"Is everything prepared?"

Her favorite South African minion nodded her cowled head. "As per your instructions, mistress."

If the woman lived through Samhain, Rhiannon might go to the bother of learning her name. She had proven herself most obedient and useful.

Behind the closed hall doors, the chanting permeated into the hallway where she stood. Many of her followers had only heard rumors of her power. Tonight, she would give them proof and cement their loyalty for the looming battle.

Five minutes earlier, the minion had informed her the hall was packed. They'd been forced to open the doors to accommodate the overflow into the school's quadrangle.

Rhiannon drew a small amount of power and blew the doors open.

She nodded to the two minions positioned at the front of her procession. Those places used to be reserved for Edana and Fiona, but those two had failed her.

The hall fell silent. Candlelight made elongated shapes of the gathered faithful. Smoke hung in the hot, fetid air created by too many bodies pressed into the space. One day soon, she would have Baile's great hall for her gatherings. Then she would burn down this broken-down, old school Alexander had purchased for her. Then she would have a venue befitting her status.

All heads swung her way, eyes feverish with devotion as they settled on her.

Rhiannon basked in their admiration. They had seen only a pittance of what she could do, and already they adored her.

Like a wave sweeping the assembly, people dropped to their knees as she made her way down the aisle toward the altar. Behind her came another four of her current favorites, each dressed in a corresponding color to represent each of the four elements. The elements would be hers come Samhain. Hers to command and master.

On the altar, arms and legs spreadeagled and tied, lay her offering to her followers.

The woman turned her head and watched in horror as Rhiannon approached.

When Rhiannon had Baile in her grasp, she would erect a fitting altar and not a reconstituted desk like she was forced to use now. She would stain those stones with blood until they lost their natural color.

The Canadian witch whimpered as Rhiannon drew closer. She had been drugged but not gagged. Rhiannon wanted her followers to hear her scream as she bled her dry. Already, Rhiannon's pulse quickened at the prospect of the power the witch's blood would release. For so many years, she'd had to make do with sacrifices that held barely a whisper of power. But this Canadian witch, direct descendent of a cré-witch, her blood would hold some of the power Rhiannon craved. Not as much as one of the witches ensconced in Baile, but soon enough she would have their blood too.

Her mouth watered, and wetness slicked between her legs at

the prospect of how much power killing one of those witches would release. Rhiannon would bathe in their blood. Draw it into her through her pores and set the entire world aflame if she so desired.

The sacrifice's whimpers had grown to keening moans. "Please, please, don't do this. I have a family. I have children."

Not anymore, the woman didn't. Rhiannon's people in Canada had made sure to hunt down anyone with power from that coven. Other than that tiny little grouping hiding in their cave behind their wards. When Baile fell, and Goddess died, they would be hers as well.

The chanting increased in volume, drowning out the woman's cries as Rhiannon reached the altar.

Behind her stood Alexander's replacement. A useful man, but an idiot all the same. And he had no magic, but he had power in this modern world, and he was part of bringing Baile down.

Positioning herself behind the altar, she faced her faithful.

Her hair was brushed and shining and falling loose down her back. The diaphanous white gown she'd worn would reveal her form to them. She chose white because blood showed so beautifully against it. White for the truth. White for purity of purpose. White for her ascension to godhood.

She held up her hands, and the congregation fell silent.

The sacrifice continued to plead, her broken sobs the only sound in the expectant hush.

She drew her magic, clenching her teeth as the pain washed over her. The faithful must never see the pain blood magic caused, never entertain for a second the idea that she was fallible. Digging her nails into the hilt of the dagger, she raised it above her head. "Behold! The holy athame."

Her faithful prostrated themselves as they responded, "Behold."

Rhiannon forced her expression into the tender regard of a mother for her babe as she gazed down at the sacrifice.

Alexander's replacement stepped up and held the sacrifice's head still as she attempted to lash it from side to side.

Rhiannon placed a soft kiss on each cheek, each eyelid, and finally her forehead. "For your sacrifice, you will be forever remembered. We will speak your name with honor, and we will raise you to be revered amongst us."

"You twisted fucking bitch," the sacrifice screamed, brave now that she understood her pleading wouldn't sway them. "You fucking abomination of creation."

"Hush, now." Rhiannon placed a finger over her lips and pushed a tendril of power through her finger to seal her mouth shut. The woman had no sense of occasion, and she was ruining the mood.

"*Eas.*" Rhiannon made the first cut at the sacrifice's wrist. Blood swelled over the lip of the wound and covered the sacrifice's hand. Dipping two fingers into the flow, she anointed the foreheads to the two acolytes wearing the yellow of the air element. "We worship the dawn. We celebrate the spring. We make this sacrifice to the waning moon, and we live this as youth."

A hum broke out amongst her followers.

Blood already splattering the purity of her robe, Rhiannon moved down the woman's body to her groin and made her second cut. "*Deas,*" she called to the south and the fire element.

West followed, and blood flowed in a steady stream from the altar and was caught in a trough beneath it.

The sacrifice mewled softly, her life already draining from her.

With a cry, Rhiannon made the final cut at her neck.

Blood magic engulfed her, tearing at her sinews and muscles, ripping through her bone and viscera, so much stronger now, almost uncontrollable. Her body lifted in the air under its power, twisting and contorting as the magic protested her mastery. Her acolytes stood back, their eyes wide, mouths gaping as she wrestled with the power. So much of it. It was excruciating and exhilarating all at once. She felt as if it would rip her asunder, and she threw her head back and screamed.

Glass shattered as windows blew out. The altar flew across the hall into the assembled followers. Through her agony, she was dimly aware that they had begun to chant again. Their fervor gave her strength as she battled the magic into submission. It settled slowly into her, filling her with power, swelling inside her like she was a tick. She let it build until she could hold no more, and then she sent it winging for Baile in an oily, viscous mass.

CHAPTER TWENTY-SIX

Noah hated the necessary confinement to Baile and did his best to keep himself outside and running free. Fortunately, his lovely mate had no problem waving him off in his wolf form. He missed Zach and thought often of him with Rachel and Cole and the small number of survivors they'd managed to gather. The devastation to the coven sat heavily within him. So many good friends had died after the attack on the Canadian commune. Shifters and witches he'd grown up with, now gone.

He ran close to the wards as he patrolled the perimeter of Baile. They smelled more off than ever. It wasn't quite the blood magic stench, but they were definitely weaker than they had been yesterday. If he could prevent what had happened in Canada from happening here, he would fight to his last breath.

Alpha nudged his awareness, and he stopped running to pay better attention. Pack had found something. The image of two men stepping through the wards had him sprinting for Pack.

He quested for Niamh and sent her the alarm signal.

Aggression surged from Pack as they surrounded the two men. Alpha led the fight and Noah pushed himself to run faster.

His packmates were at risk, and he recognized what the wild wolves couldn't; those men were armed to the teeth.

When he reached Pack, the humans had taken the higher ground. Sitting atop a small outcropping, they fired down on the wolves. Noah demanded Pack submission, and Alpha ceded it to him. But he was already too late for one cream and gray wolf who lay panting and shot in the killing ground the humans had set in front of their position.

Noah forced the wolves back from direct confrontation and back into the shelter of sparse vegetation and boulders. Her blood in the air was making Pack harder to control. Desperate for their pack mate, they resisted his control, and it took all Noah's compulsion to get them to comply.

Niamh was coming, and that meant Warren with her.

Noah sent his compulsion to the injured wolf, demanding she lie still. In her pain and fear, she fought him briefly before submitting. He didn't know if the wolves here could use the land to heal like shifters did. Yes, he had been able to shift on Baile's demesne, but the magic here wasn't the same as it was on pack land.

Alpha slunk into position beside him, ears pricked, muscles tense, nose working the slight breeze for information.

Noah sent three wolves to circle right and stop the men from being able to slip back over the wards. Then he sent another three left. They had them contained, but if the wolves got within their sights, they were easy targets for the intruders.

One of the men stuck his head up over the rocks concealing him.

Noah smelled his fear but also his excitement of the hunt. The acrid tang of discharged weapons seared his nose.

As Warren drew closer, Noah sensed him slow down and creep forward.

Noah shifted to human to communicate with him.

"What's the situation?" Warren belly crawled into position beside him.

"Two intruders," Noah whispered. "They've positioned themselves atop that rise, under cover of those boulders." He pointed. "But not before they got one of ours."

"Shit," Warren hissed. "Emma, Mandla, and Jack are on their way."

"I've got wolves flanking them." Noah indicated left and right. "The fuckers don't know it yet, but they're trapped."

Warren tensed as Niamh slid into position between them.

"I told you to stay back," Warren hissed.

Niamh bared her teeth at him. "One of my wolves is hurt."

"I've compelled her to stay put," Noah said. "But you could reinforce that."

Niamh nodded and then turned to him. "She's not doing well. We need to get her back to Baile as soon as we can."

"Fuck." Noah had lost too many in the last few weeks. He refused to let another soul pass before he'd done everything he could to prevent that. "Can she use the land to help her heal?"

Niamh shook her head. "She doesn't have the same connection to the earth magic that you do."

Emma, Jack, and Mandla arrived so quietly Noah wouldn't have known they were there without his wolf senses.

"We've got two unfriendlies locked into position up there." He pointed. "They're surrounded and can't go anywhere, but we still need to get to them."

Mandla grunted and glared at the concealed gunmen. "Plan?"

"We get behind them," Emma whispered, scanning the terrain around her. "Warren, Jack, flank from the left." She tapped Mandla. "You and I go right." She looked at Noah. "Can you keep them distracted?"

"Do it." Noah shifted back to wolf.

Niamh tangled her fingers in his ruff and whispered in his ear, "You be careful, and take care of the other wolves."

He nudged her to let her know he had it.

Noah belly crawled closer to the gunmen's outcrop. His fur might camouflage him to a point. He compelled Alpha to stay back for the moment.

A head appeared above the boulder, froze and then a gun pointed his way.

Noah dashed left.

Gunfire erupted so close that bullets blew past his fur. He dived behind a rock. Bullets pinged against stone, and he ducked to avoid the flying rock chips.

Alpha nudged his mind, wanting to know what he wanted them to do.

Noah impressed on him the need for speed and what bullets could do and sent Alpha in the opposite direction from him.

Gunfire erupted around the streaking wolf, unearthing clod and grass at his feet. But Alpha made it to the safety of a small bush.

Noah eased back into sight of the gunmen.

"Over there," a man yelled. "That fucking wolf is just over there."

"They're everywhere," his friend yelled back.

Yes, they fucking were.

Noah compelled another wolf to duck in and out of sight as they played a lethal game of whack-a-mole with the gunmen. He hoped like hell Emma and the others did what they were planning quickly because it was only a matter of time before another pack member got hit.

The injured girl labored for breath, her mind a mess of pain and approaching death.

The rattle of a semi-automatic split the quiet as another wolf made itself briefly visible.

Noah took a moment to check in and was relieved when he got the all clear.

He caught the unmistakable tinge of excitement through the

wolves. Damn things thought this was a game and were kind of enjoying it. No amount of compulsion could override instinct, however, but he did try to impress on them again the danger of being hit.

He timed his next appearance with Alpha and split the gunmen's focus. They stayed on the periphery of the clear space in front of the intruder's position. To get caught out in the open meant a bullet for sure.

A man yelled, followed by a *thud* and the sounds of fighting.

Mandla stood up from behind the boulders with one of the attackers gripped by the nape, his feet barely touching the ground. In his other hand, Mandla had a weapon trained on the concealed man beside him.

The man rose from behind the rocks with his hands in the air.

Emma came up behind him and cold cocked him.

Noah shifted to human and dashed for the injured wolf. Scooping her up, he ran for Baile. The others could deal with the humans. He had a wolf to save.

Pack ran with him, and Noah leaned on his wolf's power to give him greater speed and endurance.

Rocks sliced into his human feet as he ran, but he didn't slow. Somehow, he had to win one life back from the fuckers that were threatening everything he loved.

Alpha urged him faster, and Noah pushed his legs. He wished he could have carried her in wolf form, but his human would have to do its best. He charged into the forest, branches catching at his arms and face as he powered through. Vegetation tangled around his ankles and cut flesh as he refused to let it slow him down. He arrived in the bailey with his lungs screaming at him, and his arms shaking from the wolf's weight.

Wolves streamed into the healer's hall ahead of him, reading his destination from their bond.

As he reached the doorway, Hannah leaped out of his way and motioned the refractory table. "Put her there."

Gently, Noah laid his precious charge on the table. His arms and chest were sticky with her blood and his sweat. "She's been shot."

"Shit, shit, shit." Hannah examined the wound. "I'm not a vet. Why am I not a fucking vet?"

Simon ran through from the ward end of the healer's hall. "My family are all vets. Let me have a look."

Alpha pressed into his thigh and Noah dropped to his knees beside the wolf. Pack surrounded him, pushing their bodies against his, desperate for the comfort of touch.

"The bullet is still in there," Simon said as he checked for an exit wound. "We need to get it out."

"We don't know anything about canine anatomy," Hannah said. "I don't even know how to sedate a wolf."

"Google it," Simon snapped. "We need to at least try."

"Jesus." Hannah snatched out her phone. "We could do more harm than good."

Bronwyn ran through from where she must have been sitting with Alexander. "Who's been shot?"

"One of mine." Noah tangled his fingers in Alpha's fur, drew the scent of pack deep inside him.

"Oh, no." Bronwyn covered her hand with her mouth. "No, no, no."

"Okay." Hannah looked up from her phone. "I found something that might help."

"Whatever it is, do it fucking fast," Noah snarled. He couldn't let that sweet girl go.

"No." Bronwyn stepped closer to the table and the wolf. "I can do this."

Hannah and Simon stared at her.

"My blessing doesn't rely on anatomy or species." Bronwyn put her hands on the wolf. "It will guide me as to what to do."

Hope stirred inside Noah.

Alpha whined, and Noah pressed his head into the wolf's ruff to reassure him.

"Are you sure?" Hannah blinked at Bronwyn.

"No." Bronwyn closed her eyes. "But unless we plan on abducting a vet within the next five minutes, I'm the best chance she's got."

Scents of honey and sage filled the healer's hall. Noah sensed the pull on water as it tingled through him.

The other wolves stirred as they sensed it with him.

A soft blue light lit Bronwyn's hands where they touched the wolf. She breathed deeply and pulled more water.

Noah's hackles rose, and he shook himself to clear the eerie sensation.

He felt Bronwyn's magic through the connection with the young female. It felt sticky and sweet like maple syrup being poured through her system. Her heartbeat strengthened, and her connection to life went from a faint flicker to a pulse and then a steady stream. Her life stream strengthened and grew until he knew she was going to be fine.

Simon handed him a set of scrubs, and he yanked them on.

Alpha eyed his clothing with disdain. He didn't understand Noah's pitiful lack of fur and was contemptuous of his need to provide himself with not-fur.

Bronwyn opened her eyes and smiled. "That was…interesting." She looked at Alpha as she spoke. "She's going to be just fine."

The female blinked her eyes open and rolled to her front. She shook her entire body and stood gingerly.

Noah lifted her off the table and put her back amongst Pack.

Wolves swarmed around her, nudging her, nuzzling her fur, rubbing muzzles and sniffing. Alpha yipped and Pack ran out of the healer's hall. It was their way. The danger was over, all was good, life went on.

Noah couldn't help smiling as he watched them go. Emotion clogged his throat as he met Bronwyn's eyes, and he had to clear it before he managed a hoarse, "Thank you."

"It's what I do." She shrugged. "And at least I could help one soul."

"Noah?" Warren stood in the doorway. "We have those two fuckers in the dungeons and Roderick wants to get some answers from them." He motioned Noah to join him. "I thought you might want to join us."

"We have dungeons?" Simon blinked at Warren.

Warren gave him a grim smile. "Apparently so, and Roderick is frighteningly delighted to put them to use."

CHAPTER TWENTY-SEVEN

Roderick had gone to the dungeons to interrogate the men, willing to do what it took to get his answers, only to find them lying dead on the floor, so now he stood in Dhara's chamber doorway waiting for the three girls clustered on the canopied bed to notice him. Baile had transformed the chamber into a haven of lavender and sparkles. A haven if one enjoyed lavender and sparkles, which his years of watching witches grow up had taught him was not uncommon amongst coven members of a certain age.

Dhara, Taylor, and Gemma had their heads together as they clustered amongst an explosion of cushions over a mobile phone. Roderick was still trying to understand electricity. Mobile phones, the internet, Wi-Fi, he took Andy at his word and trusted they worked, but electricity baffled him.

"Oh my god." Dhara giggled. "He is so, like, hot. Did you like his post?" She leaned forward on her knees. "You should totally follow him."

Gemma gave her a look of horror. "I can't do that. He'll think I'm stalking him."

"Dude!" Taylor rolled her eyes. "He has like three hundred

thousand followers. He's not even going to notice if you follow him."

Eyes shining, Gemma hugged the phone to her chest. "But imagine if he did notice."

Only half of what they chattered about was comprehensible to Roderick, but it made him smile anyway. Girls this age didn't change much over the centuries. They teetered on the edge of womanhood in a delightful and endearing mix of child and adult that was a constant challenge to navigate. He remembered Maeve at their age. She had never had many friends, and she'd been all big eyes and gangly legs and arms, blushing and scuttling away any time he drew near. There were many strange things to having lived a life as long as he had. One of those was watching a child turn into an adult and having to adjust your thinking around them to accommodate the change. Watching people outside of Baile age and die was another. It never failed to hurt when people slipped into the vale, and as the years passed, coven members tended to stick to their own for that reason.

Taylor noticed him and went bright red. She snatched a purple pillow to her chest. "Roderick."

The other two started and stared at the interloper.

He didn't come here often, but today he needed to speak with Goddess.

"Good afternoon." He greeted them with a nod. "I apologize for interrupting."

"That's okay." Taylor tucked her phone beneath her leg, and he pretended not to notice. "Did you need us?"

"I need to speak with Goddess." He turned his attention to Dhara. "Could you?"

"Oh." Dhara looked surprised. "Okay." She scrambled off the bed and came toward him. "I'll try, but I'm not sure I can, you know, call her up or anything."

Roderick stepped back to allow her to leave the room. "If you would try, I would be most grateful."

She stopped in the hall and frowned. "Where do you want to, like, do this?"

"Your choice." He didn't know if Dhara could summon Goddess at will either, and she needed to feel comfortable when she tried.

Dhara chewed her lip as she glanced around her. "Library?"

"Fine." The other girls didn't need to hear this discussion. Their reality was difficult enough as it was. Let them stay amongst their pretty things, safe and secure, for as long as they could. He followed Dhara to the library and was relieved to see it was empty. Shutting the door behind them, he waited.

Dhara closed her eyes and took a deep breath. When she opened them again, Goddess's silver gaze looked back at him. She smiled her wise, ancient smile. "Beloved."

"My lady." Roderick bowed. Goddess's presence filled the room and made the air weighty and sacred. "I would speak with you."

"Roderick." Goddess laughed like bells chiming. "You were always one for questions." Her face grew grave. "But you have always carried a heavy burden in service to me, so I will answer what I can."

"The wards are failing, my lady." He had only to close his eyes to hear, smell, and see the last coven attack. So many of his witches and brothers had fallen that day. The bailey had been bathed in their blood. Those young girls upstairs should never suffer what other girls, so many years ago, had endured. He did not think he had the strength to live through another massacre. "We captured two men who breached the wards earlier this morning."

"I am aware." She folded her hands before her. "My lost child readies her followers and paves the way for them."

The question burst out of him that he had never dared ask

before. But Goddess as part of Dhara made her seem more accessible. "Why? Why does she want to destroy you and everything you are?"

"It is her nature." Goddess's sadness was a palpable presence in the room. "I knew when I first called her how it would be."

Roderick didn't understand. "Then why not call another?"

"There is a bigger battle afoot, Beloved, and one that we are all destined to fight again and again. Evil will always battle good. Hate will always try to destroy love."

"You are saying we cannot win." The futility of such a task made him want to rage against her words.

"I am saying it is the nature of the world. It is the very essence of free will." Goddess made a graceful sweep of her arm to the view outside the window. "One thing cannot exist without the other. It is the living who have named them and given them meaning."

She was speaking in riddles now, and his irritation surged. "What does that mean?"

"It means that each soul must journey and learn. It must experience the fullness of existence before it can transcend."

"Transcend to what?"

She smiled. "That I cannot answer."

"Cannot or will not?"

"They amount to the same thing." She tilted her head and studied him. "Ask what you called me present to know."

Roderick battled his need for order into submission. He hated mysteries and garbled, veiled statements. He had survived this long by knowing what to put in which place in his mind. "The men we captured this morning died before we could question them, but they are undoubtedly sent by Rhiannon. I can only speculate as to purpose. We think she sent them to test the wards and see if she can get followers through them." Fear rose and fastened grisly fingers around his throat. "If two can pass, then it means more will follow."

"Yes." Goddess nodded, her face bearing no expression.

"They will overrun us." Her serenity infuriated him, and he had to force himself to remain calm and not bellow at her. They could all die. It could happen again.

Goddess inclined her head. "That is one of the possibilities, but you already knew that. Ask me, Beloved."

"We need your help." The words burst out of him. "We cannot possibly win without you."

"You have my help." She gestured to Baile around them. "I have given you my magic, Baile, the coimhdeacht abilities. I have given you all the tools. It is your purpose to wield those tools."

"It's not enough." He could not contain his fear and frustration. "Rhiannon has thousands to bring against us. She is stronger even than the last time she attacked this coven. There must be something you can do. You're Goddess."

She looked at him with pity. "I am life, Beloved."

"If she wins, she will end you."

"Yes." Goddess nodded and folded her hands. "It is her fate to be my counterbalance."

"My lady!" He paced, unable to contain the emotions boiling inside him. "If she ends you, what was it all for? Me? The coven? Magic? What was the fucking point of any of it?"

"Beloved!" Goddess glowed like she'd been lit from within. Her presence grew until it filled the library and forced him to his knees. "Have you learned nothing in all these years of life?"

Roderick couldn't stand, but the anger in him writhed to be free. "You are Goddess. You have the power to smite her."

"Yes." Her power bowed his neck. "But it is not what I am. I am life."

His confession was forced from him. "I am afraid. We cannot win."

"Yes." The pressure on his neck eased. "You are afraid. And that fear blinds you."

Her presence vanished, and he was able to stand again.

Dhara blinked back at him. "She's…really mad at you."

"Thank you." He had to leave the library before he broke something. Because he was angry with Goddess as well. All the years of faithful service, and he got no more than double speak and vague statements.

His feet drove into the stone of the great hall as he stalked to the barracks.

She was Goddess, for fuck's sake. She was the source of the magic all the witches used. He'd felt her power coursing through him on many occasions. He didn't understand why she remained passive when she could incinerate Rhiannon with a thought. It made no sense to him that she sat on the sidelines of the battle for her existence and watched with that all-knowing fucking smile on her face.

They'd activated the cardinal points, at her instruction, and only ended up making Rhiannon stronger than ever. As per Goddess's instructions, they'd created the enemy who would destroy her.

And he had no illusions they could stand in a fight against the sheer numbers Rhiannon had amassed. For the first time in all his years of service, he doubted. Why did she even incarnate if she wasn't going to act? Why had she brought him and Maeve into this time, only to have the sacred grove move on and render them useless? Why? Why? Fucking why?

"Roderick?" As he'd known she would, Maeve had followed him into the barracks.

He didn't bother to shield her from his fury, and she winced under the full assault of his emotions. "We will get no help from Goddess in the coming battle."

Maeve paled and leaned against the wall for support. "Then how can we hope to win?"

They couldn't, and he wished with all that he was that he had a different answer for her.

CHAPTER TWENTY-EIGHT

When you lived with a man inside your heart, mind, and soul, you got to know him. Niamh may not have been bonded to Warren for long, but she knew the current silence through their bond meant nothing good. As in nothing she would be happy about.

None of the castle animals had seen him in the past two hours. He better not be outside Baile, or she had a lecture and a bitch slapping with his name on it. She checked in with the wolves. Alpha did the mental equivalent of a dog that refused to meet your eye.

Oh, she was onto her coimhdeacht.

She brushed Noah's mind and found him singing Shania Twain on repeat. So, Warren had an accomplice.

Storming down the staircase, she crossed the great hall and shouted, "Andy?"

The property tax man turned Baile's jack-of-all-trades was the likeliest one to have some answers.

It was dangerous outside the wards, bloody hell. Warren should know better than to go traipsing all over the place without telling her.

"Niamh." Andy appeared in his office doorway, polishing his glasses on a small black cloth. "Did you need something?"

"Yes." She tried to get a read on his energy. As a human animal, Niamh had some sensitivity to people's moods and energies. And oh yes, he knew something all right. Andy gave good face, but he was hiding something. "I want to know where Warren is."

"Warren?" Andy made a great show of replacing his glasses. He folded his polishing cloth into neat quarters before sliding it into his pocket. "Is he not with you?"

Niamh gave him her best don't-bullshit-a-bullshitter stare. "Would I be asking you if he was?"

"No." Andy tittered. "Of course you wouldn't." His face arranged itself into a regretful expression. "But I'm afraid I can't help you."

"Can't or won't?" She caught his inner squirming like a trout on a hook. Never having been much for verbal gymnastics, she stepped closer to him. "You know where he is, don't you?"

"Now, Niamh—"

"Don't you?"

Debra came up behind Andy. "Hello, Niamh. Are you looking for Warren?"

She and Debra would have words if she was part of this bloody cone of silence. That they wouldn't tell her made her worry even more. "I am."

"Do you know where he is?" Debra drew abreast of Andy and looked at him.

Andy's gaze bounced everywhere but meeting Niamh's. "I can't be sure."

"And Noah is with him." Niamh cut through another layer of crap. "Who else?"

"I don't know." And this time he was telling the truth. Her connection to Noah's wolf was teaching her how to read scent, and this time Andy was telling the truth. He sighed and his expression turned pleading. "They asked me not to say."

"Who asked you not to say?" Debra folded her arms and scowled at him. Clearly, also not a fan of being kept out of the know.

Andy groaned and shoved his hands in his pockets. "I told them I wouldn't be able to lie to you if you asked."

"Andy?" Hermione appeared behind his other shoulder and poked him in the ribs. "Tell us everything."

His face crumpled. "But I—"

Debra poked his other ribs. "Every. Thing."

WARREN ENVIED Noah's ability to move without making a sound as he slid along beside Emma in his wolf form. Noah's nose worked the breeze for information constantly. Stumbling along beside him, Warren felt like a clumsy oaf.

Just ahead of them, Emma raised her fist and motioned him down.

Warren crouched beside her. She pointed right, and then at her chest, then motioned his chest and left.

Unlike when they'd visited Alexander's old manor before, it looked quiet. The detritus and furniture had been cleared from the exterior. Warm squares of light shone from every window on both levels of the two-story house, but no loud voices broke the silence.

When Noah joined him, Warren didn't know whether to be insulted or flattered.

Then again, Emma got absorbed by the night like a shadow. Good call on Noah's part.

Stopping in the shadows beside the French doors leading to the kitchen, Warren waited for Noah to scent.

Three women sat around the kitchen table chatting and sharing a meal.

It looked normal and innocuous. Only the stench of blood magic hanging around the manor clued them in on how far from normal this was.

Doubling back, Warren skirted the light cast through the doors and came up on the other side. He slunk closer to the doorjamb, hoping to hear something.

"Are you going to eat that?" a woman asked.

"No, I'm full." Cutlery clinked. "Do you want it?"

A chuckle. "Go on then. Give it over."

"Aren't you on a diet?" the third woman asked.

"Yeah." A giggle. "But you know I can never stick to those sodding things."

Riveting stuff, but Warren moved on, staying close to the wall and under the window ledges.

Noah nudged the small of his back.

Warren kept moving until he came to a larger set of windows. He wished he could risk peering over the edge. He didn't know the layout of the house, and he could be anywhere, but given the location of the kitchen, he guessed a living or dining room.

Noah jerked his head toward the window. He wanted Warren to peek inside.

Oh bugger! But the wolf wanted him to see something enough to risk discovery.

Spine against the wall, Warren eased up beside the window.

A *thud* like flesh hitting flesh sounded, followed by a woman's cry.

"Christ, Jason," a man said. "She'll fucking kill you if you damage them."

"I'm not damaging nothing," another man replied, presumably Jason. "But these bitches are getting mouthy."

Noah's eyes flashed iridescent, and his lip peeled off his two-inch canines.

Jason yelled, "Aren't you, bitch!"

A woman whimpered.

Noah's low, menacing growl made Warren's hair stand on end.

"Jason!" the first man snapped. "We're just supposed to give them something to eat and then lock them up again."

"You're a fucking wimp," Jason said. "Besides, she doesn't care what we do to them. It's only their blood she wants." A *thud*. "Remember that, you stupid Canadian cunt, next time you give me lip."

"Jason!"

A woman cried out.

"Shut the fuck up!"

Warren edged around the window far enough to see inside.

Four men stood in the dining room. Two with their backs to him. Another, medium height, slim build, near an interior door. The biggest man in the room loomed over a cowering woman tied to a chair.

A trickle of blood ran down the woman's chin. She looked to be midthirties, with a sweet, round face and curly, brown hair.

The big bastard grabbed a fistful of her hair and yanked her head back. "You better be nice to us." He leaned down and laughed in her face. "Because as long as we don't spill your blood, we can do anything we want with you."

Noah pressed against his thigh, his growl reverberating through Warren. Warren grabbed the fur at his nape to warn him to be quiet.

The captive woman stared at Jason through terror-glazed eyes.

Pushing down his answering pulse to exact vengeance, Warren took in the rest of the room. Another five women huddled on the floor with their hands behind their backs. They were watching Jason with horror. One of the women, not much more than a girl, had silent tears tracking down her face.

The man near the door moved his way, and Warren jerked back into the shadows. He crouched down beside Noah and whispered, "You know the women?"

Noah bobbed his head.

"Fuck!" Indecision snarled Warren's thinking. They were on a reconnaissance mission, nothing more. "From Canada?"

Noah bobbed his head again.

Those poor bloody women were from Noah's commune. Fuck, fuck, fuck. It went against everything in him to leave them there.

"We need more information," he whispered to Noah.

Noah bared his canines but slunk to the next window.

Following him, Warren couldn't help but wonder what Emma had found on the other side of the house. There were three of them against Goddess alone knew how many inside. If they went in now, they'd be announcing their presence.

"Reconnaissance," he whispered, both for his and Noah's benefit. "I promise to Goddess we're not leaving them there. We'll be back, you can bet your furry ass on that."

He forced his brain to chew the information methodically. So, Rhiannon had brought those witches from Canada. She must be planning to use their blood for their magic. It's the only reason she wouldn't have killed them in Canada.

Samhain was four days away now. *Four days*, he silently promised the women inside that house. *We'll get you out before then*.

The next window showed a group of about ten sitting around in armchairs. A knot of six bound women sat in the middle of the living room.

A woman picked up a slice of meat from her plate and threw it at one of the captives. "Catch!"

The captive tried to duck, but it hit her on the side of the face and stuck.

The fuckers sitting around all laughed.

Noah tensed and raised his head. His nose twitched as he absorbed all he could. Warren would have to wait until he was human again to hear what he'd discovered.

From the far side of the house, an owl hooted, and Noah nudged him.

Emma had signaled their retreat.

Warren risked one more peep into the living room to find the game of throwing food at the captives was still ongoing.

Motherfuckers would pay, and those witches would be saved. Rhiannon wouldn't take their blood and their lives. Even as he made his vow, he recognized the irony. They might be saving those women only long enough to grant them a small reprieve before Rhiannon hit Baile and all of them could die.

As they slunk away from the house, Noah looked back several times as if he shared Warren's inner tussle over walking away and leaving those poor women behind.

Christ, if he had his way, Warren would blast in there and rain fucking holy hell on their heads. If he had his way, Rhiannon would be fertilizing the soil by now. Although, he doubted any self-respecting weed would deign to feed on that rotting bitch.

Emma appeared beside them so suddenly she startled him. She jerked her head and motioned them back to the churchyard.

A good twenty-minute walk, winding through houses and residential streets, saw them back at the village green. The party was going stronger than ever. Music pounded from a makeshift setup near the venerable old oaks in the center of the green. People laughed, chattered, danced, groups of twos and threes, and even fours making out as if they weren't in the middle of a crowd.

Where were those stupid coppers now? Sitting on their fat asses, sipping cups of tea, and dunking their Rich Teas in it.

They skirted the edge of the crowd, Noah sticking close to the shadows.

The wards brushed over Warren, and he let out a long, slow breath. "Fuck!"

"What did you see?" Emma pushed her black hood back.

They both winced and did their best to ignore the wet cracking noises as Noah shifted.

"They're holding Canadian witches," Warren ground out. "I counted twelve, but those were only the ones I could see."

Noah shoved his legs into a pair of sweats. "They weren't all Canadian. One of the witches in the living room smelled like Nofoto."

"Regardless." Emma looked grim. "We can all guess what the plan is for them."

Noah disappeared beneath a hoodie, and then his head popped out. "We're getting them out."

"Bloody right we are." Warren shared a hard look with Noah before turning to Emma. "What did you find out?"

"I counted another four witches on my side of the house, but they were speaking like there could be more in the bedrooms. I also heard mention of Samhain and a big plan."

That made sense, and Warren nodded. "Pretty much what Roderick suspected."

"They all know about the two bastards that got across the wards." Emma turned and led the way down into the church crypts. "They think it's funny as hell."

"Anything about Rhiannon?" Warren watched his footing on the lichen and moss encrusted stairs.

"The odd mention." Emma vanished into the darkness of the crypt. "But I got the sense she was around."

"Same." With his coimhdeacht enhanced sight, Warren had no trouble navigating the darkness.

When they reached the tunnel entrance, Emma murmured a quick spell and the rock grated open.

They took the tunnels at a fast jog, all conversation suspended for now. Jack, Mandla, and Roderick would be waiting to hear their report.

Emma stepped into the caverns and stopped.

Warren and Noah narrowly avoided rear-ending her.

A welcoming party was waiting for them; Niamh, Sinead, Alannah, and Mags. And they did not look happy.

"You've been to the village." Niamh's dark gaze bored into him. "You snuck out to the village without telling me." She pointed an accusing finger at him. "And this after making me promise I wouldn't pull that shit."

Damage control was clearly needed. "I'm sorry." He held his arms out in supplication. "We went on a reconnaissance mission. We need information."

"You should have told me." Mags scowled at Emma. "And the reason you didn't tell me was because you knew I'd object."

Emma went stony-faced and fixed her gaze somewhere over Mags's left shoulder. "It was on a need-to-know basis."

"And you wolf-boy?" Sinead tapped her toe. "What have you got to say for yourself?"

"Look." Noah drew his shoulders back. "We're outgunned, outmanned, and outmagicked. We need information." He grabbed Sinead by the hips and drew her against him. "Were you worried about me, sweet thing?"

"Don't sweet thing me." Sinead gave a halfhearted attempt to wrestle free. "I'm angry with you."

"I'm fine, sweet thing." Noah nuzzled her neck. "I'm good at sneaking around." He raised his head and smirked at her. "Wolf-boy, remember?"

"You…" Sinead narrowed her eyes and sputtered something incomprehensible, but a small smile played around her mouth.

That approach seemed to be working for Noah, and Warren took a step closer to Niamh.

"Nope." She folded her arms and glared at him. "Try it, and lose a body part."

Worth the risk, so Warren pulled her into his arms. "How come it works for him?"

"He's cuter than you." Niamh stiffened in his hold, but Warren could feel her unbending toward him through their bond.

He pretended to study Noah. "Nah." He shook his head. "He's just furrier."

"Well." Emma rolled her eyes. "I'm guessing their approach won't work on you, will it?"

Mags shook her head and then laughed. "You're at a distinct disadvantage." She tucked her arm through Emma's. "But we were all worried about you."

"We know that." Emma leaned her head against Mags's. "But we were extremely careful, and we can't sit here waiting for Rhiannon's next move. We need to plan, prepare for her."

"Okay." Mags folded like a cardboard boat. "But you need to tell me next time you plan something like this."

Emma made a maybe face. "I can promise to tell you what we found out."

"I'm still angry with you," Niamh grumbled.

"Let's call a meeting." He tucked her against his side and wrapped his arm around her deliciously curved waist. "And then you can be angry with me over some of Roderick's excellent single malt."

CHAPTER TWENTY-NINE

Kate hung up her call to Dhara and stared out the SUV window at the forest creeping past. The rough terrain had necessitated a crawling pace.

"How is she?" Zach indicated her phone.

She had finally unwound herself from him and sat next to him behind the driver. Margo drove while one of her men had taken the passenger seat. Two more military types were seated in the rear seats. Another four SUVs crammed with capable looking soldierly people completed their convoy. They weren't taking any chances that some of Rhiannon's followers were still combing the forest for witches, and the presence of their small army comforted Kate. They made Zach twitchy. He'd rather rely on wolves than humans. "She's fine," she said, but that was not strictly true.

Zach raised an eyebrow at her.

Damn wolf could smell a lie, even one that was more evasion than outright untruth. "She sounds stressed and like she's trying not to let me know she is."

"There's trouble at Baile?"

Margo met her eye through the rearview mirror. "There's

trouble everywhere there are witches right now. The South African witches have gone into hiding." Her expression grew troubled. "What we can locate of them have, anyway. Sasha managed to get our people in Russia to safety without too much damage."

Zach stiffened. "And Baile?"

"Forces gathering." Margo tightened her grip on the wheel as they navigated through a rockier section. Rocks thudded and scraped against their undercarriage. "We suspect that's where they have your missing witches."

That would make a horrible sort of sense. Rhiannon would need witch blood, closest to where she needed blood magic. "The Baile coven are expecting an attack on Samhain."

"Four days away," Margo murmured. "Lots of extra power hanging around for her to use."

Conflict roiled inside Kate. After their parents had died, mainly she'd raised Dhara, been responsible for her, and now she'd left her little sister in a different country. She couldn't think of any of the reasons coming back here had felt so necessary. Not with Dhara sitting smack dab in the middle of a storm about to break.

Zach took her hand and threaded their fingers together. "Hey." His voice softened to a warm rasp. "She's in the best place for her."

She hated how much she loved Zach's hand holding hers. It annoyed her how much his touch and his reassurance meant to her. He'd told her she was his mate when she'd been in her early twenties, and she'd been running away from the possibility ever since.

Zach was too much—too domineering, too take charge, too intense, and too tempting. He would swallow her entire iden-tity, and for someone who had spent her adult years protecting her sister and an entire commune of witches, that felt like the worst kind of danger.

And she didn't trust him. Zach went through women faster than Abe, and that was saying a lot. He kept it on the down low, but Kate had made a habit of watching him since that surprise mate pronouncement.

"Is she really in the best place?" She tugged her hand out of his grip and immediately felt bereft. "The main attack looks like it's happening there."

Zach's golden wolf eyes saw straight into her soul, as if he understood her struggle with him. She hated that too—the endless fucking patience in him, as if it was only a matter of time before she folded. "If Baile falls, we all fall," he said. "If Baile falls, and Goddess with her, we lose control of magic."

"True." And Dhara was Goddess, apparently. Her head hurt, and she rubbed the spot between her eyes to alleviate some of the pressure.

Zach cupped her nape in his warm palm. "It's not hopeless, Katy." His strong fingers worked with his words to ease some of the tension in her neck. "We have to keep believing that."

"Right." Because the alternative was too awful to contemplate. Desperate to change the subject, she pointed to the shadowy figures flitting through the trees. "Do they follow you everywhere?"

"They stick closer now." His thumb worked at the knot of tension at the base of her skull. "They've even been coming in from other areas of the country."

"Wow." Since Zach had appeared at the commune, she'd almost grown used to having the wolves around. Almost, but the human in her still had an instinctive fear of an apex predator. "And they all listen to you?"

A rare smile flitted across his face. "More or less." He shrugged. "They're wolves, so dominance challenges are pretty much a constant."

"Have you ever fought one?" Talking about wolves helped

alleviate her nagging worry about Dhara, about all of them. "I mean, as a wolf."

"It wouldn't be a fair fight." He watched the wolves. "I'm bigger and stronger and more strategic."

Of course he was. Kate barely refrained from rolling her eyes.

"Stop it." His low rumble was half growl and sexy as fuck. "You don't hate me nearly as much as you like to believe."

The confession escaped before she could edit it. "I don't hate you at all."

"Good to know." His eyes gleamed. "It's a starting point."

But to what? Kate couldn't see herself settling down to be a nice little Alpha mate. The whole submission thing made her twitch. She leaned forward to speak to Margo. "Are we nearly there?"

"Almost." Margo had the steering wheel in a death grip.

Zach's hand drifted down her spine in a featherlight touch that she felt through every firing neuron. "You should be able to feel the wards."

Closing her eyes, Kate quested with her magic. She pulled water from the damp earth and the vegetation. A nearby stream gave her an extra boost, and then she felt them. And she smiled as the wash of cré-magic seeped into her, different but the same as what she felt at Baile. "It's beautiful."

"Right." Warmth crept into Zach's voice. "Pure."

And in the midst of the shitshow all around them, Kate felt a flicker of happiness and hope. They still had magic.

She concentrated on the magic as they drew closer to it. It filled her parched spirit, like tart, sweet lemonade on the hottest day. "And Cole found this place?"

"Yeah." Zach's deft fingers worked at the tension in her spine. "He was determined to make us come this way." He dug his thumb into a bad spot. "I had my doubts, but he was right."

She should have told him to stop, but it felt so damn good. "And there's a Goddess pool as well?"

"Goddess isn't there anymore." He huffed. "Obviously, but you can still feel resonances of her." His chuckle almost made her smile again. "And now it makes a great bathing pool."

"Seems almost disrespectful." She wanted to lean into the magic of his fingers.

"It's hot, it's clean, and it's peaceful," Zach murmured. "Kinda romantic."

"You're flirting." And she wished he'd stop. It made him that much harder to resist.

"Sorry," he said, sounding anything but. He lowered his voice to a husky whisper. "You're my mate, Katy. I can't stop wanting…things from you."

His mate. Two words that resonated through her chest and spread down to her core, leaving warm tingles in their wake. She was willing to bet he could smell that as well, and she squirmed. "Don't make me Cesar Milan your furry ass."

"Maybe I like when you Cesar Milan my furry ass." Leaning forward, he nipped her earlobe. He smelled of pine needles, earth, and musk. "Maybe I like how you challenge me."

She'd always done it as a way to annoy him, but a far more intriguing possibility had arisen. "Do you?"

Those eyes glowed like molten ore. "You took half of me when you left." For once, his expression wasn't guarded, and he let her see his need for her. "I'm tired of playing games, Katy. They're such a pointless fucking waste of time we might not have."

She'd been resisting him for so long it had become habit. Not giving in to Zach had become so consuming, it hadn't given her space to question her reasons. His words stripped her defenses and left her reasons bared to scrutiny. What if they could be equals, partners? What if the mate bond didn't mean her complete and utter submission?

Zach held her gaze, allowing her to search his face for answers. "I know you're frightened," he said. "I know you feel like giving in to the bond feels liking handing over all control of yourself."

She didn't bother to conceal her surprise. "You do?"

"And I'm a dominant wolf." He shrugged. "I can't help but take control."

"You're the most dominant wolf." She felt the need to point that out. Dominance to the maximum power of infinity.

"Give me a chance, Katy." He leaned his forehead against hers. "Give us a chance." His breath was hot on her mouth. "I just want to know what it's like to hold my mate before I lose the chance forever."

"Kate?" Margo's tone was soft and apologetic. "Sorry to interrupt, but we're here."

Wards brushed Kate's awareness, followed by the most profound sense of peace. She dragged her attention away from Zach.

They were in a small clearing. As the SUV came to a stop in front of a cave opening, two of the children from the former commune, Misty and Isaac stopped the game they were playing and stared.

"It grew." Zach motioned the cave entrance. "When we first arrived, it was just a hole in the ground."

Rachel strode out of the cave and opened the door before Kate could. "Kate." She held out her arms. "Welcome back."

Tall, with ruffled dark hair and a tentative smile, Cole followed Rachel. He stood back while she hugged Rachel, and then Zach and Rachel greeted each other.

"You're back." Kate addressed the elephant in the clearing with Cole. He'd left the commune five years ago, following the death of his younger brothers. Angry and grief-stricken, Cole had sworn never to touch magic or come near the commune again.

Cole nodded and shoved his hands in his jean's pockets. "I'm back."

"I'm glad." Kate wanted to hug him but didn't know if he'd welcome her embrace.

Cole's serious face split into a beautiful grin. "Me too."

"Oh, for shit's sake." Rachel thumped Cole's shoulder. "Hug already and get it over with."

"So profound." Cole rolled his eyes but stepped closer to Kate and opened his arms.

Kate would take all the hugs she could get.

Inside, the cave took Kate's breath away. It looked like the caverns of Baile, with crystal sigils decorating the walls and ceilings. Soft, colored light from the crystals filled the cave like light reflecting off a disco ball.

Corrie walked in from a small corridor with Sage in her arms. "Kate?" She gave a smile, which didn't quite reach her eyes. "Welcome home."

"Thank you."

"Sara and Abe are hunting," Rachel said. "We try to keep our need to go near civilization to a minimum. Cole has been working with earth to grow our produce."

"Now?" In a few weeks, the ground would be blanketed in snow and frozen several feet down.

"This cave gets freaky." Rachel wrinkled her nose. "A sort of cave greenhouse thing manifested itself, and he's using that."

The cave really was like Baile, adapting itself to the needs of its residents.

"We even have coffee," Cole motioned them to a small seating area toward the back of the cave. "Zach made a run back to the commune and got as much furniture as he could, and the cave makes the rest of what we need."

A small kitchen had been set up near the seating area.

Kate's heart twisted at the sight of a few pieces of her grandmother's china in the assortment of stuff on the shelves.

Cole read her mind as he said, "Unless you feel the need for something stronger."

"Definitely." Kate took it all in with a sense of unreality. They'd somehow made a home for themselves in this cave. Cole and Corrie were the only surviving adult witches, other than the ones they suspected were at Baile. Three children and four shifters made up the rest of this tiny community. Grief pressed down on her as Cole handed her something in a glass that smelled like moonshine. Two hundred witches and thirty shifters had made up the destroyed commune, and this was all that was left.

Zach took a seat and pulled her to him.

She let him position her on his lap, the only place that felt truly safe.

"We'll rebuild, Katy," he said. "Together."

CHAPTER THIRTY

Maeve stood back and studied Dhara. Even when the teenager was dominant, Dhara certainly appeared to have access to Goddess's memories. Maeve asked, "How much do you know of the witches the sigils represent?"

"It's weird, you know." Walking around the caverns, trailing her fingers over the sigils, Dhara wrinkled her nose. "I kind of get these flashes, and I can feel other emotions inside me."

Maeve tried to imagine what that would be like. Weird was the right word for it.

"Tell me about the witches." Maeve motioned the sigils Dhara touched.

Dhara's face lit up. "Really?"

"Yes." Sadness pressed at Maeve. "Since the grove disappeared, I am no longer able to walk with them."

Grimacing in sympathy, Dhara said, "Do you miss the sacred grove?"

"Sort of." Maeve had never had to face that question. The sacred grove had always been there. Up until very recently. "You know, when I first practiced my blessing, I used to resent it for the way it isolated me from the other witches." Her loneliness had ended the day Roderick had bonded her—although she hadn't been exactly thrilled at the time. More confused than anything else. "But being able to walk the grove made me special as well, and I suppose I miss that."

"Right." Dhara nodded and chuckled. "Like loving what makes you unique and being lonely about being unique."

Well, Dhara would know a lot about being unique. It was to be expected she understood how Maeve had felt. First, she'd been carrying the earth point inside her since she was born. Now, she carried an even greater responsibility. "Are you settling in here?" Despite being Goddess incarnate, she was also a fifteen-year-old girl. "I mean, without Kate."

"Yeah." Dhara smiled but with a tinge of sadness behind it. "I miss Kate a lot. But everybody here has been very welcoming and kind, and I know I am where I need to be." She shrugged. "Noah always says: little bit of column A, little bit of column B."

"That's good." Maeve chuckled. "I'll need to remember that."

Dhara cocked her head and studied Maeve. "And you? It must be weird to go to sleep in one age and wake up in an entirely different one."

"It was." Maeve still stumbled over differences and lack of knowledge. "For one thing, the technology of this age is way beyond anything I could ever have imagined."

Dhara widened her eyes and exhaled. "Right?! I mean, you guys didn't even have like the steam engine."

"Nope." It constantly amazed Maeve how humans could be so imaginative and inventive, yet still replay the same bad habits again and again. It was like one part of their species had outstripped the development of the other. She found it sad. Intolerance, hatred, bigotry, pettiness, selfishness—those things had barely changed. "I think the biggest change for me was the way women are treated now."

"Really?" Dhara dropped to the floor and crossed her legs. "Like we have rights now and stuff."

"There is that." Maeve had never vocalized her thoughts, so she sorted them into order. "I notice it more in the way women think about themselves. The dreams you have, and the ambitions you pursue."

"But you were a witch," Dhara pointed out. "Didn't you, like, have different rules?"

"Absolutely." Maeve touched the sigils beside Dhara. Her fingertips tingled, but the grove was gone. "We had far more freedom than mundane women outside Baile. I was born in the coven, but other women joined when they were a bit older." She was glad girls like Dhara, Taylor, and Gemma hadn't grown up to see themselves as nothing more than a vessel to a man's ambition. "It would always take those witches a while to learn that they were not chattel here."

"Chattel?"

"A belonging, like a piece of land or a cow." She loved that Dhara had to ask what the word meant.

Dhara rolled her eyes. "That is so screwed up."

"It was." Maeve motioned outside of the caverns. "But the women outside of Baile were not so lucky. They dealt with abusive men, restrictive religion, having themselves defined by how many children they had—that sort of thing." Life had been harder, tougher, and a lot grimier. "I like showers."

"Showers?" Dhara laughed.

Maeve smiled back. "Don't judge until you've lived without one."

"Fair enough." Dhara stretched her legs out as if settling in for a chat. "What else do you like about this time?"

"Maeve?" Mags called from the cavern entrance.

Maeve sent a quick wishful prayer that Mags didn't bring more bad news. "In here," she called back.

"Maeve." Mags's cheeks were pink, and she was breathing hard.

Maeve's chest clenched. "What is it?"

"It's Roderick." Mags motioned her to come, caught sight of Dhara and smiled. "Hi, Dhara."

For a second, Maeve forgot to breathe. She couldn't bear it if something had happened to Roderick. A quick check of their bond reassured her that he was well. It also gave her an inkling of why Mags was here. "He's angry," she said.

"You should come." Mags screwed up her face in concern. "Before they tie him up and lock him in the dungeons."

"It's Alexander," Dhara said as she stood and dusted sand off her jeans. "Roderick is so worried about him that it makes him grumpy."

"Yes, well." Mags made a face. "He moved past grumpy to borderline ragey about ten minutes ago."

Maeve had never thought Roderick-tamer would be part of her bond with him. It did give her a thrill that she could calm him down though. Sometimes just her presence would do the trick. She led Mags and Dhara out the caverns. "Well, let's go and see what he's up to now."

"He's in the barracks." Mags trotted to draw abreast of her. "And he's giving the other coimhdeacht hell. Jack sent me to get you before Emma loses her temper with him."

That would not go well, and Maeve quickened her pace. Maeve was tempted to thump Roderick herself. He'd been irascible and impossible to reason with the last day or so. Maeve suspected the root lay in his conversation with Goddess, which he wouldn't share with her.

They hurried into the castle and took the corridor to the barracks.

Mags stopped suddenly and gasped.

Narrowly avoiding treading on her heels, Maeve turned to see what Mags was reacting to.

Face alight with wonder, Mags stood in front of one of the tapestries adorning the corridor.

Moving closer, Maeve peered at the image and tried to discover what had Mags so transfixed. "What is it, Mags?"

"The dragon." Mags pointed, her eyes the opaque of when she had a vision. "The dragon will rise."

"The dragon?" Maeve studied the tapestry. Typical for the tapestries in this part of Baile, it was a battle scene. Baile was depicted in the foreground, and above her, wings spread, flew a dragon. Maeve had always assumed the artist had taken some creative license with the scene.

Dhara leaned in and whispered, "Are there dragons coming?"

"No." Mags shook her head. "The dragon is already here."

Instinctively, Maeve looked around her, and then wanted to thump herself for being so stupid. Of course there wasn't a dragon squatting in the corridor.

"Again!" Roderick's voice drifted down the corridor.

But there was a dragon in the practice yards, and he was hers to beard in his den. The part of St. George would now be played by Maeve.

Dhara hurried to keep up with her. "Are there dragons here?"

"Ask Goddess," Maeve said, as Roderick shouted something else. His tone had her quickening her pace to a jog.

The other coimhdeacht were all gathered in the practice yards with Roderick in the middle bearing his sword. "Again." He jabbed his sword at the one lying on the ground between him and Warren.

Emma folded her arms and glowered at him.

Mandla looked a hairsbreadth away from snatching up the sword and having a go at Roderick himself.

Even Warren was showing signs of fraying temper as he took a very careful breath, bent, and picked up the sword. "Roderick," he said through clenched teeth. "How is this helping?"

"You need to be prepared." Roderick's face was a mask of fury.

"With a sword?" Mandla sneered.

"Sword fighting is the basis of coimhdeacht training." Roderick turned his ire on Mandla. "It's about discipline and reflexes."

"Bullshit," Emma snapped. "This is about you being pissed off that we went on a reconnaissance mission without telling you."

Roderick's eyes narrowed, and he peeled his top lip back in a snarl. "An unsanctioned reconnaissance mission."

Oh dear. That would be putting Roderick in a temper. He was far too used to leading the coimhdeacht and having them follow his every order. The new generation were far too free thinking to be ordered about like cattle.

"And who exactly should we get to sanction our missions?" Emma stepped into Roderick's space.

At almost a foot taller, Roderick towered over Emma, but she didn't back down an inch.

Roderick thumped his chest. "I am the first coimhdeacht."

"We know that." Warren stepped closer to the glaring pair. "And we respect your position, but you're not exactly in a good place to be making decisions for the coven."

Roderick whirled on him. "What did you say?"

"He said you're being a dick," Emma said.

Mandla chuckled and settled in to enjoy the show.

Catching sight of them, Jack took a relieved breath. "Nobody wanted to go over your head, Roderick." Jack spread his hands in a placating gesture. "You've got other things to deal with right now. We just thought—"

"What did you just think?" Roderick rounded on him.

Maeve had heard enough to see where this was heading. "Roderick?"

"Maeve." He spun to look at her. Glaring at her as he did. "What are you doing here?"

"Mags came to find me." She stepped between Warren and Roderick, giving Warren a reassuring smile.

Roderick's scowl deepened. "This is not your place."

Stopping in her tracks, Maeve had to take a minute for her brain to catch up with her hearing. What had he said? "I beg your pardon."

"What Roderick meant was—"

"Thank you, Warren." She patted Warren's chest. She didn't need his intervention with her thick-skulled coimhdeacht. Glaring up at him, she said, "Repeat what you said. I dare you."

Color climbed Roderick's collar to his cheeks. "You heard me. We are training here."

Mandla whistled and strode from the practice yard. "Good luck, brother," he murmured to Roderick as he passed. "You're gonna need it."

"Give him hell," Emma said.

"Bad move." Jack shook his head as he followed Emma.

And they were alone. Just her and Roderick glowering at each other. "Maeve." Roderick's jaw clenched, and he forced words out. "All I meant was that this is no place for a witch. The coimhdeacht need to train. There is danger coming—"

"You." She needed an outlet for her anger while she organized her thoughts into words, and she jabbed her forefinger into his chest. "Need to listen to me."

"Maeve—"

"Listen!"

He snapped his mouth shut and scowled at her.

"There is enough tension around us." She punctuated her words with a few more jabs. His hard chest hurt her finger, but she had no intention of stopping. "What this coven does not need is you bringing that tension inside these walls."

He caught her finger and held it. "They are not prepared for what's coming."

"And how will shouting and being impossible with them

change that?" She could see by the mulish set of his jaw that he was entrenching himself further in his pigheadedness. Well, she had two hands, and since he'd taken control of her one finger, she used the other. "And they are trained and capable. Far more capable of taking on the danger of this time than you, in fact."

Thunder clouds brewed and boiled in his pale blue eyes.

"They made a decision and took an action without you."

He caught her other hand and held it.

But Maeve was far from done. "Get over it." She returned his scowl with one of her own. "And if you'd stop being so bloody stubborn, you would recognize that reconnaissance, although dangerous, is what we need. We need to try to find out what Rhiannon is up to."

"They should have told me," he grumbled, not quite looking her in the eye.

Maeve snorted. "I can see why they didn't."

"Maeve." He had the gall to look injured. "I am not useless to this coven. I am not a child to be put in a corner and kept quiet."

"No." Her anger eased, and she softened her tone. "But you are a father who is desperately worried about his son. And you have seen what happens when the wards are breached, and you'd do anything to prevent that from happening again."

The fight bled out of him. His gaze lost its manic glitter, and his shoulders slumped. "I keep seeing them," he whispered. "Every time I close my eyes, I see the blood and the dead bodies in the bailey. I see them over and over again. If I have to be hard to make sure these coimhdeacht live, then that's what I need to do."

"I was there too." And she understood. As the danger escalated, Maeve had been thinking more and more about that awful night of the massacre. "And I am as frightened as you are."

His chin came up. "I am not frightened."

"Yes, you are." She cupped his obstinate chin and forced him to look at her. "We all are." Lowering her voice, she stepped close enough to feel heat radiating from his large chest. "Work with them, Roderick. Work with them to save all of us."

He stared at her for a long moment, struggle still happening in his eyes, and then he murmured, "There's more."

"Tell me." And Maeve knew they'd come to the heart of the matter.

"I keep seeing him." Roderick drew a ragged breath. "My son. I keep seeing all the times I tried to kill him. All the times we fought." He dropped his head. "So much time wasted on being enemies, and now…"

"Now you could lose him," Maeve whispered. Roderick would not respond well to platitudes about how everything would be fine. "What do you always say to me when I feel hopeless?"

He frowned. "I say a lot of things."

"Trust in Goddess." She pressed her forehead to his chest. "You always tell me to trust in Goddess."

His big chest heaved as he drew a deep breath in and let it go. Then he whispered a fear that she would never have thought to hear, "But what if I can't? What if I no longer trust in Goddess?"

The only reply Maeve could offer was thoroughly modern. "Then we're all fucked."

CHAPTER THIRTY-ONE

Simon updated Alexander's chart with this evening's readings. In three days, it would be Halloween, or Samhain as the coven called it. Not pronounced *Sam-hane*, as he'd always assumed but *Sow-ween*. However one said it, it meant trouble, and the tension in the coven was mounting.

"How's he doing?" Hannah looked tired and rumpled. The two of them had taken to sleeping nearby in beds that had appeared in the healer's hall almost on demand. Simon chose not to question the how and why of the matter, merely to appreciate a comfortable night's sleep.

Simon checked the numbers again. They hadn't changed since he'd last checked two minutes ago. "The same."

"Damn." Hannah took the chart from him and did her own check.

He wasn't offended by her need to confirm what he'd told her. Hannah had the same concerns he did. The numbers added up to one thing: they were losing him. Even with Roderick's ability to provide blood for the transfusions at a ridiculous pace that both he and Hannah knew to be medically impossible, the infection was spreading.

Already it covered eighty percent of Alexander's torso and was spreading to his arms, groin, and back. Penned in Simon's indecipherable handwriting were the other signs the end was approaching; gurgling sounds associated with his exhalations and inhalations, apnea, mandibular movement with his respiration, decreased urine output, pulselessness to the radial artery, and fever. They would be lucky if he made it to Samhain.

"It's bad, isn't it?" One hand resting on the swell of her belly, Bronwyn stood in the doorway. Her eyes glittered with unshed tears as they fixed on him. They were doing their best to keep her off her feet, and she spent nearly all her time near Alexander anyway. Her pregnancy had settled again, but he and Hannah weren't taking any chances.

Simon wished with every fiber that he had a better answer for her. "He's not responding as we would like."

Bronwyn nodded and moved slowly to the bed, as if reluctant to confirm what she already knew. She touched Alexander's cheek with her fingertips. "He's dying, isn't he?"

"Bronwyn." Hannah struggled for professional detachment, but she swallowed convulsively, and her voice sounded thick. "We won't give up on him."

"I know you won't." She studied Alexander's face, caressing the strong line of his jaw, the high jut of his cheekbones.

The utter defeat and devastation on her pretty face fastened claws around Simon's jugular, and he wanted to bellow to the heavens, or God, or whoever was out there, to do something. He'd seen hundreds of people die in his career, thousands even, but this death would haunt him forever.

Roderick had told him that Alexander had been alive for hundreds of years—certainly well past the fistful of years granted the rest of them—but it made no difference to Simon. If he could give this man another chance, he would have opened his own veins to do it.

"We're researching constantly," he said. He shouldn't offer

hope, he knew better than that, but he couldn't stop himself. "Somewhere out there has to be something that can help."

"He's beautiful, you know." Bronwyn skimmed Alexander's top lip with her fingers. "I know you've only ever seen him like this." She looked up at him, torment and loss dulling her springtime-green eyes. "But he has this life to him, like every cell in his body sparkles and shimmers with it. And his eyes." Her voice quavered, and she took a breath. "I've never seen eyes quite that dark or intense. They were the first thing I noticed about him. I knew him." She gave a soft, heartbroken chuckle. "I was standing on the village green listening to a tour guide— Hermione, actually—and I felt him watching me."

"The prophecy?" Hannah murmured.

Bronwyn nodded. "That damn prophecy. It made him mine even before I knew who he was." She choked back a sob. "I know you must hear this all the time, but I can't believe he's dying. It doesn't seem possible that so much can end."

Hannah bent her head, and drops hit the front of her scrubs as she wept silently.

Taking her hand, Simon offered what comfort he could. All his training, all his experience, and he was as helpless as Bronwyn. Jesus, he'd give anything to be able to give those babies their father, but the chart didn't lie, they were on deathwatch now.

"As far as we can tell, he's not in any pain," he said, and cursed himself for the stupidity of the statement. As humans, they were not equipped to deal with death. Doctors like himself and Hannah managed to soldier through with professional detachment. What that really meant was disconnecting your emotions, the essence of your humanity, from the event. It sat poorly with him. Death was so intrinsically human that creating distance from it seemed counterintuitive. Yet, all his training, all his years of practicing medicine had taught him detach, detach, detach.

Bronwyn managed a smile for him. Jesus, he had seen that smile on the faces of so many loved ones. That futile attempt to meet with courage the devastation heading their way. "That's good. That he's not in pain," Bronwyn said, and the unfiltered agony in her eyes was like a claw hammer in his chest.

His scientific conceit had no place in a room with so much raw honestly. "We'll leave you alone with him."

Hannah kept her head lowered and nodded. "We're in the other room if you need us."

Bronwyn took the stool by Alexander's bed. "Thank you."

<hr>

BRONWYN WAITED until their footsteps had receded before she rested her forehead against Alexander's inert hand. Her torso felt like it was being sucked inside itself, like she was the one with that awful black killer eating the life out of her.

The last couple of days, she'd been thinking a lot about Mags's prophecy, the one with the rising blood and Alexander and the threads. Mags had been warning them about this very thing. Even Taylor had seen the same vision.

Bronwyn had chosen not to think too much about the prophecy. Some part of her had refused to even admit the possibility that it foretold Alexander's death. Even now, sitting here while his body failed, she couldn't believe it was actually happening.

Regan and Rian absorbed her grief and radiated it back through her. They felt his spirit slipping away as much as she did. She wished she could comfort them, but what could she tell them? Rhiannon was winning, and she brought death and destruction in her pocket.

From that moment on the village green, possibly even before then, her soul had been interwoven with Alexander's. They had all played their parts—even Rhiannon—and now only the ending remained.

"I suppose I should have something profound to say." Her voice sounded hollow in the quiet room. "But all I can think of is the time you took me for fish and chips." She sat up and twined her fingers with his. "Do you remember? You took me for fish and chips, and you kissed me." She missed each kiss they'd never shared, and each one they now never would. "Your phone rang, and you left me confused and half in love with you already." Then she said, "And I never told you, but I don't like tartar sauce."

The muted beeping of the monitors were her only answer.

"I still can't quite believe you wanted me." Alexander was still the most beautiful man she'd ever seen. "Short, redheaded, witchling me. Nothing special until you looked at me and made me feel like a goddess."

Little witch—his pet name for her. Panic clawed up her chest as she tried to remember his voice when he called her that. Then she did remember, and her breathing calmed. She heard him in her mind, saw that slight upward tilt to the corner of his mouth, the love shining in his sin-dark eyes.

"Please." One word, which came from the very deepest part of her being. "Please, please, please don't leave me."

A hand touched her shoulder and she jumped.

Alannah said, "I didn't mean to startle you."

"How do you stand it?" Every time, when she thought she had no more tears left, when her eyes were hot and scratchy from crying, more tears flooded her eyes.

Alannah wrapped her arms around her and pulled her head against her. "I don't," she whispered. "There is no standing it, just enduring."

"I don't think I can." Bronwyn clung to Alannah's hips, pressing her face into her sister witch's belly for what comfort she could glean. Her grandmother, Dee, would have known how to comfort her. But Dee was gone, along with almost every other person she'd loved in her life.

"Bronwyn," Alannah murmured into her hair. "I'm so sorry. So fucking sorry." Alannah's body vibrated as she cried with her. "I wish…"

Bronwyn nodded, because she understood. Alannah wished she could say something that would help, wished this wasn't happening, wished she could change it—so many stupid, pointless wishes that amounted to nothing.

"Blessed." Goddess's gentle voice penetrated the fog around her brain. "My dear and cherished Blessed." Her arms went around both Bronwyn and Alannah and she held them as they cried together. "Give me your grief. Let me bear it for you."

"No." Alannah shook her head. "Our grief is part of our love. It's all we have left."

Bronwyn raised her head and looked at Goddess. "Can't you do anything?"

"No." Goddess's haunted expression calmed her and helped her fight back the abyss. "Events have moved beyond my control now. What must come to pass is coming to pass. Like you, I can only bear witness now."

Bronwyn didn't want to hear that. Anger writhed and coiled inside her. "Everything you've asked of me, I've done. Everything you asked of him, he's done."

"I can only tell you what I told Roderick. The die has been cast. What will be, will be." The air shimmered, and Dhara blinked back at her. "I'm really sorry, Bronwyn."

She was just a young girl, not even a woman yet, and Bronwyn wanted to rage and rail at her. None of this was fair, or right.

Alannah cupped Dhara's damp cheek. "We know, sweetheart. None of this is your fault."

"It's not hers either," Dhara said. "You don't know how she feels because she's not inside you, but I feel everything she feels."

She swiped her palms over her cheeks. "She loves him, and she loved Thomas. She loves all of you, and she feels your pain like its hers." Fresh tears welled and slid down Dhara's face. "She feels every witch who dies like it's happening to her. And then she feels where their souls go and what happens to them next."

Footsteps scuffed, and Simon entered with a small plastic cup in his hand. "I have these." He held the cup up with a defeated shrug. "They're just sedatives, and safe for pregnant women, but I…" He shook his head and growled. "Fuck! I don't know what I was thinking. I was just trying…"

"To help." Bronwyn finished his sentence for him. She stood, feeling every bone and muscles in her body protest like she was hundreds of years old. Rian and Regan needed to rest, and they wouldn't while she was in turmoil. "And actually, I will take one of those."

"You will?" Simon looked like he'd handed her absolution. "They won't knock you out. They'll just calm you."

Her eyes felt swollen and hard to see through. "I'm so tired of crying all the time."

"Here." Simon handed a pill to Bronwyn and snagged a glass of water from the table beside Alexander. "I promise it's safe for the babies."

Bronwyn looked at the small, white oval in her palm. Perhaps it could send her to sleep so deeply that when she woke up everything would be over, and she'd be a different person with a different reality.

CHAPTER THIRTY-TWO

There were days, this being one of them, when Warren didn't envy Roderick his position of leading the coimhdeacht. Warren honestly didn't know how Roderick had managed it without bashing heads together.

Mandla was strapping what looked like a small arsenal to his person. He already had a pistol on his left ankle, a knife large enough to gut a rhino on his right, and was busy fastening a shoulder holster around his massive chest.

"Look." Warren tried reason. "You can't launch into this rescue mission on your own."

Mandla checked the chamber of his handgun and slid it into one side of his holster. "I have my mission."

Reason only got you so far. "Don't be so bloody stubborn." Warren lowered his rising voice. "If you go out there on your own, you're going to get killed."

Adding a second handgun to the opposite side of his holster, Mandla said, "My witch's mother could be kept in that house. We are two days from Samhain, and I will retrieve her."

"Nobody is saying we won't retrieve her." Jack joined in. "But we need to plan, prepare."

"You plan." Mandla added a third handgun to the small of his back. "I will rescue."

"Jesus." Elbows propped on the table in the barracks, Jack dropped his head into his hands. "We get it. We will rescue her but going off halfcocked like this is asking for trouble."

"I am prepared." Mandla shrugged into a leather duster, completing the Wesley Snipes aka Blade aesthetic. He started stuffing ammo into his pockets. "I have waited two days. I will wait no longer."

"Well!" Emma slapped her hands on the table, causing Jack to turn and look at her where she sat beside him. "He's not going alone."

Now he had two of them. Warren wanted to thump them both. "Let me get this straight." He folded his arms to resist the temptation. "You're going to roar in there, all guns blazing and hope for the best."

"No." Mandla pounded the table. Jack had to think fast and catch his beer tankard from going over. "My witch," Mandla growled, "has lost her grandmother. Her people are in hiding, and she doesn't know if they are alive or dead. If I can give her one thing—just one thing—that will help her sleep at night, then that is what I will do." He stuffed his phone, more ammo, and a garrote into his fatigues. "I ask nobody to risk this. My witch, my mission."

Oh, fuck it. When he put it like that. Warren shook his head and grabbed a gun from the rack. "Give me ten minutes."

"Make that fifteen." Jack shoved to his feet. He looked from Warren to Mandla to Emma and Noah. "Who's telling Roderick?"

"I vote Maeve." Noah put his hand up. "She can calm the big guy down by looking at him."

Up went Jack's hand. "Seconded."

"Twelve minutes," Mandla growled.

Strapping on guns and ammo, Warren turned to Noah. "What about you?"

"Oh, I was always going." Noah kept his legs on the table and yawned. "I have my weapons ready."

Warren had seen those canines, and he didn't doubt them for a second.

"Where are we going?" Roderick strode into the barracks.

Everyone stilled, even Noah took his legs off the table. None of them had seen him since his latest meltdown, which had resulted in him nearly getting stabbed by the swords he'd insisted on training them with.

"I am going to get my witch's people." Mandla thumped his chest. "These can decide for themselves."

Roderick gave him a long stare and then nodded. "That's not how we work, brother. We are in this together."

Warren nearly swallowed his tongue. Forget Maeve calming him down, she apparently had found a way to get through his thick skull.

"Umm, not to prod the bear or anything, and generally I'm all in on a spot of bear prodding." Noah raised his hand. When all eyes turned his way, he winked at Roderick. "In case you're unclear, you're the bear. But shouldn't at least one of us stay here? Just in case."

"Mowgli makes a good point," Emma said as she shoved hand grenades into a utility belt.

Warren had no idea where she'd got those from, but he also knew better than to ask. Trying to persuade her to leave her grenades behind was a lost cause so he braced for possible future pyrotechnics.

"Again." Noah unfolded lazily to his feet. "And risking further bear prodding, shouldn't it be you who stays?"

Roderick narrowed his eyes and puffed up his chest. "And why should it be me?"

"You're the oldest amongst us." Warren could see Noah's reasoning.

Roderick glared at him.

"I mean, in terms of experience." Warren breathed a sigh of relief as he mentally tap-danced around that landmine. "You know more than the lot of us put together. If the worst happens, then the coven has you."

"You can't fault that reasoning." Andy strode into the barracks with his laptop under one arm and a black case in the other. "If the others don't return from their mission, you are best equipped to protect the coven."

Roderick looked like he wanted to argue but nodded instead.

They all breathed a sigh of relief. Soundlessly.

"And." Andy put his black case on the table with the air of a children's party magician pulling a rabbit out a hat. "You can monitor progress from Baile and coordinate the team from here."

Emma perked up. "Is that from Sasha?"

"Indeed." Andy beamed. "I have comms for each member of the extraction team, and they're all synced to a program on my laptop. Roderick and I will be able to hear and see what every member of the team does."

Warren really liked the sound of that. He patted Andy on the shoulder. "That's great."

"I hope you have more of those earpiece doodads." Niamh and Nofoto strolled into the barracks both dressed in black combats and sweatshirts.

Warren felt his temper rise. "What are you doing?"

"Going with you," Nofoto said and held her hand out to Andy for an earpiece.

Mandla swelled like a bloated kidney. "No."

"Um…yes." Nofoto waggled her head at him. "You are going to rescue my people, one of whom might be my mother. Of course, I'm going with you."

"Blessed." Roderick used his paternal tone, and Warren winced. That would not go down well. "That is not how the bond works. Coimhdeacht take the risks to keep the witches safe."

Nofoto drew herself up to her full five feet and maybe one inch. "That's how it used to work, but this is a whole new century."

"As much as I want to pound that sexist reasoning into the ground, I can't disagree with Roderick." Emma didn't flinch from Nofoto's stare. "You're not trained for combat situations."

"And you can't whip up a storm or arrange a gale force wind, or pelt the windows with hail," Nofoto said.

That left Niamh, and with a sinking heart, Warren turned to her. "And you?"

"Fire." She snapped her fingers and produced a three-inch flame. "And beasties. Lots and lots of beasties."

"Niamh." Warren desperately hunted for the right words to make her stay and not get stubborn on him. "You are forbidden from using your magic to harm people. Even if your life is in danger." He indicated the gathered coimhdeacht. "That is why you have us."

Roderick nodded. "It is our entire purpose."

"You're right." Niamh gave him a triumphant grin that told him his words had failed to hit the mark. "But there's nothing prohibiting me from burning shit down."

Warren could hardly express how unhappy he was with this latest development. "Niamh, I can't let you put yourself in danger."

"And." She clicked her fingers. Pack trotted toward her with a black and white animal whose long, low body kept up with the much taller wolves. "I come with my own eyes, ears, and protection."

Warren eyed the creature. "What is that?"

With a low whistle, Mandla put some distance between himself and the creature. "That's trouble, is what that is."

"A honey badger." Niamh grinned.

"We call it a *ratel*," Nofoto said.

Noah chuckled and studied the creature, from a distance. "Think of a wolverine with combat training. Kind of like Winnie the Pooh as a Navy SEAL. A bit of—"

"He's a sweetheart." Niamh crouched down and scratched the honey badger behind the ears. "He must have escaped from a zoo or something."

Warren bloody well hoped so. The idea that anyone would want a honey badger as a pet baffled him.

Footsteps sounded down the passage, and Noah stiffened as Sinead and Alannah sauntered in.

Sinead grinned. "So, this is where the party is?"

"No." Noah folded his arms. "Not happening, sweet thing."

Warren flinched for him as Sinead turned those indigo eyes flashing fire in his direction. "Don't even try it, wolf-boy. Niamh can make fire, Nofoto can give you weather coverage, and Alannah and I can literally move the earth for you."

"Plus." Alannah held up a hand to forestall Noah's next objection. "We have been experimenting with the wards, and we can ward you for a good distance and mitigate the risk."

Noah took a different tack. He gave Sinead a look that must have set her knickers aflame and lowered his voice to a raspy, rumble. "Sweet thing. You know I worry about you."

"Give it a rest." Sinead clicked her fingers in his face. "We're coming with you."

Warren turned to his last hope.

Roderick returned his stare and chuckled. "One of the things my years of experience has taught me, is when to give in to the inevitable." He shrugged. "Witches are witches, and when they make their minds up, we comply."

"But—"

"Come on, Mowgli." Emma cut Noah off with a hearty shoulder slap. "Get your gnashers and claws out. And we're going to need your nose."

Noah growled, but stripped off his sweatshirt and hurled it on the table. "I swear to God, sweet thing, you so much as break a fucking nail and I'm gonna lose my shit."

"I won't take any chances." Sinead rose on her toes and kissed his cheek. "We'll all stay out of the way and give you help when you need it."

"Perfect." Andy rubbed his palms together and opened his laptop. "If you will all take an earpiece."

"Fifteen minutes is up." Mandla grunted.

"Earpiece." Nofoto shoved one at his chest.

"Lovely." Andy clicked away at his laptop. "Let's run a quick test on them, make sure they're all working."

Everyone tested their earpiece, grabbed a few more supplies, and they were off, the honey badger taking point.

CHAPTER THIRTY-THREE

As they crossed the bailey and ascended the stairs to the caverns, Roderick's voice came loud and clear into Warren's ear. "Earth witches, how far can you extend the wards?"

"We've tested the distance to cover the whole village green," Alannah said. "But we can probably go further than that."

Warren wasn't a big fan of probably, but he kept that to himself. Warding the green was going to lead to some very confused partygoers, and he liked that.

Noah-wolf led the way through the tunnels, scenting constantly. The honey badger kept pace with him, snapping at his legs when he got too close. The remaining wolves distributed themselves amongst the party. There was too much tail wagging and too many perky ears for Warren's peace of mind, but the wolves were embracing the adventure.

"How about a little fog?" Nofoto said.

"Sounds good," Emma replied.

They ascended from the church crypts into a real peasouper. Gray bands of fog hung heavy in the air, thick enough that they could barely see each other.

The wolves took the outside and rounded them all into a group.

"Stay in a tight formation," Roderick barked.

They drew closer together, black clad forms in the gloom and damp.

Disembodied voices called out around them as people lost sight of each other. A loud rap song with a kickass beat provided the right theme song.

"Wards holding," Alannah whispered. "We've reached the end of the village green."

"Nofoto," Roderick said. "Can we add some rain to that fog? Let's make sure any and all sentries are not out in the open and looking around."

Nofoto sounded way too cheerful as she replied, "One rainstorm coming up."

Wind picked up and streamed the fog. Overhead, thunder rumbled, and the rain began.

"Amazing," Emma whispered as she wiped moisture off her face.

"Why thank you," Nofoto chirped.

Noah slunk through the streets, staying visible ahead of the rest of them. He stopped and raised his head.

The honey badger stopped with him and wove his head side to side as he sniffed. Warren tensed.

Changing direction, Noah led them down a side street.

The honey badger stood a moment more before following.

"They have an incredible sense of smell," Niamh whispered. "And they're absolutely ferocious fighters."

The rain grew heavier.

"Wards weakening," Alannah whispered. "We'll take you as far as we can hold them."

"Don't take any chances," Roderick said. "We still need to keep Baile warded."

Jack turned and looked at Sinead. "What's happening to the folk who are not coven as you extend the wards?"

"They won't see us," Sinead said. "They'll experience a slight feeling of disorientation and maybe a bit of a visual distortion, but unless you walk right into someone, they won't know you're there."

The honey badger and Noah seemed to have reached a sort of accord, as long as Noah didn't get too close that was. The bad-tempered badger wasn't shy to hand out the occasional nip or head butt. After another twenty minutes of winding through residential streets, moving ever closer to the manor, Alannah held up her hand. "That's as far as we can stretch them." The rose and clove scent of her and Sinead's earth magic hung heavy in the air. The twins crouched in someone's garden and dug their fingers into the soil. Green light glowed around their hands as they called earth. "We'll hold them here for you."

Noah hesitated and trotted back to Sinead. He pushed his muzzle into her neck and made her giggle. "I'll be fine, wolf-boy." Sinead kissed the spot between his eyes. "You make sure you get back behind these wards safe and sound."

He nuzzled her again before slinking back to his badger buddy and taking point again.

Warren tried to gauge the distance they traveled from the wards by slow counting in his head. It would be useful to know how far they had to run to find safety again.

"Two blocks from the manor," Roderick murmured in their earpieces. "Andy said to tell you there is half a kilometer between you and the edge of the wards."

Or they could use technology. He laughed softly at himself.

Noah and the honey badger stopped and waited for the rest of them to catch up.

The houses thinned into an open field that skirted two sides of the manor. The rain stopped, and more fog rolled in.

"Look sharp," Roderick said. "Hopefully that shower kept most people inside, but you're now vulnerable to detection."

As if they didn't already know that. The faces around Warren were tight with tension. "What's the plan?" he whispered.

"Niamh and Nofoto stay there," Roderick said. "Find somewhere to stay out of sight and be ready to act if I need you."

Niamh and Nofoto glanced around.

Mandla pointed to a small arbor decorating a garden, and they nodded and slid into the shadows.

Honestly, if Niamh had argued, Warren would have put her there himself and tied her to the posts. He was already uncomfortable with how close to the manor they were. A faint red glow from the arbor told him both witches had drawn fire and were ready and waiting.

"We'll use the wolves and the…er…honey badger to locate our witches inside the building," Roderick said. "Jack and Emma take the east side of the manor, Warren and Mandla the west." He and Andy murmured to each other before his voice came through again. "The aim is in and out with as little disruption as possible. We don't have numbers on our side."

"But we do have fire," Niamh whispered. "Lots and lots of lovely fire."

Warren was starting to worry about his witch and her desire to set shit alight. He needed to remember that next time he pissed her off.

Mandla tapped his shoulder and Warren moved into his assigned position. The honey badger came with them, while Noah slid into step with Jack and Emma.

Wiry tail in the air, the honey badger trotted forward. They were trusting Niamh to communicate what they were looking for.

Light shone from windows in the manor, and forms crossed the windows as people moved around inside.

Mandla motioned Warren to stay while the honey badger moved closer. With his black and white coloring, and smaller form, he melted into the night.

Mandla stood preternaturally still as they waited. Only the gentle rise and fall of his chest and the movement of his eyes gave proof of life.

Goddess, he hoped the others were doing okay.

A blast of loud music from one of the downstairs windows made them both jump. Someone had turned on the party. He doubted Rhiannon would have allowed that, and prayed it meant she wasn't in the manor.

He was beginning to wonder if the honey badger had stopped to hunt when the small creature emerged in front of them. Through the bond, Niamh prodded him to follow. Her voice in his ear gave him the shot of courage he needed. "From what he's showing me," she whispered, "he's found a room behind the kitchen. There are women in there who smell of our magic."

"How many?" Mandla asked.

"Eight or nine," Niamh said. "It's hard to know exactly because he can't count, and I'm going from the images he is sharing with me."

Eight or nine witches waiting to be slaughtered by the homicidal cunt. Not today. Warren slid into position behind Mandla.

The big man moved with graceful silence closer to the manor.

A man wove into the kitchen and went to the fridge. "Who wants tequila?" he yelled.

Voices answered him from another room. Warren could go for a shot himself. Later.

They waited while the man fucked around cutting lemons and finding a saltshaker.

With a feral gleam in its eye, the honey badger watched

Warren and Mandla. It wanted to get on with the mission and create a little hell in the process.

Tequila man was about to leave the kitchen when a short woman barreled through the door. "What are you doing?"

"Tequila." The man held up the bottle.

"We are not supposed to—"

"She'll only know if you tell her." The man got right into the woman's face and loomed over her. "You planning on telling her, Reba?"

The woman stepped back and shook her head. "Just make sure you clean up after yourselves."

"That's what we have that fucking lot for." He jabbed his finger at a closed door on the far end of the kitchen.

Much obliged for that confirmation. Warren stayed tight on Mandla's heels as they moved closer.

"From what I can see," Niamh whispered, "there is only one door in and out of the place. The women smell terrified."

Mandla's jaw tightened. "More fog," he snapped.

"Say please," Nofoto came right back, but the fog thickened around them.

Warren split from Mandla and stood to the right side of the French doors that led to the kitchen. From here, he could see the heavy bolts on the interior door. Fortunately, no other padlocks, and the key was on the outside of the door.

The entire expanse of the kitchen lay between them and that door. There was no way across it without being spotted by someone entering the kitchen.

Mandla tested the French door closest to him.

Locked.

Mandla dug into his coat and pulled out a lockpick kit. He had the door open with the sort of speed that made Warren want to ask questions about who he'd been before he'd become coimhdeacht.

The interior kitchen door opened again, and another woman came through.

Mandla pushed the French door closed and ducked back into the shadows. The woman strode to the island and opened a wine fridge. She spent about two thousand years making a selection. Shivering suddenly, she looked at the French doors. With a tut, she moved over and locked the door again.

Motherfucker.

"We need them out of the house," Mandla murmured.

Niamh's chuckle was pure evil as she said, "One distraction coming up. Emma, you lot ready?"

"Give us two more minutes," Emma said. "We've encountered a small hitch."

They didn't need any hitches. They were flying ass in the wind as it was. Mandla picked the lock a second time, and they waited. Seconds stretched to hours before Emma finally said, "In position."

A fireball streaked over the roof of the house and landed in the front garden. It hit a parked car and caught it alight. Another fireball streaked into a shrub and set it aflame.

"My fucking car," someone yelled.

"Fire!"

"What the fuck?"

Voices rose, and footsteps clattered.

Warren and Mandla were through the door and across the kitchen in seconds.

Warren slid the bolt. Someone had oiled it, and it moved back smoothly.

Inside the dark room, women clustered.

"Mandla?" a woman whispered.

"Let's go." He motioned them frantically through the door. "No time."

They dashed through the kitchen and out the French doors.

"Hey!" A man yelled from the front of the house. "The witches. They've got the fucking witches."

"We've been spotted," Emma panted. "Going for the extraction point."

"Niamh! Nofoto!" Roderick whisper-yelled through his comms. "Get to the wards. Now!"

"After I do this." A giant wall of flame sprang up and encircled the manor.

Warren dashed straight for the flames and pushed the women with him toward them.

Two of them balked but the honey badger took care of that. On a low growling hiss, he charged them. The women were through the wall of flame before they'd registered it hadn't burned them.

And then it was a flat out run.

Wolves materialized around them, running alongside them, nudging stragglers.

Niamh better be behind the wards when he got there, or he'd —he couldn't think what he'd do, but she'd fucking regret it for the rest of her natural life.

The honey badger had taken lead again, winding and weaving them through gardens and houses. One of the women was limping badly and Mandla hauled her over his shoulder. A younger woman, little more than a teen, wept silently as she ran beside Warren.

He took her hand in his. "Keep moving, sweetheart. We've got you."

Sounds of a fight broke out behind them. Wolves snarled and growled, people yelped, gunfire crackled in the night. Warren wanted to turn and help the others, but first he needed to get his party to safety.

The distance hadn't seemed this long when they'd arrived, but now the streets and back lawns seemed to stretch on forever. Someone's dog got curious but backed off with one whiff of their furry fury leading the charge.

A second woman stumbled and went down hard on her knees.

Warren scooped her up and cradled her against his chest. Her hands dug into his shirt. The young girl transferred her grip to his belt, and they kept running.

Noise grew behind them. People spilled out of their houses to see what the fuss was about.

A man yelled to call the police.

Silk brushed his skin, and Niamh stepped in front of him. "Warren." Her green eyes locked on his. "Stop. You're behind the wards."

"Take them." He lowered the woman to her feet. "And don't stop until you're inside Baile."

Niamh hesitated. "But—"

"Niamh." Warren ran out of words and packed everything he wanted to say into a look. A look filled with—*don't try me now, I've given as much ground as I can, I need to know you're safe.*

She took a breath. "Okay." She pressed her mouth to his. "You take care of yourself, and I'll see you back at Baile."

"You as well." He turned to Sinead and Alannah. "Back to Baile."

"Nope." Sinead glanced up at him. She was pale and looking exhausted. "Holding these wards and not going anywhere until my mate crosses them."

Warren contacted Roderick. "We need an update on Noah, Jack, and Emma."

"Heading your way," Roderick said. "Taking some heavy resistance."

"We're on our way."

He crossed the wards and ran in the direction Roderick told them to go.

Wolves streamed after them, and somehow the honey badger's short legs kept him hanging on at the back of Pack.

Jack and Emma were herding a group of about fifteen witches, trying to keep them moving and fighting off a growing group from the manor.

Noah's wolf was everywhere, snarling, biting, tearing into limbs. His muzzle was covered in blood and matter, and his huge canines dripped saliva and gore. He looked like a nightmare creature. Everywhere the big wolf went, screams for help followed.

With a belly roar, Mandla threw himself into the fray. His knives flashed as he moved faster than Warren could track. Then he lost sight of Mandla as four men closed on him.

The honey badger latched on to an ankle and sank his teeth in. The man screamed and tried to kick him off, but the honey badger clung. A wolf grabbed his arm and pulled him to the ground.

Warren faced the other three. A wolf launched itself at the closest man and took him to the ground by the throat. The honey badger darted in and finished the job in a gruesome display that Warren never wanted to witness again.

"Christ." One of the two facing him dropped his weapons and raised his hands. "Fucking take them."

Warren stepped into the last man. Finally, an outlet for his tension and fury. He didn't want a weapon for this; he craved the feeling of flesh under his fists. The man went down after his first punch, and Warren followed him down, raining blows until the honey badger took over for him. Only then did he stand and look for his next opponent.

"Let's go." Jack grabbed his arm and hauled him away. "Wards are up ahead."

They fought shoulder to shoulder as they backed the witches over the wards.

In the distance, sirens wailed, and blue police lights flickered.

From the surrounding houses, faces pressed to windows, phone cameras blinked in the darkness.

And then they stumbled across the wards.

Noah waited for the last member of Pack to cross before he crossed.

They were missing someone. Or rather something.

Warren searched the milling wolf bodies for the honey badger.

Sinead and Alannah were retreating, walking backwards, and bringing the wards with them. The strain showed in the sharp brackets around their mouths and their pallor, but the group kept moving.

"Noah?"

Noah glanced at him but didn't leave Sinead's side. He pressed his furry body against her leg as if he could somehow lend her strength. "The honey badger?"

Noah scented and glanced at Alpha.

Alpha trotted to the wards, but before he could cross them, the honey badger trotted through. Tail whisking the air, his little legs moving twice as fast as his actual forward momentum. He groaned and spewed up a mess of blood and bits Warren did not want to know about. That done, up went his tail, and he trotted for Baile.

They'd done it. Warren wanted to drop on the ground with relief. They had the witches.

CHAPTER THIRTY-FOUR

Rhiannon stared at the empty storeroom beside the kitchen. Behind her, minions cowered and tried to make themselves invisible. All her Canadian and South African witches were gone, including Lerato, and she'd had real magic, not the dribble of nothing the cringing cowards in her kitchen laid claim to. Without turning, she asked, "What happened?"

"Umm." A portly prick stepped into the loaded silence. "We were outnumbered, mistress. We didn't stand a chance."

And now he thought to add lying to his list of crimes. She arranged her face into a pleasant smile as she turned. "Outnumbered? How unfortunate."

He wheezed out a sigh of relief and straightened his shoulders. "We didn't see them coming, mistress. They neutralized our sentries and had us surrounded before we knew anything about it."

"I see." Real magic. Rhiannon could have used that power, and these dullards had allowed it to walk out the door. She breathed deep and kept her temper in check, for the moment. "You were aware, were you not, that those witches had powerful magic?"

"Yes, mistress." He bowed. "And we did everything we could to keep them safe for you."

Had they, though? Rhiannon rather thought not.

Her favorite minion pulled a kitchen knife from the block and slashed her palm. She bowed her cowled head and held her bleeding palm up to Rhiannon. "Mistress."

The woman didn't know what she wanted, but she presented her blood without question. She was the sort of minion Rhiannon demanded. Drawing power from the proffered blood, she approached the lying, duplicitous swine.

His eyes widened, and he swallowed. Trying to step back, he encountered the kitchen island and was forced to stop.

She used the pain from the blood magic to fuel her fury. "There are four coimhdeacht," she kept her tone low and silky. "One wolf shifter, another thug who serves Magdalene. Would you like to revise your story of being outnumbered?"

"Perhaps I misspoke, mistress." His gaze fixed on the blood. "But they tricked us. They made us think there were more of them."

"Stop," she commanded and pressed her fingertips to his shirtfront. "Your lies will not save you." Pulling more power, she sunk her fingers into his skin and muscle. Her hand sunk into his chest, seeking the useless organ he called a heart.

The pig screamed and thrashed, but she had him in her power.

A life for a life, but hardly a fair trade considering what he had cost her.

Choking and spluttering, he coughed up blood as her hand fastened around his heart. He stared at her in horror.

Beneath her fingers, his heart pumped, and she tightened her grip.

"Please," he wheezed. "I'm sorry."

"Not sorry enough." She leaned close enough to whisper in

his ear. "But you have cost me, and your miserable life is the price for my forgiveness."

Rhiannon crushed his heart in her fist.

He jerked, went magenta in the face, and with a hiss, tumbled to the floor.

As her bloody hand slid from his chest, Rhiannon stepped back. She looked at the minions surrounding them. "The price for failure." She toed the corpse at her feet. "Mark it well."

<hr>

LENNOX'S CUP of station coffee sludge cooled on his desk as he read the incident report from last night. He was getting that twitchy feeling again, the one that warned him there was a lot more happening than met the eye.

According to the report, a call had come in at 10:28 from Greater Littleton's posh neighborhood. The caller had complained of noise and wild animals. Fast on the heels of the first caller, another five calls had come in between 10:28 and 10:43 with complaints varying from gunfire to wolves to men fighting in the street. Units had been dispatched, but when they'd arrived, the alleged combatants were gone leaving only blood spatter behind them. With no bullet casings, there was no proof the gunfire had actually happened.

But here's what got up his nose. Greater Littleton was the back of beyond, so sleepy it barely even needed a police force. In the last five months, guns or the suspicion of guns were cropping up like it was a borough of Manchester.

Bracing for the stomach acid burn, he sipped his coffee and reread the report.

Nobody had gotten a good look at the perpetrators, but there were several vague descriptions of large men and wolves. Several mentions of fog and rain making it difficult to see. One person reported seeing a small, raccoon-like creature who attacked people, but there were always the outliers in witness reports, and he put that aside.

But the bloody wolves gave him pause.

The only place Lennox had seen anything approaching a wolf—outside of a zoo—in England was at Baile Castle. Braithwaite had fobbed Acharya's questions about the animal off and called it a wolf dog. That coincidence was a little too close for Lennox's peace of mind.

The other thing refusing to leave him in peace was the manor on the edge of the neighborhood where they'd received the complaints. The manor belonged to Alexander Donn, the same Alexander Donn who currently resided at Baile Castle.

Coincidence number two.

Although his name was still on the deed, Donn didn't seem to live there anymore. Instead, a group of out of towners had taken up residence. They'd recently quieted down, but there had been several noise complaints about the manor before last night.

Lennox couldn't prove it, but the folks at Baile were linked to what had happened last night. He'd love to get up there and have a chat, but he hadn't been able to get near the place since they'd been magicked out of there.

"Guvnor." Acharya tapped on his doorframe. "Meeting with the brass in the pit in three minutes."

Fucking meetings were the bane of his life. But the brass had come down from London, no less, and had been closeted with his boss for two days. "Any idea what this is about?"

"Word is they're organizing a big operation." Acharya looked like a kid on his way to Disneyland. "Top secret strike."

Coincidence number three? The London lot had been very interested in Baile Castle. Lennox pushed to his feet. Only one way to find out.

ALANNAH FINISHED CLEANING the kitchen in the aftermath of a sudden demand to feed new mouths. They'd returned with the witches to find Andy, Hermione, and Debra had swung into action. They'd set up a sort of triage station in the great hall with Hannah, Simon, and Bronwyn assessing the incoming witches for injuries.

Roderick had been a calm, reassuring presence for the frightened women they'd rescued. He had this air of permanence around him, like a living mountain, that seemed to reach through fear and confusion and invite you to rest a moment. They all relied so heavily on Roderick, it must be exhausting for him, particularly now.

Bronwyn had thrown herself into healing everything from minor scrapes and bruises to broken bones. Distraction helped as Alannah knew only too well.

For her part, she'd gone straight to the kitchen and made pots of soup for their visitors. She'd also quadrupled her bread dough for the next day and set it out for a slow proof overnight. There would be many more mouths to feed for breakfast.

After assessing the witches, and healing whoever needed it, Andy's team had found bedrooms for everyone and scrounged what clothes they could to get the traumatized witches settled. Baile did her part and provided places for everyone to sleep.

It was late now, and the honey badger had fallen asleep beside Alannah's range, looking almost smug. The other animals had exited the kitchen the moment the creature had entered. She rather liked him. He had the sweetest little face. Niamh assured her looks could be deceptive and to give the animal as much space as it needed.

Footsteps sounded down the stairs from the great hall, and Alannah looked up as Simon wandered into the kitchen. His hair was rumpled, and lines of fatigue made him look older. He started when he saw her. "Hey. You still up?"

"Just getting a few things ready for the morning." She felt

awkward around him since their chat on the battlements, like she'd revealed too much of herself and needed to tuck all those messy ends away again.

Simon yawned and arched his back. "Things are never boring around here, are they?"

"Not lately." They used to be boring before Bronwyn had arrived. In fact, she and Sinead used to sneak away to London for an escape from the monotony of Baile life. "It used to be a lot quieter."

He shoved his hands in his pockets. "Ummm…actually, you caught me on a secret kitchen raid."

"Are you hungry?" She hadn't noticed who had or had not eaten in the steady pressure of supplying more food.

He cleared his throat. "I was more hoping for a glass of wine or something."

He looked so boyishly guilty that Alannah couldn't resist messing with him a bit. "We have Sinead's elderberry wine."

"Er…no thank you." He flushed and stared past her with a guilty expression. "I am not really much for…er…not that it's not excellent."

"It's hideous." Alannah laughed. "But none of us have the heart to tell her."

A relieved smile spread over his face. He really did have a lovely smile. "Good…I mean…" He chuckled. "I'm making a right bollocks of this, aren't I?"

"A bit." Some of the awkwardness between them faded. "And I have options for you."

He looked up and cocked his head. "Lay them on me."

"We have regular wine, we have beer, we have my experiments with mead, but I wouldn't recommend those, and we have Roderick's single malt." Then because it was what she did, she grabbed a loaf of bread and sliced it. Once a feeder, always a feeder.

Simon looked impressed. "Will Roderick lop my head off with that great bloody sword if I drink his single malt?"

"He's a sharer." She grabbed cheese, tomatoes, and ham from the fridge. "It's on the dresser over there."

Simon turned and located the single malt. He held up the bottle. "Will you join me?"

"Yes, please." She didn't sleep much anyway, and it was either that or keep cleaning parts of the kitchen that didn't need cleaning.

She finished putting his sandwich together and added some crisps to the plate before putting it on the table. "Eat." She motioned the sandwich. "I can't let you drink on an empty stomach."

Simon looked at the sandwich like he'd just seen Nirvana. "Thank you," he breathed. "I got too busy to eat earlier, and I just this minute realized I'm bloody starving."

It pleased her that she'd read the situation right. "It's just a sandwich."

"That's where you're wrong." Simon took a seat and put both glasses of scotch on the table. "This is a fucking miracle."

She laughed. "Maybe a minor one."

The peaty scent of scotch hit her before she sipped. Smooth, rich spice and smoke made her tastebuds prickle. Roderick had a stash of this somewhere in Baile. The scotch eased down her throat in a warm embrace, and she sighed.

"Wow." Simon stared at his glass. "This is amazing."

"Right." She motioned his now empty plate. "Another?"

"No, thank you." He pushed his plate away. "That did the trick nicely." Stretching his legs out beneath the table, he sprawled in his chair. He cupped his glass to his chest and closed his eyes. "I saw an honest to God miracle today." He gave a dry chuckle. "A bunch of them, actually. I still can't quite believe I saw what I saw."

The atmosphere in the kitchen was mellow and serene, and she took a seat at the table. "Bronwyn?"

"Yup." He opened his eyes and sipped his scotch. "I watched her put her hands on people and make the bad thing"—he clicked his fingers—"disappear."

"She's a healer." The warm burn of fine liquor radiated from her belly to the rest of her muscles. "It's incredible what she does."

"I'm a medical doctor." He took a deep breath. "I know thousands of ways to help people with science, but what she can do…" He shook his head. "It's…well…miraculous."

"She was glad to help." Bronwyn's inability to help Alexander must be eating at her. "Roderick always says the healers are the most driven of the witches. They have this imperative to ease suffering wherever they can." She studied the quietly handsome lines of Simon's face. "A bit like you."

He frowned and took a sip, letting the scotch roll over his tongue. "Not quite like me." His hazel gaze sharpened on hers. "You know what I think is the main difference between vets and doctors?"

He'd said something before about his family all being vets. "What?"

"Vets do what they do out of a genuine love for animals. Doctors." He pointed to himself. "Doctors, on the other hand, do not necessarily love people."

"Do you?" Something about Simon made her want to understand him better.

"I used to." He frowned into his empty glass, and Alannah pushed the bottle nearer. "I guess somewhere along the line, I got jaded and stopped caring so much."

He had kind eyes. Beneath the detached intelligence and the keen observation, she could see it. "I don't believe that. I think you still care."

"Maybe." He sat up and splashed another inch into his glass, leaned forward and topped her drink. "It's one of the things I always hammer residents and interns about. We tend to describe people in terms of their ailments." Rolling the tumbler between his palms, he studied the gleaming amber contents. "Like we have a thirty-year-old, male acute appendicitis. We are trained not to think of them as Frank Dawson who has a wife and a young baby and also an appendix that needs removing."

She'd never thought of doctors and their patients like that. "Is that because it makes it easier to think of them as conditions if they don't make it?"

"Partly." He took a deep breath and smiled at her. "You grew up at Baile?"

"Yes. We all did." She savored her next sip of scotch before finishing. "Sinead and me, Mags, and Niamh that is. Bronwyn came later. And the rest have kind of wandered in over the last few months." It seemed like years ago instead of a handful of weeks. "Now, it's like everyone has always been here. I like it."

"That's because you're a feeder." He grinned at her. "You feed people and nurture them that way."

She loved having people at her table, enjoying what she prepared. It gave her a deep sense of satisfaction. "Is that why you cook?"

"God no." He laughed. "I learned to cook after my divorce. At first, it was a way to unwind on my own after a long day. Then I grew to enjoy it. For me, it's more about the science of cooking than filling other bellies."

The mood encouraged her to delve deeper into him. "You said something about having an ancestor linked to Baile?"

"Ah yes!" He downed his glass. "I forget her name, but some kind of great many times over aunt or something." With a shrug, he pushed himself away from the table. "I should call my mum and ask her about my great auntie or whatever. It might be interesting."

She felt slightly bereft, as if he was taking their nice moment with him when he left. "Do that. I'd love to hear about it."

Looking past her shoulder, Simon frowned and pointed to the window. "Is that a hawk? Sitting on the window ledge."

"A kestrel." Alannah didn't need to turn to know Kai had joined them. The bird never let her near enough to touch her, but she often popped in. "Don't tell Niamh, but Sinead and I named her Kai."

He studied Kai as he asked, "Niamh doesn't let you name the animals?"

"She says they don't belong to us. They share space with us." Niamh had the advantage of not having to name animals because she could communicate with them. "She's a guardian, so protecting them and being a voice for them is her thing."

"Makes a kind of sense." He looked at her with those kind, beautiful hazel eyes. "We have a kestrel on our family crest, you know?"

A hot prickle snaked up Alannah's nape. "You have a family crest?"

"Oh yes." Simon gave her a boyish grin. "My older brothers both have it on signet rings." He pulled a face. "I never went in for that sort of thing."

She was tempted to pull out the pendant around her neck and show him, but she was also too frightened to follow through. Lots of family crests involved animals, and she'd bet her left arm a good portion of those animals were birds of prey. It could mean everything. It could mean nothing. But Simon's eyes were so familiar. She saw them in her dreams almost every night. "Let me know what you find out about that ancestor. The one connected to Baile."

"I will."

They sat in silence for an uncomfortable moment. Alannah no longer felt so easy in his company. There was more between them than she wanted to deal with.

"Well. I need to get back to Alexander." He pushed to his feet and strode for the kitchen door. Opening the door, he stepped into the chilly evening. "Good night, then, and thank you for the sandwich and the drink."

"You're welcome." And he was. She wasn't sorry he'd come into the kitchen tonight, and him leaving with awkwardness between them felt wrong. "Make sure you get some rest."

From her perch on the window ledge, Kai watched him in the doorway. She turned her head and stared at Alannah. Maybe it was fanciful thinking, but Kai seemed to be trying to communicate something. Kai was her last connection with Thomas, and the loneliness of his absence swept over her. He used to pop into the kitchen and keep her company, make her laugh, make her want things she could never have. And now he was gone.

"Um…Alannah." Simon half turned to her, and she might have almost thought he was blushing. "I don't want to overstep or anything, but…er…would you like a hug?"

"A hug?" The question surprised her into stepping back from him.

"Right." He nodded, and he definitely was blushing now. "Stupid bloody question. Forget I even asked. I honestly don't know why I did."

And suddenly Alannah did want a hug. More than she wanted her next breath. Before she could overthink it, she stepped into him. "I would love a hug."

"Really?" He gaped at her. It took him a moment to recover his wits, and then he slipped his arms around her and drew her against him.

Funny, she hadn't realized how tall he was until the top of her head rested against his chin. Or how broad and strong he was. His arms fastened gently, tentatively around her, as if he didn't want to frighten her. The heat of him seeped into her and melted her against him, and Alannah relaxed into the sensation. It had been so long since she'd been held by a man that the sweetness of it brought tears to her eyes. Even before Thomas had left, he had never been able to hold her. She'd forgotten how comforting being held in a pair of strong arms was. "Thank you," she whispered.

His deep chuckle rumbled through her. "I can say with absolute honesty that you are most welcome."

CHAPTER THIRTY-FIVE

Jack peered over Andy's shoulder as the man tippy-tapped away at his laptop, interspersed with some fairly colorful swearing. Not the sort of invective Jack would have expected from a man like Andy, but the situation warranted it.

"Son of a pustulant whore." Andy sat back and cracked his fingers.

Warren glanced at Jack and raised his eyebrows. "No luck?"

"Not yet." Andy set his jaw and went back to keyboard finger games. A bright, crisp day outside Andy's office windows stood no chance of lightening the atmosphere in the room. "The raid is set for tomorrow. I'm trying to scramble it and create confusion."

And tomorrow just happened to be Samhain. Coincidence? Yeah, fuck that bollocks. Rhiannon was behind this up to her black-souled eyes.

"You can't stop it?" Warren narrowed his eyes at the screen, but Jack got the sense his attention was on the problem more than Andy's computer. Especially considering Warren wouldn't know his ass from his elbow with technology. Even Roderick was better at computers.

"I'm being blocked from the system." Andy hit Enter and sat back. "Rot-infested rabbit feces!"

Jack was guessing that meant still no luck. "I think we need to assume this raid is happening."

"Yeah." Warren rubbed his jaw. "And normally I wouldn't give a shit but…" He shrugged.

With the wards compromised, the police could make it through. "We're going to need to get the twins involved."

"Right." Jack couldn't stand around anymore, however entertaining Andy's swearing. "I'll have a word with them."

"Do that." Warren nodded.

Jack was almost out the door to Andy's office when Warren called after him. "And be discreet, Jack. We don't want everyone panicking."

Nodding, Jack left, but he did wonder when the time to panic would be, because sooner or later everyone was going to notice the nasty fuckers pouring into the castle.

He tried the kitchen first for Alannah.

A group of four women had taken over Alannah's domain, and all activity ceased when he entered the kitchen. He couldn't remember if these women were from Canada or South Africa, but they all looked haunted and exhausted. "Morning." He managed a congenial smile. "I was looking for Alannah."

"Outside in the kitchen garden," said a short, honey-toned brunette with huge dark eyes. "Sinead is with her."

Perfect. Jack went through the storerooms and the laundry—trying not to breathe in Alannah's fuel of the future—and out the back entrance.

Brisk wind rushed out to meet him and stole his breath with its icy bite. The door to the kitchen gardens was open, and he found the twins huddled in coats and crouched together in the orchard.

They both looked up at his approach. Noah sprawled nearby

under an apple tree, doing a crappy job of not studying Sinead's ass.

"Morning." Jack jerked his thumb toward the kitchen. "I see your kitchen has been invaded."

"I don't mind." Alannah wrinkled her nose. "Feeding all the new mouths is turning into a full-time job."

In that oddly graceful way he had, Noah unfolded to stand. Wearing only a T-shirt and jeans, he seemed impervious to the weather. "What's up?"

"We've got trouble." If Warren wanted this done with a verbal two-step, he'd chosen the wrong man to deliver the news. "Police raid planned for tomorrow."

Sinead blinked at him. "Police raid? What?"

"Andy reckons somebody is pulling strings, and we can all guess who that somebody is."

"Motherfucker." Noah shoved his hands on his hips. "And they might get through with the wards the way they are."

"We thought you might be able to do something." Jack turned his attention back to the twins.

The twins glanced at each other as if having a mental debate on the matter.

"Like what?" Noah narrowed his eyes at Jack.

"I don't know, mate." Jack could see Noah buckling into his protective armor. "I'm not a witch. Not even a coimhdeacht."

"Maybe." Sinead chewed her lip as she looked at Alannah. "I mean, it could work, but it would take almost constant contact."

Noah moved to loom over her. "What could work?"

"We can't strengthen the wards," Alannah said. "We've been trying again this morning, but we could maybe hold them."

From the unhappy look on his face, Noah didn't love that idea one tiny bit. "Hold them?"

"When we push earth through the wards, they do get stronger," Sinead said. "But the minute we drop the connection, they weaken again. So, in theory, if we kept feeding power into them…"

"But we would need to stay plugged into them." Alannah chewed her lip. "And the constant energy required to do that would be draining."

Sinead stared out over the sea. "I mean, we could conserve energy by keeping the main thrust of power to the places the wards are the most threatened, and I don't know how long we could hold them."

"What about the new witches?" Jack had to believe a bunch of new witches meant new magic.

Alannah thought about that. "We could ask who pulls earth and see if we could get them to link into our bond." She shrugged. "But it's not something we've tried before."

"Before we do that"—Noah's voice went low and menacing —"I need to understand the danger to you."

Sinead gave him a fond smile. "We'll be fine."

"Nope." Noah folded his arms and tucked his chin into his chest. "Not taking your word for that."

Jack gave Sinead credit for a good attempt at an innocent look as she said, "You don't trust me?"

"Nope."

Yeah, Jack didn't buy it either. The twins wouldn't hold back if the coven was at risk.

"Noah!" Sinead glared at him. "We're the only ones who can do this."

"And I'm the one who will stop you both being a danger to yourselves," Noah said.

Apparently, the wolf had taken responsibility for both twins.

Alannah stood and put her hand on Noah's arm. "You can trust me."

"About an inch more than I trust your crazy sister," Noah said. "If you think you can save this coven, neither of you will stop at anything, and I'm not going to let that happen."

"Now, listen up." Sinead shot to her feet. "Nobody lets me do anything. I will do what I think—"

"You keep talking, sweet thing." Noah glowered. "But I'll lock you both in your rooms if I have to."

Being a mediator was a new one on Jack, but he gave it a go. "Look, before we all start yelling, there's middle ground here."

Nobody looked away from the three-way glare-off happening in front of him.

"First step is to see if any of those new witches call earth and can help." Warren was so much better at keeping the peace than him. Jack's approach was more of the banging heads together variety. "Then we need to test how long you can go before you risk burning out."

"We won't burn out." Despite Sinead's airy wave, her words didn't carry much conviction. "We'll get tired and have to stop."

"Which would be burn out," Noah snapped.

Sinead jabbed her finger in his chest. "You're so bloody stubborn."

"Right back at ya, sweet thing."

"Nobody is going to burn out." Jack would start by thumping some tact into Noah. "Because we're not letting that happen." He softened his tone. "We need you two too much to risk you."

"We know that, Jack." Alannah turned her beautiful indigo eyes his way, and Jack felt himself softening. "We'll start as you suggested. This is new territory for all of us."

"And I'm gonna be watching you." Noah narrowed his eyes at the twins. "Very fucking carefully."

Jack didn't doubt Noah would stop the twins from doing something stupid. "In the meantime, let's increase the patrols to the weakened areas of the wards," he said. "And try to isolate where we can expect this police raid to try to breach the wards."

"I'll have a word with Pack." Noah nodded.

Jack left them arguing and made his way back to the kitchen. He stopped in the doorway and addressed a woman who seemed to be in charge. "We need to know who of you calls earth."

All four women turned to stare at him.

"Alannah and Sinead need earth witches," Jack said. "As many as we can muster."

"Now?" A tall blonde blinked at him.

The sooner, the better, and Jack nodded. "Now, please."

———

LENNOX COULDN'T SAY for sure what had him sitting in his personal vehicle, partially concealed in the shadow of a large elm and watching the manor house. His gut was working overtime right now, but he had learned not to question it. He popped another antacid. Jesus, that station coffee played havoc with his stomach lining. Combine that with bloody Acharya, and his stomach felt like it was cradling hot coals.

Tomorrow's raid sat like sour milk in his throat. The entire thing reeked of overkill and manufactured grounds. Acharya had looked too fucking happy about the entire thing as well.

Acharya had left the station with an air of suppressed excitement this evening that raised questions in Lennox's mind. Through this morning's briefing, Acharya had stood to one side of the briefing room with a small knot of younger coppers. He'd never taken the time to notice the contingent of coppers who surrounded Acharya. To a person, they looked like the prospect of the raid factored right up there with an unplanned school outing when you were a kid.

There was nothing exciting about weapons and people sharing space in an explosive situation. People got dead and hurt when you let bullets drive your point home.

Lennox had been on his way home, mulling over Acharya and his cohorts when he'd found himself passing the manor, and he'd stopped.

Unless he missed his guess—and he very much doubted that —the people oh-so-casually hanging about around the manor's perimeter were guarding something or someone. In his experience, you had to have something you were afraid of losing to guard it. Or you were keeping a secret you didn't want anyone to know.

A woman walked down the drive to one of the guards. They spoke for a while, and then the guard walked back to the manor, and the woman took his place. Shift change?

From what he could piece together of the reports from the other night, a group had entered the manor and then left with some women in tow. Residents of the manor had chased them and then lost sight of them. Neighbors described the way the first group had suddenly disappeared. Combing through various descriptions of the participants, Lennox had a fair idea Jack Langham and Warren Masters had been part of the disappearing party.

If he hadn't been poofed the fuck out of Baile himself, Lennox would have dismissed that portion of the witness statements.

A dark-colored Vauxhall sedan appeared in his rearview mirror. The same Vauxhall he'd watched Acharya get into not two hours earlier. The prickle at his nape sharpened.

The car turned into the drive and stopped abreast of the guard. The window lowered and Acharya's face appeared as he spoke to the woman.

The woman nodded and stepped back.

Acharya drove up to the front door and parked. Getting out, he glanced around him before trotting up the front steps and letting himself into the house. Funny thing, Acharya must have neglected to mention how at home he was in a place that had been involved in a possible crime a few nights before.

CHAPTER THIRTY-SIX

To accommodate all the new residents, Baile produced large tables in the great hall. The assault to his ears and nose almost had Noah skipping dinner, but a wolf had to eat, so he forced himself not to fidget beside Sinead.

The rescued witches had produced six earth witches, most of them Canadian, and Alannah and Sinead had no trouble merging them into their gift. They were working on a way to get those witches to hold their power so the twins could get a rest, but no luck so far. The moment one of the twins dropped the bond, the earth magic subsided.

The rescued witches had also included Lerato, Nofoto's mother, and they were sitting with Mandla at one of the tables talking quietly. Lerato had managed to get Nofoto's younger brother into hiding before she'd been taken. It wasn't much in the glowering thunderhead of trouble heading Baile's way, but these days, they would take the wins where they could.

Alpha brushed his mind, and Noah tuned in to the wild wolf. The furry big guy was sending out some major alpha compulsion. Noah hadn't noticed that sort of clout from Alpha before. He opened himself up wider to the compulsion.

From another table, Niamh stiffened and raised her head. "Who is that?"

She felt it too, the unmistakable stamp of a powerful alpha wolf. *Ah, man.* Noah knew that alpha touch like he knew his own scent. He might not be Zach's beta anymore, but he would know his alpha anywhere. Pure joy rushed through Noah.

He must have said or done something because Sinead turned to look at him. "What is it?"

It took Noah a hot minute to get a grip on his delight. If he'd been in wolf form right then, he would be wagging his tail. "It's Zach." Saying his alpha's name made a lump in his throat. "He's real fucking close."

"Zach." Dhara perked up on the far side of Sinead. "Is Zach here?"

"Who's Zach?" Roderick glared at him.

"He's the best thing to happen to us since I arrived." Noah was already on his feet.

"Zach?" A Canadian witch murmured. "Does that mean Kate is here too?"

Noah hoped with everything in him that was true.

With shining eyes, Dhara followed him out of the castle and into the bailey.

Wild wolf howls filled the night as Pack welcomed Zach.

And there he was, strolling into the bailey with his long-legged lope. Kate was almost jogging by his side to keep up with him. Zach had brought company as well. Big, dumb, and the absolute best wolf to have by your side in a fight, Abe trotted behind.

"Nice place you got here." Zach stopped about six feet away and grinned.

Dhara was already hugging Kate like they'd been apart for months.

Wild alpha slunk into the bailey and approached Zach in a submissive crouch.

Zach welcomed him and the wolf bounded over.

"Are you okay?" Kate had Dhara by the face and was studying every inch of her. "We heard through Sasha that you had trouble."

"We left Rachel and Cole to take care of our people," Zach said. "And thought we'd bring the fight to that bitch."

<hr />

HANNAH WAS aware of some kind of commotion outside her lab in Bronwyn's healer's hall, but she ignored it. For the past hour, she'd been studying a slide of Alexander's latest blood test.

Simon sat quietly on the large leather sofa and let her concentrate. They were onto something, and both of them didn't want to break focus.

A rescued witch had brought them both dinner an hour ago, but it lay spoiling on a tray as she and Simon teased out their thinking.

"We know whatever that thing infecting Alexander is, it functions by destroying healthy blood cells." Speaking her thoughts out loud sometimes helped. "But something is fighting back."

Hannah had seen enough of those cells destroying Alexander to know them well, but this latest blood test had shown her something different. She'd almost missed it at first. Alexander's cells were fighting back. In fact, she wasn't even sure the cells doing the fighting even belonged to Alexander. Larger than red or white blood cells, and pulsing with a pale blue light, the newcomers were not only fighting the infection but were colonizing the infection cells and mutating them.

Unfortunately, there were far too few of the colonizers and they were losing the battle to sheer numbers.

"We can make a fairly accurate guess that Alexander is not

producing those fighting cells on his own," Simon said. "If he had this ability, he'd have been doing it from the beginning."

Hannah went back to her slide. The blue cells had been surrounded by the black, infected cells and were being slowly, but surely, destroyed. "What we need is more of those fighters." Hannah was too scared to even dare to hope.

"Could they come from Roderick?" Simon pointed to Hannah's collection of culture slides.

Hannah didn't need to study Roderick's blood again to shake her head. "Nothing in his bloodwork indicates that those cells are present."

"So where did they come from?" Simon picked up a cold chip and dipped it in ketchup. He stared at it before popping it in his mouth. "And where can we get more of them?"

"Oh my God." The possibility hit Hannah like a smack to the back of her head and left her momentarily giddy. "Remember when Bronwyn tried to heal him?"

"Yes." Understanding dawned on Simon's face and he gaped at her. "She said she stayed in his cells."

"Yes, she bloody did." Even admitting the possibility made her worry she'd jinx it. "Do you think she somehow did something on a cellular level to create the ability for him to fight back?"

Simon scarfed four more soggy chips before he replied. "I mean, she can heal people with a touch. A week ago, I would have told you that was impossible."

Possibilities! Glorious, agonizing possibilities swirled through her brain. "And we know she can't touch him. But what if we could get her to work with his blood cells."

"Outside of his body." Simon kept going at those gross chips like they fueled his brain. She wasn't going to stop him. Whatever worked. "And then we reintroduce fighting cells into his blood."

"Shit, shit, shit," Hannah breathed. "If we introduce enough of them…"

"Yeah." Another fistful of fries followed that possibility.

"We could use Roderick's blood to carry the cells." Hannah might start on those chips herself. She had to force herself not to get carried away. "Assuming Bronwyn can manipulate cells in a petri dish."

Simon stood. "What have we got to lose?"

"Nothing." Hannah stood with him. "We have nothing to lose, and everything to gain."

BRONWYN EYED the petri dish with misgiving. "You want me to heal Alexander's cells in there?"

Hannah and Simon spoke together. "Yes."

Hannah motioned her closer to the microscope. "I want to show you something first. Give you an idea of what to do."

Stepping up to the microscope reminded Bronwyn of school biology classes. "What am I looking for?"

"What you'll see is Alexander's blood cells. You will also notice some dark cells, which Simon and I believe to be the infection."

Bronwyn stared at the blobs through the eyepiece, dividing them into what Hannah described. "Blood magic," she whispered. It was a weirdly disturbing experience to see the blood magic at a cellular level. And something she may have use for in the future, but she pushed that aside. The air of repressed excitement in the healer's hall had her fighting not to grab the iota of hope and run with it.

"And you should see one or two blueish blobs," Hannah said from right beside her. "They're not immediately obvious and are surrounded by the infection…er…blood magic."

"Yes." As Bronwyn watched, the blood magic attacked the

blue thingies—a scientific term if ever she'd coined one. "They're being destroyed." Her magic sparked and snapped beneath her skin. She wanted to get in there and help the blue thingies along.

"We think those are your magic," Hannah said. "They don't come from Roderick, and as you're the only being who has reacted with Alexander's cellular structure, we're guessing they belong to you." Her voice grew softer. "We're really fucking hoping they belong to you."

"They're so tiny." Bronwyn pulled a tiny tendril of her magic, then reduced it even more and fed it into the petri dish.

The dish exploded, and blood spattered the microscope.

Bronwyn jumped back. "Shit! I'm sorry."

"Okay." Hannah stood there blinking at her. "Not ideal, but we have more blood."

"I tried to feed my magic into it." Bronwyn felt like she'd been caught breaking the rules. "And it exploded."

"Too much power." Simon leaned on the refectory table opposite her. "We need less from you."

Bronwyn didn't know if that was possible, and she took a deep breath. "If I can do this, and those blue thingies are me…" She let her question hang in the air between them.

"It's a good sign." Simon nodded, his expression guarded.

Hannah prepared a second petri dish as Bronwyn cleaned up the mess.

Taking a bracing breath, she tried again. This time she didn't reach for her magic, just let it flow from her in a near imperceptible stream. In amazement, she watched the blue thingies pulse and then grow. The blue color grew stronger, and then a blue thingy twitched and absorbed the blood magic cell. It pulsed, and then gobbled up the blood magic beside it and grew bigger. "Oh." The gasp was wrenched from Bronwyn as she reeled back from the microscope.

Hannah and Simon were fixed on her.

"What?" Simon looked tense. "What happened?"

"It ate it. The blue thingies are eating the dark blobs." Her school biology teacher would be losing his shit if he'd heard that. Bronwyn went back to the microscope to confirm what she'd found. Her blue thingy had done some more gobbling. As she watched it, more blood magic tried to attack it, and she let her power leak into the petri dish. Damned if she was going to stand by and let parts of her get consumed by that nasty shit.

Hannah nudged her aside. "I need to see this."

Bronwyn and Simon waited, both barely breathing, as Hannah studied the petri dish.

Finally, she sat back with flushed cheeks and shining eyes. "It's absorbing the infection, growing stronger as it does."

"No." Simon still looked scared to admit the possibility as he lined up his eye with the viewfinder.

Face taut and brow furrowed, Hannah paced away from the table. "What we know is that it's definitely your magic doing this." She raised a hand, as if lecturing a stadium. "We also now know that it grows and absorbs the infection. So, if we get enough of your magic cells into Alexander's bloodstream, they will propagate themselves."

"And the healing with happen incrementally," Simon said.

"Right." Hannah clapped her hands. "Let's get Roderick in here. We need carrier blood and we need Bronwyn to"—she waggled her fingers—"magic Alexander's blood."

Chest aching with a tangle of hope, dread, and stark terror, Bronwyn voiced the question that threatened to freeze the breath in her lungs. "Will it cure him?"

"It's hopeful." Simon gave her a carefully vague smile.

Bronwyn swallowed and tried to keep it together. It was the only hope they had.

CHAPTER THIRTY-SEVEN

As evening fell, Maeve stood beside Roderick at a tower window watching police move into place around Baile. Tomorrow would be Samhain, and already her magic was reacting to the thinning of the veil. It was like a shot of whisky to her blessing, but it also felt wilder and less predictable.

She and Roderick had watched a scene like this once before, many hundreds of years ago, and the coven had fallen that awful day. Many lives had been lost, and the coven had almost died out completely.

Thus far, Alannah and Sinead were holding the wards, and the police couldn't get through. But the twins had to rest sometime, and they were unable to get the other earth witches to hold the wards.

"I can create enough bad weather to discourage them," Nofoto said, she and Mandla standing at the next tower window. "But I can't hurt them."

"I can," Mandla growled.

"And me." Noah shared a nasty grin with Mandla. "The animals and I can create enough havoc to keep them too busy to think about crossing the wards."

Zach had shifted and was out in the falling night with the wild wolves, doing what he could to patrol the wards.

But they were interim measures at best and would buy the twins an hour or two at most before they had to hold the wards again. They were siphoning strength from the other earth witches, so they were able to hold the wards for longer.

She's coming. Maeve read the thought in Roderick's mind. Tomorrow, Rhiannon would make her move, and she'd set her stage well. Joining the thinner line of blue police uniforms on the wards were a growing mob of Rhiannon's followers. More arrived and dispersed their numbers to surround the wards.

The coven waited for news on Alexander, the only tiny glimmer of something positive in the growing sea of trouble. Roderick had provided the blood Hannah and Simon needed. As much as Maeve knew he wanted to be in the healer's hall with Bronwyn while they waited, he was needed more here now.

"Will she attack in the night?" Warren's jaw was tight enough to break rock as he stood beside Roderick.

Roderick shrugged. "I wouldn't think so. She will wait until the full power of Samhain is at her disposal."

"When will that be?" Warren studied the disturbing view outside the window.

"Midday tomorrow," Roderick said. "Let's ensure the twins are most rested for when she attacks."

Noah nodded and left the room.

Maeve couldn't drag herself away. The night of the coven massacre felt as fresh today as it had when she'd lived it. Images of death and fighting lurked behind her eyelids, waiting for her to allow them to take over her mind. Slipping her hand into Roderick's, she drew comfort from the warm clasp of his calloused fingers.

Tomorrow, Mags's vision of a tide of blood covering Baile would come to pass.

THE BREEZE COMING in through the open windows carried the faint stench of blood magic. Outside the healer's hall, Rhiannon's forces were gathering. Bronwyn could sense them out there like a storm heavy sky, but she couldn't think about them now. Not with Alexander fighting for his life.

A blood bag dripped her magic cells into him.

Hannah and Simon wanted to go slow in case there were some unforeseen side effects. Not that it mattered at this stage. It had been several days since she'd seen Alexander's chest exposed and she struggled to look at it now.

The dark invader covered most of his torso, making him look like he'd been severely bruised from throat to groin. Thick, angry black lines spread down his arms to his wrists. The constant beep and murmur of the machines monitoring him became a distant backdrop as they waited.

The breeze stiffened sharply, and Hannah hurried over and closed the window.

Thunder rumbled, and lightning forked across the sky.

Nofoto was bringing one of her storms.

In Bronwyn's womb, the twins had gone almost unnaturally still. They were waiting too. Scared like her to admit the possibility that this would work. Horrified to consider the alternative if it didn't work.

"Two hours," Simon murmured and checked the flow of the drip. He took out Alexander's chart and wrote. "No noticeable change."

Hannah paced. "We could draw his blood."

They both looked at her. "No." Bronwyn didn't want to see this not working. "Let's wait a bit longer."

Nodding, Simon replaced Alexander's chart. "We should eat something," he said and gave her a pointed look. "You should eat something."

The mundanity of his statement almost made her laugh. They might not have tomorrow, and he was concerned for her nutrition. She already knew whatever happened she would survive tomorrow. For as long as she carried the twins Rhiannon wanted so desperately, she would live. Whether she wanted to or not. To make Simon happy, she nodded her agreement.

"Let's give him some more help." Hannah inserted a syringe into the blood tubing and added more of Bronwyn's cells. "Any minute now." She stood back, gaze intent on Alexander. "Any minute now."

SIMON STRODE INTO THE KITCHEN. New faces now held sway in the kitchen, and they were not who he wanted to see. He left the request for food to be taken to Bronwyn and Hannah.

Someone nodded and said right away, but he barely registered her face as he passed into the main part of the castle. Tension was palpable in the air, carved into every face he passed, carried through taut muscles and whispered conversations as if everyone was too frightened to raise their voices and disturb the powder keg they all sat atop.

In the twins' suite, Noah was wearing a barely concealed snarl as he sat in an armchair beside the fire.

"How are they?" Simon motioned to the sleeping twins. Even in sleep, they looked strained and their faces gaunt, as if the magic they were using was eating them up from the inside.

"Resting," Noah said. "They can't keep this up for much longer."

Simon unpacked the bag he'd brought with him. "I've brought some tricks to keep them going if we need to."

Noah growled and Simon took an instinctive step back, but

he was grateful the shifter was here. The man would take care of Sinead, and by extension, Alannah.

"Nothing that will hurt them," he clarified. "But I might be able to keep them going."

Alannah's long red hair spilled over the white of her pillow like a sunrise. The fine, beautiful lines of her face tugged at his chest and invited him to touch, but she hadn't given him the right to do so, and he restrained the urge. Stroking a sleeping woman's face was just creepy.

"You like her." Noah fixed his yellow gaze on Simon.

There was no point in denying what was obvious, so he nodded. "She's not in a place to deal with me right now, though."

"Hmm." Noah studied Alannah's face. "She is my pack now."

Simon didn't miss the warning in Noah's words. Noah would protect his pack and didn't intend to be nice about doing so. "I'll bear that in mind."

"You planning on sticking around, Doc?" Noah tilted his head, exactly like a dog would.

"I don't think anyone is making plans past tomorrow," Simon said. "But whatever the future holds, if she allows me, I'd like to be part of hers."

Noah shifted his head forward and sniffed. "Something about you smells vaguely familiar."

"I'm positive we've never met before." Simon would have remembered a man like Noah Winters. Even if you didn't know he was a shifter, there was something predatory and primal about him that made him stick in your mind.

Noah shook his head. "No, it's not that. It's like you're part of the smell of Baile."

"I'm told I have an ancestor from here." He'd never given his mother's claim much credence, but being at Baile made it real to him. "Apparently, I have a witch in the bloodline."

"Maybe." Noah shrugged. "Without a reference point, it's nothing more than a familiar scent."

"Well." Simon needed to get back to the healer's hall. "You'll take care of them?"

Growling, Noah threw him a hard look.

That's what Simon had thought. "Let me know if I can help in any way."

Noah nodded. "We're all hoping for good news from you."

So was Simon.

CHAPTER THIRTY-EIGHT

Thick fog, courtesy of Nofoto, shrouded the bailey outside the healer's hall. Moisture dripped from the eves and plopped to the ground and increased the sense of otherworldliness. Bronwyn had sat by Alexander's bedside until Hannah had bullied her into taking a nap on the leather sofa. Her babies had sent her into a dreamless sleep for a couple of hours.

No change to Alexander's condition.

The door opened. Fog swirled and coalesced into Roderick and Maeve.

"It looks like the sacred grove used to." Maeve indicated the gently rolling clouds of silver-gray.

The clock above the door showed it was approaching one in the morning. Maeve and Roderick brushed moisture off their clothes and shed coats and boots. She didn't ask if they should be sleeping. Roderick would be as anxious as she was, and she understood his need to be close.

"No change," Bronwyn answered their question before they could ask it. "Simon is monitoring him now."

Hannah lay curled around Charlie on a spare bed.

"We will wait." Roderick took Maeve's hand and kissed her knuckles as if he drew comfort from her presence.

After so many hours of near silence, their voices seemed almost intrusive in the tense, expectant atmosphere. "How is everything?"

Roderick didn't need her to break her question down into specifics, and she was grateful for that. "The fog is keeping our unwanted guests back." Roderick took a seat on the leather sofa and tugged Maeve down beside him. "Zach is with the wolves watching the border. Everything is quiet for now."

For now. Tomorrow—or today really—all hell would break loose, but Bronwyn could only concentrate on Alexander.

"I thought I heard voices." A grim-faced, disheveled Simon strode through from the patient section of the hall. "His vitals are stable."

Which meant nothing new to report, and Bronwyn died a little more inside. As much as she'd tried not to, she'd pinned her future on what Hannah and Simon had discovered.

"I brought supplies." Roderick stood and unearthed a bottle of scotch from his coat pocket. "It might ease the waiting."

Except, not for her, and Bronwyn pulled a face. No relief for poor Bronwyn. *Agh*! She wished she could be strong and stoic and an example to all, but she mainly wanted to curl into a ball and beg.

Simon fetched beakers of varying shapes and sizes and placed them near Roderick. "Alannah told me you had a secret stash of that stuff."

Roderick grunted. "Left it here before Maeve and I went into stasis. Apparently, nobody found it."

"So." Simon studied the amber liquor. "I'm drinking five-hundred-year-old scotch?"

"Something like that." Roderick handed a glass to Maeve.

The door opened, and Warren, Niamh, and Taylor stomped in. Under her coat, Taylor was dressed in a pair of unicorn pjs.

"Hi." Niamh gave Bronwyn a hug. "None of us were sleeping anyway. We gave up and came to where we all wanted to be."

Simon looked around the hall. "We're going to need more chairs."

A second leather sofa appeared beside Bronwyn's indoor herb garden near the window.

"Jesus." Simon scrubbed a palm over his face. "That takes some getting used to."

Andy poked his head around the door. "Oh." He blinked at the other occupants. "Looks like we had the same idea." Opening the door wider, he let Debra and Hermione into the healer's hall.

Debra went to Taylor and cupped her chin. "Couldn't sleep?"

Taylor shook her head and cuddled closer to her mother.

Two armchairs blinked into being, and to his credit, Simon barely started at all.

Next through the door came Kate, Dhara, and Hermione.

"I should have brought more scotch," Roderick grumbled.

Simon saved Bronwyn from having to answer their questions. "Vitals are holding stable. No other discernible changes. Yet."

Bronwyn appreciated his optimism even as each passing hour ate at hers. Her twins sent her a gentle spike of reassurance.

Putting his empty glass on the table, Simon said, "I'll just do a check."

Bronwyn appreciated the coven's support, but she also resented their intrusion. She didn't want to answer their questions or see the concern in their expressions. She followed Simon to Alexander's bedside.

Low lighting created haunting shadows on Alexander's beautiful face. If she didn't know better, she would think he was sleeping.

"I'm trying not to let the light disturb him." Simon went into his observation mode, checking the machines, neatly jotting down results on Alexander's chart.

Bronwyn smoothed the sheet over Alexander's waist. It was all she could do for him. Hannah and Simon had revealed his torso since the treatment had begun.

"It's only been a few hours." Simon swapped the nearly empty bag of blood with another one. "The body takes time to heal."

Not Alexander's body. He'd been alive for long enough to have an accelerated and greater healing ability than the average person. From everything, apparently, except blood magic eating him alive. She brushed his skin with her fingertips, careful to keep her blessing locked tight inside her. His skin felt cool and silky to her touch.

For the hundredth time, she studied the thick black striations on Alexander's chest. It looked like someone had taken a marker and drawn on his skin. Bronwyn stopped and leaned closer to the marks on the arm closest to her. She couldn't be certain, and she blinked and then rubbed her eyes. "Simon?"

"What is it?" His full attention turned to her with dizzying intensity.

"This line." She indicated a thick, black mark that curled over his bicep and pooled in the crook of his elbow. "Does it look different to you?"

With a frown, Simon snapped on a small torch and trained it on the spot she indicated. He studied it for so long she had to force herself to breathe.

When he looked up at her, the expression in his eyes made her breath catch in her throat. "I think it does. But tell me what you're seeing."

"It looks less black." Bronwyn's voice came out as a strangled whisper. If she spoke aloud, maybe fate would take another swipe at her and make it not so. "And slightly shorter. I could have sworn it extended down his forearm."

"Hmm." Simon took a marker out of his pocket and made a dot on Alexander's skin where the mark ended. "Not scientific, but it'll do the job." Next, he dug his phone out and took some photographs. "Let's watch that."

Neither of them voiced that they should keep it to themselves.

"We should have known everyone would be here." Sinead's voice drifted in from the room next door.

Roderick answered her. "Shouldn't you be resting?"

"Tell me about it," Noah said. "I couldn't get them to stay put."

Simon stiffened as Alannah spoke, "We can hold the wards as easily here as we can from our suite. And we want to be here."

"Looks like you'll have some company tonight." Simon touched her shoulder. "They're good people."

"The best." Bronwyn's throat tightened. As one of the strange Beaty women in her hometown, all the support and love offered by the coven still surprised her. "I just can't deal with anyone right now."

"Stay here then." Simon pointed to his dot on Alexander's arm and handed her the marker. "And keep an eye on that."

Bronwyn wasn't surprised when she heard Jack, Mags, and Emma join the waiting coven about five minutes later. A low murmur of conversation came from the other room, and she found it strangely comforting.

Her vision blurred on the blue dot on the inside of Alexander's arm. Had the mark moved further away from it? Standing, she peered closer. A tiny sliver of unmarked skin was between the mark and Simon's dot.

She could totally be seeing what she wanted to see, and Bronwyn grabbed the marker and added a second dot.

Footsteps whispered behind her, and Roderick's big presence loomed over her. He studied her and cocked his head. "What is it?"

"Maybe nothing." Bronwyn didn't want to spread false hope. She pointed to Alexander's arm and explained the dots. "It's totally possible that I'm just seeing things."

Grunting, Roderick leaned over and studied the arm. "Bronwyn?"

"Yes." Her heart thundered in her throat.

"Look." A muscle in Roderick's jaw twitched.

There was now a half inch between Simon's first dot and the deadly marks staining Alexander's skin.

"Please." Bronwyn didn't know who or what she was begging, but she squeezed her eyes closed before she looked again. She made a third dot, this one higher than the last. "It's moving?"

"It's moving." Roderick nodded and locked gazes with hers.

They shared so much in that eye meet—desperation, hope, fear, their mutual love for Alexander.

"Simon woke me." Hannah strode to the bedside. "He wanted me to see."

Simon followed tight on her heels, his eyes glinting with unexpressed thoughts.

Together they studied the evidence before Simon grabbed his phone and thumbed through the pictures he'd taken. "They're lighter," he whispered. "Those fucking lines are definitely lighter."

"And they've moved again," Hannah said.

Tears blurred Bronwyn's sight as she stared at Hannah. "Don't lie to me. Please don't fucking lie to me."

"Hey." Hannah hauled her into a hard hug. "I would never be that cruel. But we don't know what this means yet. Something is happening though."

"The blood magic is lifting." Goddess glided into the room. "I can feel it's hold on him growing weaker."

Bronwyn's muscles melted, and she slumped into her chair. Her hands shook so badly she could barely wipe her tears away.

"Once the blood magic is clear, we must remove the athame," Goddess said.

Simon glanced at Hannah. "Surgery?"

"No." Hannah shook her head. "Not when we have a healer who can repair the damage faster than we ever could."

Roderick frowned. "Will it be safe for Bronwyn to do so?"

"Yes." Goddess nodded. "Once the taint is gone from him, she can heal him."

The conversation dipped and swirled around her, defying Bronwyn's ability to track its meaning.

Dhara shook her head as if clearing Goddess. "Shall I tell the others?"

Bronwyn couldn't answer, but Roderick shook his head. "Not yet. Let's wait a while longer."

"Fucking hell," Simon murmured. "Take another look."

The black streaks on Alexander's arm had retreated to his bicep and gone from stygian black to a mottled gray.

Bronwyn's head swam, and Roderick caught her before she slid from her chair "Stay with us, Blessed. He is going to need his little witch."

"It's moving faster." Hannah laughed, a bright, harsh sound that jangled the silence. She clapped her hands over her mouth. "I can see it happening."

So could Bronwyn. The streaks were vanishing, shrinking back like a dying plant.

"Um." Simon cleared his throat. "I don't want to be this person, but we don't know—"

"Then don't." Bronwyn implored him with a look. "Don't be that person right now."

Nodding, Simon went into his vitals check.

Bronwyn groped for Alexander's hand and held it. Had she felt a slight pressure?

No, that was impossible. Even before the blood magic had spread over him, he'd been unresponsive.

His arms were now almost entirely clear, and the stain lightened on the outside edges of his chest.

Alexander's fingers flexed beneath hers.

She hadn't been imagining that. No, she fucking hadn't.

Bronwyn returned the gentle pressure and stood. "You're not leaving me today," she whispered. "You come back to me."

"Blood pressure coming up," Simon muttered. "Blood ox levels improving."

Alexander's chest rose and fell on a deep breath.

It was like watching timelapse photography as the blood magic retreated to the point of impact, the athame.

"Heart rate holding at fifty-three," Simon snapped. "Blood pressure one-one-four over seventy-five. Blood oxygen eighty-seven and rising."

Roderick glanced at him. "That's good right?"

"That's very good." Hannah nodded and checked Simon's numbers. "That's very bloody good." Tears spilled down Hannah's cheeks. "Those are normal, healthy ranges."

"Come on, son." Roderick's voice broke and he coughed. "Fight this."

The black marks were now a five-inch stain around the athame and shrinking.

"Dhara?" Bronwyn motioned her forward. "Can we have Goddess?"

"I am here, Blessed." Goddess put a hand on Alexander's chest. "The blood magic is nigh gone."

"We need to get that knife out." Simon's eyes glowed as he stared at Bronwyn. "Time is of the essence as we don't want him to bleed out when we remove it."

Her legs shook so badly she didn't know if they could hold her. "Tell me what to do."

Snatching a notebook out of his pocket, Simon began to draw. His medical terms flew over her head, but what she got was find the leak and repair it.

"Almost time," Goddess murmured. "Stand ready, Blessed."

Bronwyn called water.

A glass by Alexander's bedside shattered.

"Easy now." Roderick's arm on her shoulder anchored her. "Do what you always do. Block from your mind who this is and how much he means to you."

Taking a deep breath, Bronwyn wrestled her leaping magic under control.

"Not yet." Goddess barely glanced up. "We cannot risk the blood magic jumping to you."

The stain on Alexander's chest looked like a pale bruise now, and even as they all stared, it faded to healthy, tanned skin.

"Now," Goddess snapped.

Bronwyn poured magic into Alexander. It arced to his heart and surrounded the beating muscle.

Simon gripped the shaft of the athame. "Ready?"

Bronwyn nodded.

Carefully, competently, Simon pulled the knife from Alexander's chest and tossed it to the floor.

Bronwyn's magic surged to the severed artery and knit the cells together. The injury shuddered through her, almost knocking her to the floor, and then transmuted into the earth.

On Alexander's chest, the wound closed to a thin scar and disappeared altogether.

"Why is he not waking?" Roderick kept his intense gaze focused on Alexander.

Alexander took a large, shuddering breath and expelled it though open lips.

His eyes opened and locked on Bronwyn. "Hi, little witch," he rasped. "I had one nasty fucking dream."

CHAPTER THIRTY-NINE

Samhain.

Alexander watched the sun rise over the sea and reach tangerine tentacles across the lightening sky. Just another day, yet not even slightly.

Magic sparked and crackled beneath his skin, all four elements growing stronger as the power of Samhain grew. There was a sense of unreality to the dawning day that kept him in a limbo state of objectivity. His mind understood what today would bring, and all the possible repercussions, but his humanity refused to accept the staggering importance. If the coven didn't prevail today, it would mean the death of magic. Without Goddess and her cré-witches, Rhiannon would run rampant through the world. There would be no balancing force, no good to her evil, no check to her power.

He couldn't fathom a world in which Rhiannon controlled the weft of existence.

"Should you be up?" Bronwyn slid her arms around his waist and snuggled into his side.

He had no real memory of the last few days, but the devastation they'd caused were carefully hidden in his father and Bronwyn's eyes. In so many ways, the last few days had been easier on him than those around him.

Pressing a kiss to the top of her head, he drew the honey and sage scent of her into himself. "I believe I've slept enough over the last few days to justify an hour or two on my feet." He hated that his little witch had faced losing him forever. That she had dealt with the all too real possibility she would raise their children without him.

Of course, if Rhiannon's plans came to fruition today, they wouldn't be raising their children at all.

Alexander caressed the swell of Bronwyn's belly and felt the twin life forms sleeping inside her. Not even born yet, and already they carried the weight of expectation on their tiny shoulders.

Growing light chased the remaining shadows into the bailey's corners. From here, he couldn't see over the walls to the crowd waiting on the edge of the wards. He'd been part of that crowd the last time Rhiannon had attacked Baile. She'd been poorly prepared that time, impatient for victory, and it had led to her failure. She had managed to disastrously weaken the coven and Goddess, but ultimately, Baile had repelled her.

She wouldn't make the same mistake twice.

"None of this seems real," Bronwyn murmured. "Like it's all some huge bad dream, and we'll all wake up."

Alexander wished he could tell her it was a dream.

"Good morning." Roderick strode into the room.

Alexander shouldn't be surprised the tireless bastard was already up and about and wearing an air of grim resolve. "Morning." He returned Roderick's smile.

Roderick studied his face, as if trying to see inside him and if he was truly free of the taint that had almost killed him.

Alexander nodded, and Roderick's tense shoulders eased a tiny amount.

After holding a weeping Bronwyn after he'd regained

consciousness in the wee hours of this morning, he and Roderick had endured an awkward hug, a few throat clearings, and hastily wiped tears, and gone right back to the way they always were.

"What does it look like outside?" Roderick would give it to him straight.

Roderick made a face. "Not good. The number swells constantly. Alannah and Sinead are holding the wards." He folded his arms. "It stinks of blood magic."

"She won't want to take any chances this time," Alexander said. "She'll wait until noon to maximize her chances."

"Warren tells me the police are poised to attack as soon as they can clear the wards." Roderick curled his lips around the word police, and Alexander almost laughed. The notion of centralized law and order rankled Roderick.

Regardless of what Bronwyn and the two doctors said, Alexander's coven needed him, and he despised waiting. "I best get a good look at what's happening."

Bronwyn frowned up at him. "I don't think that's a good idea."

"Little witch." He kissed her nose. "I cannot lie here while everyone I love is under attack."

Her frown deepened, and her need to argue played in her expressive eyes. After a moment, she sighed and looked at Roderick. "You'll keep an eye on him?"

"Definitely." Roderick nodded.

Alexander could give the babysitting a miss, but after what Bronwyn had gone through, if this put her mind at ease, he'd deal. "You need to rest." He pulled her tight against him. "We're going to need you before this day is over."

Reluctantly, she let him go.

Baile was quiet as he and Roderick let themselves into the kitchen. After a weepy reunion earlier this morning, the coven had all gone to rest. The specter of today hung like a reaper over all of them.

"Are you well?' Roderick stopped him before they climbed the stairs to the great hall. "Truly?"

"I am." Other than feeling weaker than he ever had, he was well. "It was worse for you lot than for me."

"Hmmm." Roderick's stern pale blue gaze studied him like a science experiment. "You are certain?"

"Roderick." Alexander needed to set the big man straight. "Even when I hated you, it was a point of pride never to lie to you."

Roderick scoffed. "That was a lie you just told."

"Eh." Alexander shrugged. "More of a stretch of the truth."

Roderick chuckled. "You lied straight to my face when it suited you."

"You may have a point." He slung an arm around Roderick's shoulder. "Come on then, Daddy-o. Let's see what we're up against."

RHIANNON STUDIED her reflection in the speckled glass of a full-length, oval mirror that had once belonged to a queen. Rhiannon forgot which one. Now it belonged to a goddess.

She had chosen a royal blue gown. The color caught the blue lights in her dark hair and turned her complexion creamy. Today, she would finally take her proper place. It wasn't the day for anything as obvious as black or red.

"Mistress?" Her favorite minion scratched at the door. Rhiannon should make a point to learn her name.

"Come."

The door opened, and the woman slunk through the narrow opening. "All is in readiness."

Rhiannon allowed herself a girlish moment and faced her minion with her arms spread. "How do I look?"

"Like a goddess," the minion said, admiration gleaming in her dark eyes. "Perfect."

"Good." Soon, the world would tremble at her feet. Petty politicians and world leaders would be swept away beneath her power or die. "Let us proceed."

"All your generals have been briefed," the minion said. "They will attack on your command."

Rhiannon nodded. She expected nothing less from those who served her.

A SEA of people surrounded Baile as the sun climbed toward its zenith. A motley collection of uniformed cops, those roadside freaks from their makeshift caravan park, thuggish types sporting leather and chains, Wiccans wafting sage and brandishing makeshift weapons, weekend warriors in camo, and more concerning knots wearing black combat gear interspersed amongst the masses. The mob's organization concerned Alexander even more than the numbers. Thousands of Rhiannon's followers clustered in what he recognized as attack formations. "Fuck."

"They're waiting for something." Warren joined him at the turret window.

"Rhiannon," Roderick replied. "They're waiting for her."

Pale and determined, Andy strode into the room. "Sasha has sent what help he can. They will be arriving shortly and will attack from the rear."

"So many," Emma whispered. "Sasha doesn't have anywhere close to the numbers out there."

"What's the plan?" Jack looked to Roderick.

"If the wards fall, we draw everyone inside the castle."

Roderick's jaw was tight enough to break rock. "Even without the wards, I built her to withstand a protracted siege."

"The twins are holding the wards," Noah said, standing with one shoulder propped against the wall. "So far, nobody is pushing against them, so it's not taking too much effort." He motioned the view outside the turret windows. "Zach is still out there with the wolves. We can call them in if we need to."

Alexander didn't mention what they were all thinking. They would need to call Zach and the wolves in.

"Something's happening," Emma said, her voice low and tense.

A ripple ran through the crowd nearest the gatehouse, and a figure in a blue dress parted the masses. Sun gleamed off her crow-black hair as she moved to the ward's edge. As if she knew they were there, she stared up at the turret.

The crowd grew more focused, heads all swung her way, and quiet descended.

"Roderick." Despite the distance, her voice reached them clear as a bell. "We can end this now."

Roderick moved in clear view in the window. "You surrender?"

Mandla chuckled. At least someone appreciated Roderick's medieval parley smack talk.

"Send me Goddess, and we will allow you to leave Baile unhurt," Rhiannon said.

Warren's low grumble carried in the silent tower room. "Like hell she will."

"Nay." Roderick called back. "You have brought this fight to us, and we have no option but to engage."

"Very well." A smile spread across Rhiannon's face. "War, it is."

Whispers susurrated through her followers.

A blade flashed as she drew it across her palm. Crouching, she pressed her hand to the ground. "I call earth to serve me."

A rumble shook the earth as a large, jagged crack opened beneath her palm. People jumped away from the two-foot wide split in the earth as the shaking grew stronger.

"What is that?" Emma leaned forward.

"The wards," Roderick said. "She's attacking the wards."

From the widening fissure, a thick, oily mass rose like pus seeping from a wound. It touched the wards and made them visible as thin, silver streams of light surrounding Baile. The ooze spread over the wards.

Timbers creaked, and dust rained down from the ceiling as Baile absorbed the impact.

"Call Zach in," Roderick snapped. "And check on Alannah and Sinead."

Noah sprinted from the room.

Up and over the gleaming silver of the wards, the inky black climbed. The wards shimmered and sparked, and the spread stopped for a few minutes.

"Earth! Cede your power to me," Rhiannon shouted, and tremors rocked the floor beneath them. Blood magic continued an inexorable climb up the wards.

Again, the wards glowed bright as they fought back, Alannah and Sinead's earth magic trying to stop the rising tide.

From inside Baile, a woman cried out and then Sinead's screamed, "Alannah!"

"Get Bronwyn," Noah yelled.

The wards flared and blinked then vanished.

With a roar, Rhiannon's people surged into Baile.

CHAPTER FORTY

"Do something," Noah snapped, Sinead lying limp in his arms.

Bronwyn grabbed for her blessing and touched Sinead.

She was out cold but still breathing. She fed healing magic into Sinead first, and then Alannah.

Alannah's eyes blinked open. "What happened?"

"The wards are down." Noah said.

Sinead groaned and rolled to her side. "That magic was too strong."

"We can try again," Alannah said.

Noah growled and opened his mouth to argue as Roderick strode through the door. "There is no purpose. We are overrun." He gestured the room. "Everyone, follow me to the great hall."

Outside, the crowd raised their voices in a steady roar. Pounding echoed from all the exterior doors.

Bronwyn obeyed Noah and stayed clear of the windows as they ran for the great hall.

Most of the coven was already gathered when she joined Alexander standing behind Roderick.

Standing on a table, Roderick raised his hands for silence.

"The wards are down. Baile is holding for now, but we need to get the witches out."

Out? Bronwyn stared at Roderick. Not sure she understood his meaning.

Alexander looked down at her and nodded. "We need to get you out of Baile and away from here."

"How?" Emma jammed her hands on her hips. "There's a fucking mob between us and the nearest exit point."

"No." Bronwyn raised her voice to be heard above the noise coming from outside. "I'm not leaving."

Alexander frowned at her. "Of course you are, little witch. You and the other witches need to escape. We'll keep them off your tails for as long as we can."

"No." Niamh appeared at her shoulder. "We're not leaving."

"Blessed." Roderick's voice lashed at them. "You are all that remains, and you must be kept safe."

"No." Maeve joined them and glared at Roderick. "Once before, good men gave their lives to get us safe, and we ended up here anyway. We fight together. And if we lose, and Baile falls, we fall together."

"Little witch." Alexander turned those devastating dark eyes on her, full of pleading. "We can't protect you."

And she understood that, but that ship had sailed. "And we don't want to be protected." Faces of the women, her coven sisters, reflected her words. "This is our fight too, and protecting the witches last time only brought us right back to this point. I've made my choice."

Niamh raised her hand. "Me too. I'm staying."

Honey badger nudged her calf muscle and glared at the assembled men as if stepping in as Niamh's backup.

One by one, the witches echoed Bronwyn's determination.

Frustrated men glared back at them.

Emma moved beside the witches. "Together," she said.

Jack glared at her, and then a reluctant smile slid over his face. "Okay, then. Together."

"I cannot be happy with this," Roderick growled.

"Noted." Andy held up a hand. "I'll minute your objection."

The shouting outside grew louder and a dull *thud* reverberated through the hall as something heavy hit the doors.

"Beloved." Goddess stepped forward and held her hands out to Alexander. "I have one gift I may bestow on you."

Bronwyn tried to step between them. Alexander wasn't well enough for anything. Her feet stuck to the ground and wouldn't move. The twins shifted violently in her belly.

"*No.*" Bronwyn felt their objection to her interference rather than heard it. Helpless and panicked, she stared at Goddess approaching Alexander.

"Earth," Goddess called and raised her hand.

Alannah and Sinead crouched and placed their palms against the floor. Green magic swelled around their twined hands, growing stronger and deeper green.

Goddess drew it to her and molded it between her palms like a giant glowing green ball. She looked at the rescued witches. "Give me all the earth."

The rescued earth witches joined Alannah and Sinead, their own magic swelling the magic until it was as large as a boulder.

"Fire," Goddess called.

Niamh, Nofoto, and Lerato drew fire and sent it to Goddess. Two additional Canadian witches added a stream of red to the growing sphere between Goddess's outstretched arms.

Mags and a Canadian witch gave her Air, and yellow magic swirled in and around the red and green already dancing and sparking, casting light over Goddess's face.

Bronwyn and Taylor added water.

"All four elements combine as one." Goddess raised her voice over the hum of the magic. "I bring spirit onto the path of power."

The four colors flared and exploded outwards, driving coven members back. A vast sucking sound filled the space as the four elements streamed back toward Goddess and exploded into a brilliant white sphere easily three times her height.

Alexander's skin prickled. His heartrate accelerated; magic pounded in his blood. Spirit swelled and pulsed and then shot straight at him. Spirit magic hit like a truck, blowing his hair back, and driving him to his knees. His muscles screamed in protest as they tried to contain the power coursing through him. And he knew what he had to do.

BRONWYN SCREAMED as the light engulfed Alexander. His molecules blew apart in a shower of sparks that grew and spread, filling the entire great hall.

She tried to get to her feet and reach him, but the magic held her pinned to the ground.

Roderick's face contorted in agony as he fought against the same force holding him down.

And then the spirit magic stopped, suspended for a moment before rushing back to the place Alexander had stood.

Light sparkled and shimmered, so bright her eyes streamed, and her retinas burned.

Magic pulsed on a low, resonant *boom*, and the lights vanished.

A massive white dragon stretched his wings. He shone like millions of diamonds had been embedded in his skin. Air whooshed around them as he opened his giant wings and fanned them.

"Holy fuck," somebody whispered, but Bronwyn couldn't take her eyes off Alexander.

Throwing back his head, he bugled and blew a stream of crystalline light at the stained-glass window.

The window shattered into thousands of pieces, and the dragon launched himself through the gap.

Taylor helped Bronwyn to her feet as the entire coven rushed to the jagged remains of the broken window.

"Give him all your strength," Goddess yelled. "Give him everything. Open your elements wide. NOW!"

Bronwyn joined her sisters, magic streaming from them, more magic than she'd ever felt, more magic than she could ever have imagined pouring from all of them toward the great, majestic beast winging across the sea.

It hit the dragon, and he got even bigger, his wings the size of a commercial airliner's as he tipped them and stroked the air back to Baile.

The front doors to the great hall blew out.

In the bailey, Rhiannon's followers froze and stared at winged, white death heading their way.

Several screamed and started to run; others dropped to the ground and tried to cover their heads; still others stood and stared in paralyzed wonder.

Rhiannon stood in the center of the bailey and screamed. "Nooooo!" Frantically, she turned to a follower. "Give me blood. All of it."

Bronwyn was dimly aware of people crying out and the coppery tang of blood. The stench of blood magic made her retch and convulse, but she couldn't take her eyes off Alexander. And still, the magic poured from her.

Blood magic coalesced into a black cloud and covered Rhiannon, growing and stretching, as her followers dropped around her.

Alexander exhaled, his mighty chest swelling.

Bronwyn felt the yank on her magic, and her knees collapsed under the force.

Blood magic rose around Rhiannon in an oily, inky cloud, shot from her like a spear and slammed Alexander in the chest.

Alexander faltered, his wings snapping back against his body, and he plummeted.

"More," Roderick bellowed. "Give him all you have."

Bronwyn pulled every ounce of magic she could. Around her, her sisters did the same.

Alexander spread his wings.

Nofoto threw a thermal to catch him.

Blood magic boiled and snarled around him, engulfing him, shrinking his great body.

His wings swept down and then up again, and he rose.

Magic poured from the coven into his body, and he swelled with it.

A ray of sunshine struck his body in a multifaceted light array that turned him into a glimmering shaft of light.

Two more beats of his wings, and he rose higher.

Light reflected off the faces watching him.

He inhaled and grew even larger, casting his shadow over Baile, and released a stream of diamond fire at Rhiannon.

Bronwyn felt the draw, like her magic was being sucked out of her. Even her twins' magic was drawn from her womb. The world grew dim around her, her vision blackened, and blood trickled from her nose.

And Rhiannon exploded.

Blood and matter showered her followers.

Everything stopped.

Parts of Rhiannon stilled in the air.

Goddess staggered to her feet and into the bailey. "The two become one," she said, her voice carrying like clarion bells and hurting Bronwyn's ears. "Thus, is balance restored."

Silvery light streamed out of her and surrounded what was

left of Rhiannon.

Dhara collapsed to her knees, and with a cry, Kate ran for her.

Particles of Goddess and Rhiannon fused into a ball and crashed to the ground, shaking the earth beneath Baile. Mortar dust rained down around them. Windows shattered. The great wooden rafters groaned in protest. In the bailey, Rhiannon's followers were flung off their feet. Those farther away scrambled for escape.

Alexander landed, and as his feet touched the ground, the dragon morphed back into man, a man who swayed and collapsed.

Simon scrambled and reached him moments before Bronwyn.

"It's over," Alexander whispered as his eyes drifted closed. "It is done."

"No, no, no." Bronwyn's hands shook as she touched Alexander. She couldn't have come this far to lose him again. She couldn't—

"He's okay."

Bronwyn became aware of Simon shaking her.

"Alexander is fine. As far as I can tell, he's sleeping it off."

Sword drawn, Roderick raced for the mass of matter that had been Rhiannon and Goddess.

Slowly, like wax melting, the light and dark fused. A head formed first, and then the rest of her limbs, as a naked female form took shape. Dark, shiny hair streamed down her naked back as she looked up at them.

Even Roderick stilled as Rhiannon but not Rhiannon rose gracefully to her feet. Silvery light beamed from her eyes as Rhiannon achieved her goal; she became Goddess. But not as she had envisioned it. Light and dark, evil and good, blood and cré-magic combined into a new being, and one with so much power it pulsed like a tangible presence from her.

CHAPTER FORTY-ONE

Roderick didn't know if he'd ever get used to Rhiannon in this new incarnation, but she stood beneath the stained-glass window—the new one—light playing off her beautiful face as she studied it.

By the time they'd all recovered from fueling the dragon and Goddess reforming into Rhiannon, the window had repaired itself into a new image. The first witches were gone, and in their place stood Bronwyn, Alannah and Sinead, Mags, Niamh, and hovering in the background, a gleaming white dragon. A new coven, a rebirth for cré-magic.

His hand twitched and landed on his sword hilt. Some part of him was hardwired to want to take that head off those shoulders, and he wasn't sure it would ever go away.

She turned and grinned at him. "Roderick."

Despite knowing the Goddess he'd served was half of this new being, he couldn't bring himself to bow to her. All he could manage was a nod. "What happens now?"

"Now we do what was intended all along." She tucked a strand of shining dark hair behind her ear. Her eyes had changed to an eerie silvery gray, the only outward sign that she wasn't that Rhiannon anymore. "Now we bring magic back to the world and heal what has been broken."

"We thought we'd head back to South Africa," Mandla said from behind him.

Roderick turned.

The honey badger had made a new friend and stuck to the big South African's side with a cocky swagger. "We have our own coven to build."

Dhara tucked against her side, Kate came up from the kitchen. Zach flanked them, his wolfish eyes always searching for a possible threat around them.

"We're headed home as well," Kate said. "Now that Dhara is Dhara again, and we have what's left of our witches, we can also start to rebuild."

Jack, Emma, and Mags had announced ten minutes earlier that they would be doing something similar in Moscow.

"I can help with that," the new goddess said. "Goddess pools are now portals that will link us all."

"Portals?" Dhara blinked. "Like magic gates?"

"Exactly." *She* chuckled. "Never again will my covens be left to flounder in isolation, and as my covens flourish, so will my strength, and so will magic grow in the world."

"We're not going anywhere." Noah strode into the hall with Sinead by his side. "We're staying right here."

Roderick glanced at *her* and got the distinct impression she knew all this already.

The rescued witches would be returning home as well. He and Maeve, along with Alexander and Bronwyn had decided to stay at Baile.

Andy, Debra, and Hermione would help them build a new Baile, a learning coven, a training ground for new witches and a center of magic. The mighty old castle would be the hub of magic going forward.

Warm, sweet light flooded his being as Maeve bustled down

the stairs toward him. All those hundreds of years ago, he'd had no idea of where the bond he was called to make with a tiny, blonde spirit walker witch would lead them. Would he have accepted the challenge had he known?

Roderick had to laugh at himself. Of course he would have. He was born to rise to the needs of cré-magic, then, now, and into the future.

SIMON LOOKED around the healer's hall that had been his home for the last few days. It still fucked with his head that so much had happened in such a short amount of time. He changed into the scrubs he'd been kidnapped in. His phone rang, and he checked caller ID. With all the excitement and news coverage of the last couple of days, he should have expected this call. He answered, "Hi, Mum."

"Simon?" His mother's voice sounded strained. "Thank God, we got you. Your father and I have been watching the news." She clicked her tongue. "We were so worried. What's happening there? Are you okay?"

"I'm fine, Mum." He'd like to tell her the reports winging across the world from Greater Littleton were exaggerated, but that would be an outright lie. "I was never in any danger." He'd just secured his place in the pocket of hell reserved for people who lied to their mothers. "Things got…weird for a while, but they've settled down now." Into what, Simon couldn't say, so he went for a subject change. "How's Greece?"

"Hot," his mother said. "And you know what your father's like. He won't listen, and he's got that bloody heat rash again."

"Did you take the cream I prescribed with you?"

"I packed it." Mum growled. "But can I get him to use it?"

Simon settled in for a chat, hoping his diversionary tactic had gotten her off topic of what had happened at Greater Littleton. There were no words in his vocabulary to describe it. Alexander was fully recovered and showed no signs of either his brush with blood magic death or morphing into a dragon. Jesus, that would never not do his head in.

Mum went through the boat trip they'd taken round the islands, the great beach they'd discovered, and the food before she wound down and asked, "What did happen there? The internet is full of the strangest things."

"You know the internet." He forced a light chuckle. "You can't believe everything you read."

"Right." Mum sighed. "Well, just stay away from the odd castle."

Not if he could help it. "Speaking of Baile, I've been meaning to ask you something."

"Yes," Mum's tone got perkier.

"Didn't you tell us that we had a woman in our ancestors who came from here."

She laughed. "Oh God. I forgot about that. I kept telling your dad there was something about the place that kept pinging around my brain. I'd even forgotten I'd told you boys that story."

"Do you remember her name?" On the cusp of his departure, Simon felt the need to find all links he could with Baile Castle.

"Not her name, darling." Mum laughed. "It was a man, a younger son. The story goes, he was supposed to be a parish priest but refused and went to that castle and never came out again." She lowered her voice. "They say he was quite the lad, and the priesthood was not for him. If you know what I mean."

Simon laughed with her, even as the hair on his arms stood on end. "Do you remember his name?"

"Gosh now." His mother tutted. "You're determined to challenge my memory today, aren't you?"

The piercing whistle of a kestrel sounded from outside the healer's hall and Simon looked out the window.

A brown speck against the sky, Kai rode the thermals.

"It was something like John or Luke. Something old fash-ioned like that," Mum mused. "Thomas!" she declared. "That's it. His name was Thomas." She chuckled. "I can't believe I forgot that, because we kind of named you for him, Simon Thomas."

"Right." Simon's head spun. He'd managed to glean from chatter around the castle the name of Alannah's lost love. His ancestor, apparently. He couldn't begin to fathom what that meant.

"Why did you want to know about Thomas?" Mum asked.

"Just curious."

Alannah stood in the doorway and waved at him.

He managed a smile that he hoped didn't look too consti-pated. "I have to go, Mum."

"All right, love." She sighed. "Call your mother more often."

"I will."

"And take care of yourself."

"I will."

"Don't work too hard. You know you need to take care of yourself before you're any good to your patients."

"I know, Mum. I'll speak to you first."

He said goodbye and hung up before meeting Alannah's gaze. "Hi."

"Hi." She cocked her head. "You all right?"

Instinct warned him not to blurt his discovery out to Alannah before he'd sorted it through for himself first. "Yup, fine."

"All packed?" She glanced around him for bags.

He'd come here with nothing, and that's how he'd leave. "Yup. Nothing to pack."

"I'm your lift home." She dangled the Landy keys from her forefinger.

His life would resume as if nothing had happened, yet so much had. He tucked his newest knowledge away for another time. A time when maybe Alannah didn't wear so many shadows in her eyes.

Hannah had decided to stay at Baile with Charlie and work with Bronwyn to cure disease before it could even develop, but that wasn't his future. He was an A&E doctor, a doer, not a researcher, and he had no place here.

Hell only knew if once Hannah and Bronwyn got started, there'd be much use for people with his skills for much longer.

He forced himself to return Alannah's smile. "Let's go."

Heart in his throat, he followed her out to the stinky old Landy and climbed into the passenger side.

Alannah eased them out of the bailey and onto the road.

Most of Rhiannon's followers had disappeared as she'd—well, he didn't quite know how to describe her ending and her beginning. The diehards had been rounded up by a group of coppers under Lennox and taken away. Sasha's people had disappeared with Rhiannon's generals and close followers. Simon didn't want to think what had happened to the followers, but he also felt no sympathy.

"Thank you." Alannah's sweet, calm voice fell like a salve on his wounded heart. "For all that you did here."

"You're welcome." His time at Baile hadn't started on the most auspicious note, but he was leaving knowing he'd done the right thing.

Simon wanted to fill the silence in the Landy with words and feelings, but he kept quiet. Alannah wasn't ready to hear what he had to say, and she definitely wasn't ready to receive the way he felt about her.

The village green was once again a quiet, peaceful place with one or two folks wandering around. The serenity wouldn't last long. Once word got out about Baile and what was happening there, Greater Littleton would be flooded with the desperate and the dreamers again. Everyone looking for a miracle would find their way here, and Baile would deliver.

He supposed that some part of him should be honored to have been present at events that would change the world forever. Instead, he felt heartsick and exhausted.

"You could visit." Alannah glanced at him out of the corner of her eye as she drove. "I mean, if you didn't have anything better to do."

Joy bubbled up inside him, and he had to clench his hands to keep his tone light. "Would that be okay?"

"It would be more than okay." She grinned at him. "I would look forward to seeing you."

It was far from the declaration of love he wanted, but he'd take it. And one day he'd tell her about Thomas, but not today. "Then I'll visit."

Alannah nodded and grinned out the windscreen. "Good."

CHAPTER FORTY-TWO

"Good evening." The news anchor found her camera and smiled—not too widely to be accused of being flippant, but just enough to be trustworthy. "In tonight's news, authorities continue to be baffled by the appearance of what several eyewitnesses claim was a dragon off the coast of Devon. Whilst speculation is rife, scientific sources continue to be skeptical. More on this story after the break."

"Can you describe, in your own words, what you saw here this evening?" The reporter shoved a microphone under the aging blonde's chin.

Bonnie had waited a lifetime for her moment on telly, and now that it had come, she wasn't about to waste it. Her best pink shirt shared enough cleavage to show the world out there what they were missing. "I absolutely can, Ron." She smiled into the camera, thanking the foresight that had told her to get her veneers done. "Well, it was a regular night at the Hag's Head." She worked a little plug in for the pub. "And something told me to look outside." She leaned a little closer to the microphone. "I get these feelings, you know, Ron. The blessing runs in our family, you know."

"Blessing?" Ron, bless his cotton socks, asked her exactly the right question.

"That's what we who practice the craft call our abilities." Bonnie gave the camera her best weighted stare, the one she'd been saving for this moment. "Most of us in Greater Littleton have special abilities. And we're not at all surprised by what happened tonight."

"Ah, come on." The nighttime host shot a sideways eyeroll at his studio audience. "Dragons! What's next? Pink elephants on parade."

The band launched into the jaunty Disney tune from *Dumbo*.

"And they say England hasn't legalized weed yet?"

Bada-boomp-pa.

GETTHEFACTS.COM:

Q: Do dragons exist?

A. No. No scientific evidence to corroborate the claim can be found.

Read the full question and answer.

SOCIAL MEDIA POST

I don't care what you say, that looks like a dragon to me. #dragonsarereal #cremagic #magiclives

Comment: *One word: Photoshop*

Thus concludes the cré-witch chronicles. An ending, but also a beginning.

EPILOGUE

*T*wenty-eight years in the future.

REGAN CLIMBED THE WEST TOWER, as she'd done every year since she could manage to toddle up here on her own. Today was her birthday, her twenty-eighth birthday, and she hated it as much as she'd hated the twenty-seven that came before. Mum and Dad had some big party planned for tonight, at which they'd all sit around and pretend the other part of the celebration wasn't missing. They did it for her, Regan knew that, and telling them she didn't want it would just cause more heartache than she could handle.

So, she'd go along to her birthday party, smile and laugh, open her gifts, joke with the rest of the Baile coven, and play her part. Mum would do her best to pretend her heart didn't break a little more with each passing year, and Dad would stand by all stoically and try and make her laugh until they both couldn't bear the pretense anymore and would slip away somewhere to mourn in peace.

Roderick—because let's face it, calling the strong, vital man granddad was just a joke—would step into the gap with Maeve and try and keep the party going. For Regan's sake. Because the Baile coven never wanted her to feel like she wasn't enough for them, never wanted her to feel like the absence of Rian wasn't an aching wound inside her nearly every waking moment. Rian, her twin, her brother, missing since three days after they were born. Not dead, not kidnapped, and not hidden in some forgotten pocket of the world—just gone. One minute, Mum and Dad had been leaning over their crib cooing at their twin babies, and then a flash and Rian was gone. Of course they'd searched, they still did, but sometimes Regan felt that she was the only person who still knew he was out there somewhere. But she did know it, like she knew the beat of her own heart, and she would never stop looking for him.

She reached the small, arched door at the top of the tower and dug the key out of her pocket. Cool, sweet air rushed through the open door to greet her. Baile never let this room get dusty or stale. Regan didn't know how the massive crystal had come to be here, or what had made her come looking for it all those years ago. She'd grown up around Baile, and weird stuff happened here all day, every day. From the bailey, hundreds of feet below Niamh's voice drifted up as she taught her newest flock of fledgling guardian witches. In the great hall, Mags was locked in a meeting with several spiritual leaders as she tried to provide them with guidance on what the next few years would bring. Andy had a summit organized for later in the week to settle a centuries old dispute in the middle east. Yup, the weird and wonderful happened at Baile all the time.

In the bright morning sunlight, the labradorite crystal glinted pink, blue and green from its pewter depths. Bracing for the familiar shock of questing, Regan placed her hands on the smooth, cool surface. She closed her eyes and whispered, "Where are you?"

AND WE CLOSE this part of the **Cré-witch Chronicles.** The Cré-witch Chronicles is a complete five-book series consisting of **Born In Water, Purged In Fire, Raised In Air, Cradled In Earth,** and **Joined In Spirit.** Read the prequel and origin story , **Cast In Stone**, to discover Maeve and Roderick's story. **PLUS** a bonus novella that fits neatly between **Cradled In Earth** and **Joined In Spirit**, called **Forged In Fate** for more on those Canadian witches and their sexy wolf shifters.

WHAT'S NEXT? I'M GLAD YOU ASKED...

Welcome to the Hell Bound

It's not every day you find a naked, angry man in your basement...

Edme Ward is a woman with a problem—or three. She's the not-quite-official guardian of a portal to Hell, the diva-wrangling stage manager of a community theatre group, and — most recently— host to a sexy, angry Hell Prince who she's accidentally summoned from the underworld.

For the seven Hell Princes, war is a way of life. But when the balance between Heaven, Earth, and Hell is unexpectedly skewed, it threatens to destroy the ancient hierarchy forever. Asmodeus, guardian of Lust, is locked in a battle with eternal foe and fellow Hell Prince, Wrath, — but this time, Wrath is out to destroy his domain and banish Asmodeus forever.

It's an inconvenient time to end up in some woman's very earthly basement.

Drawn to Asmodeus, Edme risks losing her heart to a being who is the very definition of lust. While Asmodeus must overcome his desire to punish the all-too-human Edme—and accept her help.

As the Hell Princes lose their grip on their domains, the end of days looms. With existence itself teetering on the edge of annihilation, Asmodeus and Edme must turn enemies into allies to defeat a hidden foe.

And the secrets they unlock will either save everything or end the world as we know it (probably on a Wednesday)...

Lust *is the first book in the* Hell Bound *series by Sarah Hegger. Filled with snark, steam, and sexy underworld princes, fans of* Buffy *and* Lucifer *will love succumbing to the charms of the Hell Bound.*

Pre-order now to enter the domain of the Hell Bound.

For first dibs on news, deals, and giveaways, and so much more, join the @Home Collective

Or if Facebook is more your thing, join the Sarah Hegger Collective

Anything and everything you need to know on my website http://sarahhegger.com

ABOUT THE AUTHOR

Born British and raised in South Africa, Sarah Hegger suffers from an incurable case of wanderlust. Her match? A hot Canadian engineer, whose marriage proposal she accepted six short weeks after they first met. Together they've made homes in seven different cities across three different continents (and back again once or twice). If only it made her multilingual, but the best she can manage is idiosyncratic English, fluent Afrikaans, conversant Russian, pigeon Portuguese, even worse Zulu and enough French to get herself into trouble. Mimicking her globe trotting adventures, Sarah's career path began as a gainfully employed actress, drifted into public relations, settled a moment in advertising, and eventually took root in the fertile soil of her first love, writing. She also moonlights as a wife and mother. She currently lives in Ottawa, Canada, filling her empty nest with fur babies. Part footloose buccaneer, part quixotic observer of life, Sarah's restless heart is most content when reading or writing books.

PRAISE FOR SARAH HEGGER

Drove All Night
"The classic romance plot is elevated to a modern-day,
wholly accessible real-life fairy tale with an excellent mix of
romantic elements and spicy sensuality."
Booklife Prize, Critic's Report

Positively Pippa
"This is the type of romance that makes readers fall in love not
just with characters, but with authors as well."
Kirkus Review (Starred Review)

"What begins as a simple second-chance romance quickly
transforms into a beautiful, frank examination of love, family
dynamics, and following one's dreams. Hegger's unflinching,
candid portrayal of interpersonal and generational
communication elevates the story to the sublime. Shunning
clichés and contrived circumstances, she uses realistic, relatable
situations to create a world that readers will want to visit time
and again."
Publisher's Weekly, Starred Review

Hegger's utterly delightful first Ghost Falls contemporary is what other romance novels want to grow up to be." –
Publisher's Weekly, Best Books of 2017

"The very talented Hegger kicks off an enjoyable new series set in the small Utah town of Ghost Falls. This charming and fun-filled book has everything from passion and humor to betrayal and revenge." –
Jill M Smith, RT Books Reviews 2017 – Contemporary Love and Laughter Nominee

Becoming Bella
"Hegger excels at depicting familial relationships and friendships of all kinds, including purely platonic friendships between women and men. Tears, laughter, and a dollop of suspense make a memorable story that readers will want to revisit time and again."
Publisher's Weekly, Starred Review

"…you have a terrific new romance that Hegger fans are going to love. Don't miss out!"
Jill M. Smith – RT Book Reviews

Blatantly Blythe
"Ms. Hegger has delivered another captivating read for this series in this book that was packed with emotion…" Bec, Bookmagic Review, Harlequin Junkie, HJ Recommends.

Nobody's Fool
"Hegger offers a breath of fresh air in the romance genre." –
Terri Dukes, RT Book Reviews

Nobody's Princess
"Hegger continues to live up to her rapidly growing reputation

for breathing fresh air into the romance genre." – Terri Dukes, RT Book Reviews

"I have read the entire Willow Park Series. I have loved each of the books … Nobody's Princess is my favorite of all time." Harlequin Junkie, Top Pick

My Lady Faye

Conquering William

Defying Roger

Henry's Honor

Love & War Series

The Marriage Parley

The Betrothal Melee

Western Historical Romance

The Soiled Dove Series

Sugar Ellie

Standalone

The Bride Gift

Bad Wolfe On The Rise

Wild Honey